ALICIA II

Also by Robert Thurston

BATTLESTAR GALACTICA

(with Glen A. Larson)

ALICIA II

by

Robert Thurston

Published by
BERKLEY PUBLISHING CORPORATION

Distributed by
G.P. PUTNAM'S SONS, New York

 Published simultaneously in Canada by Longman Canada Limited, Toronto.

SBN: 399-12219-2

PRINTED IN THE UNITED STATES OF AMERICA

Library of Congress Cataloging in Publication Data

Thurston, Robert.
Alicia II.

I. Title.
PZ4.T557A [PS3570.H86] 813'.5'4 77-28897

For Joan

DOROTHY: You're a very bad man!

WIZARD: Oh no, my dear, I'm a very good man. I'm just a very bad wizard.

—From the film *The Wizard of Oz* (1939)

ALICIA II

PART I

1

All my life, Alicia, for you. Even when you were nine years old—blond, happy, and narcissistic—I wanted to be your age. Or perhaps a more mature ten. There was nothing untoward or suspect about my wish. I merely wanted to be small enough and light enough to skim along the edge of the lapping water instead of plunging my heavy feet through the barely visible ripples of your wake. My footprints, caverns in the wet dark sand.

But when Alicia was nine I was twenty-six. Officially. Multiply that official number by three, add a decade or so, allow for the period of darkness. The solution is the gap of years between my age then and my genuine birthdate. Old in my new body, I was at the same time younger than Alicia. I was a retread, terrible word, still clumsily transmitting carefully composed messages to his muscles who, suspicious of their sender, took their time about responding.

All retreads had to go through a "mandated-renewal-period," as they called it in bureaucratic circles. I chose Atlantica Spa, which turned out to be a wise decision because, with its aged buildings, collapsing boardwalk, rarely operating concessions, and uncrowded beach, it was one of the least popular vacation resorts on the entire continent. I enjoyed the place because I needed to be separated from the masses who, because they could slide so easily through the small spaces between each other, laughed behind their hands at clumsy retreads. Retreads were always colliding with other bodies, which seemed to us like a wall that was continually re-forming, conspiratorially, at each step. I had always been mildly claustrophobic (perhaps a secondary reason why I rushed so quickly to the stars) and I could not easily have endured trying to adjust within four moving human walls.

Years ago, in my real childhood (genuine childhood, pre-retread childhood) a relative gave me a red and black checkered kaleidoscope. For my birthday, I think. I cannot remember a single thing about the relative but the toy, a well-made kaleidoscope that survived many collisions, occasionally interrupts my thoughts. When you turned it, six silhouettes of men walked along its inner rim. It first fascinated me—until I perceived the little men as trapped inside that small circle. I stopped turning it, the six men came to a halt. I felt what it must be like to be trapped inside the tube, and I could not easily put my eye to the kaleidoscope any longer. And, while I was genuinely terrified, I was also a little proud. This foolish extension of a real fear proved me to be sensitive. When my parents berated me and repeated mercilessly how much the toy had cost my poor unmemorable relative and how it came from some mystical place called the Museum of Modern Art, I felt even better about my rejection of it. Each refusal to be sensible reinforced my belief in my fathomless sensitivity. Not too many months later, the toy became a permanent fixture on a shelf, and I could look in it, or not, as I wished. And it was useful as a tool or weapon.

If my claustrophobia, or fantasy of claustrophobia, hadn't created in me a need for the expansiveness of the Atlantica Spa beach, I would not have met Alicia. But that is milk gladly spilled, a thread justifying all of Fortune's web. Children, rarely seen or heard in my former circles, were strange to me, freakish. I had not been really close to a child since the time I had been regularly assigned the care of my youngest sister, who grew up to be such a swaggering tyrant that I cannot believe the memories I have of her childhood. My first day at the Spa, as I sat exhausted from sunlight, shriveled from a short morning walk, I watched Alicia from the vantage point of a collapsing collapsible chair on a sagging porch. My attention was detached, curious, much like the audience gaping through cages at the local zoo. where the objects of their awed attention were holograms of African animals, many of whom were already extinct. They are people who never experienced a real zoo, as I have. They could not apply emotion or sense, fear or odor, to the hollow-looking creatures in the cages. (In a museum we cannot really view a painting unless we can feel something of the pain or joy in the brushstrokes, in the realization of a difficult concept—but that is another kind of zoo). I sat low in my unsteady chair and studied the habits of the child playing on the beach. Attached unsurely to the threads of my new body, I was impressed by her freedom of movement and envied her easy happiness. I commented to myself on the grace of her gestures, caught my breath at the savagery of a sudden splashing attack upon the sea. She bounced and flew and performed balletic dances. Once she fell and faked some tears in an attempt (vain) to draw some kind of reaction from her frozen-faced father, who looked away at something else. My hand made an involuntary movement in her direction, an inefficient mime, a reaching out to dry her tears.

Perhaps I fell in love with Alicia during that idle exhausted time when I sank into that chair and watched her go through her paces. I gazed at a beautiful child and, in my mind's eye, grew her up (quite accurately) to the beautiful woman she would become. Odd and perverse of me, perhaps, but the kind of imagining appropriate to a convalescent.

When I later asked formal permission to become her playmate, her father hardly reacted. Perhaps he saw I was too weak to have misguided motives. Without emotion he passed her to me like a coin to a panhandler.

She dubbed me Uncle Vossilyev and made me follow the leader, just to show off her grace at the expense of my clumsiness. "Do it again, Uncle V.," she'd cry as I looked up from the ground, helpless, waiting for my body to cooperate.

Since I was under orders to rest most of the day, we played mostly at sunset, when the rays of the red sun sent myriad-reflections, of both sharp and dull intensity, off the oil, algae, and assorted scum on the water's surface. Sometimes the glare did actually blind me and I, hoping that some planted synapse had not gone awry, sent a hasty message to my eyes, who reluctantly executed a shimmery blur, coming to a slow focus merely to tease, to assert a bit of independence against the body's invading rebel. Sometimes my lungs offered a tedious resistance, trading me a series of sharp pains in the ribcage for the air I needed. Sometimes my limbs fought each other in a tournament to see which could embarrass me more.

Nights we searched for seashells, but found few in a beach which, after all, had been scoured by the last beachcombers before they abandoned it for the artificial substitutes—the plastibeaches or plasbeas—to become slickerjobs, salaried beach-boys as phony as the terrains they were assigned to patrol. Well, what the hell, not for me to snub that way of life. It was, of course, one of the better paradises that rejects sought in the few years allotted to them before they lined up at the retread chamber. I remembered the line of rejects I had seen in my first go-around, standing slump-shouldered and empty-eyed, feeding like a long strand of spaghetti into a retread chamber entrance, supplying for the selfish qualifiers, like Uncle V., bodies for their reincarnations. When I started thinking this way, I stopped begrudging seashells.

Alicia seemed too bright to be a reject, too intelligent to have failed even the most penetrating of test batteries. If she was a reject, I told myself, retesting would qualify her irrevocably. The question, the doubt, gnawed at me so much that I promised myself to ascertain her status at the first opportunity.

2

"Come on, Uncle V., let's swim," she said after I, sprawled (again) on my back, had conceded her the game. Any game.

"I can't swim."

"Don't you know how *yet?*"

"I know how. I've known how since Methuselah and Solomon were tots."

"Then you lied before."

"I did *not* lie. I can't swim. I know how, but I can't make my legs work right. They flop when they should flip."

"You always flip-flop. Flip-flop. Flip-flop."

She enjoyed the sound of the word and circled around my prone body, chanting it like a formula for ritual sacrifice. Gritty sand seemed to penetrate my skin, while the sun tried to burn out my eyes. Tiring quickly of her ceremony, she raced to the water, hollering:

"You don't know if you can't swim if you don't try. Scaredy-cat!"

"You little serpent, I'll get you for that."

I said that in a sitting position it had taken years to reach.

"You can't catch me. Not if you can't swim."

She scurried into the water, her long legs working up and down like the spindle of an old-fashioned sewing machine. For a while she just stood, splashing threats as well as water upon me. When I made an awkward lunge toward her, she shrieked and stumbled backward, slid underwater briefly, came up doing a graceful backstroke.

"I'll get out to the float before you will," she screamed. And of course she did. I could not even get a quarter of the way and had to force my angry muscles to return me to the beach, where I collapsed, looking, I'm sure, like a puppet whose strings have just been cut.

"Don't go any farther than the float, you wretched child," hollered a voice above and behind me. Alicia's father, Mr. Reynal. He rarely came down to the beach. He put hesitant feet upon the sand in the way the rest of us toed the water on a breezy day, and he always wore clothing that covered up his body from neck to foot, although—incongruously—he always went hatless. Up until that moment he had rarely spoken to me. Toneless greetings each time he relinquished his daughter, grunts when he took her back, graceless refusals to all invitations. His shouting at that moment was a pleasant surprise, as was his angry expression. An astrophysicist, his day-to-day look was as blank as a reject's in the waiting line.

"She's always threatening to leave the unpolluted area," he said. "She wants to swim out from the float to the reef and find the places where, legend has it, men can walk on water."

Two sentences in a row from him was something of a bonus, irony an extra-special award. I searched his face for the emotion behind the comments, but his anger had vanished and his usual passivity had been reinstated.

"Kids always threaten," I said, though where I had acquired such worldly wisdom is a mystery. "It's all a kind of compromise with life's compromises. You have to fight it before you can join it. Alicia's a very bright child."

I was dismayed by my own tactlessness, felt an urge to bite off my tongue. Innocuous enough when applied to a satisfactory, the remark was a pathetic insult to a reject, and I had not established in what category Alicia belonged. But her father did not react to the remark. Which did not prove anything considering the rarity of his observed reactions.

For a long time we sat and watched Alicia romping on the float. She did a jerky little dance she had cribbed from *Holo-Causts of 2133,* a show we'd watched the previous night. She rubbed gobs of mud, that had collected on the float, all over her arms and forehead.

Her father offered no conversational openings through which I could rush with the subject I was frantic to discuss. If he had said, "Been a nice day," I would have shot back, "A perfect day for all, retread, natural, satisfactory, and reject alike. By the way, speaking of rejects . . ." If he had said, "How are you feeling today?" I'd respond, "I feel a bit rejected. By the way . . ." But he would not say anything I could use. He just stared ahead, the glare from the water losing intensity in the dark ashes of his eyes. Finally I spoke. Politely, tactfully, cleverly, and with due consideration:

"Alicia, is she a reject?"

Besides the need to obtain the desired information, I also perversely longed for a flicker of emotion in the man's face. My heart leaped to my throat for both reasons as he looked toward me.

"No," he said, no clue to his mood in his voice and face. He must have observed my relief.

In case he was thinking, Why did you ask?, I said:

"She's allowed such latitude I wasn't sure which way—I mean, some of us had to—that is, reject-shells are in such demand now and—well, standards being—"

"Do you generally call them reject-shells?"

There was no criticism in his voice. I felt some anyway.

"Well, it's the . . . the common term."

"Yes, I know."

He went back to watching his daughter as she skidded to the edge of the float, almost fell into the water. She looked ridiculous, a white face above a body that was almost completely brown with mud. Mr. Reynal spoke again, so suddenly I almost lost command of my body and fell at his feet.

"I'm afraid Alicia may face the danger of losing out on retesting."

The statement, and the toneless way he said it, chilled me.

"What do you mean? I thought you said she wasn't a reject."

"I said that, yes. And, for the moment, it is true. But I am a scientist. A realist, if you'll accept that."

"Naturally I'll accept it, but what does science have to do with it?"

"Everything. Science and politics. And Alicia could lost out with both. But there's no point in pushing her. She'll either work it out or she won't."

I wanted to beg him for an explanation, but instead waited through his long silence.

"Originally she tested out just above the minimum. She's become that rare occurrence, a satisfactory marked out for retesting. I'm not entirely sure the reason for the ruling is her test score. I have, well, certain political sins they might be punishing me for. Her score might have been quite fine, in fact. Best thing for her might be for me to remove myself from official view. I'm thinking of that. Anyway, she might fail upon retesting."

"Well," I said, reaching for the cliché, "most of the time you retest the same. That's what they say. Only a statistically insignificant number of child-satisfactories who are marked for retesting ever show general quotient-loss and retest as reject. Satisfactory is satisfactory, sounds safe to—"

"Her mother was a reject."

His chief political sin, no doubt, I said to myself.

"Oh, I'm sorry.

"Nothing to be sorry about. She was a lovely woman."

Hollering to us, Alicia hopped back into the water. As she swam toward us, her wildly moving arms beating down any water resistance, I conjectured her as that rare statistically insignificant loser, and I felt a little sick. If what her father said was true, she did have a couple of strikes against her, according to prevailing theory. A politically damaged father was one thing, a reject as either parent was even worse.

"So you see," Mr. Reynal said, "Alicia is more in danger from politics than from science. From people whose specialty is to keep track of the backgrounds of candidates, nose around thick files and come up with thickheaded conclusions, all backed up with especially researched data."

"But scores are scores."

If it had been his custom to laugh, he would have laughed at me. Instead, he hid behind his gray eyes and too many clothes, a fugitive from normal conversation.

"No. Scores are adjustable. We're all adjustable, for that matter."

"I don't understand, sir."

"Of course you don't. When you're fresh in a new, as you say, reject-shell, you believe in permanency. Right now, you're like Narcissus staring at only one reflection, satisfied with only one pond. Ah, well, Alicia will be all right, I'm sure."

He gestured: end of subject.

I gestured: no, you don't.

"Shouldn't you be hard at it working with her? To ensure her passing on the retest?"

"She's only nine."

The definitive answer.

3

I don't know how many times I tried to trick Alicia's father into talking about her mother, how many times I searched those cold gray eyes for a reaction to my sly inquiries. I also interrogated Alicia, who had no memory of her. I don't understand why I *needed* to know. Perhaps it was just that, retreaded at twenty-six, I reinstated the romantic notions of my youth almost a century before. Fingering coarse sand, ignoring the fishy odors of decay that the breezes carried to us from the restricted beach areas, I contemplated beauty and continued on a quest. As I became adjusted to my new body, my romanticism increased; the decades since my actual twenties seemed a series of brief interruptive dreams. I began to believe, even before I had hard information, that Alicia's father was a genuine tragedy of his age, doomed always to seek the one love of his life who could not be restored to him by retreading or any other means.

It was not difficult to amass information about Alicia's mother. Information is always available to the enterprising snoop.

She, the first Alicia, had won Claude Reynal's attention because she projected a gaiety untinged with the ironic bitterness that was frequently found in a reject. She had only a few years of life—so what?—those few years could be spent fully and richly. It was a more permissive age then. Escapism was a catchword. Satisfactories frolicked with rejects, and retreads led the way to all kinds of loud diversions and lovely habits. (I remember myself at the time—an old codger, purple-veined and pockmarked, barely able to lift a spoonful of soft-boiled egg-substitute, inveighing foolishly against those freedoms which had not been allowed in his own youth.)

Alicia's father and mother were married with little fuss and, for that matter, little notice from a world that had not realized the importance of priorities. She was a vibrant eighteen. He was handsomely entering middle-age, and was quite popular in reject circles for some political pamphlets he had written. I am told that the wedding guests threw him into a pool of champagne and he came up laughing. But I find that story apocryphal, not merely for the callous treatment of such a rare commodity as champagne (though for some reason a penchant for destruction did accompany the escapism, or perhaps it always does), but for the impossible-to-imagine picture of Alicia's father emerging from that bubbling pool laughing—smiling even.

I did manage to make him tell me how, after a few years of childlessness, he deliberately impregnated her near the end of her alloted life-cycle. Just to keep her around. It astonishes me, now that I think of it, how well he was able to wield political power even in those undisciplined days. Who did he know that would allow the birth of a child rather than prescribing abortion or womb-transferral? Or, more likely, were they so reject-shell-happy that they were hoping for a babe that would eventually test out as unsatisfactory? All types of political deviation may be forgiven, if there is a chance of a reject-shell at stake.

When the time came for Alicia I to be sent to the retread chamber, Claude Reynal scrambled through piles of red tape, searching for a loophole, a special dispensation. A particularly annoying lackey told him he'd been lucky to get the time extension for her pregnancy, and now there would be no way out. Yet he demanded and obtained a second retesting, unprecedented as it was, but to no avail. As before, she tested out a shade below satisfactory. There were no exceptions.

What was she like in the reject line? Did she, always in contrast to others of her status, smile all the way to the chamber entrance?

Her story, that part of it which I could glean from Claude Reynal's reluctant musings, plus some data I was able to obtain by other means, would have ended there for me. However, in my final days at Atlantica Spa, an aunt of Alicia's, on her father's side, made a surprise visit. Mr. Reynal evidently couldn't stand her, and he managed to find excuses to avoid her, so I had plenty of time to sit at the feet of this gossipy woman, all retreaded and already aging in her new body, and listen as she supplied the last part of the story of Alicia I.

After retreading—when the consciousness of Alicia I was blotted out forever; when, as a reject-shell, the yet-throbbing body was sucked through a series of tubes to the Inspection Chamber; when, after inspectors had marked out in red strokes the necessary repairs and surgeon-mechanics had completed their task of adjustments and part-replacements, the shell whipped through another series of tubes to the Nurture Chambers where care and feeding proceeded until the old wreck who was to inherit Alicia I's body either passed on or was put away; when, after a journey through still another series of tubes, the new inhabitant of the shell was implanted and connected—after all this, the former Alicia stepped unsurely out of a convalescent area as Martina Skotch, the famous cybernetic psychiatrist who, in her new life, made quite a name as a leading lady in the textureflicks. Before they were banned. In other words, she used Alicia I's body appropriately. Functionally.

(If she had known this, would the second Alicia have attended a Skotch t-flick with a different attitude, have fought with her own hates against the emotions the flick attempted to force on her? Attached to a simulation of Martina Skotch's nerve centers, tuned in to the emotions approximated by her for the story-line, seeing through her eyes and touching with her spidery fingers—in that part of her which remained detached and unaltered during a t-flick showing, would Alicia II have contemplated that this housing, now a simulated part of her, once belonged to her mother? That this womb heaving tentatively in passion once had her curled up inside? Questions more perverse than these have occurred to t-flick viewers in the midst of a showing. No wonder they were banished, their detractors claimed later.

(Would Alicia II have paid extra for that titillation of the audience known as Opposex, the female being switched into the male role and vice versa? Then she could have, in the persona of Arch Kral or Steve Dimond or whatever play-stud was in vogue at the time, watched the shell of Martina Skotch, subtracted a few years [but not all of the years since Alicia I's death, since Martina made a fetish of keeping herself young cosmetically and surgically], and pondered the beauty of her own mother. Perhaps studied her own beauty at its source.

(But Opposex was abolished after a short term of use, and Martina Skotch faded to her retirement, her flicks gladly forgotten, unrevived even for untextured showings. I am told Martina's t-flicks were really dreadful, but still I am sometimes sorry that I missed them. The one or two t-flicks that I saw toward the end of my first lifetime, when they were of little practical use to me, seemed imperfectly synchronized. Love scenes transmitted unresolved tactility and unfelt emotions. Rain stung faces but left them dry. Food odors tantalized, then frustrated because taste could not be transmitted.)

Alicia's father, paying off a specialist in revival techniques who had slipped him information, sneaked into a lobby where the new Martina made her first grand entrance into the world-at-large. He approached her and tried to find Alicia I in the sad tired eyes, the awkward movements, the limping gait. He told her who he was and, I'm afraid, made a proposal which the as-yet-inexperienced Martina found indecent, even by the standards of those escapist times. When she turned him down, he became desperate and begged her to just let him accompany her for a while, a decade or ten minutes, it didn't matter. Again she refused. He kissed her anyway. She slapped his face. He left.

An ugly story, perhaps, and one wisely kept locked in the family closet. I wonder if Alicia's father, transplanted at his own request to another world, continued to carry that aging torch. And Martina—these old stars, where are they now?

4

That day on the beach Alicia's father and I said little more to each other. We watched her play and let her taunt us for our lethargy.

When she was not proving I was a fool or inventing ways to draw a veiled clue of affection from her father (a gentle but brief contact of the back of his fingers with the back of her hair, a slight body-tilt forward to acknowledge the importance of what she was saying), Alicia often left us on little sulky trips of her own. Her father, when I asked him, never knew where she went, nor did he seem to worry. A couple times I tried to follow her, but she was too adept at escaping shadows.

To break the long silences between Claude Reynal and myself, I continued to force him into conversation. That was how I managed to draw meager gossipy tidbits out of him. He never seemed to care what he told me, he just clearly preferred I would shut up as soon as possible. I learned a conversational technique that worked well with him: the concise introduction of a subject without any sensible preface. One day I needed to talk about myself—desperately, my body's inability to learn anything was pushing me toward insanity—and I said to him:

"You don't remind me at all of my father, not one bit."

God, that time I got a movement of his lips that, if worked with a bit more, might have been shaped into a smile.

"I was not aware of any resemblance of even the remotest

interest," he said. He sounded friendly—sarcastic, but friendly—so I plunged onward.

"My dad was sensitive, too sensitive for his times, too sens—"

"Then of course there could be no resemblance."

He did nothing with his face to indicate even the slightest awareness of humor.

"Well, I didn't mean that you are insensitive. Of course not."

"Of course not."

"My dad was an escapist."

"Perhaps we're not so unalike. I have a tendency or two in that direction. What was he like?"

I was almost too stunned to answer. Claude Reynal had actually asked *me* a question. Finally, shying away from that body-tilt forward, those cold gray eyes, I said:

"Well, he reacted to his time, the issues, the crises. You know, crime, scarcity of food, cramped living quarters, hatred, bigot—"

"I have dim memories of some of those conditions. Like many others, I have conveniently changed them into history."

"Oh. Yes? Anyway, my dad tried to escape, as I said. He dragged us, the family, way the hell all around the country, trying to find a—a better life, I guess you'd call it."

"Yes, I would."

I wished that he would tilt his body back the half-inch he had moved it in my direction.

"Well, my dad just escaped to where he'd come from. In effect, that is."

"In effect, yes."

I could not perceive the game Reynal was playing with me, I could just feel his manipulation of the pieces.

"We found essentially the same conditions everywhere. The cities suffered from overcrowdedness, the small towns were barricaded. See, the easier times, the times of the world government and the miracle of retreading, were yet to come."

"The miracle, yes indeed."

I was getting the urge to shut up, but this time the suggestion for it was not coming from Reynal.

"Well, I don't know, I guess. Things were just screwed up for him."

I paused, waiting for him to say something like, screwed up, yes, but he remained silent, staring at me.

"He tried to help us all through it. He tried to, I remember this now, I'd forgotten, he tried to counsel me to do the best with my life, to benefit mankind, to do all I could to spread intelligence and human compassion. I guess this all sounds pretty silly to you."

"Not at all."

"Ah, but people's life stories are so mundane. I don't want you to be bored by my, well, by my autobiographical wanderings."

"Not boring. We both should hear it."

"I don't understand."

"No, you don't. Go on."

I was sitting in a plastic-cloth lawn chair that suddenly seemed made of hard wood.

"Well, he spent a lot of time giving me advice like that. Later, in his declining years, he became a bit senile. More than a bit. He kept threatening to kill himself. In his last days I kept a deathwatch during which I vowed to dedicate my life to working for humanity, just as he'd wished. After his death, I supervised the whisking away of his body to the nearest retread chamber and few days later the bad news came."

"Bad news?"

I think he tilted another half-inch forward.

"Yes. You see, because of some defect in himself, or maybe in the retreading process, there couldn't be any transferral from his natural body into a preservation container that would've held his soul until a body became available for retreading. They sent a message that he couldn't be retreaded, we'd never see him in any form again, he was—as they always put it then—*officially* dead."

"Ah, yes. And that's the bad news?"

"Isn't it?"

"Depends. You haven't mentioned your mother."

"Yes, well, that's a bit unpleasant. She took the news that my dad couldn't be retreaded quite badly, was never the same again. Like my dad, she moved us to a few new places, but it wasn't the same. There was no, no reason for the moves. And when she died, she didn't sign the retreading renewal agreement. She refused to be reborn in a new body, she said, she was quite satisfied to die in the old one."

"And that was bad news, too, was it?"

"Of course it was."

"Had he planned to return to your family?"

"He said that, but he *was* senile, acting strangely."

"Do you miss him?"

Reynal was turning the tables on me, interrogating me just as I had interrogated him the preceding two days. I had trouble answering.

"Miss him? Guess so, haven't thought of that for years. His death, then the news he couldn't be retreaded, those shocks pretty well knocked me out, as you can imagine."

"I can."

"I got into a long depression. Months really. But maybe it was to the good. I came out of the gloom with dedication. Whatever I did with my life it had to be for him, for my father. So I applied for a government job in retreading research."

"Retreading research, oh."

"You sound disappointed."

"Not at all, but perhaps we have differing concepts of dedication. Did you get the job?"

"Not exactly. Nothing available in retreading research as such."

"A popular area of interest."

"Exactly. My credentials made me eligible for some research on cloning being done deep in an Arizona research complex. The American government, on its last legs by then and more paranoid than ever, had buried all its research and development areas in various underground locations."

"I inspected a few. Much later, of course. Cloning's always interested me but I've failed to follow the research."

"Yeah, maybe if we'd been more successful, well—all I remember is how I welcomed the thought that, not only could I work on a project that was in congruence with my father's wishes, but I'd be able to escape the ugliness of the everyday world in a clean and socially healthy environment."

"You were an escapist like your father."

"If you want to put it that way." I did not, and I was feeling the strain of autobiography. I yearned for his signal to shut up. "So anyway, I came to the enclave. That's how we styled ourselves, as 'the enclave.' Probably other enclaves did, too. For many years we worked unsuccessfully to create human clones. In the early days we were so enthusiastic, so confident we would grow human beings from cells. Clones were such a wonderful idea. If we could develop clones, we wouldn't need rejects, retreading would be available to all, bodies would be supplied by us, the enclave. Later, after the world government had taken over and its representatives had begun to deny us funding for any further cloning research, we, the enclave, wound up embittered over the duller areas of study that'd been assigned to us. Study! All we did was hold long discussions, more talk than action. A very silly group, in a way, mad scientists still pretending our work carried importance in the real world. I'm glad to be out of it."

"Some of that bitterness you spoke of has carried over."

"Yes, well, in my last days, I was a curmudgeon. Selena always said—"

"Selena?"

"My wife. She was a—"

"Oh. I wonder where my child has gone this time."

There it was. The signal. Reynal's command that the conversation was over. It had come too abruptly, even though I was looking for it. I felt angry, as if the as-yet-unmentioned parts of my first life held no meaning for him. Then it occurred to me that he just could not admit the subject of wives into the talk, could not allow the memory of Alicia I to intrude once more.

5

The rest of that unfortunately-too-brief week I happily accompanied Alicia on all her improvised tours. We explored the incredibly preserved remains of a dance casino, scraping away sand from a marble floor and talking to wallflower ghosts in the shadows. We found an abandoned bridge and invented a ballad-singing troll for it, life-history and all. We stole into other people's cabins and examined their belongings. The more I saw of Alicia, the more confident I became that her father's speculations she might yet follow her mother's fate were the exaggerated woes of a loyal parent. Intelligent? She topped the list of all the children I had ever known, not to mention a few allegedly satisfactory adults.

We romped through the weakling hours of several hot afternoons and danced comic jigs to welcome the reluctant risings of the moons. Her pretty face displayed many facets as she whirled through many lights—the cunning shadows of the natural moon, the steely flicker of the satellite-moon, the python attacks of a beach fire, the aura of manmade lights peering from hilltops, the reflections from these sources upon the impenetrable waters. In each light a different expression, no face repeated twice in any given hour.

Gradually my body became used to me ordering it around and took up its duties with less reluctance. Perhaps it realized that it already had a suitable revenge for my interlopement and figured that to continue these minor tortures was unrequired sadism.

Mr. Reynal's vacation ended at the same time that my Renewal Period Permit expired, and we agreed to head back to the flooding mainstream together. I regretted leaving such a quiet and, especially, unpopulated area. During my whole stay at the Spa, I saw fewer than thirty people, spoke to maybe half of them.

Even now I recall that desolation with nostalgia, but today in my sleep I dream of a ravaged city with Paradise printed in greening wrought iron above its entrance. Small wonder that the Spa was converted finally to a plasbea (what was the official and scientific term for plastibeaches—I forget), pale imitation of the original but carefully ordered, fancy-colored and glossy, with more comforts than civilized man desired, a stunning collection of diversions so encyclopedic that it is offered to you alphabetized, and with the frequent rubbing of skin against skin that makes a trip there really feel like a vacation.

I suggested taking the raptrain (the official and only occasionally used term for the cross-country rapid-transit system), instead of the cheaper, faster, and more convenient choices of transportation. Mr. Reynal said it was all right with him. Everything was all right with him, it seemed. Perhaps he succumbed to my transparent romantic need to participate in all the dying arts.

Some of us preferred raptrains in their deteriorated and less rapid state. They offered a leisurely trip when you were in no mood to get someplace quickly—without discomfort, gas pollution, and fear—and you could reach most of the major areas on the American continent in them. The passing of the cross-country subway system may not be a serious matter but, in an era when progress is measured in forward stumbles, it seems regrettable that raptrains were phased out in favor of underground shopping areas and econo-conapts.

I recall thinking, as we waited in the turnstile line, how desperate a problem overpopulation had seemed to be two centuries before, when prophets predicted inevitable Malthusian doom. Instead of succumbing to the obvious trends, we had turned them into advantages—expanding outward and downward, inventing nutritious food-substitutes and reviving arable land, finding new space in abandoned raptrain tunnels, underground caverns, buildings plunging deeper into the earth or soaring to the heavens. Now we had come full circle. In spite of the raucous demands to reproduce, to flood the planet with inhabitants in amounts above the levels thought safe by the ancient prophets, we found our population balance threatened in a different way. All of our genetic studies and experiments could not force the reproduction of more rejects, more bodies to serve as shells. Why don't you people have more babies? the desperate society screamed at the too-lethargic reject parents. Not only was the birth rate too low, the reject childbearers did not supply enough reject babies, in spite of the proper genes. They kept producing too many satisfactories and not enough of their own kind. Some thought it a diabolical plan to keep the population balance screwed up.

There are never enough bodies, said the retread specialists. Periods of darkness, during which the individual "soul" awaited his new shell, grew longer and longer. The medical world was at fault, some said. If only they would preserve lives beyond the average fourscore and ten. The medics, in turn, blamed the media for urging, practically forcing, the masses into an advanced stage of sexual stimulation so that we might receive more babies. The political and social analysts then said that the solution of more babies was specious, and failing. While there were more bodies available for retreading, there were also more satisfactories to be eventually scheduled, more housing needed, more blame to be spread among the various population sectors.

Well, I thought, at least I've come through it all with a new body; then I shuddered, appalled at my own cynicism.

6

The air of the raptrain station, thick with stench, seemed to lie in layers of heated bodies, inefficient urinals, the debris of indifferent lives, the rust and dust that easily evaded sanitation crews. I waited, Alicia's hand in mine. With her father in front of us, we were walled in on the remaining three sides by other travelers. I thought I could feel them leaning against my back, shoulder, chest. I had worn a netted shirt and trousers made out of the so-called "icebox" fabric, which was supposed to retain cool outdoor temperatures but which (as I discovered then) malfunctioned in the middle of a large crowd. I stood on my toes to gulp in some air and my heels came down on someone's arches. We both muttered our excuses, though he was not more at fault than I since he'd been pressed forward by someone to the rear of him, perhaps several rows back.

Not able to turn around, I twisted my head as much as protesting neck muscles would allow, and looked out the side of my eyes at the redfaced gentleman behind me.

"If you could spread your feet apart," I began, "then perhaps—"

"Hey Ernie!" Redface said, "I didn't recognize you from behind."

He touched my bare arm with fingertips that felt calloused.

"I'm sorry, but you must be . . ."

My apology was drowned out by the elongated howl of the train coming into the station. We made it into the car just as the quota sign flashed on and those behind us were blocked from entrance. Except for the redfaced man, who squeezed through in the short delay before the airlock sealed.

"That was a close one, hey, Ernie?" Redface said, smiling, pulling tighter a checkered (red and white, the white ridiculously transparent) robe. "But what the hell, I'm going to go soon anyway. They offered me double the insurance payment to my wife if I'd go ahead of time. But I told 'em something they could do with *that* money. Hell, my old lady'd only have a couple of years to spend it anyway. So it should go to the kids? Let 'em shift for themselves is what I say. One of 'em's a goddam satisfactory anyway. They say I should be proud, but I'm not gonna leave that little bastard any advantages, bet on that. Funny, but I thought I heard you already bought it, Ernie, but that's no—"

"It's probably true. I'm not Ernie. This body may have belonged to him, but he, I'm afraid, is gone." I suppose I sounded like the prototypical cold fish. Ice gleamed in rays off my scales. Ernie's friend nodded, hooked a calloused thumb into the belt of his robe.

"Sorry, excuse me," he muttered, holding in anger, then squeezed his way to another part of the car. During the rest of the trip, he often glanced my way with his cloudy regretful eyes.

7

I suppose I could romanticize my parting with Alicia at the mobbed Lakeshore Station in the Cleveland Meglop. Embellish the details, see a glint of future affection in her tear-filled eyes (which actually were quite happily bright and looking around for new adventure, I thought). But we should not strew love's path with artificial roses. Everything was rushed. Breathless statements, reunion promises to be broken, a mad dash to exit. Perhaps I tested a blond curl or two for spring, patted her head affectionately in a dutch-uncle fashion, felt a brief moment of sorrow at parting, that sort of thing. But I was more concerned with getting my second life started. Eager to test my body's resources now it was beginning to function properly. I looked forward to enjoying long-lost pleasures.

I had been so much of a recluse in my first lifetime, I knew I needed a fuller life this go-around—something better than burrowing into a deep underground cavern with an enclave of experimenters who were as much inclined toward the hermit's life as I was. Looking back on that first life from the vantage point of now, a whole lifetime away from it, only the mundane details of everyday existence remain in my memory. With my knowledge so disused and now out of date, I have even forgotten those facts and theories which dominated every waking minute of my time in the enclave. Nothing of my experiences there would conveniently blow up into an old man's tall tales of the great long-ago. I married within the group, we all did that sort of thing, one of us was even a specialist in inbreeding, which gave rise to some odd but funny jokes. Selena's specialty was sociogenetics. She was a softfaced girl with a paperclip figure. Though we worked together superbly, we did not stimulate each other to sexual passion too frequently. Eventually the sexual act became redundant and we abandoned it. Our bed sagged at the sides instead of the center.

In early middle-age, when such things are so appropriate, I had an affair with Lanna Petresen, a functionally attractive brunette programmer who, although she played more sexily than Selena, was really not much different in bed.

My life's work is compressed into a footnote of a rarely consulted journal. Selena died. I became crotchety. Selena retreaded as a chubby underdressed blond. I died in my sleep.

During the renewal period, I had given heavy consideration to the possible content of my new life. Selena had hinted (begged) that I could come back to the enclave, resume life with her. She said she was enjoying the enclave's comforting sameness under a world whose confusions were too much for her. But I crankily told her no, not that life again, Selena darling. No, this time around was going to be a lark, a ball, a wingding lollapalooza. Lusty new experiences, sources for old-age tall tales this time. I wanted dangerous adventures, the luscious fruits of dissipation, regularly scheduled orgies. As it turned out, I could not have all of that. Contrary to popular belief, two out of three is not enough.

Before the beginning of my whirlagig life, I had to pay a call. In his first life Dr. Ben Blounte had been my father's closest friend. They grew up together, married in a double ceremony, even died only weeks apart. The only thing that did not work out companionably was retreading. When my father's did not take, Ben mourned with the family. I recall thinking that his sorrow had a bizarre look to it—a vigorous young man shedding tears over a dead old man who had not even recognized him at their last meeting, when Ben had been freshly retreaded and eager to show off his new body.

Throughout my life I had allowed myself to break my enclave

asceticism only for yearly visits to Ben, who pampered, checked and double-checked me with a plodding thoroughness. The last time we saw each other, he demanded that I come see him as my first official act after R & R, retreading and renewal.

Cleveland, one of the last cities to adopt modern city planning and architectural methods, had not changed much. It was still laid out impractically on the grid system, with buildings rising vertically, and underbuildings going straight into the ground. Streets went more or less in a line and came roughly to right angles with each other. Monorails clogged along. There were even, here and there, moving sidewalks that worked. And the usual traffic that made one regret that so little advance had been made in the progress of vehicular transportation over more than two centuries. Cleveland was an illogically modern city, as if shells and facades had been positioned to hide the industrial atrocity, the great lake destroyer, that it had once been. I get the feeling that, wherever the times go, Cleveland will be behind them. I felt comfortable there.

Ben operated out of the same digs he'd used for almost a century, in the ninetieth understory of an old building. In Ben's waiting room I gave a fake name to the rusty old robosec, even though I knew the machine garbled every message anyway. Ben's voice grumbled in the next room, swearing at the robosec's misinformation.

"Come in, whoever you are," he shouted. The signal light above the door flashed on. I placed my hand on the strip marked enter and the door, another piece of outdated equipment, slid clumsily away from me.

In front of me was the same old office. Ugly black swivel desk which tilted uneasily on its pivot. Twisted contour chairs for patients (you had to be sick to even contemplate sitting on one). The leaning tower of an examination cubicle. The holographic hunting and fishing pictures that had replaced the earlier Great Moments in Medicine series (their pastoral simplicity was a lot pleasanter and, anyway, the great moments series had been a bit too bloody). The various devices and instruments of Ben's profession were scattered in disarray about the room. Ben came around the desk (which tilted further as his hip brushed against it) as if his outstretched hand were leading him. There were tears in his eyes. And in mine.

"How in hell did you recognize me so fast?" I said, as he embraced me.

"No matter what kind of face you inherit, you'll still come into a room wearing that same dumb look on it."

As Ben backed away from me, I looked him over. He had become much older, no surprise there. His face was heavily lined and his body bore the thinness of old age. But the alert brown eyes still examined every inch of you with a doctor's vision, even though you were not there on a medical appointment and were just standing casually in front of him. He ordered me to sit down. I did my best to fit my body into the unnatural position required by the contour chair. I seemed to feel the rough threads of the cushion (Ben always bought factory seconds and leftovers) through the thinness of my clothing.

"Want to be examined right now?"

"Not now. Too official. I'll come back tomorrow or the next day for that. Make me an appointment."

"Tomorrow morning, nine o'clock."

"All right, all right. Whatever you say. But today's for us. I insist on that. I've looked forward to—"

"Me, too. Thought of you a lot lately, especially as time dragged on."

"Periods of darkness are getting longer all the time."

"So I hear. Eventually they'll just have to let some of us die straight out."

"Morbid. I think—"

"No, it's not morbid at all. Common sense is what it is. How many lives do you need, for Christ's sake?"

"How many do *you* want?"

"I think maybe one more will just about do it."

"But that's it. Don't you see that? We'll always want one more."

"Maybe. I can't see it, actually. I can't see why anybody can't do everything he wanted within two, or at least three, lifespans. But you may be right—"

"All I can say is I'm glad to be back and willing to take things one lifetime at a time."

"That's the name of a song. Must've been out while you were in darkness. Yes, I believe it—"

"What in hell are you talking about?"

"One lifetime at a time. There was a song by that title a few years ago. Really annoying song. 'One Lifetime at a Time'—everybody was going around humming the damn thing. Here, let me sing it for you, I think it—"

"No, not that. Let's save cultural matters for a little bit."

"Well, okay."

"And I've heard you sing."

"You're still the same little bastard your father brought me almost—what?—eighty years ago. Called me names then but—"

"It was more than ninety years ago, and I was the politest, gentlest kid patient you ever had, I even—"

"Ha! I was going to send you to the Pope as the best argument for abortion *I'd* ever seen."

We lapsed into a friendly silence. I could hear Ben's equipment rattling. Still uncomfortable with myself, I was made even more uneasy by Ben's big affectionate smile. I looked away, out the window with its fake view of a rural countryside. I remembered years ago when the scene used to move. But it had broken and Ben had not bothered to get the view fixed in all those years. The same tree still bent in the wind, the same collie in mid-leap, the cow stuck with its nose in the cardboard-brown grass. I looked back at Ben, at all the age in his face, at the way the years seemed marked off like the circles within tree bark, and I wished that I'd been able to stall time the way that window scene had.

"I just can't believe you recognized me so easily," I said.

"Well, it was no big thing. After all, you did send me this."

He produced a postcard that I'd sent the day I was retreaded. I had deliberately chosen one with a flat picture on it instead of the ugly 3D repros that cluttered the counter. The Boston

Retread Chamber Center was depicted on the front, and there was a message on the back: "Made it fine. As expected am wobbling like a rubber duck. See you soon, Voss."

I handed it back to Ben.

"I'd forgotten about this. I sent it my first day. An attendant had just picked me up off the ground for about the twelfth time."

"The card just came through the reprofax machine two days ago, so, aware of the service's regular screwups, I figured you were about due. My recognizing you was not exactly clairvoyant."

"Well, I never figured to fool you for very long."

"You lucked out fine with that body. Looks strong, fit."

"Thank you. I guess."

"And with that face, at least people will be able to look at you without revulsion this time around. But the body especially: whoever had it first was in real nice shape. Don't get many rejects who care to body-build these days. Let's give you that checkup right now, hey?"

"I refuse to subject myself to the indignities of you and your satanic devices today."

"Fifteen minutes and we can get a complete readout."

"On *your* equipment?"

"Well, twenty-five at the most. C'mon."

"Tomorrow morning, nine o'clock."

"All right then. But this lifetime let's be a little more prompt in keeping your appointments, okay?"

"I'll be here at nine-thirty and you know it."

"What good is a second lifespan if you can't break old habits?"

"What good is the first lifespan if you don't apply your learning from it to the second?"

"You might very well ask that. You, especially, might—"

"You seem pretty eager to get me into a checkup stall. Why the rush? You losing patients?"

"That's true, but it's not the reason. Let's say that, due to better equipped clinics and new doctors who have to pass Advanced Bedside Manner before they're allowed out of med school, the day of the irritable and foible-ridden old doc operating out of his own office is just about over. It's been over for nearly a century but a certain brave few of us have refused to recognize that. There's already been many hints that next time around types like me'd better find a proper clinic and join up, or else consider a new profession. Anyway, I've managed to keep and overcharge a few patients and so lead rather a gentleman's life here. Here, look at the viewer. See? I'm already up to Book IV of *War and Peace.*"

Ben pointed to a dusty viewer which was out of focus, so he'd probably not been reading his Tolstoy too carefully.

"So," he said, turning away from the viewer, "I like to shove bodies into the stall as often as I get the chance."

"Tomorrow morning, nine o'clock. Prompt, I promise."

"There's another reason for a quick checkup that I'm positive the Center avoided briefing you about."

"What's that?"

He stood up and walked to the rural window, looked out it as if the scene genuinely throbbed with life. He crossed his arms and looked thoughtful. I recognized the signs, he was assuming his professional manner.

"Sabotage is the popular word for it, my dear Voss."

"What? Are we in another anarchy cycle or something?"

"In a way, in a way. Particularly in the sense that anarchy generally involves the attacks of the downtrodden upon some of the more fortunate people above them."

"And they're blowing up buildings? I don't see how—"

"No, this time the sabotage is on bodies, not property. It's very new and has only been showing up on bodies retreaded in the last few months. Myself, I haven't examined anyone whose body has been tampered with, so I don't have any first-hand experience with body-sabotage. I suppose the sabotages would have been seen merely as defects, or in some cases failure of the retreading process, if one of the radical doctors had not supplied an anonymous confession. And that started people checking records and—"

"Wait a minute. You've lost me completely. Sabotage? Explain it."

"In this case sabotage is simply the altering of the reject's body before he or she goes to the chamber. Something is removed or something is implanted or something is altered just enough to make things, well, uncomfortable for the new possessor of the body. At least for a while."

"*Something.* What something?"

I could tell he was carefully preparing me, as if for surgery, and I didn't like that.

"Usually body organs. Though all kinds of tricks have been tried. Last I read about, a bone had been removed and been replaced by a plastic replica that had been treated so that it would gradually dissolve in the body inherited by the retread. The shell, as so many people inelegantly call it. A shell, as if it had never had life in it before. Or was a castoff by somebody who didn't care—"

"Look, I'm shuddering enough, so you can bypass the philosophical asides. My bones feel okay at the moment but—"

"Take it easy, there's only been one revealed case of the bone thing. Most of the cases involve the vital organs of the body."

"Well, that's comforting certainly."

Mentally I was exploring my insides. I detected all kinds of possible malfunctions I had never noticed before.

"Removal is one of the key sabotages. Say, one kidney will be taken out. At the retread chamber, where all the qualified personnel are overworked (to say nothing of the majority of unqualified personnel), nobody checks the body—the shell—all that carefully. One little scar looks like another, and there's no reason to be overly observant. So the fact of the removed organ isn't discovered until the retread's first physical. Even then it's not such a big deal unless the kidney that's left is not functioning quite properly, in which case a transplant can after all be arranged. It's just an annoyance factor, you see, a little bit of revolution put aside for the future by the reject with a date at the chamber."

"I'm not sure exactly what this is all about, Ben. You're saying that rejects have operations before submitting themselves for retreading in order to *hurt* the body in some way for its new owner?"

"Yep. They go to the so-called radical doctors, who do all of these things in an underground sort of way, and have whatever destruction or discomforting alteration they choose performed. Actually, operations like the removal of a kidney are, although simple enough, fairly rare because they can be detected so easily and compensated for, even with chamber inefficiency. Most of the sabotage is more subtle and less detectable—and, for that matter, more painful. There's a tricky implantation in the aorta that causes mild pain and is extremely dangerous to operate on. And there's a time-bomb technique they can use on the spinal cord—makes it virtually collapse a few days after the retread receives his new body. Fortunately, most rejects are as cowardly about pain and operations as the rest of us, and don't have anything done. Most who do frequently opt for such sabotages as having a lot of back teeth pulled or an eardrum punctured or—"

"Stop for a minute. I can take just so much picturesque detail and then—"

"Sorry."

Ben walked to a window of a deer leaping away from some hunters. The brown fur-covering of the jumping figurine was shredded and patches of wiring and red cloth were revealed. Ben turned and stared at me. Little pains were developing all over my body, I thought I could hear bones cracking in my arm.

"Why don't they check us out more thoroughly at the retread chamber?"

"That's been suggested. By me and a very few others. But my *doctor friends,* most of them won't hear of it. It's an old AMA thing, really, since before the sabotage began. Years ago the plan was to have clinics right at the chambers; the AMA forbade it with the argument that it would be better if the retread voluntarily went to a doctor or clinic of his own choice. Thereby assuring proper desired care, and more money for the doctors. Now they add the argument that there's enough adjustment necessary after retreading, and if a checkup revealed a major defect in the body, the shock might be too much for the new retread. A sound argument, perhaps, if a bit too rationalized. Think of all you've had to go through in recent days—how much psychological shock could you take?"

"Not much."

"Right. Anyway, there's a further problem, a stupider one. The bureaucrats in charge of the chambers *refuse* to acknowledge that bodies are being tampered with. They insist that the talk of defective shells, as they call them, is exaggerated and, since it comes from obviously self-seeking doctors, as they call them, it is probably untruthful. Whatever their logic, the main thing is that the rumor of defective shells hurts their precious public image, not to mention making them apprehensive that their customers will demand more of them than they're able at present to give. You can almost see their side. There's not, after all, been much cogent information about sabotage so far. No solid research, certainly. They can pooh-pooh it all rather easily right now. But they'll have to come around—"

"Why are the bodies sabotaged in the first place? How did all this come about?"

"Nobody knows for sure, but it's an easy guess. Think of how you'd feel if you knew your body was to be given to a new inhabitant and your life would be snuffed out forever at twenty-six or seven."

"Of course I've thought about that often. Everybody does, but—"

"But nothing. I don't want to get into the argument for and against retreading. We all went through that, at college or someplace. Hell, at that time I agreed thoroughly that the best qualities of humanity were worth preserving, and that retreading was a miraculous way to do it. I was completely convinced that the retreading laws were logical and that the move toward elitism was only natural for an overpopulated world. So few would have to be sacrificed for so many, remember that little idea? I believed all that garbage. I suppose that underneath, in some self-loving way, I still do."

We could not look at each other. That always happened when the ideological underpinnings for retreading were discussed. One time when we were discussing the subject in the enclave's rec room, Selena shut us all up by pointing out that, as long as we stayed safe underground and ventured outside so rarely, we weren't qualified to judge such matters. She said we looked on ourselves as the chosen among the elite who could make decisions for everybody else, when we really were hermits who hid in dark underground caves, avoiding all contact with real progress by pretending to be contributing to it.

"Anyway," Ben continued, "the early days of important reforms, scientific advances, and the straightening-out of world problems that had been in need of solution for decades—all seemed to justify retreading. Even seemed to justify those suppressed beliefs in elitism. Now, I don't know. Some people'd like to abolish retreading. Doubt they'll succeed so long as it's big business, but they might. So, rightfully or wrongfully, the masses are revolting. A small percentage of them anyway. They say it was the original revolutionaries who submitted to the first operations. Which says a lot, I guess, about dedication and sacrifice."

"Where do they get the doctors?"

"Romance, I suspect."

"What?"

"There're times when you want to get in an old-fashioned operating room and get blood all over your surgical gown, just for the nostalgic adventure of it. And the danger, think of the danger. If they catch you, no more retreading for you! That's some good danger, you've got to admit."

"All a bit gruesome for romance."

"I think you don't understand romance."

He rubbed a hand against his shirt, as if wiping it of blood.

"Well," I said, "is it really so serious a problem? What I mean, can't you just transplant for the defective organs?"

"Not at all, my dear Voss. Organ banks are mere transfer points nowadays. On the rare times when an organ, or set of them, arrives at the bank, they have long waiting lists for disposal. That's the paradox of retreading: we need whole bodies, and so few parts ever become available. What parts *are* available, are jealously hoarded by the retread chamber mechanics. Parts of bodies in whom retreading doesn't take are chopped up to use in replacement situations. Top of that, sabotage increases the waiting lists, while also keeping the retread specialists in fits, since sabotage is becoming the chief reason for the need of new organs. You can't even trade organs any longer. You used to be able to barter a kidney for a heart, a lung for a liver. Now you can't get them to take an arm for a fingernail. Only in cases of vital necessity is there a chance anything can be done. Life in danger, they can sometimes come up with a deal. Sometimes you can get an artificial organ on the black market—although the Christian Lobbyists are doing their best to stop that—but usually it doesn't work too well and anyway creates too many problems for both patient and doctor, keeping the things adjusted and that sort of thing. I'm afraid if the body's been sabotaged there's nothing much that can be done about it."

"All the more reason for avoiding that checkup today. But, don't worry, I'll be here prompt—tomorrow morning, eight-thirty."

"Good. C'mon, we'll go out, get some supper. And, since it's my treat, we'll cash in the fortune and get some real food."

"Well, if it can make you take the lock off your wallet, I should get retreaded more often."

He smiled.

"Come to think of it, you're a good argument against retreading. Maybe I'll send a letter to the insurgency group."

8

We ate at a phony seafood restaurant. That is, the restaurant was phony, although the food was quite acceptable. There was a delicious sole almondine (soyabeans instead of almonds, but what the hell), with the fish cooked just right, neither wet-rag soggy nor throat-catching dry. Plus all kinds of side orders. Like beets. It had been years since I'd tasted a juicy red beet but there they were, grown on new altered land and superior to any substitute I'd ever come across.

What made the restaurant grotesque was its pseudo-nautical decor. One room even swayed gently in imitation of the gentle rocking of a ship. We didn't dine in that one. Since the place was lakeside, the windows looked out upon Lake Erie, but with special tinted glass that transformed its dead ugliness into an apparently uncontaminated and lovely lake scene. They might as well have installed a mammoth version of one of Ben's completely fake window views, green fields and leaping deer. That, to me, seemed better than this amelioration of a repulsive waterscape. I complained about it to Ben, but he just shrugged and said:

"That's Cleveland."

I told him my plans, how I wanted my life to be more adventurous this time around.

"Second lifespan syndrome," he said.

"What's that?"

"At the end of first lifetime, one has the natural tendency to review things. Most reviews are a catalogue of losses—missed opportunities, tastes and pleasures that went untasted and unpleasured. What one missed turns out to be what he wants to do first after retreading and renewal."

I did not like the way Ben, with his professional manner, was deflating my dreams, so I changed the subject. Later in the evening he returned to it.

"If you want to sow wild oats, or whatever natural grain appeals, you'd probably best go down to the Hough District. It's organized there now, in sort of a carefully programmed disorder. They've rebuilt the whole area. It lay in ruins for decades after the big fires destroyed it and the order went out to let it lay rather than just reconstruct the ghetto. So they, in effect, moved the ghetto to Cleveland Heights. What with its reclaiming as a pleasure area, Hough's pretty classy now. Dangerous, but classy."

"Why dangerous?"

"Well, a certain amount of violence breaks out regularly. The rejects see it as a kind of symbolic haven, and they sometimes like to stir up a little trouble, inflict a few punishments on the more fortunate. There's a lot of bitterness and resentment just hanging there in the air if you know where to look for it. But, if you keep attention on your own pleasures and needs, you can get by pretty well. Also, there's a lot of police around and—"

"Don't tell me they've revived all those blue laws against

prostitution and drinking and gambling and doping and—"

"Spare me the catalogue of your favorite things. No, it's a free enough area. But there's a lot of hiding of rejects who're trying to prolong their lives, and there's a market in things to help them, like false papers and fake death reports, that sort of thing. The police won't bother you once they know you're all right. If you go, just take care, that's all. It's really no different than it's ever been historically in areas where the fun is."

After dinner I became restless, eager to get moving, test my new life. But Ben was so full of opinions that I played the game of after-dinner coffee (real) and cigars (cabbage leaves). His age finally got the better of him and we escaped the restaurant just as something in the window broke down. The tint failed and patrons got a long glimpse of the real Lake Erie before a waiter pulled a curtain.

I walked Ben home, which was close to the restaurant. Streets were emptying as people scurried to find shelter from a programmed twilight storm. I wanted to walk in the rain, Ben didn't mind. We arrived at his place pleasantly damp. He offered me a drying-out drink, but I didn't care for the cramped smallness of his apartment, where everything attractive had to be slid out of walls and his old Great Moments in Medicine pictures hovered over you threateningly. I could not stop thinking about Hough District, so I made poor excuses, Ben accepted them, and we parted. There was about five minutes of rain left, I rushed out to enjoy them.

9

I took a cab to Hough. For some obscure governmental reason, cabs had been banned during the last years of my first lifetime. Although I rarely questioned the policies of the world government, or even of the American Sector of it (the enclave survived on its grants, after all), I had been puzzled by the vehicle-restriction laws. Apparently a sufficient percentage of the population had also regretted them, for all the restricted types of vehicles were now returned to the streets and roads. My cabdriver said that a dozen new and harmless types of fuels had been invented to make vehicles safe again, and the bans had therefore been lifted. I reclined in the cab's plush back seat and muttered that of course they had presented us with new fuels. Enclave research had shown that such miraculous developments were generally at hand whenever the government leaders needed them, and had usually been so for some time.

I arrived at Hough too early. A few people roamed the streets. They passed me hastily, clearly not yet interested in pleasure-seeking or seekers. That suited me, since I liked to survey an area first, particularly an area like Hough where it's important to know the escape routes. A policeman stopped me and looked at my papers, then advised me to button the top buttons of the light coat I wore. It was the current custom here, he said, and I would not look so much like an outsider. He winked and wished me a good time.

Even in the quiet earlier hours, Hough showed promise. The rainbow streetlamps made me think of circus tent roofs as their rays of light found solidity in twilight mists. As darkness fell and colors sharpened, I noticed the strange abstract designs painted on several buildings. They had not been visible in daylight. Some of them reminded me of Pennsylvania Dutch hex signs. Each facade seemed done in a different style, as if the designers had deliberately chosen to provide an unchronological survey of abstract and expressionistic art since the twentieth century. Later I saw the buildings with landscapes and figure studies on them, so perhaps the intention was, after all, more historically inclusive.

There was no lettering on any building to indicate what went on inside. A shrewd device, since it stimulated the investigatory instinct and kept a steady flow of people in and out of entrances. During my first few minutes within the borders of Hough, I peeked in several doorways.

While my eyes were soothed by the changing and slowly focusing colors, I found many Hough sounds and odors unpleasant. The music that came out of some of the buildings was nerve-wracking and a bit horrifying. I never quite accepted that period's frenetic overtempoed and undermelodied music with its nonsense syllables interspersed with obscenities and longish quotes from classical literature. Odors, though not as annoying, employed more devious methods of attack. In between acceptable food, air-modifier, and other smells would come quick nauseating whiffs of those kinds of perfume that intentionally duplicated animal odors (considered the height of sexiness at that time), or of the kind of rayheated food which is less palatable than the cartons it comes in, or of ghost-tenements from past centuries. I tried to escape from the unpleasant odors by moving to the center of the street but I found the air there more oppressive, so I retreated to the buildings and learned to get used to the smells.

When the sky was sufficiently dark, a man dressed in an old lamplighter's outfit walked the streets. He gave me a greeting but, since it was in some kind of slang, I could not understand him, so I just nodded back. Using an electric-eye wand, he set the rainbow lamps into slow revolutions. As they turned, each surface of each ten-sided lamp cast its color on buildings and people—and on the street, which was especially treated to glow with soft bands of color, all changing with the shifts in the lamplight. The activity of the light made you feel you were moving even when you were standing still. Glowing bands moved like an assembly line beneath your feet.

I gazed at the sidewalk with so much concentration and for so long that I drew a businesswoman to my side.

"Up to anything worth my while?" she asked.

I looked up. She seemed quite worthwhile. A tall, voluptuously designed young woman whose face was so childlike I couldn't believe it was she who'd made the proposition. I realized later that the innocence in her face, on many Hough faces, was a carefully calculated blend of cosmetics and ritual, reinforced by the pastel shadows that swept across the face in the moving lamplight. She moved in closer, spoke again:

"If you're good to me, well, all I can say is I got a bed that can do almost as many tricks as I can."

"That must be some bed."

"I'll let you press all the buttons."

Her dress, which clung to her body from neck to thigh without a single symmetry-destroying wrinkle, changed color from blue to light green. It, too, was treated to respond to the rainbow lamplight. I glanced at her slipper-styled shoes. They made similar color changes, but in darker, deeper tints.

Taking my arm and leading me up the street, she named her price. Ben had prepared me for the current Hough rates, but I was still surprised when she whispered to me a list of her rates, charges that I found exorbitant even with my newfound feeling of extravagance. She saw my reluctance and, experienced businesswoman that she was, made her voice sexier as she pleaded her case. Her final ploy was to stop me beneath one of the lights, where the color changes were more intense, and to kiss me with some passion. Her soft lips and adventurous tongue should have out-argued the remaining bits of enclave puritanism left within me. It disturbed me that they did not. Although this firm-bodied and sexy woman was *exactly* what I had been anticipating in my renewal-period fantasies, I did not feel properly responsive to her. Intellectually, I desired her, but I could not summon up a reasonably good physical or emotional response. There was no increase in heartbeat, no anticipatory jitteriness, no stirring in the loins. I wondered if my years of only slightly marred fidelity to Selena had warped all my sexual attitudes. Well, hell, forget it, I told myself, you're just out of practice. I kissed the woman back and agreed to the deal on her terms. She demanded half her money in advance. Ben had warned me about this, too. In Hough, he had said, the only cheating came from outsiders—unusually bitter rejects, and retreads who took delight in cheating inferiors. I had been surprised about the rejects. Ben said that many of the customers who came to Hough were last-fling rejects, an embittered breed who did not care what they did, even to their own kind.

As I counted the bills, while taking sidelong glances at my new purchase counting right along with me, I pictured Selena laughing about my buying of a whore. I remembered the times in bed with Selena when I could not evince even the slightest sexual attraction for her. Such failure usually led to Selena's gentle reassurances that it did not matter (and of course it did not matter much to her, at least not after our early years), and I could not help thinking (but could not say) that it goddamned well did matter. Generally when I reviewed my earlier lifetime, I took the easy way out and blamed my impotent periods on Selena. She was just not desirable. More than that, she did not care about sex. Her idea of a perfect relationship had been working together side by side in metallic laboratories and grossly lit conference rooms, then reviewing the workday (side by side) in the evenings. In my darker moods, I sometimes thought she had a better chance of orgasm with a test-tube dildo than with me. Selena had contributed more to the enclave than I had. It occurred to me, at least in retrospect, that her sexlessness might have been responsible for her success. Even my fling with Lanna had not proved a great deal. As men frequently do, I chose for my mistress a woman so much like my wife (kind to my failures, politely grateful for my successes) that I made no real advance in my sex life. I forced myself to accept the excuse that there were men who simply did not have the carnal needs that others displayed so blatantly, and so I spent the rest of my life contributing to the footnote I left behind. Toward the end, I formed my vow to make up for the sexual missed opportunities the next time around, when I would have a functional body and a new set of stimulations. I had what Ben had called the second lifespan syndrome in abundance. There were, in fact, so many new experiences I wanted that it might take an entire second lifetime to accomplish them.

And, to make matters worse, the first step on my new road was obviously not going to be easy.

However, looking at this eager friendly young woman—

"Thanks," she said, accepting the money and discovering an opening at hip level of her tight-fitting dress in which to deposit it.

—I realized that I would not, after all, mind the effort.

10

"Part of the lease agreement, friend, is buying me a few stimulants first."

Again she took my arm. Her touch made my neck feel warm. Hopeful.

"Not that I really need stimulation to react to a guy of your build." I felt suddenly ecstatic with my new body. It was, after all, so much taller and broader than the natural one I'd been born with and lived a full lifetime in spite of. "No, it's just part of the routine, flattering you. You don't need flattery, when it's the truth. You know, don't you? Of course *you* know."

I liked what she said, the way she cajoled me into confidence. On the other hand, I suspected that it was still a routine–sly instructions to a hick. We walked along silently for a while before it occurred to me that talking might also be part of the routine. I asked her name.

"Mary. Just plain grand-old-name Mary."

She tightened her grip on my arm. Intimate. Her hip kept brushing mine as she began to walk closer, almost to hang on my body. Now I felt warm all over, which made me relax a bit. Embarrassment was a good sign. Hopeful.

"My ma had good instinct. She looked into my cradle, took one short look, and decided Mary, a simple name was good enough for a simple child. Ma wasn't a reject. Strange, but she sure knew one when she saw one. She brought me up like I was somebody else's kid. When I tested turndown the second time, she moved all my junk into the front hallway and told me to let her know when the moving men'd come."

In the false and unfair lighting of this carnival street, with her dress changing color every few steps, Mary seemed like a walking copy of a human being–but also like a painting that one should grab and preserve from the barrages of an outside war. I often forgot that there were people inside what we sometimes callously called shells, people who despaired at the hatred of their mothers, joked about the inevitability of their fates. *Sentimentalist*—I could hear Ben's voice raised in accusation. *Bleeding heart*—and of course Ben understood, he was the biggest bleeding heart sentimentalist of us all. We cry, then we laugh, then we cry because we laughed, then we laugh because we cried—and that's why Ben and I are the simpletons of our breed.

"Turndown, that's the crap they hand us in filthy silver spoons, in triple-dip cones."

I noted that she said *us.* The lie of camaraderie would make everything easier for me, I thought.

"But I guess you don't want to hear much more of that, not when we're both so close to the charnel house."

I almost asked her what she meant by *charnel house,* but it was clearly slang and I knew I should be wary of slang that might give away my retread identity. A moment's thinking, and the obvious and disquieting connection between charnel house and retread chamber came to me.

Since she accepted me as a reject, I chose to build on the pretense.

"I'd like to dodge the charnel house, I sure would," I said.

"Yeah, well . . . yeah."

"When my time comes, I might hide out—"

"Submerge."

Her correction was offhanded, casual.

"—here in Hough. I know it's futile but, if it looks like they're going to catch me—"

"Hook you."

"—I'll take care of my body, sabotage it. Maybe you know of a place I could hide—*submerge.*"

Some suspicion in her eyes.

"Might be, friend, might be."

I did not like the negative sound of her assurance. Maybe I had misstepped. I decided to back off, utilize the tone of despair I'd picked up from her:

"Ah, well, it's no use, I'll line up at the charnel house like any other . . . any other . . ."

"Gift package to a lifer."

She turned her attention away from me, studied passing people and fronts of buildings as if she were taking a poll of the jury. I was momentarily frightened.

"C'mon," she finally said, pulling at my arm to make me walk faster, "you got the money and we got nothing but turndown time to use, let's get someplace."

Relief, I was just a paying customer to her, no matter what she might suspect. I figured that status must be unimportant in the Hough pleasure games. Which shows the kind of innocent I was.

She led me to a building stippled in dots, something like a Seurat painting but with larger circles. Light passing across its surface created a peculiar wavelike effect. I stopped, fascinated. I could have spent hours staring at the design upon that building, but Mary pulled at me and ordered:

"Inside."

Inside. Well, inside was a surprise to me, too. Inside was not at all like outside. No soft, softening lights, no faint circus mist, no sense of emollients or purifiers.

We ascended a stairway upholstered in a plush gray rug. On either side of us were velvet-covered walls, deep red, in a diamond pattern. The high mahogany door at the top of the short stairway was bordered with inlaid carved statues that looked vaguely pre-Raphaelite. The door was opened for us by a cadaverous man in butler's attire. He bowed as we passed, and I thought I heard a hinge somewhere around his waistline creak.

The room we now entered was designed and laid out like a gentleman's club, vintage late-nineteenth century. Wide and high-ceilinged, layers of cigar smoke entwining and disappearing, massive armchairs, solid tables, bookcases lining the walls, books in handsome leather bindings, waiters holding trays high and moving comfortably across the room, serving people in armchairs. Incongruous to the usual ideal of the gentleman's club was the presence of women, almost all of them as sensually dressed as my companion. There was also an ungentlemanly raucous sound to the actively conversing voices. Perhaps, I thought, a stag night at a polite club would have such a semblance.

Mary, still tugging at my arm as if I were a stubborn dog, led me to a corner alcove, where we sat together on a Victorian love-seat. I got a little woozy staring at the cupids and flowers surrounded by curlicues that formed the fabric design of the chair. My finger traced the pattern. Mary jabbed at my arm. I looked up to find a snobbish-looking waiter, who obviously saw the riff-raff in me, waiting for an order. I asked Mary to order for us, to cover the fact that I had no idea what to ask for in a place like this one. She told the waiter, two gin and tonics. He included her in his disdain.

"Gin?" I asked. "Real, live gin?"

"They claim it."

"Interesting."

"You slipped off gin? You can order something else."

"No, fine with me. I've never had it."

"Then you won't know whether it's real live or not."

She was sounding more professional. I did not like feeling like a business item, especially from the debit side of the ledger.

"You like it here?" I asked.

"Something wrong with it?"

"No, I just wondered."

"It's nice. Only place in Hough quite like it. They say it has something to do with social aspirations. But you know what I'm talking about."

"Sure."

Of course I did not understand at that time. Now, I think perhaps such clubs represented the kinds of life which the reject was denied. Rejects could mimic, and in some ways even improve on, the privileges of the chosen. The first time Mary approached me she asked if I would be worth her while, and I had taken the phrase to be a casual conversation opener. But I think now that being worth her while was more important than a profitable evening.

The waiter brought the drinks. Although I had never had gin, I knew that I still had never had gin when I drank that stuff.

There's something about ersatz flavor that you can recognize even when you haven't tasted the original. But I pretended it must be the real thing, and Mary seemed pleased.

Three swallows of gin and I realized something new about my new body. It was not at all used to alcoholic refreshment. I could feel the blood—or something—flowing through my arms and legs. In my first lifetime I had been able to drink just about anything with only the slightest side-effects. My fear of appearing foolish had always held back drunkenness for me. But this time—with no Selena, no fellow workers, no Ben Blounte around—I didn't care how I acted.

Mary spoke to me. I heard all the syllables, but they did not gather together into a comprehensible sentence. Blinking my eyes to clear my vision and sitting up straight, I regained some concentration.

"I really don't," Mary was saying.

"Really don't what?" I asked, with fairly clear enunciation.

"Don't believe you know your way around a flagpole."

"Why on earth would anyone want to go around a flagpole?"

"If you don't know, I'm not going to tell you. Drink up."

"Something tells me that might not be the best idea."

"On the way to the charnel house you'll regret every swallow not swallowed."

"You say that like a proverb, a maxim."

"You've never read . . . No, never mind."

"Never read what?"

"Value the tears of this life as well as the laughter, prolong the pain *and* the pleasure, place hate on equal par with love—any of that mean anything to you?"

"Something."

"What? What exactly?"

"You're grilling me."

"On hot coals. If a man offend thee, let him know, or find graphic ways to show him. How about that? Can you do anything with that?"

"What should I do?"

"You don't know, I can't tell you."

"The worst guidance for life is a proverb that merely sounds good."

That stopped her. She squinted at me.

"What the matter?" I asked.

"That one seemed right. I should remember it."

In spite of my general confusion, I could take a cue when I heard it.

"Thought you'd know it right off."

"I don't know them all. Who the hell knows them all? Who wants to read the whole book? I couldn't–"

"There you are. I read my part, you read yours."

"But I should know the one you said. I saw it, and it wasn't quite like you said it."

The farther I carried the bluff, the easier it became, particularly as Mary supplied more clues.

"Well," I said, "I won't claim to have it exact. I haven't opened the damn book in a long time. Who needs it ? I mean, we should live by the words inside us, not those in that damn book."

She was now thoroughly muddled. Downing the rest of my gin, I felt confident I could bluff my way through any of her suspicious conjectures.

"I don't know," she said. "Around here everybody quotes. Never knew anybody that–"

"We travel in different circles. Mine takes pride in screwing up the quotes. Mine laughs at your precious book. We believe in action."

A bold move, but I could see that it got to her.

"I'm sorry, I didn't realize that you–"

"That I what?"

"Be careful. Don't talk so loud. Don't you know they send spies down here?"

"Bah! Forget about spies. Too late for them."

"Really?"

Mary became so wide-eyed that I regretted the stretching of my bluff. My newfound skill at inference could too easily backfire.

"I'm sorry," I said, "perhaps I've said too much. Maybe we should leave."

She agreed, a bizarre respect for me in her eyes. I paid the bill, finding its amount only normally astonishing. Mary set a brisk pace across the room. I followed unsteadily. Before we reached the door, a voice called out to Mary. She turned, and responded to the wave of a short, pudgy man almost buried in a leather armchair near the exit. He looked like a king who had retired and gone to seed.

"God, it's Sam," Mary whispered. "Sorry, friend, I *have* to stop for him. A matter of social etiquette."

"Why?"

"He controls about half of this area. For that matter, he controls me."

She turned on her charm as she sat on a divan beside his chair. I sat beside her, and Sam glanced at me. I thought I had seen distrust in Mary's eyes, but Sam's glowed with the real thing. For a minute I thought he was going to require credentials. I sank back into the plushness of the divan, trying to keep Mary between us as an obstruction to Sam's line of vision.

They exchanged pleasantries. Sam shifted his body forward and gave me a long once-over with his doubting eyes. I felt myself sobering up.

"The word's come through," he said to Mary. "Got a better deal than ever."

"Sam, what do I need with a better deal? I hate the one I've got enough, I couldn't hate a better one any more."

"No, listen. That last deal was a splintered shaft, I'm ashamed I brought so many of you in on it. You got to allow me mercy."

"If I know your deals, you've probably sold your ticket on the charnel line to the devil and been promised retreading as God."

"Join emotion to mind when time's on the block."

"Do not hearken to the voice that whispers, 'Early.' "

"C'mon, Mary, that's not fair. I only perform a service."

"Service is the corrupt man's word for selling out his brothers."

Mary's facility with the proverbs made me wonder how I had ever bluffed her.

"Listen to this, Mary. Now, if I remember right, you got the policy that provides a good supply of funds and other needs from your twenty-fourth to twenty-fifth birthdays."

"Didn't used to be a 'good supply of funds.' When you sold it to me, you said it was more than I'd ever need for a comfortable year."

"Jargon of the trade, my dear. But *their* jargon, not mine. I believed it. I really believed it was the best possible policy ever provided in the history of insurance companies. I really *believed* that."

"You gave that impression."

"Sure, I'm always searching for the best for my people, I'm—"

"Best conditions, a better share of the intake for you."

"Unfair, Mary, unfair. I'm a businessman, sure, but not your cheating run of the mill—"

"The stealer of years cannot properly be called a mere thief, he is justly condemned as a kleptomaniac."

"Hell, Mary, you've even got that one wrong."

"Ask him." She pointed a thumb at me. "He's an expert."

They both stared at me. Nervous silence.

"I think you got it right," I said. "I *think.*"

Sam leaned toward her, his face oily, sincerity steaming out of his pores.

"This one's it, Mary, your guts'll cry out for it when you hear."

"My guts are crying out now, but not the way you mean."

"Listen!"

His voice displayed the authority of a man who controlled areas. Mary listened.

"This one's got so many options you're in danger of using up your year just trying to choose. Think of this for one: relocation to any place on earth, any vacation spot or whatever, all expenses paid by the company—even a plan where you can take in as many of the spots as you please. Let your mind roll that around. Anyplace on earth."

"But not offplanet."

Sam appeared insulted.

"Naturally not offplanet! What kind of idiots you think run the company? They don't want to have to find you when your year's run out. As it is, they don't trust nobody to turn their body in at the end of the policy year. They'll be squatting on your doorstep the day before your birthday, you can believe that."

"Which birthday? It would be crazy to hope that it would be the twenty-fifth on this one, too."

"Mary, we both know you're not that naive. Insurance wouldn't make any sense if they just bettered the deal they already gave you. You know their principle is, the earlier you turn yourself into the charnel house, the more they're willing to give you in their contracts and policies. No, what you do here is get credit for your former policy—which does, believe me, raise the ceiling on the benefits of the new policy—and I write you up one in which you agree to cash in on your twenty-fourth instead of twenty-fifth. Then, from twenty-three to twenty-four is the best year a person could have and not only that—"

"You're insane, Sam."

"Careful."

A warning.

"I am twenty-two now. Twenty-two and a *half.* It's bad enough I have to face the thought of only two and a half years before I make my early-arrival to the charnel house. You think I want a year cut off that, just so my easy-life year is somehow a bit better—"

"A *lot* better."

"Screw, Sam. I only bought the other policy to have something definite to look forward to, I don't need—"

"I know your argument. I've been in the business long enough. Since I was thirteen. All you got to do is think about—"

"I don't have to think. Not for a minute. The only real hope we have is in the length of a year, the using-up of a day, the eternity of a minute—and I'm not misquoting a word there."

"Let me tell you more of the options, this must be the *longest* contract ever offered."

"All in fine print, I expect."

"Give it a chance, Mary."

"No!"

"You hurt me. Heaven forbid that I should offer you a bad deal."

"I know, Sam. I also know I owe you a lot, and I don't want to insult your intentions, but please don't try to press this one on me. I'm happy the way things are. The best happiness is believing you are happy with the way things are. Remember that one."

"Okay, Mary, I understand."

Although his voice was sympathetic to her, he hardly skipped a beat before addressing me in a businesslike way:

"How about you, friend? What can I do about your coverage?"

He could not have knocked the wind out of me any faster if he'd stuck me in the stomach with a rolled-up policy.

"It's fine," I said. "My coverage's fine."

"What is it exactly?"

I looked, I'm sure, like the instructor of a class in squirming.

"It's . . . it's enough for my needs."

"Personal, family plan, assigned indemnity?"

"I'm satisfied with it, let's leave it at that. I don't care to do business when I'm—"

"I get it. You've opted full term. I always recognize the signs. Defensiveness, ready to dodge any sensible talk about the improvement of your life. I recognize them. Listen, boy, you're making a mistake, my—"

"Please, not—"

"You opt out a year early and I can give you almost the same terms as I was discussing with Mary here. Look, all time is alike when you've not provided for yourself."

"Company slogan," Mary said.

"Almost. Now, just give me a minute and I can outline a plan that'll—"

"You stupid leech, I don't want to hear your goddamned plan!" I had not intended to scream at Sam, and I was discomfited by all the threatening faces that turned to stare at me.

"There's no reason to—" Sam said.

"Plenty of reason." I tried to keep my voice down. "You

pretend you're doing a service when you're really asking them—asking us—to give up what precious time we've got in exchange for a few measly trinkets."

"You call these options *trinkets?*"

"Exactly. Gifts to the foolish natives for agreeing to ride the slave ship. Incense for the charnel house. Beads, my friend, trade goods, shiny toys, trinkets!"

"You think a year in Paradise is not worth trading for that extra year in Hell?"

"Don't fake it, Sam," Mary interrupted. "You used that line, or one very much like it, on me the first time around. Besides, if you want to keep your religion straight, it shouldn't be Hell, it should be Purgatory."

"I don't care what I said the first time around! Nobody talks to me the way this bastard just did. I didn't choose the way these policies are written, I just sell them as they come."

"And you're not selling me, so why don't you just let Mary and me go?"

I started to stand up, motioning to Mary to do the same. Sam leaned toward her.

"He talks funny, Mary. You sure he's okay?"

"He is okay with me, and that's enough, Sam. So long, we've got to be going."

"I don't know. He talks like a wobbler to me."

"Goodbye, Sam!"

Mary seized my arm and pulled me out of the drawing room.

"He better not be, Mary," Sam called after her.

"Why did he say that? That I'd better not be?" I asked, as we passed through the doorway. "I'd better not be what, for that matter?"

Mary stopped in the doorway, leaving the wraithlike butler holding the door open for her, and she stared at me for several seconds.

"He meant that you better not be a wobbler, of course."

I almost asked what he'd meant by wobbler, but suddenly I realized the word's meaning anyway. I had used something like it in my postcard to Ben. A wobbler was a retread, a slang term derived from the insecurity with which a retread handles his new body. I remembered my own wobbling the first days out of the retread chamber accommodation section. The word seemed quite appropriate.

"Why is he so concerned about it? I mean, why does he care about wobblers?"

She sighed.

"It's custom. Custom around here, anyway. He hardly allows wobblers into his district of Hough, only does it at all when it's clear they're carrying sufficient amounts of money. None of the other bosses are like that, they don't care whose money or how much so long as it's spent in their districts. But Sam's really out for revenge. He wants to screw wobblers out of the cash as fast as he can, and using any method available. Con job, legitimate business, or a beating, he don't care, so long as he gets one hundred percent of what the guy brought across the border. Not for himself, mind you, Sam lets us keep our usual percentage of the take, he just wants to screw any wobbler that staggers his way across the borders of Hough."

Mary apparently agreed with Sam's views of proper bossism.

"He's pretty excitable," I said.

"Sure enough. That's why it would be instant massacre if you did turn out to be a wobbler."

"I don't follow."

She regarded me as if I were too naive to be possible.

"Look, you just gave him hell, right? You're a stranger and you talked back to him like you were one of the Hough crowd. He's not too keen on us speaking up to him in the way I did and there are limits to what he'll allow. I get away with more than most 'cause I been around so damn long. And, whether it seems that way to you or not, you attacked him more than I did. Not more often but deeper. He don't like that, but he'll let you go, mainly 'cause we got out of there fast enough. But, if you'da been a wobbler, he would've gone berserk. No wobbler is gonna talk back to him. He hardly endures that when he's outside Hough and dealing with outsiders. They say he gets into fights. He certainly isn't going to put up with wobbler shit on his own turf."

"Well, I'm no wobbler, anyway."

"Like he said, you better not be."

Although she smiled, there was something secret in her eyes. A threat waiting for the right time.

11

Back on the street, I shivered at a cold breeze. The pastel lights had a moodier glow to them now. I asked Mary if they changed in intensity or coloring; she said no. Apparently the fuzziness which the lighting lent to the surroundings allowed one to see things according to his mood. For me, even the colors painted on the buildings took on a different tone. I felt as if I were traveling through a multicolored Slough of Despond.

Mary grew laconic, responding only to my direct questions. I asked her about children, and she told me she had gone through the proper childbearing period as part of a government measure to encourage (and ensure) reject-births. The law had since been revoked, but Mary had borne three children, each of which was immediately farmed out.

"They're okay kids, I guess, from what I hear. Dumb as hell. They're not going to upset any balances. Well, better a shell than a wasted life, as the book says. I have done my bit, anyhow."

I asked her where we were going, hoping she would answer, her place. I was having interesting visions of her special bed. But she answered:

"To a place. You'll see."

We walked slowly. The streets were more crowded now. I would have liked to walk a bit faster, especially when I saw that some of the passersby were eyeing me strangely.

We came to an unimpressive building without the wild coloring of its neighbors. Painted all black with white bordering around its single window, and a black and white checkered pattern on its door, the place seemed too austere for Hough district. Mary nodded toward the door and we walked to it. It parted for us, like a curtain. I touched its material as we passed. Surprisingly, it was made of metal, not cloth.

It took a minute for me to become adjusted to the darkness inside the building, then another minute to adjust to the inside of the building. As soon as the door sealed shut behind us, hands gently took our hands and led us forward. We went through another door, I think, and the guiding hands stopped us. As I began to see better, I realized we were standing at the end of a large room. Again, the decor was austere. Black and white curtains intertwined along the side walls. Down front was a massive ceiling-to-floor curtain in separated black and white panels. On the floor were seats that had to be stepped down into, cushioned holes in the floor. Out-of-tune music was being played casually and lethargically somewhere behind the paneled curtain. The sparse lighting was placed irregularly at floor level, and was one of the reasons why it was so difficult to get one's bearings in the room.

"Is it a theater?" I asked Mary.

"You guessed."

"Been a while since I've been inside one."

Which came close to being a slip of the tongue. It had been more than sixty years.

An usher came and led us to our seats. There was room for two in our floor-hole. We descended on steps at opposite sides of the hole. Once we were settled, the usher handed us programs and left. Mary asked why I looked so disappointed.

"I expected to be strapped in or wired up or something."

She laughed.

"I've heard about that kind of show. Years and years ago they had some kind of theater where you got plugged or wired into the performance. Goes back quite some time, decades at least."

"I don't know much about theater, I suppose. Only been a couple of times."

"You'll enjoy this, and it'll be something like being wired up. There are devices in the cushions behind us, sensors I think they call one kind of 'em, and they make suggestions."

"Suggestions?"

"I guess they're called that. They use that word here, I know. Look it up in your program. The sensors and other stuff can help you feel things from the play, but only as much as you want. Works on your mind in some way, instead of forcing the feelings on you. Why they call them suggestions, I guess."

In more technical language the program verified what Mary told me. Apparently the sensors sent out a wave, actually a set of them, that influenced the audience in feeling, thought, and response. However, each member of the audience could control the extent to which he was influenced. If he wanted to be free of all suggestion, he could lean forward. That action would break contact with the sensors and wave-senders that were centered inside the cushion. The waves received would themselves be subtly influenced by the state of mood and emotion of each audience member, and by the general feeling collectively of the audience. Certain aspects of the play could be altered by the intensity of audience reaction.

The program also devoted space to information about the play being performed that evening, which was entitled *Death, Exactly What You Think It Is.* It was being performed by the Theater Department of the Hough in Action Overall Protest Committee, a high-sounding title for an organization functioning in the heart of a glamorized red-light district.

A program note said:

> Once drama was structured on a system incorporating two to five divisions, called *acts.* Generally each act was somewhat shorter than the act preceding it, so that the drama had a comfortable framework to which the members of its audience could respond easily, knowing that the sequences would build in a regular fashion to climactic moments and that the play as a whole would obey regulations of tempo and pace leading to the inevitable conclusion. The audience, it is said, responded so willingly to structured drama because it provided an organization to the virtually unstructured lives they led. Although periodically plays broke with these traditional patterns, the basic structure remained for several

centuries. In recent years the old form of drama has gone out of vogue, although stodgily and arthritically preserved by our various enclaves of *approved* national theater. Now, it seems to us, the time for experimentation has come again—at a time when vitally needed. Perhaps our work, the work you will see and experience tonight, is only another cyclical emergence of unstructured art, or perhaps it is the wave of the future. We do not care. All we know is that now it is life that is structured, at least for some of us, perhaps the statistical majority if the right records could be revealed to us. It is life that, like old drama, comes to an inevitable regulated conclusion, and perhaps just at the climactic moment. Therefore, we believe that an unstructured drama, which never really ends, which reaches its climaxes without tempo and irregularly, which takes up one night from the point where it reached its weary end the night before, which sometimes ends, which is (above all) reflecting the way life used to be—this kind of unstructured drama is necessary for our regulated lives as structured drama once was for those whose futures included haphazard potentials.

The rest of the program listed cast and credits. I shut it and glanced at Mary. She seemed withdrawn. She had twisted her program into a cylinder and was trying to squeeze the cylinder tighter. Twice she looked over her right shoulder.

"Something wrong?" I asked.

She nodded.

"You might as well know. I think there's a couple of Sam's men standing in the back of the auditorium. I'm not sure, it's awfully dark, but I think I recognize them by their shapes."

"Shapes?"

"Yeah, sounds funny. But, when you been in Hough as long as I have, you get to recognize real danger by its shape. If I'm right, these two guys are the top goons of Sam's squads, the two he always sends out when he's *really* mad. Down here, we catch sight of them out of the corners of our eye, if we are lucky enough to see them first, and we scurry to doorways or safe shelters. 'Course, if they are after us, they get us anyway, but you can't stop instinct from running its course."

"And you think they're here for us?"

"I think they might be here for *you.* But who knows? They might be here for somebody else. Maybe it's their night off and they're avid theatergoers. Which I doubt. I'd just be cautious if I were you. After all, you're the one who just proud as punch walked away from Sam when he was furious at you."

Mary gave me a strange look. A cat and mouse look almost, with her the cat. I got the impression she was enjoying the threat of these hoods. I lounged casually in my seat, getting my head as close to floor level as I could without dropping out of sight completely.

The play began suddenly. All lights went out. The cast members started to utter emotional sounds. First there was a moan from a forward corner of the theater, then happy laughter broke out among a group somewhere to the rear. A soft humming drifted in from the left, and was countered by a snort of disgust from the other side. New sounds were added, sounds of joy and contentment mixed with sorrow and pain. I sensed cast members moving around the spaces between the audience compartments. They became quite loud. A girl crawled by our floor-hole, purring sexually in my ear. I found myself trembling uncontrollably and could not understand why, then I realized it must be caused by the devices in the cushions. I leaned forward, breaking contact with the cushion, and my trembling stopped. I reached over and touched Mary. Her skin was cold, and she was shaking.

The sounds of the actors around us subsided. When they seemed acceptably soft, I leaned back against the cushion. Immediately a sense of relief, which I understood as a release from violent emotion, overcame me. It seemed as if I had never interrupted the flow of emotion when I had broken contact with the cushion.

The lights went up on a scene already in motion. The program notes had said that one night's performance started where the previous one had left off, and that seemed to be what was happening. An actor dressed in conventional streetclothes stood over an actress who performed the last writhing movements of what was intended as a particularly painful death. Behind them a chorus line mocked and exaggerated the death motions of the actress. Their movements were clownish and grotesque. They laughed often in an agitated staccato.

I felt joyful as the girl neared her final death throes. I glanced at Mary, who was looking sideways at the stage, sorrow in her face. She kept rubbing the area just below her left eye, causing a red blotch to form there. A pair of actresses walked through the audience, each carrying a small purple and yellow striped box. As one of them passed me, she offered to play cards, chess, checkers, or any other games that would provide distraction from the main drama. She suggested the diversions first in a sensual voice, then in the manner of a hawker selling goods. To our right a frightened man took up an offer from the other saleswoman. They started playing a game, their heads carefully turned away from the action of the play.

A moment before the onstage actress finally stopped throbbing with exaggerated pains of death, I felt a sudden emotional change. A profound sorrow came over me in a wave. Mary's sorrow appeared to have diminished, for she was now smiling. I was puzzled by the differences in our reactions to the same scenes. The actress finally lay still, and the man began to strut through the audience. A door in the ceiling opened and balloons drifted down. The chorus began dancing in the style of formal ballet. First they danced around the dead girl, then picked her up and passed her from dancer to dancer. I felt exultation, a sense of glory. My mind was suddenly full of poems that I did not recall ever reading, although I was certain they derived from classical sources. Along with the chorus line, I (and presumably the entire audience) celebrated death. Apparently the machinery of the cushion provided several impulses simultaneously, for I was also aware of the fact that what I was celebrating was a traditional religious view of death. In spite of my own religious cynicism, I now knew for certain that, no matter how bloody and painful the actress's death, the glory she would attain justified all. The actor, whom I knew to be her murderer, stopped in front of Mary and me. Staring down at me, he said:

"That's a decent death she had, isn't it?"

Not only was I self-conscious at being addressed by an actor who should have stayed within his play, I was also uneasy because it was possible he had seen through me, recognized me for the filthy retread I was in his eyes. All of this feeling, plus a bit of confusion, intruded on the joy and ecstasy that the cushion was transmitting.

"It is glorious, isn't it?" he continued.

I nodded my head, feeling as if he were pulling strings on it. I was dimly aware that Mary nodded, too.

"Sir, you look like a wise owl, offer up your body today, let me kill you now, before your time, before the charnel house gets you. Defraud the system, deprive them of one more body and we beat them one more time. C'mon, let me have you, I can give you your choice of many enjoyable and painful departures from this world."

I shrank back into my cushion, afraid I would die any minute. Mary did the same. Clearly she was afraid of his offer, too. I could not tell whether our fear was natural or induced by the cushions. Instead of continuing his offer, the actor smiled and said:

"No, of course you won't accept my proposal, nobody ever does. We're all in the charnel house line this very minute."

The man's eyes seemed to be lighted from the inside. To avoid them, I looked back at the stage. The actress was still being passed around the line of dancers. For a moment I was convinced that she actually was dead, that the actor had made his offer and she had accepted. I forced myself to lean forward, away from the cushion. My feelings did not leave me so easily this time. The actor broke into a smile and said:

"Stopper the sweat, mate. You live, and she does, too."

Suddenly the actress revived. As she leaped down to the floor, color returned to her face. She ran down the center aisle to me, and slid to the floor by our compartment. She grabbed my head and kissed me firmly on the mouth, while the actor laughed. His laughter was part joyful, part insulting, as if he mocked both death and me. As the actress kissed me, she gently pressed me back against the cushion. Her tongue entered my mouth briefly and left there the taste of blood, an effect that I would have thought beyond the sensory equipment. Yet the taste was not, I was sure, real.

Standing up, the actress did a couple of easy ballet steps, then picked up a balloon rolling by her feet. She tapped it to me, and I tapped it back to her. Although the cushion was clearly sending out happiness, I felt some genuine contradictory fear. I was afraid of the way these performers were centering on me. What did they know? Was the fact I did not belong so evident?

The rest of the cast sauntered through the audience and duplicated her balloon-tossing act with others. Some raucous music blared out. The performers reacted to it by returning to the main stage area in automated fashion. One of them recited a poem on the meaninglessness of death at any age, coming to the predictable conclusion that the dictated death of a reject was an insult to hallowed human values. Although I thought the poetry wretched, the cushion apparatus forced my eyes to fill with tears. I felt a beauty in the lines that I could not perceive. It was bad enough to have to sit through a terrible play, but to have to respond to it in a manner alien to one's intelligence was too much to bear. There was suspicion in Mary's eyes when I leaned forward, so I tried to look as if I appreciated what I saw and I sank backwards.

After a pair of sardonically comic segments which made light of the charnel house line and the imminency of death, the actress who had kissed me was pushed forward by the others. She looked around the theater as if she wondered what she was doing there, then she began to sing. Her voice was delicate, childlike. It quavered on high notes, became a whisper on low notes. But it was beautiful, and so was the song. The melody seemed formal, almost classical. The lyrics were simple. All of the other music I had heard so far in my new life was strident and unpleasant. The actress's song was effective not only for its musical beauty but for the way it treated the sadness of an individual death, the singer's own, as a single tragic matter—in contrast to the exaggerated and polemical way the subject of death was being treated in the rest of the play. Even when I leaned forward, I still felt the song's, and the singer's, beauty. When I had seen her up close, when she'd kissed me, I had thought she had a nymphlike but not extraordinary attractiveness. Now she seemed a pale perfect vision of beauty. While she sang, I fell deeply in love with her (still realizing that the feeling was, at least partially, bestowed upon me) and I did not want her to die, ever. I had an overwhelming urge to try to save her, hide her out from the charnel house robbers. But, I thought, everybody could be found if they had to be. I began to cry, vaguely aware that Mary, too, wept. Overcome by emotion, I made the key mistake. In the midst of my sobbing I began to chant:

"I'm sorry, I'm sorry, I'm sorry . . ."

I should have seen that Mary and the rest of the audience were reacting to the song by crying about their own fates. I was the *only* audience member who was loudly begging forgiveness. I could not stop shouting how sorry I was, even when my back had broken contact with the cushion. I did not realize for a moment that the singer had stopped her song and was staring at me. I brought my hands up to my face to wipe away tears.

Beside me, Mary began to laugh softly.

I looked at her. She was sitting up straight, a vindictive gleam in her eyes. I knew what she would say and I stood up, trying to discover the location of the exits.

"I knew it, you're a wobbler!" she screamed. "I knew before Sam did, damn it! I gave him the signal when we were all sitting together."

I started climbing out of the floor compartment. Mary stood up. All over the room, people in the audience were staring at me, their eyes just above the level of the floor. They looked like children peering out from hiding places. Turning, Mary made a broad hand-signal. The two men she had pointed out to me as Sam's flunkies were now running toward me, their fists clenched, tear streaks running down from their eyes.

I ran toward the stage, where the actors were now milling about. Trying to change direction toward an exit, I stumbled and slid across the polished floor, almost into a floor-hole, whose two inhabitants backed to the further edge, holding out their hands as if to ward off contact with a plague victim. I tried to stand up, but my left hand slipped out from under me, and one of the flunkies stepped on it. The other one pulled at the back of my collar and would have pulled me upright, except that his partner still had his foot on my hand. The collar-holder grunted, and the foot-crusher let my hand go. When I was more or less back on my feet, one of them punched me in the stomach while the other delivered a chop to my back. I fell back, received a sharp kick in the ribcage. While still down I was hit in the face twice by the ex-collar-holder. A large ring on his bulky fist tore my skin. I saw the blood on his fist as he drew it back for the next blow. At the same time his partner was giving his attention to mangling my body. He showered a downpour of hard jabs at my stomach and groin. I heard Mary laughing. The man with the ring grabbed my belt, picked me up and hurled me as if my weight was no more strain on him than a light beachball. I fell hard to the floor and slid into another floor-hole, one which had been vacated by its inhabitants. My body twisted and fell against one of the sensory cushions, which was still transmitting. In the midst of my pain I felt a joyful happiness that there were, after all, so many wonderful aspects to death. I looked up and saw a flunkie reaching down toward me, clearly inviting me to further rollicking with him. Mary stood above him, looking delighted.

The flunkie, from his awkward position, managed a back-handed swipe, his ring doing further damage, while his colleague, grunting and cursing, pulled me out of the floor compartment. Mary hollered encouragement. So did a few members of the audience.

The lights went suddenly out. The darkness was so absolute that I was certain it was the initial phase of death, a state in which I might find welcome relief. My fading consciousness noted that the flunkie's hold on me was abruptly released. With some force, it seemed. Other, less muscular hands lifted me up. Help came from several other sources and, as I passed out, I knew that I was being transported in the general direction of the stage. Perhaps, I thought, I had merely become part of the performance.

12

When I came to, I felt pain fading, a signal that repair work had been performed on me. Just a twinge or so remained of the fight. Although I was in a strange place, I recognized it immediately because of the curtains and technical equipment. It was the backstage area of the theater.

Someone touched my arm. I turned and saw the actress who had kissed me, whose singing had preceded the brawl. She no longer appeared so beautiful. Streaked make-up and lines of sweat gave the illusion of a mask dissolving off her face.

"Lie still," she said as I started to sit up. I was on some sort of cot. "Let the ointments and chemicals work. You're almost as beautiful as you were on the day somebody else's mother gave birth to you."

"Somebody else's . . . mother?"

The minute I spoke, I knew how groggy I was. The actress picked up a towel from her lap and began wiping make-up from her face. I dreaded seeing the woman underneath the artifice.

"Whoever supplied the handsome shell you inhabit so unjustly."

"Oh . . . politics."

"Yeah . . . politics."

Her natural look was neither nymphlike nor beautiful. An arch in her eyebrows and a crookedness in the line of her mouth made her appear sinister. But her brown eyes were kind and her nose turned up in an appealing schoolgirlish way.

"What's . . . your name?"

"Brunnhilde."

"Your . . . real name?"

"Of course it isn't, but you don't get my real name out of me. What's your name?"

"Voss . . . Vossilyev Geraghty."

"Your real name?"

"Yes."

"Not a stage name?"

"No . . . Irish father, Russian mother, born in this country, what used to be this country."

"Okay, Voss, but if you ever want to go into show biz, that name'd look sharp on a marquee."

A man, dressed in chorus costume, walked to the cot and stared down at me. I might have been a morgue corpse for all the interest he showed.

"He better, Bru?"

"Seems to be. Give him another minute or two."

"Well, all right, but we better get him out of here pretty soon. Anybody figures we got him, and they'll pounce on all of us at the stage door. But, well, the coast's clear so far, and we're closing down the show for the night after the next number, so we can all fade into the wings and out of trouble."

He walked away.

"Okay, Pet," she hollered after him.

"Pet?"

"His stage name. Sue me."

"They don't know I'm here?"

"No. Pet slammed off the lights. One of our acrobats tripped your attacker up, and a few of us carried you away. When the lights came back on, we convinced your friends that the darkness was an accident and that you must've slipped away out the front. A ploy with moss growing on it, but those guys are none too bright so they took off after you. Expecting, I suppose, to find you swimming through your own blood in a gutter. Your doxy didn't look like she bought the story but she left anyway and took off in a different direction from your buddies."

"Good of you, all of you, to save me."

"Don't thank us. We just treat everybody else like we would one of our own. A tradition of the theater, to be helpful in a crisis, or so Pet says."

"Well, anyway, I'm lucky to get out of that."

"I wouldn't start shouting lucky yet."

"What do you mean?"

"You're a little bit lucky to be saved from those orangutans, but you shouldn't really consider yourself lucky until you get through the night or, more especially, out of Hough. In about five minutes Pet is going to put you out alone in the back alley, like a cat nobody'll take. You know your way from here?"

"Afraid not. Could you explain it to me? Draw me a map?"

"I couldn't draw your blood if I had a hatchet. No, this time of night, I couldn't trace any kind of route through that pastel and misty maze out there. Look, in daylight I've no sense of direction and get lost at least once an hour. Even if somebody here *could* help you, doubt if they would. Pet wouldn't let them, for one thing. This theater is sacred to him, and it's here only by the grace of the district biggies, and they will not take it too kind if one of his troupe is caught helping you out."

"Well, don't worry. Let me rest for a bit more, then throw me out and I'll smell my way to Dover."

"Lear."

"Glad to see you avant-gardists still know the classics."

"I do a number sometimes called *As Flies to Wanton Boys . . ."*

"Judging from what I heard you do out there tonight, that song, I'd like to hear it."

I lay back on the cot. Well, I told myself, you're a terrific success at trying out your sea-legs. I missed most the chance of settling Mary into that bed she had bragged could do tricks of its own. Still, as I recalled her vengeful laughter while I was being beaten, I did not miss it much. So my planned night of debauchery was ruined, and there might be more violence from Sam's bruisers. If they did kill me, and secreted my body in some Hough dungeon before the authorities could find me and transfer the implantation of me, my soul as it was called, to the retread chamber vaults or into a new body, I would then meet the real death of which Bru had sung so plaintively. Thinking of that, I shuddered involuntarily.

"What's the matter?" Bru asked.

Her voice was so compassionate that, for a minute, I was going to tell her. However, empathic as she might be, she would soon experience the hopeless death of her song. How could she care about the end of a wobbler fresh out of the charnel house?

I simply told her I was afraid that my assailants would return, and she nodded.

"You're about as cowardly as I've seen, but you got reason enough, I suppose."

"I should probably be going." I sat up. "Longer I stay, the more dangerous it is for you."

"I don't care. Death's death. It could come today, and okay with me."

"You've been singing that song too long, Bru."

"I wrote that song, Voss."

Since I could still feel the song's beauty and her beauty as she sang it, I was disturbed that such a talented young woman should not have qualified for long life. In the enclave I had always argued that the artist should even be excluded from the testing procedures. People always threw back the tired counterargument of who is to define what art and artists are—and that anyway only a small amount of worthy art ever originated with rejects.

"It's a beautiful song, Bru," I said.

She smiled.

"Thank you. I absorb even undeserved flattery."

"I wish I could hear it again. I would even go through the beating again to hear it."

"You deserve the beating then."

"*And* the one I'll receive if I don't clear out while there's a chance."

"No!"

She grabbed my arm. She had not done a good job of make-up removal and orangy patches all over her face looked diseased.

"I'll take care of things," she whispered. "My place, it's close by. We can get there and you'll be safe. Even if they trace you to me, I can easily get you out of the building."

"But you could get hurt, killed."

She shrugged.

"I could. Um, the performance is almost over. I'm not needed. This is the time to go. I'll get Pet to let me."

She waved to Pet, who was watching from the wings.

"This is . . . kind, what you're doing."

"Think nothing of it. You've aroused my pity. But that is all you will arouse tonight, know that."

"What do you mean?"

"I just don't want you to think that, just because I'm an actress, you can have your way with me."

"I didn't think that."

"You *are* strange then."

She told Pet her plans. He glared at me with a paternal scorn that disguised his youth, but he did not refuse her. All he said was:

"Bru, Bru, Bru . . ."

"Pet, Pet, Pet—goodbye, Pet. See you at rehearsal bright and early. I think tonight has given me an idea for a new song."

"Well, that's better than most ideas tonight could give you."

"See, even actors believe the legends about actresses," Bru muttered.

13

Bru's place was in a different section of Hough, where buildings were tenementlike, in moods of gray and black, with tilted stoops, swaybacked stairs leading up to scarred doors. Ghetto odors replaced the perfumes of the pleasure streets. Bru's apartment was on the third floor of an especially decaying structure. She guided me through shadowy dimness up stairs so rickety they reminded me of nightmares where staircases led nowhere. At her door she selected a card to open it. After a short and dark delay a bell rang softly and some lights went on.

"What's the bell?" I asked, as I looked around the small

sparsely furnished room. There were a few wall shelves holding objects whose casual arrangement suggested that Bru was not much interested in planning; an adjustable table dominating the center of the room; a couch so decrepit it had a certain antique prettiness; a couple of stark chairs; some blurry pictures from cheap stores.

"It's an alarm. Rings only when nothing's happened. If I don't hear it, I don't go into the room."

"Never heard of that sort of thing. New?"

"Hardly. This is a very old building and that's part of an old alarm system. It's a miracle it works at all, but it's saved me at least a couple of times when creeps had snuck in here. Sit down."

I chose an armchair which fitted itself to me so well I almost expected emotions to be transmitted from its seedy upholstery. Bru pressed a button on the wall and cupboard doors slid open.

"Something to drink? Not much here."

"Anything. Must be ancient, that alarm system."

"Very. Speaking of ancient, how about an old-fashioned?"

"Sounds appropriate. I didn't think there was much need for alarms anymore."

"There is around here."

She placed three small bottles onto movable shelves of an old mixyerdrink machine. I had not seen a mixyerdrink in several years, had forgotten about them. I wondered if the popular artifacts of the past disappeared like people into districts like Hough. Bru pressed a few buttons on the side of the mixyerdrink. The shelves slowly upended, tipping the bottles. The liquid from inside each bottle ran down tubes into the main mixyerdrink container where they were mixed. The newly made old-fashioneds went through another tube into two waiting glasses. Bru carried the drinks to me with a smile and handed me one.

"This always works. Don't just hold it, take a sip."

I sipped. It was delicious.

"Delicious," I said.

"Of course." She took a long swallow of her drink. "We shouldn't need them."

"The drinks or the alarms?"

"Alarms. We prey on each other down here. We should be preying on you."

"Well, I'm certainly vulnerable enough."

"I don't mean you specifically. Your kind, I mean your kind."

"I'm not so kind. Just normally decent."

"What? Oh. You should come down to the theater and write jokes for Pet. He adores the old ones."

"Don't think I want to set foot in your theater again, not after tonight."

I could not seem to shake the nervous tension that had come on me after the fight, and I took several more sips of my drink to calm myself. Suddenly I discovered that I had sipped my way to the bottom of the glass, and was merely catching ice-cubes with my teeth.

"Another?"

For an answer I handed her my glass.

"All I meant," she said while repeating the drinkmaking procedure, "is that we should find ways to get the kind of breaks that retreads have. We deserve as much of a chance to extended life."

"I won't argue with you about that, but how then are you going to get the bodies in which to continue your lives?"

"The ones we got might be good enough. Or why don't we just switch things around? Why don't you give us your bodies to ride around in for a change?"

Her resentment made me uneasy. I didn't stop for sips with the second drink.

"Watch it, lifer. I'm mixing them pretty heavy."

She was right about that. Again my body was demonstrating its inexperience with alcohol. Bru and the room went slightly out of focus.

"I'll hold off on the next one."

"Sure. Say, I'm sorry I lit into you. We don't often get one of you alone to rage at, we sometimes get overexuberant."

"Wouldn't call it rage but go ahead and be overexuberant. I'm sure it'd be enjoyable."

"Enjoyable? That's just the kind of remark I'd expect from one of you."

"So now I'm sorry. Hey, let's get away from this 'one of you' crap. I'm Voss, remember?"

"Better refill those glasses, calm us down."

"I'm not so sure about that."

While she mixed the next batch, I tested my equilibrium. I made it to my feet all right, but my walk around the room was a bit unsteady. She met me halfway with an old-fashioned.

"What's that?" I asked, pointing to an ornate statue on a corner shelf. It was small, painted in many colors, and was surrounded by objects I could not recognize.

"Just a statue, statuette really," Bru said.

"What kind of statue?"

"Religious. A saint. A martyr, actually."

"Saint? That surprises me."

"I don't understand."

"Just didn't expect to find one of you being especially religious."

" 'One of you,' huh? My name, dear Voss, is Bru."

"Okay, right."

We toasted each other and drank.

"It's a shrine then, a goddamn—a shrine."

"That's what it is, all right. Everybody around here has one. It's St. Ethel."

She made her hagiographic declaration as if I should understand her immediately.

"You're a Catholic then," I said.

"Not on your life, lifer. St. Ethel's not a Catholic saint, far from it. They wouldn't canonize her for millions of dollars. Not after that Papal bull that argued its way into a justification of retreading. No, sir, Ethel reached sainthood by the true act of the true God."

"How's that?"

For a moment she looked as if she might prefer a way out of the conversation, then she sighed and said:

"Ethel . . . well, Ethel was just one of us. Lived out in Denver, maybe seventy-five years ago. Before she was six, she began hearing voices and counseling the people around her."

"A regular Joan of Arc, I guess?"

"You can guess what you want. I don't know anything about Joan of Arc. Ethel heard her voices and first she began simply giving advice. You know: be patient and your true love will arrive within the month; have faith and you'll achieve great wealth; pray and happiness'll come to you. Nothing special, just strange when you realized they came out of a little kid."

As she talked about Ethel, she moved as if summoned to the small shrine and flipped a switch at its base. Diffused light illuminated the statue, which was of a rather plain-looking girl staring upward with innocent eyes, not much different from icons of any religion. The statue was well made and lifelike, especially for a miniature. In a beveled semicircle around its pedestal there were typical shrine trappings—candles, small plastic flowers, prayer cards.

"Later she said the voices were rejects who had passed on. She said they were writhing in suffering as they roamed this earth and viewed its horrors."

"Roaming the earth? Ghosts, you mean?"

"Not exactly, although they pass among us like ghosts. But the word smacks of superstition. Better for us to think of them as souls."

" 'Souls' has the better tradition, I think."

"Please don't mock."

"I'm sorry. Really, I didn't mean to mock. I've always hated the way the word soul is applied to the retreading transference. I'm just a bit surprised and confused by this side of you."

"I'm no different from others of my kind. The belief in St. Ethel has increased among us in the last ten or fifteen years or so, although the large majority of rejects still favor worldly pursuits."

"Tell me more about her. I've been . . . out of touch for a long time and know very little about anything."

Bru smiled. Just enough to be friendly, not enough to be anything more. Her eyes glistened and reflected the flickers of the candle she was now lighting.

"St. Ethel said the souls said they were condemned to walk the earth for as long as their bodies were used by retreads. Although the period of their wanderings was rarely more than a hundred years, she said, the emptiness of their existence made it seem like an eternity to them. They were not made free until the possessor of the body had given up his soul to be transferred to a new body. And with that the cycle actually continued, as the invading possessor forced another soul into an eternity of wandering the earth. Only the earth death of a retread shell could shorten the earthly wanderings of the doomed souls."

"You said they were made free. Free to go where?"

"To heaven, St. Ethel said. She said we were all to go to heaven."

"Isn't that better than what most religions offer? Purgatory could go on for centuries, hell forever. A *relatively* short period of consignment to wandering this earth, and then eternal salvation in heaven. Not a bad bargain, I think."

"There are those who would argue that, and do, but I'm not able to discuss the facets of my belief so coldheartedly. According to St. Ethel, we were allowed heaven only because man had interfered with God's own plans for us on earth. She said that He had allotted certain lifetimes for us—the initial predestination, it's sometimes called—and these lifetimes were being cut short by the retreading process, which was a sin in His eyes. Later she said that, when He allowed us heaven, He condemned to hell those who accepted our bodies. See, that's why you people have such a drive toward immortality. Once you give up or lose your right to be retreaded, you will be consigned to hell, where you'll accept all the accumulated suffering for the centuries that've intervened."

"Whooo. That's pretty heady stuff. Better for me not to get to believing in your religion. I don't much like the thought of hopeless eternal damnation."

"But you're not eternally damned. Not necessarily."

I backed away from Bru, seeing the light of potential conversion in her eyes, hearing panacea in her gentle but actorish voice.

"You have the ability to repent. If you recant your life, and give up your body to free the soul of its rightful possessor, and denounce the ways of your kind, you can be saved from hell—and, after a period of pain that corresponds to the intensity of your sins, you too are allowed into heaven."

"Well, that's merciful, I guess."

Her voice, so soft and appealing onstage, had become the harsh and forceful voice of the convert. Or fanatic. I began to doubt my safety; perhaps I should try the street again. I had already managed to misread the intentions of Mary, how could I be sure of my rescuer, Bru?

"St. Ethel brought the message to us for a decade and a half of her life. In that time she not only made predictions of future events, both of disasters and closely personal happenings, but on occasions she performed miracles."

"Miracles–"

"I can guess what you're about to say, the sarcasm that's coming. Miracles are also *tradition.* Well, God allows us miracles so we may see the truth. They're brief flashes of truth meant for those who can see and understand them. St. Ethel cured sickness. She placed her hands on the heads and bodies of suffering children and said to them: 'You are cured so that your body may be preserved until the time of the charnel house comes to you, and then your soul may reach salvation after the long time of agony.' "

"Hmmm, I'd think it'd be preferable for the child to die–save his soul as well as his body from the indignity of retreading."

Bru looked victorious, I had played into her fanatical hands.

"That exact question was asked of her and she said we *must* accept our suffering in order to be worthy of the attainment of heaven. Again, I suppose you'd say that's merely the repetition of a belief common to many previous religions."

"I thought it, but I wasn't going to mention it."

Some of the zealotry disappeared from her eyes.

"I'm sorry, I don't mean to go on so. You have to understand that I am totally involved in the little life I have, and so I do have moments of getting carried away. Sorry."

"No need to apologize. Tell me more about your saint. What happened to her?"

She was pleased at this question, too. There were echoes of litany in her voice as she continued. The light of God was in her face, and was quite sexy.

"When Ethel became older, in her early twenties, she said that she would have to go, to face death, *ahead* of her time. Somehow she managed to get the Retread Directors to accept her at the age of twenty-two, four years early. No insurance policies involved, just a voluntary early submission to the charnel house. However, as her appointed hour neared, she became moody, began to meditate at length, and could hardly communicate with anyone who came to see her. They said she spoke in disconnected phrases, nonsense words."

"Maybe she was just afraid."

"Maybe, but when she emerged from this distressed period, just days before she was scheduled to appear at the retread chamber, she no longer encouraged benign acceptance. She said that accepting our reject status was actually a *violation* of our souls rather than the means to their salvation. People asked her if that meant, then, she had been wrong before. Did her voices lie to her when they said heaven was at the end of the wandering soul's suffering? She said no, God was merciful and would continue to open the gates of heaven to us. But He wanted something else from us. He wanted us to defy the retreaders, to do anything to keep our bodies from becoming their property. She said we must risk salvation in order to stop the defilement of our bodies at the hands of our enslavers. Her voices now told her that we must do anything in our power to resist retreading and, if we could not resist, then we must not merely accept so passively. Her followers asked her what they must do, but she said they had to find that for themselves in their own time."

"From what I've heard tonight, they seem to be beginning to find out."

"I don't know what you've heard, but it could be many things. Anyway, they asked her what *she* planned to do, did she plan to resist the retreaders actively, go into hiding, attack them, what? She said to come to the charnel line and see. On her scheduled day, crowds stretched from the charnel house to the horizon. Most of the crowd knew when they arrived that they wouldn't be able to see whatever St. Ethel did as an example to her tormentors. Police had to be called in to separate those scheduled for the chamber from those who were merely viewers. A riot almost developed, but St. Ethel soothed the mob's angry members, shouting to them from her place in the line. The police kept weapons trained on the crowd throughout the intervening hour. People called out to St. Ethel and she answered them. The answers are all recorded and form part of our rituals. As her part of the line was being called into the chamber, St. Ethel stepped out of line, toward the crowd. The front of the crowd began to surge forward, but the authorities held them back. After taking perhaps half a dozen steps, with the eyes of the crowd and police riveted on her, St. Ethel stopped. She had been carrying a bag. Out of it she took a small can of what was later verified as gasoline and she doused herself with it in a quick motion. Almost as quickly she had drawn a match and applied it to her clothing. The flames surged up around her before anyone quite knew what had happened. You can imagine the rest of the scene—the crowd's reactions, the rush of police toward her, the attempts to put the fire out—"

"Self-immolation, that's—"

"I know—again, a tried and true method of martyrdom. But I'm not through yet. Their attempts to put out the fire were unsuccessful. While the helpless frightened crowd watched, it raged on. They say the flames reached almost to the sky. Several viewers at different locations in the crowd claimed they heard St. Ethel's voice quite clearly from a point at least fifty feet off the ground. Not only did they hear her, they said she was laughing quite happily."

"Impressive, I'll say that for your martyr."

"We're not through yet. You see, the flames eventually died down and, instead of revealing a woman whose about-to-be-retreaded body had been burned to a crisp or reduced to a pile of bone and ashes, St. Ethel stood in the same spot where she had originally set fire to herself. Her body was still intact, not a burn on it. And she was alive."

Bru paused. I suspected that most St. Ethel proselytizers took their pause at that point.

"Well," I said, "I'll admit that her little fire show must have been a convincing display, perhaps it very well could have been a miracle. I don't doubt the possibility. But a self-immolation can be faked with the aid of chemicals and the right kind of clothing."

Bru sighed.

"And *you* must realize that any objection you can bring up has been argued over and over in the years since. Not only by doubters but even by believers who needed to go through the ritual of criticism in order to shore up their faith. All I can do is refer to the same evidence we all have to, when the question comes up. In addition to the crowd's testimony, there are sworn records of people, technicians, who inspected her clothing later and found no residual evidence of either chemicals or specially treated materials. She was wearing the same kind of clothing she always wore. A simple print frock. The fire was genuine. Take that on belief, if you must, but we *know* the fire was genuine."

Bru glanced at the shrine as if she expected it to go up in flames at that moment in order to verify her belief.

"After the fire, St. Ethel resumed her place in line, and the people stared in silence as she disappeared into the charnel house. They stood there for hours, a vigil. However, the last part of the miracle would not be revealed for some time. We have friends, sympathizers of a sort, working within the retread chamber and they brought the story to us. At the moment of her extermination, St. Ethel passed away quietly, almost beatifically if you can accept that description as something more than just faith in a legend. Her body was treated in all the ways in which your people treat one of our bodies as part of the preparation process. All the chemicals were applied, the body was passed from hand to hand, the right wires were attached, the body was cut open in the right places. All the proper retreading preparation was done to her body. At the moment when the transference of one of your retread souls was scheduled, the right buttons were pushed, the correct power was set in force. But the transference did not take, it didn't work, the scheduled inhabitant of her body did not take possession, her body remained still, a shell without a soul."

Her hagiographic tale conjured up memories of my father and the failure of his retreading.

"When the first attempt failed," Bru continued, "the technicians did what they no doubt always do: said a few kind words for the person whose chance at a future had failed, and then they set up for a new operation, obtained a fresh transfer, and tried again. Again it did not take. They tried several times, it is said, although that might be an embellishment to the tale as it was transmitted among us. However many times they tried, each time the process failed. They had never before encountered a treated shell that had not *accepted* its new possessor. All previous failures had been blamed on the process or the inheritor-to-be. I'm sure they did not believe that it was possible for a reject-body to reject its successor. Finally, after so many failures, they had to believe it. St. Ethel's body was moved out of the retread chamber and disposed of according to burial customs. Call it what you will, miracle or simple scientific failure. Or perhaps, if you wanted to substitute the psychological for the religious, perhaps St. Ethel's will was strong enough to influence her body even after she was dead. Perhaps she strongly willed that no one could have her body, after all. Miracle or not, we believe she did accomplish the impossible, achieved the ideal of a reject rejecting, and that she is now with God—Who, incidentally, sanctions whatever we do in her name."

Bru's look was defiant, daring counterarguments. She was as beautiful as she had been onstage, and I wanted to be closer to her, but her eyes declared territorial boundaries. I began to feel woozy, the drink working on me.

"I don't think I've converted you exactly," she said, more anger in her voice than humor.

"No, but I'm willing to toast St. Ethel, if you like."

She grabbed my glass from me and walked steadily to the dispenser.

"You're drunk already," she said.

"Apparently something to do with not being used to this body."

"Say shell."

"I don't like to think of it that way."

"Say it anyway. Body's too tame a word, hides the truth. Shell reminds, or should remind you each time you use it, of the sin."

"His name was Ernie."

She turned away from the dispenser, a full glass in each hand. "Whose name was Ernie?"

"The former owner of this body. Shell."

She asked me how I knew. We sat down again and I told her about my experience with the redfaced man in the raptrain. After I finished the tale, Bru held my hand for a moment, soothing me. She asked more questions, served more drinks, became obviously drunk with me, and soon I was telling her about Selena and Lanna and my life in the enclave.

I suddenly realized that Bru's head lay on my shoulder, and that her right hand traced an ambiguous pattern on my outer thigh.

"You're friendlier than I expected," I said, as clearly as I could under the circumstances.

"You're nicer than I expected."

"What brought you to that judgment?"

"I don't know. You're different, been hid away most of the time. Makes you excusable, not so easy to hate as the others."

She pulled back the side of my shirt collar and kissed me at the base of my neck.

"That's almost affectionate," I said.

"It is affectionate. Meant to be, anyway."

"Why?"

She laughed.

"You are careful. And dumb. You're one whole lifetime ahead, didn't you learn anything from it?"

"What I think I learned doesn't apply logically to these circumstances."

"How impressive of you to say so."

She leaned forward and kissed me again, first on the cheek, then the mouth.

"You said I shouldn't believe the legends about actresses being sexually promiscuous."

"That's right. That's true. That's a myth that should be destroyed."

"Then, you don't mean this to be ... that is, you're not intending to ... you're kissing me only as ..."

She laughed.

"I just said not to believe the old story that actresses' favors were easily obtained, it's wrong to equate us with prostitutes. But I didn't say I never did it."

Her kissing became more passionate. At first I was unwilling to respond—feeling something like a cad of the old (theatrical) school, as if I would be taking advantage of a woman whose mellowness had largely been achieved through the influence of strong drink. But I had felt affection for Bru ever since she had first sung and the theater machinery said I must love her. In our short time together, I could have been persuaded that I would fall in love with her, or indeed had fallen. Whatever, I could only cope with the ethics of the situation for a short time.

"Let me make things appropriate," she said. "Move for a minute."

She pressed something at the side of the couch, and it began to roll sideways. At the same time trap-doors in the floor began to open, revealing what appeared to be a made-up bed beneath. The doors abruptly stopped and their mechanisms began to whir. Bru gave one of the doors a nudge with her foot and it completed the opening procedure. As soon as the doors clicked to their proper stop, a soft, blowing sound developed and the bed began slowly to rise. At normal height it stopped.

"Magical," I said.

I lightly kicked at the side of the bed facing me, expecting my foot to meet wood or metal, but the bed covers merely sagged inward. Bru laughed.

"What's funny?"

"What you did. Everybody who's never seen one of these does that, and they always look stupefied to find there's no structural framework to the bed."

"How is it done?"

"It's just air currents, just simple controlled air currents. The little machinery it has buoys up the bed and normally keeps the air going so that the bed won't collapse."

"It, it *does* collapse?"

"Sometimes at the most embarrassing times. That's one of the things that makes it fun."

"I'll bet."

"You wouldn't get hurt even then. The main technique is to learn to get on so you stay on, and to keep enough wits about you so you don't fall off later. You see, it's pretty old and just doesn't maintain its shape as well as it must've when it was brand new."

"It's very interesting."

"Don't be afraid. Come on. Try it."

Taking my hand, she led me to the side of the bed and sat me down. At first I thought I would slide right off, but I heard a rush of air and the bed seemed to take form under me. Gently pushing me backward, Bru climbed gingerly onto the bed, hesitating at each major movement for the mechanism to catch up with the new positioning of its inhabitants. Soon we were both in the middle. I clung to Bru with more than just the tenacity of a lover. Helped by her imprecations, I relaxed. Once my body became adjusted, I learned to like the feel of the bed which was, quite literally, like floating on a cloud.

"Like this?" Bru whispered.

"Very much."

"Thought you would. This is always more fun, more sensual, when it's your first time on it. More fun for me, too."

"Well, let the revels begin."

She laughed and poked me in the ribs.

"Are you absolutely sure you're not a ringer? An actor sent to set me up in some way? Are you an actor, Vossilyev Geraghty?"

"No. No, I don't think so."

"Ah, an element of doubt. Well, we'll just have to check out your performance, won't we?"

As Bru helped me off with my clothes I found the air currents made disrobing easier. For Bru the process was even simpler. Kneeling, she reached back and touched the back of her dress. Its neck widened to shoulder-width and slowly the dress dropped down her body, clinging to her figure so that the action was slow and sensual. Her body, not at all adequately suggested by her clothing, was thin, but in the kind of slim proportions—tiny breasts, narrow hips, small waist—which all together approach a classic kind of perfection. But I should not resort to such tired phrases to describe her. Bru was beautiful. At least she seemed so at that moment. As I looked at her, I could not help thinking how pleased the inheritor of this body—and it would have a new possessor in just three or four years—would be. I don't enjoy remembering that now any more than I liked thinking it at the time.

She leaned down, edged her body onto mine, ran her tongue along the line of my lower lip, and whispered:

"You were saying something about revels?"

It was my first real contact with a woman's skin in such a long time. I could not remember the last time Selena had rubbed against me sensually.

I should have responded immediately, felt goose-bumps all over my skin, eagerness all over my body. But I felt as detached as I did during the last couplings with Selena. I desperately wanted a sudden response, a flood of emotion surging through my body, that terrible zeal to get it all over with, mixed with the caution for delay, any kind of reaction to Bru's body twisting itself on top of mine. But instead I felt cold, as if my blood was being pushed through my body by an Arctic wind.

Bru sensed my lack of response and she began to shush me as she might have done a small child, cooing in a soft voice. I touched various parts of her, consciously, almost clinically, seeking erogenous zones, desperately trying to force physical reactions in myself.

"Don't worry," Bru whispered. "We've got plenty of time."

"It's not that, it's—"

But I could not find the words to explain what I felt.

Bru slid off my body. I could feel the bed adjust to the change, as a soft wave passed under me. In between nibbling my ear and stroking the nipples of my chest—the two areas which, even with Selena, usually initiated some genital response—Bru attempted to comfort me.

"It's all right. You've been through a lot tonight. And you probably aren't adjusted to everything yet. Happens all the time, I've read."

"Read?"

"I read a lot of material from—from your world. Envy, I suppose. I don't know, it's more interesting than what we're fed. All our publications are guided and run by your people, anyway. Our art is the only thing that seems vital to me. Here, how does this feel?"

She kissed me, slowly forcing my mouth open with the action of her lips and certain maneuverings of her tongue. Her tongue, when inside my mouth, had what seemed to me a phenomenal reach in its explorations. At the end of the kiss, she said:

"There, is that better?"

"Depends on what you mean. I loved it, it felt marvelous, but my body is still playing its game of detachment."

"You're too nervous, or maybe a bit too drunk. Take it easy."

"I wish I could. But this is too reminiscent of too many past nights, when I—when I, well, when I couldn't get it up for Selena. She was nice about it, too, like you are. She wasn't too fond of sex anyway. But the problem was worse than she imagined. I would feel the beginnings of stimulation, and I'd feel there'd be no restraining me, that I'd be so aggressively sexual that I would not even be able to control my techniques. Then something happened, it would be as if I suddenly stood outside myself, watching the foolish, passionate, animalistic me performing this absurdly awkward and dumbly motivated act of sex. It seemed to me stupid to give in to the emotional pretenses, the easy substitutes for a simple urge, a mechanism that in itself was no better than a rhesus monkey's or a walrus's or that of all the laboratory mice we studied in the enclave. I thought—"

"Wait, I'm not up to the subtleties of all this. Maybe it's better if you don't talk about it. Just relax and I'll—"

"But I can't relax! I—I looked forward to this change from my former life more than any other. I thought my—my problem'd be cured with a new body, maybe it won't. The anticipation of retreading was the main focus of the last third of my life. I couldn't—"

"Ssshhh, easy. There's nothing wrong now. Forget all this. You're—"

"It's not that simple, Bru. It's just not that simple. Don't you see what it means?"

"How could I? How—"

"It means—it means that, whatever body I inherit, whatever its healthy physical characteristics, it means that this screwed-up set of sexual attitudes will remain with me. It means retreading doesn't change you, does not change me. I am still the same. Nothing ever changes, nothing ever improves, nothing—"

Bru stopped my ranting by kissing me. A tender, calming, almost chaste kiss.

"I do believe," she said, "you're stupider than most retreads I've seen."

I laughed. Gradually, reacting to her gentle ministrations, I felt less nervous.

After a few minutes, we tried again. And another time beyond that, each attempt as unsuccessful as the first. Bru used most of the traditional and some not-so-traditional methods of stimulation, but I continued unresponsive. Finally, we agreed there was no more use trying.

I dozed off. The next thing I knew, daylight was slipping through pinpoint defects in the window-darkener. Bru awoke right after me. In an almost reflex move she began to caress my shoulder. I gently removed her hand from my skin.

"No," I said, "I don't think we're going to do any better this morning. You're an actress, you know it's unwise to attempt a production that flopped the previous night."

"Self-pity's what's unwise just now."

"Probably, but it's better for me to just slip away unnoticed, I think."

"No, stay, I'll feed you some breakfast. I got—"

"That'd be fine, just fine."

Delicately, she half rolled off the bed, landing on her feet. I wondered if I would be able to roll off the bed so easily. As she walked away, I remembered my appointment with Ben.

"No, damn," I said. "What time is it?"

"Around eight. But the clock—"

"I've got to go. I'm sorry. I have to be somewhere in a half-hour."

I dressed while Bru fed me pieces of croissant. She was still naked, and I could not help surveying that body and wondering how in the bloody hell I had failed to respond to it.

"How long is your appointment?" Bru asked when I was ready to go.

"Shouldn't take too long, unless Ben's machines are out of order, which they frequently are, but I doubt the whole thing'll take the morning."

"Come back here when you're done."

"I don't—"

"Please. Don't go on with the protests, they've been overdone since the first star-crossed lovers crossed their stars."

"You're sure you can—"

"I don't care. I don't care about any of it. Just come back. It doesn't matter what we do, or what happens. I'll feed you more croissants, we'll talk philosophy, we'll pray to the St. Ethel shrine, I don't care. Just come back."

"All right."

She kissed me, chastely, then removed croissant crumbs from my lips. Standing in her bare feet, she seemed tinier than ever, as if she had shrunk some during the night. I left, savoring the thought of my return to her later, not knowing I would not return. Perhaps I should have gone back to her after my meeting with Ben. I started in the direction of Hough once, tried to call her a couple of times. But what could I have said to her? She would not have believed lies, and I could never have told her the truth.

14

Ben mugged an exaggerated shock when I arrived at his office only three minutes late.

"Didn't expect *you* for another couple of hours. At least."

"Well–"

"I was positive you wouldn't show up until I was halfway through my busy time."

"You have a *busy* time?"

"Don't be sarcastic. Get your clothes off."

"I thought you didn't need clothes off in one of those things."

"That's heretical Medical-Association-endorsed superstition. Clothes impede the accuracy of the instruments, especially in such antiquated equipment as mine, which has been known to mistake a key ring for ruptured blood vessels. Anyway, I want to see up close what kind of sexy body they gave you."

"Sexy's not exactly the word for it. Not after last night."

"Why, what happened last night?"

A most desirable and provocative question. I told him easily, calmly, about my experience with Bru. He dropped the joking manner and began nodding, once in a while grunting his professional grunt. At the same time he guided me to the examination cubicle, positioning me and arranging the recording devices so that they were aimed at all parts of my body. He interrupted my story to ask me to hold my breath at certain times or to turn sideways for further examination. I was only faintly aware of the various noises the medical devices made as they focused on different levels and depths of my body. Ben's equipment appeared to be more rundown than ever. The examination seemed to last a long time. By the time I had finished telling my tale, I was back in my clothes and we were awaiting the arrival of the diagnostic printout sheet.

"Why don't you comment?" I asked Ben, after I had tired of several moments of him pulling at his ear as if it were a defective bell-rope.

"Oddly enough, for professional ethics. I can guess at a diagnosis, but it would be only a guess. Let's look at the analysis on the printout and see whether it confirms my suspicions or confirms your more creative psychological interpretation of impotence carried over from your previous lifespan."

"Suspicions?"

"Well, theories, conjectures . . . suspicions, yeah."

"Ben, for a friend you can be very frustrating."

"For a doctor I can be especially frustrating."

"You should say that with a Jewish accent."

"In medical school I substituted a course on *shtick* for the regular classes in bedside manner."

I could not wait uncomfortably in Ben's uncomfortable chair. I started to pace around the room.

"I thought printouts were supposed to come almost immediately."

"No, it's all more careful than that. More information-storage banks to be searched, more correlations to be tested from the data. Or maybe it's just my equipment. Be patient, it's all there, it'll come out when it's ready. Let me check something."

He walked to the console, pushed against the base of the keyboard with his thighs and slapped the machine on its sides. The printout paper began to roll. Ben read it as it arose from the machine. His subsequent sigh was much too audible.

"What's the matter?"

He did not answer, so I asked again. He turned around.

"What I suspected, I'm afraid. What I told you about yesterday."

"I don't remember what you told me yesterday."

"Sabotage. Your body was sabotaged before the reject even presented himself at the retread chamber and—"

"Charnel house."

"What?"

"Never mind. I don't even know why I said that, why that's

more important than—tell me what you mean. What have they done—what did he do to my—to this body?"

"Excuse me. I don't mean to present things this badly. I'm getting old and—"

"Never mind questions of style. We'll vote later on whether you have flair. Give me the diagnosis. Now, Ben!"

He sat on the edge of his desk, looking down at me. Rather too paternally, I thought.

"No, you do have to excuse me. You're my friend and, frankly, this is unpleasant for me, quite—"

"What, Ben, what?"

"Voss, your—your difficulties with that girl last night had no psychological overtones, no traumatic reappearances from your first lifetime. Don't interrupt, listen. You had no, no chance for success sexually last night. Whatever doctor worked on your body did a thoroughly efficient job, one that I'm sure would've passed through most inspections at the retread chambers. What they've done is complicated, and diabolical. And, unfortunately, it's a sabotage performed with the most unconscious irony, if you'll excuse me pointing out ironies, on just the right inheritor of the body. They couldn't have chosen a better target if they'd known. It's a most, a most delicate operation, in more ways than one. Many-faceted. They have altered and even removed some of the nerves leading from the sacral or lower segment of your spinal cord; these are the nerves that control your sexual reaction to stimuli and begin the process of engorgement that enlarges your penis during sexual activity. Tampering with the sacral neurons is not all they did. They have also affected the nerves in your penis that also create sexual responses. Besides that, they seem to have done something to the urethra, or the interior of that tract, which would cause intense pain if sperm did enter it. And, the bloody goddamned jokers that they are, they have also removed your prostate gland, which is merely extra cruelty since that was the one thing that was transplantable, and they didn't have to worry about goddamn transplants with the other goddamned alterations. Whoever did this has got surgical technique to spare, believe me—the machine detects even further tampering of the genital region that could not be clearly detected with my equipment. Look, if I hadn't set this diagnostic procedure into the program, this is a kind of defect that'd be generally overlooked in a regular examination. So you see, your impotence had nothing to do with the fact that you couldn't get it up a few times with Selena back in the old days. This was sabotage and only sabotage and—I'm going on too long and much too methodically. You should say something. You look very sick, what can I—"

I laughed.

"I don't know why you'd think me sick. What's a missing prostate gland and some sacral whatevers between friends? I mean, I can—forgive me, Ben, I just don't know what to say. I could accept impotence as a tragedy I'd have to live with, or some kind of worthwhile psychological condition. But just plain physiological impotence, some disconnection and incompleteness in my sexual apparatus—that's, well, that's comic, that's not tragic. They pulled a good one on old Voss. Bru would love this. I can play any silly scene I want. Devastatingly sentimental in the soap opera mode, courageous acceptance and all that; witty and ironic, amusing you with sexual innuendoes; warm and human, the old doctor and patient bit; bitter cynicism, the—"

"Shut up, Voss, for God's sake. Okay, self-pity's in order, but such stupid dramatizing—let's skip all this, and take some time to absorb the facts and we can get you to adjustment in your usual sensible way."

We took the time. After some talking, and some thinking, it began to seem to me both funny and sad that Ernie had gone to all this trouble for his personal revenge on the unknown, as yet unselected, receiver of his body. His shell. I started to have a little respect for good old Ernie. I wondered what kind of person he had been, how he had lived his short life, what kind of resentments had boiled within him. It was frustrating not to know anything about such matters. Still later, I became used to the idea that what had happened was neither, as I had declared so pompously, comedy nor tragedy. Aside from a few memories of my meager sex life that might make me regretful on occasion, living without sex seemed no worse than going through this lifetime with poor eyesight or a defective kidney.

I could put up with it.

I thought.

I could be free to lead a more intense productive life.

I thought.

Nothing would make me despondent over what was, after all, a mere physiological deficiency.

I told myself, confidently.

Why I chose to go offplanet, I am not entirely sure. I think it was because the world itself seemed no longer acceptable to me. I was a retread, though an incomplete one at that, yet I could not see things in an elitist way. In my worst moments I wanted to lead a useless life, perhaps in some enclave like the Hough pleasure area. Yet it was in my nature to be useful. I had to work in some way that would be beneficial to mankind, or some small segment of mankind. Although, if I had been asked to give a reason for my loyalty to my fellow man, I would have stuttered or collapsed without an answer. Or maybe, after thinking about it a while, I would have said it was a habit I picked up in my first lifetime.

Perhaps my reasons for going offplanet were not all that altruistic, especially since I did not particularly connect with most of my space service colleagues. Perhaps I thought I could lose myself in the rougher life, the riskier day-to-day activity of one of our outposts. I asked for difficult duty, after all. The woman filling out forms became interested in my request, tried to ferret out the reason why I would volunteer for that which drew so few volunteers. She pointed out to me that, as a retread, I had no assurance that, if anything happened to my current body (she called it that, as if it were merely an item from the stock room—our "current body" supply is depleted, order another gross), I could be preserved long enough for transportation to a retread chamber and transference to a new shell. Most difficult-duty assignments were not safely close to planets that had retread chambers, she said. They were so difficult to maintain that only certain planets provided the proper setup for a retread chamber.

Charnel house, I said. She asked me to explain why I should use the vulgar term for it. I explained, and she stopped prying. My training period, filled with (as it turned out) outmoded fighting and survival techniques, went by quickly. After my refusal to accept any extended leave-time on earth, I was placed on a ship heading toward a high-hazard duty post, all of this in less than a year after following a lovely child's footsteps across wet sand.

PART II

1

Stacy became my friend on the planet blandly named Coolidge, the assignment that used up most of my offplanet time.

Before putting me aboard the shuttle to Coolidge, orbiting-station personnel did a redundant test of my adaptation pack—adaptapack—which had been surgically implanted in my chest. The adaptapack adjusted for the differences between Coolidge's atmosphere and what was breathable for my body. Primarily it allowed me to inhale without harm the traces of methane in the planet's air, along with other, not identifiable by Earth standards, elements that were part of the atmosphere.

As we descended toward the planet, I studied the lines of various intense colors, arranged almost in series, spotting the surface. They were distributed among other, Earth-normal, colors of land, sea, and clouds. It looked to me as if paint had been casually applied in many places by an artist more concerned with testing hues and tints than committing his talent to a masterpiece.

I decided to ask the pilot about it.

"Do you know what all those colors on the—"

"I just drive."

"But hasn't anybody ever said any—"

"Nobody talks to me."

"That's hard to be—"

"Not after you get to know me."

"Will I see you that oft—"

"Business at the satellite or landing stage, this's the only shuttle you'll use."

"And you're the only—"

"Correct."

"And you don't—"

"Not to you people unless you talk to me."

"I see that you're not exactly—"

"I keep to myself."

"You sound like you come from New Eng—"

"Lotta people think that."

"Do you?"

"Nope."

"Where, th—"

"Toronto, Old Canada, New Whatever-they-call-it."

"Cold climate, anyway."

"Almost every first-timer makes that remark."

"You win."

"I usually do."

"What's your—"

"Stacy."

"First or—"

"Last."

"I'll be sure to remem—"

"You do that."

I gave up on talking to him. We descended onto the planet with the businesslike efficiency of two people who would see each other again only on an official basis.

I was astonished when Stacy presented himself at my quarters several months later, his gear slung over his shoulder. For a moment I could not quite remember him. When I did, I was *really* puzzled. He stood at attention for a long time while I stared at him, wondering when he would say something.

"You're not going to tell me what you're doing here until I ask you first, right?"

"Right, sir."

"Okay, what are you—"

"I'm assigned to you now."

"But who'll pilot the—"

"New man, just arrived, good credentials."

"Why'd you—"

"I needed a transfer, change of scene."

I had requisitioned no aide, and had in fact always said I preferred to work alone, that I *liked* to be alone.

"But why me, Stacy, why'd you want to—"

"Practicality, Mr. Geraghty."

"Prac—"

"I don't put myself where I won't be useful, and I don't put myself where I can be stepped on."

"And I—"

"You were the only choice."

"But I can't see—"

"Oh, you'll get used to the arrangement."

"Are you—"

"Positive. I'm good at paperwork, I'm not clumsy, and I can shoot."

Which proved to be the proper qualifications for the position.

2

In the months that followed, Stacy took pride in staying out of my way. When I was busy with home-base work—detailed reports, mostly, about our generally uneventful forays into Coolidge's pretty but placid wilderness—he found other work to do quietly. When I needed something, he obtained it for me—even when I was not, according to regulations, supposed to have it. He kept annoying colleagues out of my way. He even did some light cooking. Half the time, he had anticipated my requirements and had completed the task before I asked.

Most of the other members of the Coolidge exploratory team

did not share my appreciation of Stacy. Not surprising, since they did not especially appreciate me. They thought Stacy a creep, wanted him returned to the orbiting station. They were disturbed at the silent way he watched them like a spy, never saying anything, yet looking—examining, critical. It was the critical they really couldn't stand, the suggestion of mockery. The female members of the team especially complained about Stacy. It was all part of their intricate courtship of me. I tried to listen patiently to their complaints, as a penance for the cruel methods I had to employ in order to discourage their courtships.

When I told Stacy what the others said about him, he just shrugged and admitted the truth of their accusations. When I suggested he could use a soupçon of etiquette in dealing with them, he said he wouldn't—it was too late to break old habits.

Coolidge had proved to be something of a disappointment for our exploratory team. It was a very Earthlike environment. With some color differences, the greenery was amazingly similar. Little of interest had been discovered by our geologists, zoologists, and anthropologists. The only mystery worth keeping a conversation going was the strange multicolored mist which had been scheduled for later investigation, although some data had been derived from distant sightings. Because it covered large areas of the planet, it was decided not to study it closely until more data had been gathered. With the single exception of the mist, then, Coolidge was unexciting for a group of hazardous-duty volunteers. I did notice, though, that most of the team settled into ordinary routine with some ease. Myself, I couldn't stand the life in the bubble. Too much paperwork, too few trips into the wilderness. I complained too loudly and too often about the dullness. My colleagues, who claimed to be too involved in their own trivial projects, were only too eager to let me assume the role of troubleshooter. Stacy and I became the men who chopped jungle ahead of the rest, looked into dark places with them peeking over our shoulders, exposed ourselves to the planetary subjects for future study.

One day Stacy and I took one of the birds—a bird was a

complex combination of old-style helicopter and more modern shuttlecraft—and plotted a course for a destination where, on an earlier flight, a large animal had been sighted from a distance by a pair of geologists. We arrived at the point of sighting quickly. Stacy took back manual control and set the bird down into a clearing. Our equipment showed no sign of animal life for a few miles' radius. I decided we should take a lookaround. Outside the ship, the clearing seemed less peaceful than it had looked from above. To our left a bunch of Stoka trees were in furious motion. Stoka trees, named after one of the more obtuse officials at the orbiting satellite, resembled Earth trees in bark and foliage, though with streaks of red and lavender throughout both leaves and branches. From time to time their branches tended to start bobbing up and down, usually in a 1-2-3 up, 1-2-3 down pattern. (Later it was discovered that the trees' movements were connected with the production of an apparently useless sap.) When several of the trees fluttered their branches at the same time, it was an enchantingly rhythmic sight.

"Sense anything, Stacy?"

"Not much."

"But something."

"Not much."

"There's something out—"

"Yes, I know."

"What do you think—"

"Dragons. Moby Dick."

"What do you—I get it, you think we should go back."

"Affirmative."

"Well, I'm not going to, I am going to—"

"I know that."

The attack came suddenly. The beast made no noise, voiced no attacking howl, sent no formal declarations of war.

It attacked Stacy.

All I saw first was a grayish blur. It looked to me like a mass of wiring insulation suddenly enveloping Stacy. He was knocked down immediately and appeared immobile. I reacted instinctively, drawing out my handgun and shooting full-charge at the attacker. To no effect. The creature had grown larger, even as I shot at it, and now pinned Stacy to the ground.

"It's . . . it's piercing me with something," Stacy said. There was no panic in his voice, he merely wanted to provide me with relevant information.

I leaped at the beast, grabbed at its surface—I have to say surface, it didn't feel anything like skin. It had the consistency of accumulated dust. After my hand had sunk well into its surface, which gave way easily, I felt the beast's body or heart or core or whatever. My feet were still touching ground and I was able to get enough leverage to pull at it, lift it off Stacy with surprising ease. Turning its attention to me, it seemed to reshape itself. With a force that did not jibe with its light weight, it pushed me against a Stoka tree. Now it began to envelop me, surrounding the tree as well as my body. I began to feel the stabbing pain in several places. Stacy, unable to rise from the ground, laboriously worked his hand down to draw his gun. His movements were slow, as we concluded later, because whatever the beast injected into us had a numbing effect on our bodies. When Stacy had finally drawn the gun, he found that, if he aimed it at what appeared to be the creature's head, the line of fire would also include my head. Ignoring his own pain, he pulled himself with great effort along the ground to a position beside the creature. I was losing consciousness. For a moment I seemed to read the beast's mind, wherein a quite logical philosophical basis for my death was, I thought, presented to me. Whether this was hallucination or telepathy I never knew. I would probably have died if Stacy had not lined up his shot and sent a fatal charge through the creature's head.

As the beast fell away from me, it seemed partially to dissolve before it even hit the ground. I passed out. When I came to (inside the bird, where Stacy had somehow dragged me), Stacy told me the beast had dissolved further, leaving only a pile of gray ashlike matter. As my head cleared, I said to Stacy:

"Thanks, you saved my—"

"You saved mine, too. Even."

"But I feel I should say anyway—"

"No."

"Why not? Why can't I have the satis–"

"I couldn't stomach it."

"You don't put much value on life-saving?"

"I didn't say that."

"Well, do you?"

"Value enough."

"When you were down and that beast was stabbing you with whatever stabbing thing it had on its body, did you want to be saved? Weren't you glad when I pulled the creature off you?"

"I suppose so."

"You suppose–did you feel no gratitude that I'd saved your life due to my quick thinking and physical agility?"

"I was a bit concerned with how to make myself move and save you."

"But I saved you first, damn it."

"That's true."

"And for me you–"

"It was your duty."

"My duty to save–"

"We have that duty for each other. And for the rest of–"

"Oh, shut up, Stacy. I'm too weak for this kind of–forget it."

He nodded. Of course he nodded. Shutting up and forgetting it was what he wanted to do in the first place.

3

Stacy and I often saved each other from serious injury or death, although not usually from creatures as exotic as our mystery-beast. I concocted elaborate drama out of the simple act of thanking him for saving my life or limb, partially because of his taciturnity and partially because I always felt ecstatic after a narrow escape. I derived a special joy out of risking not only my life, but my future retreading, and beating the system by staying alive.

But Stacy never said thanks. His life being saved was just another event in his daily routine.

I said to him once:

"Don't you value your life, Sta–"

"If it's marketable, others'll put a price on it."

"But it means nothing to you?"

"Didn't say that."

"Where is the instinct to preserve yourself, to keep your body intact so that you'll make it to your next retreading?"

"Where's yours?"

"We're not talking about me."

"Whatever you say, sir."

"Don't pull that sir on me. I want answers from you."

He shrugged.

"Is life, your life, meaningless to–"

"No."

"Then why do you pretend it has no–"

"I pretend nothing. What you want is the pretense. You want to verify that I'm an echo of you."

"Explain that."

"No."

"You are infuriating, you know that?"

"I suppose."

Looking back on such an exchange, a routine discussion really, I find it appears that much of what I said was underlaid with an awareness of my own absurdity. I had no such awareness at the time.

4

Stacy and I had been teamed for more than two years when the attacks from my colleagues increased. They would drop by my quarters alone, in pairs, sometimes as many as three in a diffident nervous group, and make their charges. Always there were drawbacks to the prosecution arguments. They said he stole from them, but left no solid evidence they could use to convict him. When I asked why they didn't search for the stolen goods, they stuttered that his cutpurse achievements tended to be limited to, well, perishable goods. Food, soap, cleaning materials, toilet tissue. When they saw I could not take such trivial thievery seriously, they told me that he did all the stealing for me—to make my life more comfortable. I saw that they resented the fact that they couldn't shower every day, that their personal hygiene supplies were limited, that they had to eat the slop the mess-hall served up.

Seeing that I did not respond properly to their picture of Stacy as a common thief, they kept adding to the list of his offenses. Quite a list: insubordination, petty sarcasm, grand sarcasm, contemptuous stares, misplaced laughter, disregard of personal property, accidental breakage, tramping mud around the recreation area, insulting honesty in direct responses, disgusting personal habits used in defiant social warfare, rebellious attitudes and contempt in delivering them—plus much more. I always said I'd see what I could do to tame Stacy, but I knew I would not be able to modify his behavior.

On a dreary day when Stacy had been absent for some time, and I was beginning to disintegrate from the frustration of not being able to find anything I needed, I decided the only solution was to find my vanished aide. I found him all right, and immediately wished I had never gone looking.

Right before I reached the recreations hut, I heard a Stacy-like howl and the sound of a body crashing into some very hard substance. Thinking Stacy might need my help, I ran to the doorway. I sensed several of my colleagues running behind me.

Sally Aden—the prettiest, kindest, and most sexually active of our research team—was just sliding down the far wall as I came through the rec-hut doorway. Her head seemed to roll on her neck as if it had just been disconnected and was about to fall away. A thin stream of blood from her nose ran sideways across her cheek. Her mouth was open, jaw slack. Her laboratory coat, already beginning to collect spots of blood from the nose and a jawline cut, was torn at the shoulder seam. Her arm was twisted behind her, and I heard something in it crack as I watched her finish her fall and then lie unconscious on the floor. A pool cue rack, which her leg had lightly brushed against, wobbled on its stand and then fell over. Stacy, who had been blocked from view by a high sports equipment case, now ran toward the unconscious Sally, his fists still clenched, his throat making strange guttural noises. He looked ready, eager even, to inflict further punishment upon her prone body. I hollered his name, twice. The second time he stopped immediately, as if programmed to switch off at the sound of my voice. His body went slack and he looked at me, as usual, expressionlessly.

The others ran in and, while some attended to Sally, the rest hurled vituperous accusations at Stacy and me. *Both* of us. I took Stacy by the arm, saying nothing to him, and led him out. Our accusers parted like a Red Sea about to revoke the miracle.

Back at our quarters I threw my own accusations Stacy's way, but he would not explain what had happened or why. He just kept telling me to draw my own conclusions. I said I did not want to rely on inference, I wanted truth. He said to ask around and see how much truth I could collect. I gave up, strode out of the place, and went to the hospital to check on Sally's condition. The doctor said she was all right for the moment. The diagnosis was a hairline jaw fracture, a broken arm, some damaged ligaments, possible concussion, but she would survive okay, she just wouldn't be attractive again for some time. He allowed me to look in on her, although I felt he stood too close to me the whole time, as if he feared some further violence on my part.

As I stared at the bandaged, lumped, and distorted face, some memories of Sally Aden came back to me. She had been the most ardent pursuer of me after my arrival on Coolidge. She said that she was open to any sexual activity outside of sado-masochism. I thought her attractive and appealing, so I felt foolish at having to resort to the many dodges with which I discouraged her attentions. She had renewed her offers from time to time, and I remembered fondly the way she rubbed her body against mine when she was in an especially sexy mood. Looking now at her damaged face, I wished I had not had to hide the secret of my absent sexuality, had revealed the secret and then offered to service her, satisfy her at the expense of my own ridiculous detachment. I went back to my quarters, considered attacking Stacy myself, pummeling his face until it was as lumpy and distorted as hers. He was not there. I went to sleep.

In the morning a delegation of my colleagues came to me and announced in pious tones that something must be done about Stacy. Trying to stall, I asked them what for. Even though they knew I had been the first witness at the scene, they described what they knew of the assault in what must have been for them pleasing, if somewhat embellished, detail. Then they stood back and awaited my defense. In spite of the fact that I did not respect the customs and mores of my colleagues, I had to concede they had a case. I could not dismiss them in my usual flippant manner. I asked what they wanted. Their spokeswoman said they wanted Stacy sent away, reassigned to some new planet which he could wreck at will. I replied that, of course if our commander wished it, I wouldn't stand in their way once Stacy's guilt was properly adjudged. They began hemming and hawing collectively. It turned out that Sally Aden, now conscious, would not accuse Stacy. She said that she had merely tripped over a pool cue stand. She wouldn't go on report accusing Stacy. Of course I had seen the fall of the pool cue rack after her own fall and Stacy's subsequent charge at her, but I asked the delegation again what they wanted from me. They said that, since I was the first witness to arrive at the scene—really the only witness since the tension had gone out of Stacy's body before the others had arrived—I should go to the commander. Realizing that I was the only witness who could make the charges against Stacy stick, I knew suddenly I had the advantage over them. They sensed my knowledge of technically circumstantial evidence, but did now know what the evidence consisted of. I said I would not be a witness. After more hassling, they conceded and said that at least I must request Stacy's transfer, or get him to request it himself. The only decent thing, my unfriendly colleagues pompously declared. My turn to hem and haw, I said I'd see what I could do.

When I confronted Stacy again, he again refused to provide a defense. He admitted the assault, which was no help since I already knew he was guilty, at least technically. What was frustrating was that he would not even suggest any mitigating circumstances, or even tell me what had provoked him to the assault, no matter how much I prodded him. I felt helpless. As he was about to leave my interrogation, he asked if he should make preparations for transfer. I had wanted to delay any decision, to procrastinate as long as possible. But there was no reason for that. I was already the judge who had heard all the evidence. On top of that, I was a corrupt judge. I knew my verdict before the defendant took the stand and pleaded *nolo contendere.* I told Stacy not to pack, he was staying. There was no justification for that decision. I just wanted him to stay. I could not be alone and I could not join my colleagues—a stubborn decision, perhaps, since I knew they would not change toward me even if I had decided their way. I felt defeated, and I was. I could hope that Stacy assaulted no other women. (And the fact that he didn't in no way attests to any prescient wisdom on my part.) And I could hope that I would never have to make a decision like that again. A foolish hope, as the events of my life were to work out.

5

By that time we had discovered that the multicolored mist, which I had thought looked so lovely when I had been shuttling down to Coolidge, might be both poisonous and sentient. There were several patches of mist around the planet that could move at various speeds across vast areas of land. A mist-watch had been set up early to see whether it would come close to our base at the bubble, and emergency procedures were carried out each time a patch of mist seemed to edge toward us. Technicians sent exploratory missiles for atmospheric measurement into the mist to see whether we would need further adjustments to our adaptapacks if we ventured into it or it decided to visit us. Data were inconclusive, although all findings suggested that the air within the mist was breathable. There was nothing to do but to send a man into the mist. I volunteered but our commander decided that the assignment was not yet sufficiently dangerous for me to tackle.

The first man sent into the mist was gone only a minute or so. He came out screaming that his lungs were on fire. Before our eyes he died, life going out of him a bit more with each breath until he finally fell. The rest of the team retreated quickly and returned to the bubble, where the sensory devices and adaptapacks were again tested. Nothing in the data showed any atmospheric element which we did not already know and had not made adjustments for. A second exploratory team, which I observed from a safe perch—flying one of the birds—held back too far from the mist, as if it had placed a slide in a microscope, then walked away and tried to see through the lens from the other side of the room. I complained about their reticence, but was told that they were not ready to take undue risks. They were saving me for any undue risk missions that might come up. My particular skill, one of them told me, was being able to risk death and come out alive.

The second team's sensory devices recorded nothing that would contradict what we already knew. They decided to return to base. If they had immediately, the important breakthrough might not have been made. A risk-taker like one of the warriors in *The Iliad,* uncharacterized but fierce, sneaked away from the research team encampment that night. Using some exploratory equipment he had stolen, he located the patch of mist and headed right to it. Nobody ever found out what he was trying to do, or whether he had some reason to suspect he would be safe within the mist. He was not. He entered the mist, stayed in it no longer than the first penetrator. Some people in the camp were alerted or awakened by his screams in the distance. It took them a long while to figure out what had happened, but fortunately the recording equipment operated without distraction. After they had carried the man's body back to camp, one of the technicians discovered, while examining some data on one of the printouts, that there were some slight differences in the patterns recorded. Subsequent study showed that a part of the mist had changed in composition just before, and during, the penetration of our adventurous defector. Though the change was complicated and many-faceted, and the resulting amalgam like nothing previously discovered on Coolidge, the elements that composed it were analyzable, even including the steps from something known to something unknown. Adaptapacks could be adjusted for the changed-force within the mist, our experts said. But there should be a test first, to see if their hypothesis was correct. The time was ripe, I was told, for me to try my luck inside the mist.

The mission was explained to me: There was a possibility my colleagues were wrong. The surgical adaptation of the packs that made breathing possible could, after all, malfunction. There was no guarantee that a phenomenon like this one could be measured accurately by instrumentation that had been designed and redesigned to record what was already known. There were many variables. And, I was told, I did not have to go. That was, of course, my kind of challenge.

6

I requested Stacy be assigned to the mission to man the instruments, small components which would relay detailed information back to more sophisticated equipment at the team site. After I told Stacy, I countered his silence by saying:

"You want to come, don't you?"

He did not respond.

"Didn't say that."

"What did you say?"

"Didn't say anything?"

"Oh. Yes."

I left it at that. When I went to the doc for discussion of the adaptapack surgery, I found that no such operation had been ordered for Stacy. I stormed out of his office and confronted our commander in the botanical lab, where we argued within a twisted jungle that looked nothing like what we encountered on the planet's surface. He said the operation had not been ordered for Stacy, who had not after all been scheduled for duty *within* the mist, because of its intricacy and expense. I demanded that Stacy be properly equipped in case of emergency, or I would not attempt the penetration. After some spluttering, he did a few bureaucratic turns and agreed to my demand. I went to Stacy and said:

"I just saved your life."

"I hadn't noticed."

Feeling very much the gallant leader for whom protection of his comrades was a prime virtue, I explained how I had wrangled his adaptapack adjustment from our commander. He listened without apparent interest.

"So you're scheduled for surgery later this evening, same time as me. Well, do you want to thank me?"

"No."

"Why not?"

"Surgery."

"What's wrong with surgery?"

"Hate the thought of it."

"Ah, come on, Stacy. Would you rather not have the operation?"

"Given the choice, yes."

"Well, you're going to."

"I realize that."

Stacy went under the knife without showing his reluctance. We were both conscious during the operation. Myself, I enjoyed the sensation of watching a doctor cut open my chest without any pain to me, physiologically or psychologically, knowing there would be no postoperative pain. Watching the doc study my insides for a moment, then motioning the technician over.

Watching the technician, in specially sensitized gloves, delicately work with the adaptapack—unlatching a portion of it, making transistor inserts, changing a few elements, relatching, doing something with dials. Watching the surgeon do me up again, and watching in the mirror as my operation scars slowly faded and disappeared, leaving no sign on my skin that any surgical work had ever been done in that region. I was so impressed with the way the surgical and technical procedures had been performed that I wondered, in a rare moment of reflection on the subject, whether the sabotage done on my body back on Earth could somehow be repaired by them. I doubted that it could, but I almost was willing to ask. However, I had never been able to admit to anyone on Coolidge that I had the problem, so it was a bit difficult to contemplate solutions.

After my operation I stayed around, lying on a cot, for Stacy's. He stared at the ceiling and watched none of it, displayed no reaction to my occasional kibitzing. Afterwards, I tapped him on the chest and said:

"Feel any different?"

"Physically or philosophically?"

My final instructions were not to take any chances, or act on any assumptions of my own. All I had to do was verify that the adjustments to the adaptapack were correct. I nodded my head and agreed, knowing I wouldn't stop for the caution of scientist-bureaucrats. But I agreed because it's always easy to agree when you know what you're going to do anyway.

The next day Stacy and I were flown to the team site and the following morning we headed toward the point where the nearest patch of mist had last been observed.

7

The jungle surrounding us seemed composed of nothing but blacks, grays, browns, and odd streaks of green, as if all the actual color of the landscape had been absorbed into the brightly colored mists. There was not even much sound disrupting the dank placidity of the area. As we walked, and hacked our way through particularly dense growths, I told Stacy about my instructions.

"We can't be hamstrung on this kind of mission," I said.

"Perhaps."

"What do you mean? You agree with them?"

"To an extent."

"In what–"

"You'll risk the mission. You shouldn't."

"Oh, hell, Stacy, why–"

"You asked."

"But you don't think I should–"

"You do what you think best."

"I will."

"You always do."

A tracking device, which Stacy had clipped to his belt, located a patch of mist nearby. We set off in pursuit of it. Curiously, it seemed to maintain its distance from us.

"What the hell do you think it's up to, Stacy?"

"Being polite, diplomatic."

"What do you mean?"

"It's detected us maybe. And is staying out of our way."

"But it does remain close."

"Didn't say it was a coward."

We stalked it further, detected little change in its behavior.

"I *knew* it," I said. I waited for Stacy to ask what, but he didn't. He continued walking beside me, each hand touching a piece of the equipment he carried, as if he felt he must protect them.

"I knew it was a living thing," I said. "A creature, like all the nightmarish monsters we've feared we'd find in our explorations of the galaxy."

"And've found few of."

"But some. I've heard about—"

"I've heard a bit, too, but not seen anything."

"Take it on faith."

"On Faith they've discovered only desertlike conditions."

"What? Oh. I—well—"

"You're not used to me making jokes."

"Well, yes."

"Yes, there's a difference between making jokes and being one."

"I've never heard you—"

"Sorry, something about the atmosphere, I guess."

"The atmosphere."

"Or the mission."

"Stacy, what—"

"Or the company."

A tone in his voice that I had never heard before, or perhaps had never perceived, made me shut up.

The mist finally stopped moving. As we approached it, the air around us seemed to change. The colors of the jungle deepened in hue, some yellow was now in evidence on leaves. There was a hint of an odor, perfumelike, which you could not quite define, no matter how much you concentrated on it. Stacy sensed the changes, too. He looked down at a device strapped to his wrist, examined a dial or gauge.

"We're close," he said. "A bit too close, maybe."

"You stay here. As soon as you're set up, I'll go seek out the prey."

"The prey?"

"My language a bit too fancy for you?"

"In a way."

"Why?"

"It suggests an attitude."

"Oh? I'd think you'd know my attitudes better than anybody."

"True. That's why I'm scared."

He set about his work. Then he spoke suddenly, as if the subject had been gnawing at him for some time:

"What's wrong is, we talked about it once before, you don't care about your own life."

"Of course I do, I–"

"No. You don't."

"How can you know?"

"You're too reckless. You've had one entire lifetime already and it's spoiled you maybe?"

"Spoiled?"

"Some retreads are too willing to risk an inherited body."

"And I suppose you're protecting your own, as you say, inherited body."

"Not inherited."

"What? Oh, I see, then you're an even more reckless individual than I am–coming out here as a natural and facing the chance that you'll never be retreaded into another–"

"I won't anyway."

"What?"

"I never qualified retread. I was a total reject, as they call them."

"Then how–"

"At that time, the time I would've come up for disposal, they desperately needed spacers, so they passed a law allowing rejects to volunteer for space duty instead of giving up their bodies."

"Oh. I remember that law, but I never suspected it had anything to do with you, I–"

"Never mind. That subject's taboo here."

He returned to setting up his equipment.

"Were there many of you?"

"Many of us what?"

"Who volunteered for space duty."

"Too many, I suppose—they repealed the law. Now they select their own, no volunteers."

"Is there anybody else here?"

"Anybody else here what?"

"Anybody else who's also a reject. Among our colleagues."

"We don't advertise. We don't get many planetside jobs, unless there's garbage work. Mostly we're assigned to ships, landing platforms, people like you, duty like that."

"Well, who else is—"

"Sally Aden."

"Really? Sally?"

"You satisfied?"

He was not treating his equipment as gently as usual, so I decided not to examine the ramifications of his revelations.

"I'm satisfied."

"And I'm all ready. You can go—"

"Stacy, I didn't mean to—"

"Are we going to do the mission today?"

Without replying, I started in the direction of the mist. At first, while I should have been concentrating on my objective, images of Sally Aden kept coming at me. I pushed the thoughts of her out of my mind and sharpened my concentration on the mist. I expected to see it everywhere. I came upon it suddenly as I walked into a clearing that I had not anticipated. The mist hugged the ground like a normal fog, wisps of it came to me in thin strands.

"Okay, fella," I said aloud, "we'll do this right off."

I strode toward the main body of the mist without slowing my pace.

The mist stretched from one side of the clearing to the other, and seemed to go beyond the borders into the adjoining trees and shrubbery. To my right a pair of Stoka trees gestured wildly, their branches vibrating more agitatedly than usual. I thought for a moment they were trying to warn me off, but suspected that the difference in their branch-waving rate had more to do with the presence of the mist than with my entrance into the clearing.

Although I felt some tension, I was not ready yet to succumb to questionable omens. I took a deep breath just before penetrating the main body of the mist.

Entering the phenomenon I felt a damp tingle on the surface of my skin. It seemed much like the touch of an earthly fog, or walking through a misty rain. I had not expected the similarity. I had mentally prepared for a thicker texture, perhaps because I did not trust surface appearance.

I walked further inward. As I did, the sweeping and swirling colors deepened, took on darker hues. In spite of the distraction and seeming density of these mist-colors, I observed some specks of light, in contrastingly bright yellows and reds, but could not tell their distance from me. They might be small and quite close, I thought, or large and far away. There was a pleasant aspect to them, perhaps because of their brightness shining through the darker and pastelish mist-colors. They looked something like little fireflies or jumping sparks. I felt drawn toward them, and wanted to walk immediately in their direction.

Looking around the adjacent area, I let out a little air. I knew I would have to take what might be my final breath in a minute, and so I needed to stretch time as much as possible. The longer I could stay inside the mist before dying, the better data, after all.

A darker area of the mist hovered a few feet away to my right. Although it looked to be just a clump of mist, a blob of condensed moisture, I felt that it was watching me, studying me. I took a step toward it. My step provoked a response, and it rushed toward me. I knew right then that this clump of mist within the larger mist was what had killed the others. Well, come away, I thought.

As it reached me, my chest seemed to erupt with pain but still I knew I could hold my breath a short while longer. Rather than let it surround me, I walked right into it. As I penetrated each new aspect of the mist, I felt something like a person opening boxes within boxes. The area of thicker mist was only four or five feet across, and perhaps a foot taller than I was—if tallness is a proper dimension for a creature that drifted at different levels. Inside, this area of mist was like the outside, except for additional darkness and fewer colors. I could no longer see the specks of light in the distance. My skin detected less of the feeling of fog, less dampness. I tried to focus on texture, define it. It felt oppressive and yet seemed to have little substance. Outside, I had felt I could almost grab balls of mist; inside, I was afraid to bend my hands.

The strain upon my chest of holding my breath became too painful. There was nothing left to do but make the proper test, see if the adaptapack had been adjusted successfully. I let air out, then inhaled. And almost choked. Not on the mist itself but on the ugly odor that came with it. It made me think of bad eggs and drowning in lye. I held back the choke and, in a second stage, completed the breath. And then waited for pain.

The technicians had done the job. There *was* no reaction. I took a couple more tentative breaths for verification. Nothing happened inside me. Oh, it felt like something there was attempting from the inside to pull my lungs into a collapsed state, but it was not killing me. The adjustments were successful. As I breathed, the mist's poisonous material was being extracted, then funneled out through my exhalations. Because of the mist's foulness, I was more aware of the adaptapack operation than ever before, reminding me of the early days after its installation when I was made uneasy by the instrument's forced exhalation mingling with my own natural. Getting into sync with the adaptapack was one of the earlier hardships of having one inside of you. But we all became adjusted and generally breathed in rhythm with it, or at least did not notice it. I had not been especially conscious of it earlier when I had entered the mist holding my breath.

As I continued to breathe the foul air around me, I felt exhilarated. I tried to holler out defiant words to the mist, but the thickness around me hampered my speaking ability. So, in case the creature was telepathic, I sent out antagonistic thoughts.

Well, okay, I said to myself, I have met the enemy and have breathed it to its knees. What now? Our commander had ordered me to clear out once the adaptapack test was completed, but I was feeling too victorious for that. I decided to explore the area outside the thick and odorous mist-clump. Walking sideways, I made my way out. The outer mist felt like fresh air to me, with the same stimulating qualities. Beside me the thicker mist continued to hover. I surveyed my surroundings in blithe disregard of my former attacker. Since there was little else to focus on, the distant specks of light drew my attention. They reminded me of fireflies I had seen on a visit to an uncle's farm. I was only seven or eight then, and I made it my business to chase the night's flickering gadabouts. Sometimes I caught one and imprisoned it in a jar, watched it die or found mercy and let it go soon afterward. I had not seen a firefly in so long I had to investigate these seeming-fireflies that inhabited the mist. At the same time, I had to remain attentive, to see if the mist had any other lines of defense. If such phenomena materialized and killed me, my death would supply that much more material for the measuring devices.

I decided to allow myself five minutes to research the firefly lights. As I started toward them, I could almost hear Stacy cursing me, since his equipment would have informed him immediately of my defection from the mission plan. However, I knew Stacy would stay right where he was, unless ordered otherwise or unless I became enmeshed in genuine trouble. One thing he would not do was chase in after me without cause.

At first I thought the light-specks were maintaining a distance from me, since they did not appear to become larger as I approached. This impression proved to be either an illusion or a temporary retreat on their part. Soon they were enlarging before my eyes, and I could distinguish dots of color inside each speck. Each firefly light had several colors bouncing around inside it. Specks within specks. Purples and oranges predominated, and there were apparent blue links connecting some of the inside specks. As I neared I could see that the movements of the firefly lights were less random than they had originally seemed. Some flew a more or less circular pattern; others danced in more complex, nearly geometric figures. There was little rhythm to their floating ballet, or even beauty, yet I was certain that it was being done with some kind of organization. As if there were a mind behind the manipulation of the lights, the mind perhaps of the mist itself or of some entity within it which I had not yet seen.

I came close enough to one of the lights to examine it in more detail. It was almost round, not especially large, had a diameter of about five or six inches. There appeared to be some substance to it, although the materials that composed it were evanescent. I had expected some transparency, but could not see through it at all. I reached out my hand to feel if there was any heat or other sensory aura around it, but it moved sideways away from me. The blue connecting links shimmered and there was some movement of the dots of color. I became excited. There did seem to be life here, even possibly intelligence. As I edged up to the light again, my movements were slow and I felt like a sea-diver in deep water, an analogy that had more truth to it than I knew at the time. I tried to touch the light, but each time I walked toward it, it moved away. In a different direction each time. So we're playing a cat-and-mouse game, I thought, but why then doesn't it use its mobility to just flee from me? What kept it within the limited distance? What made it stop after it had moved slightly away from me? I envisioned Stacy, tracing my movements, wondering what the hell I was doing. I was afraid he might interpret my odd moves as trouble and rush into the mist, so I resolved to get my observation of the firefly light over quickly.

Finally it stopped without retreating when I approached it. Tentatively I reached out my hand to it. I felt nothing, so I cast the hand out further, almost to the visible border of the light. Still no sensation. I decided, what the hell, I'd try touching it, and did. My hand slid easily into the firefly light. This time I felt nothing and something at the same time. There was no surface touch, my hand seemed to be in normal air. Yet, inside the hand there was some agitation, as if all the nerves there were suddenly tingling. Around my knuckles there was a slight pain. I pulled my hand out and these feelings went away. I repeated the act, to similar results. Irritated nervous feeling inside the light, everything normal outside, not even an after-tingle.

An intriguing sensation, but I would have to leave interpretation to experts. I could not afford to spend any more time within the mist. Waving a sort of goodbye to the light, I turned and began to make my way back to Stacy. For several steps I was not aware that the light was following me. First I sensed it, then I looked over my shoulder and started to turn around. It was just in back of me. When I stopped my forward movement, it kept moving right on. Before I realized what had happened, it increased its speed and rushed at me. I startled backward, but not fast enough. I watched the firefly light enter my body. The effect of watching it disappear into my chest was strange, a little spooky. At first I felt nothing from its penetration and I was tempted to look backward to see if it had perhaps gone through me and continued on its path, unmindful of my corporeality as if I had been nothing but an intersection on its daily trip downtown. Then I felt the first twinge of pain. It came from inside my chest, just past the point where the light had entered. The pain was neither violent nor intense. It was similar to the agitation that my hand had felt. Only this time, since the pain was centered in an area near my heart, a feeling of pressure was added to the tension. For a moment I thought it was going to kill me by pressing my heart inward until life was squeezed out of it, or whatever would happen to the heart if it were trapped in a vice. However, it turned out to be only a localized small pressure. If this light was a creature, I thought, the area where I felt the keenest point of pressure was probably where its intelligence or consciousness lay, sending out rays of agitation in all directions.

I decided that the best course of action would be to return to Stacy as quickly as I could, and so I started in that direction. The pain added to my pace, gave me an incentive to reach my best speed. Meanwhile, I could feel my visitor moving around inside me, as if sightseeing my interior, testing me out as a phenomenon the way I had just walked through the mist with the same objective. Breathing became more difficult as it seemed to penetrate and explore a lung. In my mind, or perhaps my imagination, it walked or drifted along the lung's inner lining.

Up ahead the clump of mist drifted, in apparent ignorance of my approach. I skirted to the left of it, watching to see if it would make a move, maybe act in concert with the thing inside me in a kind of inside-outside pincer movement. But it maintained its aloofness and I passed it easily. The firefly light had wandered from my lung to my upper shoulder and now seemed headed for my neck. I almost panicked, envisioning it interfering with my breathing and choking me to death. As I felt the pain enter my throat and seem to push out its sides, I noticed the thinning of the mist. I was coming to the edge of it. The rays that my visitor sent out seemed longer now, reaching up and down through most of my body. I wanted to dissolve in a complete nervous rage. Thrash about, run against trees. Even though I could simultaneously analyze the feeling in an objective manner, I knew I could not control it. This must be how madmen feel, I thought, when they are on a rampage.

When I ran into the clearing, it looked to Stacy like I had fallen victim to the same attack as the previous adventurers into the mist. He stood up, quickly began to disengage himself from the equipment still attached to his body. I ran toward him, trying to cry out for help. The light inside me had passed through my throat and now seemed to be exploring the lower borders of my brain. My face felt on fire. Stacy could see my pain and he started toward me.

Then my intruder passed into the center of my head and the pain increased to more than just agitation and pressure. I felt it was going to grind its way through my head, leave my skull in dust and ashes. This realization, plus the added pain, made me finally cry out. The fierce intensity of my cry stopped Stacy, and he began to circle around me to make sure it was safe to come near. It was not, for I lunged out at him and might have killed him, choked him—if he had not already become wary. He dodged to one side. I felt terribly angry at him, and I did not know why. I wanted to punish him, make him feel inside the way I felt. What I wanted from him may have been what all people who think they are dying want from those left behind—others to share their pain, or perhaps others to die right along with them. I was positive that my head was breaking up into small pieces, my body disintegrating into liquid. There was no way out. I had no chance. Suddenly I did not want to die. I had believed I could face death calmly, that my recklessness might be just an excuse to dispose of myself in some heroic fashion. But, no, I did not want to die. That wasn't it at all. I wanted others to die. I wanted to watch death around me. Anybody but me could die, that would be all right. Stacy could die. I would not mind it if Stacy died, even in front of me, even at my hands. I could accept that more eagerly than my own death. I was supposed to live forever, or almost. I was one of the chosen. Stacy was not. He could die. It would be all right, ordained. He was not chosen. But I must live, I thought. I could not let this thing kill me. I took another lunge at Stacy, and this time caught him full and hard on the side of his head. He staggered away from me. My blow had been strong, powerful beyond my abilities, as if the creature was guiding me, adding to my strength. Stacy fell but recovered quickly, and was on his feet again before I could kill him.

Briefly I regained some control and moved away from him, expecting him to exercise proper caution. I hoped he would run like hell out of the clearing and let me die alone. I did not figure that he would remain, staying out of my way, looking to see what could be done.

I must have looked comic, thrashing about in the center of the clearing. I could not stop it. The firefly light was intent on modulating its torture, letting up for a brief moment, then bearing down more painfully. The rage took control again and I ran at Stacy like a stampeding beast. He backed up and slid around a tree, a comical escape from a comical attack. Clown-villain that I was, I followed him around it. He ran past more trees, further into the forest, then with feints and dodges worked his way back to the clearing. While I chased him, I experienced several moods, each one with a fiercer intensity than I had ever felt before. My anger was fury, my tears were plentiful, my self-hatred at a new high. I seemed to be experiencing every emotion in the extreme. Once I felt joyful and laughed uproariously. This caused Stacy to stop for a minute and stare back at me. Then the monster inside me stepped up the level of pain and I lunged at him again. He reacted quickly, ran away from me again.

We headed back to the clearing. The mist had edged closer. It had passed the area where Stacy had left the measuring equipment, almost as if it had come nearer just to watch the little fracas we were staging. Stacy had no choice but to run into the mist. I had to follow.

The mist made the chase more difficult, more so than ordinary mist would have. Since I had been in the mist alone, I had not suspected that a man's outline would become so indistinct. Only Stacy's movements, jerky countermoves against the flow of swirling colors, enabled me to track him. If he had stopped, stood still, I would have become confused, lost sight of him.

The firefly light loosened control again. I slowed down and tried to holler to Stacy, but I could not quite speak. What came out of my mouth was more shouted gibberish than anything sensible. Nevertheless, Stacy turned to look back at me. Then I saw the thick clump of mist again, moving toward him. I realized that each new penetration created this reaction within the mist. It rushed to Stacy, who was not looking its way, and enveloped him. He disappeared into it, and for a long moment I could not see him.

When he came out, he came out screaming.

He ran toward me, pointing at his chest. In the way he screamed while running, he looked very much like the mist's earlier pair of victims. He fell before reaching me, his hands clutching at his chest. I ran to him, intending to grab him and drag him out of the mist. As I leaned down to him, the firefly light again took control of me and I found myself wanting to rain blows upon Stacy's prone body. He looked up at me, his eyes wide. I could see he was holding his breath. Something had altered. His breathing was affected by the mist in some way. I realized that, even as I clenched my hands into fists and reared my arms back with the intention of hitting his face and chest. Stacy saw what I was going to do, and shut his eyes.

In my mind I addressed the light, felt like I was shouting at it: No, goddamn it, no, you are not going to make me do this. Not this. Not goddamned this.

I forced my fists to unclench. In spite of everything in my body telling me otherwise, I reached down and, taking Stacy by the shoulders guided him to a sitting-up position. With my arms wanting to crush him, I carefully grabbed the clothing at his shoulders and began pulling him out. Even though I desperately wanted to kill him, I got him outside the mist and into the air. With every muscle in my body wanting to exert itself against him, and with believing it would be better to crush him with the added power in my hands, I was able to work a kind of artificial respiration. For a moment he did not seem to breathe. Then something clicked into place, and the breathing started. The click, I knew, had something to do with the adaptapack.

Then, as suddenly as it had entered my body, I felt the firefly light leave. I did not look to see it return to the mist, nor did I notice when the mist had retreated back into the forest. I felt that all organs, bones, blood vessels—everything in my body had collapsed and crumbled, was now lying in uneven piles within my skin. I was sure that I would die, and now I didn't care. Instead, I looked at Stacy and watched the rise and fall of his chest in breathing as if it were a choreographed ballet.

8

Later, we discovered that the firefly lights and the attacking mist-clump were only two of many creatures inhabiting the mist. Each new being discovered within the mist added to the achievements of the research team's mission. The mist itself was not sentient. It was merely an ocean in which the other creatures swam or used whatever form of mobility natural to them.

A woman named Louise Libman (one of many, incidentally, whose attentions I had to discourage) managed to communicate with the light-creatures by allowing them to enter her mind. According to her, what passed to her from them was not exactly language. It was more a transmission of pictures and patterns, none of which were discernible in human terms. She felt she was getting somewhere interpreting their transmissions, without knowing what they did with what she tried to transmit to them, when one of the firefly lights went haywire and caused her death. Her thrashings about before she died resembled mine when I had emerged from the mist. A later, less sensitive communicator concluded that the light-creatures were not really aware of us, at least not as living beings, and that what passed between human and firefly light was not genuine communication. We were something like paintings in a museum to them; they stopped by and examined us once in a while. He, too, was nearly killed by one of them and we had to halt our research on the firefly lights.

After the mist had drifted away, men came and removed Stacy and me from the clearing. I blacked out on the way back to the base and don't remember much of the next few days. Quite a long time passed before I recovered. There were days of just lying in bed and not talking to anybody. Not even Stacy–which was something of a switch, as he pointed out in an unsuccessful effort to elicit a response from me. Then there was a period of just walking around like a village idiot and watching people do things.

The doctor told me, at a time before I was ready for any diagnosis, that the emotions the firefly light caused within me had resulted in some psychic damage. The way he put it, I was afraid to offer any emotion to anybody. I had seen the extent of my emotions and was afraid they might become extreme again, might again force me to run amuck. I did not respond, wondered what was supposed to be different from the way my emotions worked before I penetrated the mist, and after.

Stacy functioned for me as a kind of nurse/therapist. Took care of my schedule, planned activities, saw that I ate properly. Whatever he did, it worked. Being a walking shell can't last forever. It is good protection, but it can't last forever. I started puttering around my quarters on meaningless but enjoyable tasks. Gradually I started giving Stacy orders. I could tell from the alacrity with which he performed them that he knew I was getting better. And, soon, I was better.

* * *

Nobody really knew why Stacy had lived. His adaptapack adjustment had obviously failed when he had entered the mist. Under the attack of the thicker clump of mist, when he breathed in what should have been the fatal dose, he had felt ravaging pain in his lungs and especially in the region where the adaptapack had been implanted. He said it was like breathing in acid. Perhaps what saved him was that he had the presence of mind not to exhale immediately, and therefore did not allow his attacker to force more of its poison into him. Instead, he was able to maintain enough self-control to run out and look to me for help. If I had not been able to overcome the guidance of my own invader and perform the artificial respiration, he no doubt would have died. It was not so much my fumbling attempts at resuscitation that worked the wonder, but the fact that, in performing it, I pushed against his chest and made a mechanism in his adaptapack slip back into its rightful place.

"Well, I've done it again," I said to Stacy, during one of my earlier days of feeling well.

"Done what?"

"Saved your life."

"Oh. Yes."

"Well, if I hadn't—"

"Right."

"I think this time you might thank me. I mean, the other times I could see your side of the matter. But this time—"

"This time you tried to kill me first."

"Oh. Right. If I hadn't done that, you wouldn't've run into the mist and—"

"Correct."

I tried to see victory in his face, but could not.

"Well," I said. "Well, I fixed your adaptapack, right?"

"Yes."

I tried to find a way to force his gratitude. I made only a few attempts because the next thing I knew he was presenting me with his transfer papers.

"Where did this come from?" I said, holding the papers away from me, as if they were dripping with acid.

"I requested them."

"You *want* transfer?"

"Yes."

"Why? Why the hell why, Stacy?"

"It's what I've, what I've decided."

"Okay. Okay, but why?"

He remained silent. His body was stiff, at attention even though his hands were in the at-ease position.

"You're not going to tell me why?"

"No reason. Nothing that can be said easily, anyway."

"But there must be something. I mean, you're not just transferring within the system, you're going offplanet entirely to some idiotic new planet. You don't want to assist me any more?"

"Didn't say."

"No, you didn't. But what do you expect me to believe? You don't do things idly. There's something more important here than a wish for transfer. What could be more important?"

"Life, sir."

"What does that mean? Your life, my life, what?"

"Mine."

"What—"

"But yours also."

I tried to get something less cryptic out of him, but he was not providing any. The transfer was immediate, designed to hook him onto a supply ship just about to leave the orbiting satellite. Very slowly it dawned on me that this would be our last conversation. That he was going in a minute, and had waited until the last moment to tell me.

"What a damned stupid thing to do," I said to him.

"Yes," he said.

"Well, you might as well go, damn it."

"Yes."

"You have everything you need? When the hell did you get your equipment together?"

"Some time ago."

"You've been planning this for—"

"Yes."

"Damn you, Stacy."

"Yes."

"Get out of here."

Picking up his gear, which I then realized had been stashed in a corner for a couple of weeks, he walked to the door. I started to holler, wait, but I could not force the word out. At the door he turned.

"Goodbye," he said.

"Yes, well, right, goodbye then."

Without smiling, without altering a facial muscle, without even a friendly inclination of his body, he said:

"And, oh, thanks."

"For—goddamn it, what a stupid, sarcastic, miserable thing to say now when—"

But he had left. I was screaming at an afterimage.

During the rest of my tour on Coolidge I never heard anything from, or about, Stacy. There was the usual rumor that he had been killed on some foray in his new assignment, but I discredited that. So did most of my colleagues, who knew that such stories often popped up after a departure. I doubted that he died, it wouldn't have been like him.

When I left Coolidge I tried to locate Stacy. The space bureaucracy being what it was, it wasn't really too difficult to find him. We reunited on a planet named Oddment. At first he resisted hooking up with me again but apparently he perceived something different in me that changed his mind. Anyway, Oddment was a rather peaceful place and there was not much trouble to get into. (The only individual to whom I ever revealed my sexual deficiencies was a rather stodgy Oddment native. In his culture the loss of sexual equipment was no catastrophe since it gave them ability to concentrate on higher things. They believed that sexual energy was displaceable and, not only that, worth displacing. So he never took the subject seriously and, in fact, cooperated with me much more after I revealed my physical defect.) If anything, Stacy and I functioned better as a team on

Oddment, or perhaps merely refined the relationship.

Eventually I got tired of the troubleshooting nature of most of my assignments, and I decided to return to Earth to see what kind of trouble I could get into there. Stacy said he would come too and, in typical Stacyesque fashion, gave me no reason for it.

PART III

1

They say that, for the returning spacer, Earth is never quite the same, which does not mean that it is really any different. My return, after nearly fourteen years away, had little nostalgia attached to it. I remembered no embroidered picture of Earth. If anything, I remembered worse than I had left.

Stacy had even less reason to look forward to his return. He had already done more than the twenty years of space-time required of him when he had volunteered for duty in lieu of the charnel house. He probably would have continued in space service if I had not decided to return.

On the last day of our long journey homeward, I began to feel a small amount of anticipation for our destination. I tried to excite Stacy, but he was not interested.

"Stacy, look out here, just out—"

"Why?"

"It's Earth. You can see it now, quite—"

"I've seen it."

"But—"

"There're pictures of this view in every headquarters of every mission in the galaxy."

"But that's pictures, this's the real—"

"Doesn't matter."

"Yes, it does! Just look once."

"No, thank you."

"It's not a picture. It's, well, authentic."

"The dirt in my shoes'll be authentic enough for me, thank you."

"I give up."

"What you usually do."

I looked in his gaunt face to see if I could find even a hint of humor in it, some clue that he was making fun of my pomposity. Instead, he just sat impassive, slouched in a crewman's chair, his rubbery body apparently in an uncomfortable position. Of course, if I had asked him if he felt any discomfort, he would just have said that he was comfortable enough, thank you.

By this time, I was frequently annoyed by his contradictory and sometimes peculiar habits. A food he would eat voraciously one week would be left intact on his plate the next. He had a propensity to dress in one color when we were at liberty, but he seemed to have no particular favorite color for his ensemble. He would take no baths or showers for a long time, then start bathing or showering hourly. Drink nothing, then stagger around as if drunk. Drink a lot, and be soberer than anyone else around. He was graceful, except when he was exceptionally clumsy. The major contradiction was that we were friends.

2

Disembarking procedures passed quickly. We sat in narrow low-ceilinged cubicles while proper bureaucrats asked the proper questions. There were few questions to ask, no delays worth evoking for a couple of rough old spacers. We were soon off the space station and on a shuttlecraft. I asked Stacy:

"What'd you like to do first?"

"Nothing special."

"You've been away from here for over twenty years, isn't there anything—"

"Not anything special. I have less reason to be coming back than you do."

"Then why are we here?"

"That is someplace in your head. I don't know."

"No, neither do I."

"Thought not."

"You're so goddamned smart, Stacy."

"Not too smart. I'm here with you."

At the Earthside receiving center, a small woman behind a big desk presented me with a surprise, a message from Ben printed on vellum-substitute, which always irritated me because it never crinkled. I was not surprised to find a message from Ben awaiting me. He had always known my whereabouts.

DEAR VOSS,

You are, I hope, through with all that outer space crap. I thought you'd never come back. Hope to see you soon, I need somebody repulsive like you to measure my own life by. I am living in New York, having been thoroughly annihilated by Cleveland, and you can reach me at the above address. Come up and see me sometime, and bring whiskey. There's a lot of it around nowadays.

Yours perpetually
BEN

I showed the message to Stacy, who was not impressed.

"It's great, isn't it?" I said.

"What?"

"To be welcomed back after fourteen years, that's great."

"Suppose so."

"Wouldn't you be thrilled to hear from a pre-spacer friend like this? I mean, a person from your past?"

"You find me a person still alive and in his rightful body from *my* past, and I'll be happy to be thrilled about it."

"Okay. Sorry. Didn't mean to rub you the wrong way."

"You didn't."

Before leaving the receiving center, we established our credit with the bank. The printout and credit notes (which looked suspiciously like good old-fashioned money, in spite of the variable amounts they could stand for) displayed the fact that each of us had what amounted to an easily disposable fortune earned from our years in the space service. Now I understood all those old yarns about how long it took a good spacer to waste his accumulated income after he returned to Earth.

Some delegates from a convention of Third Lifetimers, "the aristocracy of retreads," were generally raucous during the shuttle flight to New York. One sip of bourbon, for which my stomach had not yet adjusted to Earth gravity, made me quite sick. A conventioneer tried to help me:

"Take some deep breaths, sonny."

I did, and threw up again.

"There, that oughta do it," the conventioneer said. "Sit back and rest. Gotta take care of your body these days."

"Sure," I murmured.

"Now more than ever."

I made no sense out of his remark as he chattered on, but when I was feeling better I asked him what he had meant about taking care of the body "now more than ever."

"The 'now more than ever'? One of our slogans. Well, you've been away. You don't know how scarce new bodies are becoming, especially intact ones. Those that aren't sabotaged or cremated or utterly destroyed. There are so few bodies to inherit nowadays that it is incumbent on all retreads to preserve themselves as long as possible. Whatever you do, however long you last in this lifetime, you got a long period of darkness ahead. The backlog is so long right now that, once you die, *anything* can happen before you get retreaded. So it's best to take the best, the very best, of care. Hell, what am I talking to you for? You're a young man yet, in good shape obviously, by the time you pass on, this body-logjam'll probably be over."

"Sure. You, too. You're still young yourself."

"Well, I may look it, but . . ."

"But what?"

"Ah, I don't want to burden you."

"Go ahead."

"Well, this body may be young enough on the outside but

inside it's a wreck. Doctor tells me my third lifetime may be somewhat foreshortened. This body's been sabotaged in so many ways, there's no way they can keep up, nothing they can do. I'm just carrying on until the end comes, until I sink into what may be a damn-near eternal period of darkness. Now, you take Jorgen over there . . ."

In the next two hours I listened to more life stories than I wanted to. My companion, who did look young and fit, knew what was wrong physically and internally with each of his fellow conventioneers. All his talk made me very uncomfortable. It just served to remind me of the sabotage done on my body, that body that looked so damn good to him. I nearly revealed my secret to him, but I had been silent about it for so long that I could not see this sodden Third Lifetimer as a proper recipient.

3

I asked Stacy if there were any particular sights he wanted to see before searching out Ben's office. He said no, so we hired a taxi and I gave the driver the address on Ben's message. As I relaxed my body into the plush ease of the taxi, I felt relieved to find that cabs had not changed much in my fourteen years away from Earth. They were still driven by laconic crazy men, and they still offered, for extra fare, dozens of luxury comforts to distract the passenger's mind from the erratic driving. I contemplated one of the luxury services—a drink, some taped music, old TV programs—but decided I would be more entertained by our driver's assault upon the highway than by any sideshows. Stacy, interestingly enough, chose a private pornographic globe which he attached to his head. He sat there the whole drive, his body apparently unresponding to the illusory pornography around him. Not a twitch, not a single shifting in his seat. I wondered what kind of activity might actually stimulate him.

The driver, after rattling the papers of my payment as if they had to be counterfeit, released us from the locked cab at Ben's building. Stacy got out first. As my feet touched the sidewalk, someone to the right of me screamed, "Duck!" Space-training instincts took over and I plunged to the ground. So did Stacy. Almost immediately the street seemed to explode with gunfire. I felt, or thought I felt, the vibrations of several projectiles hitting the sidewalk close to me. The shooting stopped almost as abruptly as it had started. Stacy and I glanced at each other, then crawled to the doorway of the building.

"What do you think that was all about?" I asked Stacy as we stood up.

"Somebody out to kill somebody."

"Us, do you think?"

"Doubt it."

"Because who would be after two spacers just off the–"

"Not so much that."

"As what then?"

"I suspect if they were after us, they woulda got us."

I examined the scene in the street. A crowd was collecting around what appeared to be two dead bodies. Our taxi had left. I turned around to find a very tall man watching the scene over my shoulder.

"What happened out there?" I asked him. His brow furrowed and he obviously thought I was crazy for not knowing, so I quickly added, "We've been away from the city for some time."

Understanding, he nodded and replied:

"Looks to me like it's the shortlifers."

"Like *what's* the shortlifers?"

"They're responsible. One of their insurgent teams, killer squads. We've been getting an especial lot of trouble from them this summer, what with practically no police force and all."

"No police?"

"They're on strike. Can't say as I blame them. Rotten working conditions. And one of those slugs mangles your brain, it's bye-bye retreading. A lot of cops've gone to the retread chamber with not a prayer for a new life."

"I don't understand what you mean by insurgent teams."

He gave me another quizzical look.

"Even if you've been outta the city, you should know—"

"Never mind, just tell me."

He responded to my surly tone and explained patiently, crisply:

"The insurgent teams, the killer squads, are groups of rejects who are taking advantage of our helpless situation and are going about killing us, picking us off in the streets, at home, in restaurants, you never know where. Is that clear?"

4

Ben's office was on the fifty-first floor and we traveled to it in a remarkably slow elevator, one with nicks and scars all over the compartment. We stepped off the elevator onto a floor that had also seen better days and, probably, better shoes. The corridors, once the epitome of modern mirrored chic, had become dim due to too many burned-out fluorescents that had not been replaced. The mirrors, which ran at shoulder level through every corridor, were thick with dust and exhibited vague and distorted images. Some of them had crayon writing on their surfaces.

Finding Ben's office took up a good deal of time and good guessing. We proceeded down unmarked labyrinths, where signs denoting office numbers had been removed or switched, where people you met looked at you dreamily and claimed they had never mastered the numbering system of this floor or, for that matter, any other floor of the building. We passed several windows that had been painted to allow the sunlight to force its way through dust as thick as that found on the mirrors. Within the borders of some mirrorlike windows were gray fragments of an unrecognizable fake landscape.

When we reached the proper corridor, we found that Ben's

office was the most obvious. The glass of its door had been cleaned and the lettering stood out clearly. Underneath Ben's name were the words "medical consultant." He had never called himself that before, whatever it was. I took a deep breath before opening the door.

Instead of the dustiness and disarray I had become accustomed to in Ben's previous places of business, the room I confronted was remarkably clean and efficient-looking. Spare modern furniture was placed neatly around the square of the room, and reading material spread in an attractive fashion on mirrored tables (the furniture, no doubt, had originally been coordinated with the general decor of the building). A pretty brunette receptionist sat behind a desk with mirrored sides. That impressed me. Ben had never before had a receptionist, because (he always said) he could not afford one. Things *must* have changed. The receptionist was reading a book in a viewer propped up to her left.

"What're you reading?" I said, more to get her attention than to find out the content of her book.

"Oh! I'm sorry. Dr. Blounte is always saying I should hang a little bell on the door. It opens *so* quietly."

"Yes, it does."

"The Reject Crisis."

"Excuse me?"

"The name of the book I'm reading. *The Reject Crisis.* It's about there not being enough bodies and what should be done about it. Did you want to see the doctor?"

"Yes, please."

"Who should I say?"

I gave her my name and Stacy's and her eyes brightened with joy. They were attractive eyes. A deep brown.

"Dr. Blounte has been waiting for you for days, expecting you any minute. He said this morning that he'd given up. He'll be overjoyed."

"Why don't you announce us, or should we go right—"

"Oh, no. We can't interrupt him now. His door's on time-lock, and can be opened only when the time's up. He's busy. Absorbing."

"He's what?"

"I'm sorry, you couldn't know about that, being away from Earth for so long and all. Absorbing–it's a new technique for gaining knowledge, something like the old sleep techniques. The subject goes into a meditative state while hooked up to an information-provider. In the meditative state, he is more receptive to knowledge and very much of it can be projected, and absorbed by the subject, in a short time. But it's a tricky process. The subject must be in the right state for it to start and it's dangerous to interrupt him in the middle of absorbing."

"Dangerous?"

"They say brain damage can result. I don't know if that's so, since people who absorb are always extremely careful about their procedures."

"One would have to have a great desire for knowledge to want to receive it under those conditions."

"Well, Dr. Blounte certainly does."

"Are we talking about the same Ben Blounte? Don't answer."

The Ben I remembered had always been casual about intelligence, knowledge. He would have cringed at being called intellectual. Still, he always seemed to have information and commentary ready when needed, so perhaps he had always been a devotee of absorption in its various forms.

"We'll wait then," I said to the receptionist. She nodded and returned to her book. I tapped the viewer and said:

"What *should* be done about it?"

"Pardon me. Done about what?"

"The reject crisis. What should be done about it, according to that book?"

"Well, the authors put forward a number of solutions. They seem quite big on more selectivity in breeding and stiffer tests to divide the satisfactories from rejects. They say that even the term 'satisfactories' is wrong because it suggests a level just above mediocrity. There should be another word, one with more weight to it."

"Something like 'superiors.' "

"I guess that'd be the gist of their argument, although I think that word just might be a bit too much. Too disturbing, don't you think?"

"Don't ask me. I don't think I'd change the word in the first place."

"Might agree with you on that. Satisfactories has done well enough for us as it is."

"Maybe 'excellences.' "

She stared at me to see if I was joking. Seeing that I was, she smiled. The corners of her mouth turned up in a childlike way.

"Silly to quibble over the words, I guess," she said. "I read another book that suggested we ought to dump the whole system, give up our immortality or some such thing. Of course, there's always been some radical thought around about the process. Always will be, I suppose. I can see the point, but . . ."

Her voice trailed off. By her tone I gathered I should understand her but I did not. I was going to ask her about it, but Stacy shocked me by beating me to the punch:

"But what, ma'am?"

"Well, if they stopped it all, I'd kinda miss getting a second lifetime. I mean, it's easy if you've been retreaded once or twice to endorse radical theory. But, when you haven't had your chance and they threaten to do away with it, you begin to feel, well, cheated."

"You've never been retreaded then?" I asked.

"I'm only four years past my final satisfactory rating. A natural, as the term goes. I've a long way to go, and many years of anticipating future lifetimes, so it's only logical to be a little wary of radical thought. It's just so hard to weigh the balance, you know?"

"I wouldn't know," Stacy said. "I have no prospects."

At first she was confused by his remark, then she realized what he meant and her eyes saddened.

"Oh. I'm sorry. I hardly ever, I mean, I never—"

"I know. You never saw an *old* reject before. Ain't very many of us around."

"Yes, I see. It's a, well, it's something of a privilege, a—"

"I am aware of the breaks society has given me, miss."

Stacy said this as if it were a ritual incantation.

"I–I'm–"

"What's your name?" I asked her. I meant the question to relieve tension, but she looked at me as if I were going to put her name into some report. Nevertheless, she answered, a dutiful sound in her voice:

"June. June Albright."

"Hello, June Albright. Pleased to meet you."

"Um, thank you. Oh, look, Dr. Blounte's time-lock light is on. You can go in now."

She pressed a button and a door in the wall, with some creaks, slid open. Stacy and I stepped through into the inner office, a large room done in several soft colors and textures. I almost did not see the man behind the desk. He was a young man, with curly blond hair and an open, smiling face. His shoulders seemed massive and he appeared too big for the normal-sized desk in front of him. I wondered for a moment where Ben was. The young man sprinted around the desk, holding out his hand to me.

"Jesus Christ, Voss," he said, "You look terrible, like you've been out in space for fourteen years or something."

At first I was disturbed by the young man's familiarity, then I realized.

"Jesus Christ, Ben, it's you!"

"Of course it's me," he said, taking my hand and shaking it with energy even greater than that present in the usual Ben Blounte handshake. "I know, I can tell. You're as dense as ever. You forgot. You expected the dear old gray-haired doc, stooped over his patient's records and his rusty diagnostic machines. Admit it, nitwit."

I was uneasy. This was Ben all right. I recognized the inflections, the tone of his voice. But, even though Ben had always treated me in this offhand way and I had never minded it, what he said seemed inexcusably rude and brash now that he was in this muscular young body. Clearly, Ben's retreading had been fairly recent.

"Well," I said, "I was a little disconcerted. I mean, I hadn't thought–"

"You hadn't thought as usual. What do you think you need me around for? Hello, I'm Ben Blounte."

This last was addressed to Stacy, who noncommittally took Ben's outstretched hand, saying:

"Stacy."

"Last name or—"

"Last."

"Any other names?"

"None I admit to."

"Okay then, Stacy. What are *you* smiling about, Voss?"

"Nothing. Just that that conversation you just had nearly duplicates the first words Stacy and I ever exchanged."

"Well, sit down, you two. Did you remember to bring the whiskey, chum?"

To Ben's delight I produced a bottle of whiskey I had purchased at the terminal.

"Great! I've a couple of my own bottles but they're so damned expensive I prefer drinking somebody else's."

"You're lucky. At the moment I can afford it. I can afford a lot of bottles till my spacer money runs out."

"Well then, it *is* certainly good to have you back." He laughed, then added more seriously: "I mean that, by the way. Have a drink, *spacer.*"

We had several drinks, and talked. Mostly just Ben and I talked. Stacy spoke only when spoken to, his custom. Ben addressed him from time to time. Once he admitted that he had liked Stacy right off, a comment that drew no reaction from Stacy.

Ben had died about six years after I last saw him. He had been retreaded a year and a half ago.

"That's almost seven years you were in the period of darkness!" I said.

"Yep. The time gets longer and longer now. I feel especially guilty."

"Guilty?"

"I didn't *have* to come back this time. I could have blissfully gone to an eternal rest. Only idle curiosity made me sign the retreading renewal."

"Why *idle* curiosity?"

"It's the idleness of it that's so damnable. Things were picking up in interesting ways. New techniques were being developed in medicine. Politically, the rejects were just getting organized. I had developed a certain amount of expertise in my own specialties. Good books were being written. Women were looking interesting to me again. Real whiskey was becoming more and more available, as the grain for it could be spared. And I thought I'd like to see you again. A lot of especially imbecilic reasons like that."

"They sound like pretty normal reasons to me."

"To you they would. I know, I'm not being fair. What I'm trying to say is that the normal reasons, the regular humdrum urges that drive us to leap to new lives, are no more than just euphemisms for idle curiosity."

"I don't follow, Ben."

He took a long theatrical swig from his whiskey glass before continuing.

"Used to be, we had only the one lifetime to prove ourselves, succeed or fail. Now we screw up or devote ourselves to the wrong career, we can say, pouf, so what, I'll do it another way the next time around. We can be cruel, because we can make up for the cruelty later, in all that time we have. Or we think we'll make up for it—time has a way of distancing cruelty and making it eventually excusable. So we go on, draining life of its meaning, because we think we'll get around to giving it that meaning later."

"Damn it, Ben what do you expect? It's human nature, it's—"

"Ah, sure, it's human nature. The great catchall excuse. Jesus, Voss, it's human nature to *die.* If we're going to violate that, we might as well get something worthwhile out of the violation. As it is, we've failed any ideal contained in the technological development of retreading."

"What do you mean by that?"

"Every development has an ideal inherent in it whether or not its developer realizes it. Scientific inventions enlarge the environment, or at least enhance some detail of it. Mostly they help to free man, and that's the ideal in them, to give man a better existence and therefore freedom to pursue his ideal needs. Science in the past has continually made man freer, even within political tyranny, but what has been the result? Man was freer and didn't know what to do with his leisure time. He—"

"Wait a minute. Some people made good use of their freedoms. In those goddamned political tyrannies you mentioned, there were men who used the technology to get rid of the goddamned tyranny."

"Maybe, or maybe the technology wasn't so necessary. Never mind, of course there are individuals who break out of any mold. So forget about the few individuals, I'm talking about the mass of men."

"Who lead desperate lives . . ."

"So shut up. Look, let's talk about medical developments instead. Almost all medical developments in the past have led to the extension of life. A small technique could save an organ and give the patient who knows how many years of extra life. Retreading is the ultimate in the extension-of-life-ideal. All the time you need to do all the things you want. With all these medical and scientific developments designed to free man and allow him to develop to a higher level of existence, what's happened? I'll tell you. In most areas of life today, there is little or no progress being made scientifically or medically. In regular society the most work is being done to refine the retreading process and to prevent the results of sabotaging. With all the potential for moral and idealistic progress, people everywhere are in the middle of repeating their mistakes and just finding some new thrilling way of screwing up. Jesus, this is good whiskey. I know it's good, it's making me absolutely morbid. Drink up."

Needing a change of subject, I asked Ben why he was now called a medical consultant. He explained that he came back to life to find that there was no longer any such occupation as private practice for doctors. He did not want to associate with a hospital or clinic, so instead he chose medical consultancy. He had so much expertise in so many medical areas that he was able to advise for problems and suggest new general ideas.

"How would I have the right to complain if I just spent this lifetime doing the same old things as my two previous lifetimes?"

Eventually Stacy fell asleep. Perhaps from the whiskey, or perhaps from boredom at our conversation. Alcohol never *seemed* to affect Stacy appreciably—but, since I didn't know his demons, I could never be sure.

"Do you do *anything?*" I asked. "In this job, I mean?"

"'Course I do. What makes you say that?"

"Well, we've been here an hour, more than an hour, and I haven't noticed you do anything in an official capacity. Do you have an official capacity? Except for good old-fashioned whiskey, of course."

Ben laughed, said:

"It's a *position,* really. I'm on call. Most of my time is free, and I spend it either absorbing, since I'm acquiring quite a taste for arcane knowledge, or in planning for crises that I'm sure will develop later. Boozing with old chums is slated in for only a small part of my total schedule. And, while I'm in here, the venerable Miss Albright keeps away the few wolves that come on the prowl. She's a good lady, Miss Albright. If I didn't want peace in the office, I'd tup her once in a while. But once tupped, I doubt—I don't know what I doubt—but, anyway, a good lady is she. You oughta tup her, be the best thing for you, the—"

"Don't joke, Ben."

"What? Oh. I forgot. You don't tup, can't tup. I'm really sorry."

I glanced nervously Stacy's way, to make sure he was still asleep. He knew nothing about my physical defect, at least I didn't think he did. Ben reached over and touched my arm.

"I'm really sorry, chum. It's the whiskey. And the fact it all seems so long ago. By now, were there any fairness in the universe, you should've found a magic salve or science should've provided a miracle cure. If it happened now, I probably could've done something—with my new power, I have broader resources—but it's too late, way too much time has passed. I doubt any operation would be a success, I doubt—"

"God, Ben, thanks for telling me and all that, but would you please shut up? If you're probing to find out if I'm adjusted, I am adjusted. But let's not discuss remote possibilities, huh? Let's just drink. Speaking of drink, I find a not surprising need to use your lavatorial facilities, if you'll—"

"Just a moment."

Ben walked to his desk and pressed a button. The outlines of a door appeared in the far wall. He gestured toward it.

"In there."

"Thanks."

"Don't mention. I'm glad that at least they didn't tamper with you in that respect. While they were in the neighborhood, I mean."

"Some joke."

"Only half a joke. Their sabotaging systems have become rather, well, rather more sophisticated since the days when you were a victim."

I returned from the bathroom to find Stacy awake and June Albright standing at the office door. Ben announced he was going to take all of us to supper at his club.

"It's a Third Lifetimer Club," he said. "Special Advanced-Lifetimer Clubs in every major megalopolis. Members into their third, fourth, even fifth, lifetimes."

"I'm surprised that you attach yourself to an organization advocating such exclusivity. I'd think your views might be just a bit unpopular for—"

"No philosophy on Earth'd keep me from finding and using a place where the food is."

"In some ways you never change, no matter how many lifespans."

"Agreed. Let's go."

5

In the taxi on the way to the club I told Ben about the shooting incident, asked him what was behind the assassination squads. An odd distress came into his eyes.

"There are many more, well, revolutionaries among the reject class now than there were in your day, Voss," he said. "And they're better organized, better equipped, with better resources."

"And they've become killers?"

"Some of them. A radical fringe. Best way to show your contempt of retreading is, I suppose, through violence, to deny it to the privileged individuals. Killer squads're well trained, they aim for the head with high-powered weaponry—and they hit the head with an amazing precision, just often enough to deny a few randomly chosen—or perhaps not so randomly chosen—individuals their chance for another lifetime. Many of their victims, if they're killed at all, wind up salvaged. Even that's something of a victory for the assassination squads, since those victims are condemned to a long time in the period of darkness, which is much longer these days than when I experienced it. Adjustment is harder the longer you've been in. I can attest to that. Anyway, one of the hazards of everyday life is the killer teams, so watch yourselves."

"Our space training may come in handy."

"Don't get too confident. Some of these killers are pretty efficient. There's a fellow by the name of Gorman Triplett who's become quite a legend in reject circles, something of a hero. We're almost at the club. Wait'll you taste the food. Best modern science can offer. Some of it's even real. Probably taste even better to a couple of spacers than to us common earthmen."

The food was good and the place pleasanter than it had any right to be. Ben and I drank more than was perhaps good for us.

We talked on and on and on, content with seeing each other again. Stacy kept right up with us, in drink but not talk, without showing any ill effects from either. June Albright sipped slowly at a succession of glasses of red wine. We all seemed quite convivial—at least to my distorted perspective—as we left the club. At the club's outer entrance, we were detained for fifteen minutes because there had been an assassination squad spotted nearby. But it turned out to be a false alarm. Ben and I smoked enormous cigars while June vainly tried to make sensible conversation with Stacy. Maybe not so vain, since his responses were not clouded in their usual mysteries. Sounding every year of my middle-age, I asked Ben if it were safe for decent citizens to walk the streets now.

"Safe as it ever was. Well, maybe not that safe, especially with the police strike and—"

"No police, yep, I was told. There're no police now."

"Well, the city charter requires that one-third of normal staff be on duty at all times, even when the full force is on strike. But that one-third is kept busy enough. See, the killer squads are hard to trace. Mostly they're composed of rejects who've gone underground and been absorbed into what turns out to be an efficient protection system. And their strategy is insidious. They arrange to group together at a prearranged rendezvous point, go to their assigned mission location, fire suddenly and quickly, and then just as quickly disperse. With the exception of a few teams who always work together, like the famous Gorman Triplett's, most of the squads don't have a permanent organization—you know, with the same three or four members working together. A reason the police went out in the first place is because of reject-control regulations."

"What are they?"

"A group of laws that were passed by frightened lawmakers. They came about because of the shortage of usable reject bodies. In addition to the rejects who were just plain vanishing into the underground, there were many who committed particularly horrible suicides just to prevent the use of their bodies in the future. And then there was the sabotaging, you know about that."

"When I left, there was some religion that allowed rejects to give up their bodies for a future salvation, some kind of—"

"The followers of St. Ethel, you mean."

"Right."

"Oh, they're still around, and I'm told they've even grown in numbers over the years. Most of the people standing in a charnel house line are wearing their St. Ethel medallions, whether they're believers or not."

I thought of Bru and wondered if she had theatrically held out her medallion to the charnel house porter.

"Some people think that it's good that the St. Ethel cult exists, else we might have damn sight fewer bodies for the chambers. God, we can talk of it so coldly. How's that possible?"

"The drink maybe."

"Maybe. Anyway, there're still a good many among the reject class who can't buy the St. Ethelian message. Still, the St. Ethels are responsible for keeping a difficult situation under a certain amount of control. Wait a second, the booze is getting to me. I was telling you about the laws. Did I finish that?"

"I missed it if you did."

"The laws then. The law that really gets the goat of every cop is the one that says, no matter what crime the reject has committed, he may not be killed in any way that'd prevent the further use of the body. That, as you may imagine, has made efficient precautions against assassination attempts very difficult. And has, in passing, set up quite a paradox. Assassination teams are sending too many retreads and naturals to the chambers and their subsequent overlong periods of darkness. At the same time, the ranks of the reject deviates are swelling with new recruits who're not around when their date with the charnel house arrives. At the same time, those people who're screwing up the whole system cannot themselves be effectively apprehended because the rules prevent the law-enforcement officers from killing them, or for that matter chancing a safe kill."

"Safe kill?"

"One that leaves the body intact. There've been some experiments with the kind of weaponry that stuns or paralyzes but they tend to be short-range weapons and the police never get close enough. Top of that, the killers are better shots. And they can't locate the killers in between attempts. Ah, it's a farce, Voss, it really is. The things I could tell you . . ."

"It seems the kind of farce you enjoy."

"Just what in bloody hell do you mean by that?"

"You know what I mean."

"No, I do not. I definitely do not."

"Well, I'd tell you, if I knew what the hell I meant."

"I'm sure you would. I think it's safe to go out on the street now."

At Ben's insistence we visited a couple of other watering-spots around the city. One, to see a singer he especially liked. Another, to imbibe some sobering-up materials. Stacy left us silently at some point I do not recall. Ben could not be sobered and had to be placed in a taxi and sent home. June and I proceeded to a couple of other places.

Of course June was interested in more than pleasant companionship, as she pointed out quite explicitly and indelicately after she had finally drunk too much. I had to spring on her one of my many comic ploys to talk her out of it, I forget which one. She was too drunk to worry about the sense of it, but she looked regretful. She had, I assumed, hopes for the future. I saw her home, even held her for a while, kissed her. I could do that, had done it before when I found myself in such absurd situations. I left her apartment and walked recklessly down the unusually quiet streets. Once I thought I heard gunfire in the distance.

6

After a couple of days in a rundown hotel, Stacy and I decided to use a bit of our accumulated spacer money and a part of the large amount on our credit shields to blow ourselves to a couple of weeks at the Continental-Plaza-Astoria, the city's luxury hotel.

Or, rather, I decided and Stacy nodded laconic agreement. I should have realized what a trap the hotel was from its advertising, which emphasized the feature that one could enjoy the delights of the city without ever leaving his hotel room. Translated: you don't have to go out on the streets and chance getting shot by an insurgent team.

The Conplaz (as it is called) is a kind of ornate maximum security prison, offering isolation for people who need a soothing incarceration. There was nothing the Conplaz wouldn't provide. Guards in informal dress, so as not to be disturbing, roamed the hallways in twos and threes. Surveillance devices were placed in the halls and (in discreet places) in the rooms and suites. These latter could be activated either by the guest in trouble or by keying the code of sounds that indicated something amiss. A large panel of numbered buttons (color-schemed for each room) allowed the guest to order just about any service a hotel could legitimately provide, and without the annoying interferences of officious middlemen. Even prostitutes could be ordered—a clerk assured me that they were carefully screened not only for health and safety but to insure that no rebel rejects were among their numbers. There were number codes by which you could even specify the condition of the food you ordered, the edition of the book you wanted to view, the measurements necessary for clothing done to order by the hotel tailor. In short, all the comforts and services that we have come to associate with maximum security hotels over the years. I made abundant use of the panel, and sampled several types of diversions the first days. Even Stacy made some use of the machine.

Perhaps the best, and silliest, hotel service was the tour of the city, which was accomplished with the guest staying right in his own bed. The simulation used the four walls of the room, so that pictures and sound came from all directions. A dial beside the bed allowed the guest to speed up or slow down the tour. You could "drive" around the city at a normal pace, or jump from place to place according to a previously chosen program. I selected the museum tour first, and stopped the motion of the tour frequently in order to examine specific paintings closely. Another time I did the one that emphasized the sights of the old city, spots like the reconstructed Statue of Liberty and the well-preserved Chinatown.

I did not know at that time that Chinatown was staffed primarily with Oriental rejects, who were more or less officially left alone in spite of the body shortage. First, because the Oriental fugitives would have been extremely difficult to locate in the junglelike maze of the Chinatown area. Second, and worse, because there was an unwritten and unspoken custom against retreading Caucasians into Oriental bodies—one of those strange archaic tribal rites, different from the official laws, like the one forbidding cross-sexual transfer. There had been many bizarre cases of racism during the early years of retreading, but readjustments and relocations had ameliorated most such problems.

Anyway, Chinatown fascinated me and I took that part of the tour three times, while ordering authentic Chinese food from room service. I often felt strangely ridiculous for enjoying such an ersatz tour—or, for that matter, enjoying those few days of isolation in my luxury cell.

My third or fourth day of leisure was interrupted by a call from a reporter on one of the dailies that were transmitted through most of the civilized world. He said he wanted to interview me. I asked why on Earth a reporter would want to talk to me. He said it had little to do with Earth, but instead with my time in space, which was of interest to his readership. I told him it was his funeral, come ahead and interview me.

The interview was uncomfortable. The reporter was a big man, too fat by quite a bit, and I felt the old retread's disturbance with observing a misused body. I did not like the feeling but could not avoid it. The man's questions concentrated on my space service experiences. I was sparing of detail, but that did not deter him from writing me up poignantly as some kind of tragic hero in his article, which came out a few days later. He emphasized the fact that I, as a retread, continually risked my immortality in dangerous-duty situations, an aspect of my adventures that I deliberately made light of in response to his incessant questions on the subject. He found extraordinary interest in an idea that was entirely his own: that I was somehow especially heroic for testing my "mettle as a man" by blithely ignoring guaranteed immortality to go back to our roots as men of action. He said I was testing history, or some damn-fool idea like that, and by doing so I verified history's continuing vitality. I put the article in my traveling files and hardly ever looked at it again.

The hotel's services, in spite of their variety, grew trying after a few days, and we decided to try a "real-life" trip outside the hotel. As we were readying to leave the suite June Albright called us. She said Ben had been called to a conference in Washington and she had the day off. Without asking if we had any plans, she ordered us to meet her in the old Washington Square area, near the partly decomposed crumbling arch. It was safer than most places, she said, a kind of demilitarized zone that rejects respected. That may have been so, but the drivers of the first two taxis we flagged refused to take us there. The third cabbie let us out at the arch, which was still impressive even in its ruined state. June was already waiting, carrying on a lively discussion with a pair of seedy-looking men in overcoats much too thick for the balmy day. When she turned and said hello to us, the men stepped backward, with a mixture of courtesy and apprehension.

"Hi," June said, "we were discussing the relative merits of our time and the time of Dostoevsky, nineteenth-century Russia."

"What are the relative merits?" I said.

"Actually, according to Simon here, the two eras are about the same. The privileged class had it pretty good at both times, and social responsibility amounted to about the same thing. Simon, by the way, is not a reject."

"Why do you feel it necessary to point that out?"

"Because you were thinking he was."

"I'm a suicide," Simon said in an incredibly scratchy voice. "Which means, since you were about to ask, that I have refused to be retreaded the next time around. I've had two good lifetimes and will not violate another reject's body for another go-around, merely to satisfy selfish urges for pleasure."

I was happy to meet someone with an ideal, even if delivered soapbox-style, but I was getting sick and tired of having reject philosophies thrown in my face wherever I went. June bade goodbye to her two seedy companions and walked with us away from the arch, across the reconstructed park. Groups of children, happily ensconced in whirling swings, joyfully twisting down convoluted slides, alleviated somewhat my dark mood.

"He made you uncomfortable," June said. "Simon."

"A little."

"Normal, I suppose. Most retreads are uncomfortable around suicides. Sometimes I wish they'd not go around announcing it so loudly. Might influence me, and I don't want that."

We found a small Pakistani restaurant to have lunch in. Such little places with ancient cuisines pleased me, made me happy that certain cities had gone to so much trouble to preserve styles of food preparation even when the countries from which the food derived no longer existed. Thinking of that, I suddenly wondered whether there still was a Pakistan existing somewhere halfway across the globe, sending representatives to world meetings. Did they have our benefits? Did they have second lifetimes? Again I could not get my mind off the subject of retreads and rejects—even when I wanted to enjoy a quiet lunch, the subject obsessed me. I wanted to shout out to anyone around that I did not feel guilty, I did not want to be forced into guilt, I had had fourteen years of forgetting the guilt and had lost the defenses necessary to survive.

June kept up a steady conversation, even got Stacy to respond more eagerly than usual. She seemed to have a way with him, an ability to draw him out. Afterwards, we wandered the streets, looked into many shops. I don't know at what point we left the circumscribed safe area, but soon we were walking down darker streets. There were people around, but not many, and they walked more briskly than had the crowds in the shop area. Stacy walked a couple of steps to the side of June and me, as if to define a boundary, that he was the loner and we were the couple.

June explained to me the thesis of a new book she was reading about how to effect a relatively stable retread-reject relationship in society and discourage the uprisings of recent times. Her summary was interrupted by three men dropping down at us from, it seemed, the sky. Actually, they had jumped out a second-story window. Each of them held a weapon—ugly guns, apparently handmade, undecorated and curiously misshaped, appearing centuries old—and, as soon as they gained their footing, two of the men pointed their guns at me, the third aimed toward Stacy. Our attackers were not prepared for the kind of quick reactions that our space duty had provided us. Stacy, always faster-reflexed than I, high-kicked the man whose gun was pointed at him. The weapon sprung from his hands and he fell backward. Almost in the same motion, Stacy hit at a second attacker's arm and deflected his aim while sending him scurrying sideways, his feet struggling comically to keep him from falling. After I pushed June out of the way, I jumped straight at the third ambusher. Although his gun was pointed straight at me (I had never been cautious around opponents' weapons), he was too surprised by my sudden movement to operate it. His shock lasted only a second, but that was all the time I required. If I had been slower, he might have dropped me easily. As it was, I had pushed him backward by the time he pulled the trigger and the gun fired uselessly upward. One chop to the neck, and he crashed sideways into a wall. The impact did little damage to him since he was already unconscious when he hit. I turned around to help Stacy, who was still struggling with the second attacker. However, now the first one had raised himself from the sidewalk and gone into a crouch. I dove at him, but this time he was ready and he moved sideways. My shoulder rammed him, anyway, and he was momentarily put off balance. His reflexes were good, and he twisted in my direction as I tried to recover my own equilibrium. At that moment, Stacy had connected with his assailant's jaw and the man was crumpling to the ground. As he fell, Stacy grabbed the barrel of his weapon and pulled it out of his hand. My man had taken aim at me and would have pulled the trigger if Stacy had not brought the stock of the gun he held down onto the man's head. The force of the blow, given impetus by the lunge of Stacy's body, was too strong. The man was dead before he hit the ground.

In a moment June stood beside me, asking if there was anything she could do.

"It'd be best to get an ambulance here soon as possible."

"I'll get to a—"

But she did not have to move, for we heard the ambulance siren a few blocks away. We could only wait.

"Thanks for pushing me out of the line of fire," June said. "I've had some hand-to-hand training, but these guys woulda caught me too much by surprise."

"Well, they seemed primarily after Stacy and me, not you."

"They'd've gotten around to me."

The ambulance arrived, easing to a calm stop. With it came a representative of the city's one-third police force. He escorted us to headquarters, where our story was routinely recorded. We were excused but, on the way out, a cop stopped Stacy and cautioned him not to go for the kill, please. He asked why, aside from the obvious moral implications. The cop said they had had to rush the body to a retread chamber, and that there was a chance some nerve linkups to the brain might not be possible—the body might be useless, unretreadable. Stacy shrugged and said that was too bad. The cop did not seem to take Stacy's statement as an apology, but said no more.

Because it followed so directly upon the human-interest reportage about me, and because the three men were only the third or fourth reject assassination squad to be caught in entirety, the attack merited extensive coverage by the media. One reporter obtained the fact that Stacy was a reject living out his lifespan as a natural, and played it up. People were apparently impressed that, to protect me, he was willing to kill another reject. That angle of the story infuriated me, and I am sure angered Stacy, even if he did show no reaction to it when I showed the article to him. However, I decided it would be useless to deal with the reporter and try to point out that Stacy's act had nothing to do with a feeling of class, that his instincts were that of a trained spacer and not an earthbound reject.

7

"Mr. Geraghty?"

"Yes."

"You probably don't remember me, but we've met."

"Oh, when?"

"Some time ago, I'm afraid. Fourteen years, according to the news."

"I don't know if I–"

"By the seashore. You were just–"

"I can recall the sea, but–"

"I was nine. You told me–"

"Yes, wait–"

"Alicia. I'm Alicia. You and I, we–"

"Of course, I remember it all very well. You were so beautiful then, a child that–"

"Well, that *was* fourteen years ago."

"You are still beautiful. Don't be coy about it. You know."

"Yes, maybe. I just don't think it's important."

"Beautiful people don't have to."

"You win. It's good to see you again, Mr. Geraghty."

"Voss."

"I used to call you Uncle Voss."

"Did you? Yes, you did. Uncle–"

"I remember especially exploring that casino, the ruined one, the derelict–"

"There was a big bandstand split in half and a lot of wires from the ceiling."

"Where the chandelier must have been."

"Yes, of course. That image of the place has haunted me, because I never could figure out what that was, what it–"

"You told me what it was."

"Did I? I couldn't have. I don't remember."

"Well, I just wanted to say hello. I'll just—"

"You won't go anywhere for a while. I want to talk to you."

"Oh, no. I have to—"

"It is terrific to see you again."

"Well, yes, for me, too. I said that."

"How did you find me?"

"You're easy to find. You're *everywhere,* that article, films, your adventure with the killers and—well, anyway, I was looking for you."

"You were looking—?"

"Well, I always wondered what happened to you. How your life was, what you'd become. I always expected I'd run across you someday. Then, a few days ago, in the papers, while I was doing a job in the midwest, I saw your picture in the local paper and—"

"Job? What do you do?"

"I troubleshoot mostly. Work with all kinds of social problems. It's sort of a government job, but not really allied to the government, they just send money. I, and others, try to settle disputes. Social things."

"I don't understand."

"Difficult to explain. Like my last one had to do with some physical attacks on property by a community of followers of St. Ethel. You know about the St. Ethel cult, what it—"

"Yes, I've heard about it. What do they attack? I thought they were peaceful."

"Most of the time. The attacks were on their own property, you see. They were destroying their own possessions, endangering themselves, causing quite a commotion. My agency sent me to quieten them."

"And did you?"

"A little. They're still destroying things, but less openly."

"You failed then?"

"No, succeeded. For my purposes anyway. I don't always care what I'm ordered to do, and sometimes find other solutions. I have to go."

"No, for a minute why not—"

"Let's get together later."

"In the hotel restaurant then. Supper. Eight o'clock."

"Well, okay. But I pay my tab."

"You don't have to. I've got spacer money coming out of—"

"Doesn't matter. Eight o'clock then."

"Yes."

"See you then."

"Sure. Hey, how's your father?"

"He died."

"Oh, I'm sorry. Has he returned to life yet?"

"He won't. He chose not to."

"Oh, sorry."

"Don't be. He died out in your territory, one of the outplanets. You probably passed it by hundreds of times. Sorry, I'm late. Goodbye."

"Bye."

8

Alicia did not show up for dinner. I passed up an invitation from Ben to visit a few dives, talked Stacy into joining Ben, was rather rude to a reporter who wanted to do some kind of followup story about me. And I waited in the hotel lobby for two hours. Thinking of Alicia.

When I was finally certain that she was not going to arrive, I struggled to recall a few physical details about her. We had only been together for a few minutes of the early afternoon. The lights of the lobby had been too bright and there had been too many people milling about. I could not seem to focus. It had not been enough time and my memories were more a general impression than a vivid recreation. But I had certainly been dazzled by her. I knew her hair was blond but could not recall what shade. I could not see that its vivid yellow coloring of her childhood had not significantly faded with maturity. I remembered that she was attractive, but could not recall details of her face, could only recall the brightness of her eyes, did not even remember their pale blue, almost gray color. I had noticed her body was prettily shaped, but I did not perceive its delicate symmetry until much later.

Perhaps I had such difficulty summoning up an immediate memory of Alicia because the picture of her as a nine-year-old kept intruding on my fanciful reflection. I began to reminisce, started out recalling the sweet things. More and more details about our invasion of the casino returned to me. I wondered if I should write them down so I could slowly dole them out as conversational tidbits over our meal. When she did not show, I forgot them and have never been willing to make the effort to summon them up again. At the point I decided she was not going to show up, I started seeing pictures of her in her more stubborn moods, when she'd go off by herself and refuse to have anything to do with me. When I left the lobby, I wondered if perhaps the young woman who had accosted me that afternoon was an imposter, sent to embarrass me socially.

I returned to the suite that Stacy and I shared. He was still out with Ben. I fell asleep, awoke to the sound of a quite authoritative knocking at my door. I hoped it was Alicia before I even opened the door. She commented later that she had not expected me to be so gentle with her when she materialized at my doorway in the middle of the night. Some of that came from composing my smile as carefully as I straightened my slept-in clothing. Alicia was still in streetclothes, still looking every inch a businesswoman on her way to a meeting.

"I woke you."

"All right, it's all right. I enjoy being awakened by visions of loveliness."

Odd that I, so cold to women normally, should have bantered with her right from the beginning. Maybe not so odd.

"I hope that is sarcasm, that remark. Because, if it isn't, I'm not too pleased with it."

"You've lost me."

"That vision of loveliness stuff. Can I come in?"

"Of course. Sit on the leather chair."

"Do you have anything drinkable?"

"Some vintage whiskey."

"Pour it quick."

She accepted the glass of whiskey with a quite enchanting smile, and drank it eagerly. Then she put her hand on her chest and held her breath. Her eyes watered.

"What's the matter?"

"Nothing. I should have eaten something, that's all."

"You didn't have any dinner."

"None at all. Haven't eaten since lunchtime."

"I think the hotel restaurant's still open, we can—"

"No. No, I don't want to be among people just now."

I could not understand the vehemence of her response, but did not mind going along with it.

"I'm sorry, by the way."

"For what?"

"Don't be coy. You know for what. For not meeting you for dinner as I promised."

"That's all right."

"Really? I doubt that. Did you wait long?"

"A little while."

"Which means a long while, I know. Oh, God, I don't know why I . . ."

"Why you what?"

"Nothing. I'm just not good at keeping my appointments, that's all."

"I'll take note of that for future reference."

"Do that. I ask all my friends to take notes about me. Frees me of my later responsibilities to them."

"I don't understand that."

"Simple. I only feel in the wrong tonight because you don't know me. Or else you don't realize that the child you knew hasn't changed. If you were somebody who knew me, then you'd know I'm liable not to show up for dinner dates, or any kind of date or appointment, and then I would not be guilty. Now you know me. Next time I won't have to apologize."

"And if I should choose to miss an appointment with you?"

"I'd see it as only a fair return for my treatment of you." She took a long sip of whiskey, which seemed to go down better than the first one had. "Then I'd hit you."

"I'll take note of that, too."

"Better buy a loose-leaf notebook. Do you have anything for an upset stomach?"

"No, I don't think so. I never have the problem. I'm sorry, you said you were starved. What you really need is food."

"I'm not so sure of that. But you may be right."

"I'll have something sent up."

"Don't bother."

"Why not?"

"I don't like being served."

"Pretend it's being delivered by a St. Bernard because you are slowly dying from hunger."

"Well, all right. But make the order something simple, okay?"

"Steak and salad."

"Great. I didn't know there were any left."

"Any what? The steaks aren't exactly—"

"No. St. Bernards."

"I don't know either, maybe there aren't."

Pressing a button next to the light switch, I activated the wall panel and punched out the code for the food, together with a request for the appropriate wine, according to the current ratings, to go with it. When I turned away from the panel, Alicia was not there. She had disappeared from her chair. For a moment I was terribly afraid that she had simply left again without telling me, stood me up again. Then I heard water running in the bathroom and knew where she was. I paced nervously around the room, waiting for her to come out again. Why was I acting so strangely, I wondered. I was like a young man setting up the intrigues of courtship. Which, for me, was the most absurd of activities. My sexual state had always forced me to avoid even platonic intimacy with women. Many had tried to break down my apparent detachment, and wound up hating me for their failure. But, I realized suddenly, I was simply too happy seeing Alicia again and just could not assume my normal reserve around her.

After she returned from the bathroom, she started talking eagerly about her job. About how, after she had devoured everything education had to offer—everything of interest, anyway—she had bored herself for a year or so with some job involving the classification of literature, then she applied for a position with a social-problem division of the government. (I interrupted her to ask what kind of government was in power nowadays. She replied, "The usual. Isn't it always the usual?" I tried to remember a day when the political structure of the world meant enough to me for me to want to investigate it. I always knew there were a lot of people invested with the job of running things, anonymous people who accepted the duty because it fulfilled some kind of need, and I never much worried about who they were or what they did.) After her final satisfactories, Alicia was, by her own request, sent into the field to work directly with people. She had wanted to work with rejects primarily because she had slipped into the satisfactory classification by a fairly narrow margin. Not many of the social-problem specialists at the agency cared to work directly with rejects, so possibilities were many and varied. As she rambled on about the difficulty of reaching the rejects emotionally, especially those who felt resistance to the system, I realized I had not felt so comfortable with anyone in many years. Not even with Ben, and certainly not with Stacy, who was too often unnerving and unpredictable. In fact, the last time I had felt so content in someone else's company was probably with Alicia during my beach convalescence.

The food arrived. Alicia took it from the bellhop's tray, told him she would not let him serve her any of it. She ate the steak and salad aggressively, recklessly. I imagined that was the way she attacked social problems. It was a silly unsocial thing to notice, but I was quite pleased with the way she would pick up a piece of dropped lettuce from her lap, use it in a gesture to make a point, then begin to chew on it while watching for my reaction to what she had said. When we had finished the meal, she seemed charged with new energy. She walked about the room, picking up our dishes and silverware and returning them to the tray—carrying her glass of wine from one place to another, setting it down, walking away from it, returning to it and picking it up in order to carry it some other point where she would set it down again. As if she had to keep busy, she straightened things around the room that did not particularly need straightening. If I did not understand something she said, she'd wrinkle her eyebrows and stare at me with a kind of ironic disbelief in her eyes. I would pretend of course that I understood what she said perfectly. She, of course, didn't believe that, and so explained herself in more detail—her hand hitting her thigh with a slap each time the word she needed failed to come—until she could see that I did now finally understand.

After several minutes of active movement and talk, she suddenly sat back down and settled quickly into an odd moodiness. She asked for more wine and, when I poured some into her glass, affectionately touched the back of my hand. A niecelike affection still, so it did not bother me. You're okay, uncle, she seemed to be saying by the gesture, even if you did give up thinking as a bad habit. I tried to stir up more conversation about her work, but she no longer seemed interested in talking about it. She kept interrupting to ask me the time, even though the clock was out in the open as a part of the control panel. I started to feel a little woozy, since I had been drinking at a more rapid rate than she. Finally I could no longer resist the urge to go to the bathroom. When I came out, she had fallen asleep. Her body was curled up strangely, with her head and torso twisted in a different direction from her legs. There was a small bruise just above her ankle. One of her shoes had slipped away from her heel and seemed to dangle like an ornament from her toes. I removed it, placed it on the floor. In my boozy way I became quite interested in her leg and foot. The leg was shapely but thin, and its musculature showed that she led an active life, probably not only for her work but with some exercise and sport. Her foot was long and narrow, tapering down to long and narrow toes that she curled and uncurled when she stirred in her sleep. I considered waking her, but decided instead to put a light blanket over her. Trying to find something with which to occupy myself, I kept catching myself looking back at her, watching her sleep. I thumbed through the enormous booklet of hotel entertainments, but could find nothing in it that I would have enjoyed or could even order because it might have disturbed her sleep. So I sat, and enjoyed sitting.

As I examined the features of my hotel room, I resolved to move away from it as soon as possible. In some way Alicia's presence in the room made me realize that I had failed as a gentleman of leisure and I no longer wanted to keep up the pretense.

I don't know how long Alicia had been awake when I discovered her staring at me. I was pleased at the attractive way she returned my smile.

"I'm sorry to fall asleep on you."

"Don't be."

"What time is it?"

"About four in the morning."

She stretched her arms as if it were not only early, but bright. "Good!"

"Good?"

"I needed to be here at least until now."

"I don't understand. Why needed?"

She stood up, straightened herself, sought out the removed shoe and slipped it back on her foot, and was on her way to the door before I realized that she was leaving.

"They'll be questioning you probably."

"Questioning? Who?"

"People who'll be investigating my whereabouts tonight."

"Alicia, I don't—"

"Not to worry. Tell them anything. Just establish my alibi, that I was here with you from about eight o'clock."

"But you didn't get here until much later, until—"

"I know that. Just tell them eight, and that I stayed till now. Don't worry, Uncle Voss, it's necessary."

"Don't call me uncle."

"Don't be petulant. Ask me to dinner tomorrow night. Tonight, really. Go ahead. I'll show up, I promise."

"Okay, same time, same place."

"Good. Oh, why don't you pretend that I succumbed to your every desire. Tastefully, of course. It will do my reputation good within the service."

"Alicia, that is beyond—beyond—"

"Well, too bad. I'd like to be thought of as a wench, even if I have no abilities along that line."

"I'm not so sure about that."

"Keep the petulance. It's got possibilities. Goodbye now."

She blew a kiss from the doorway, and I almost shook my fist angrily at her. Except that I did not feel angry at her. I laughed after she closed the door.

9

A couple of investigators did visit me and ask about Alicia. I told them very little, just laconically established her alibi. They gave me the kind of look that displayed their logical conclusions, refused to tell me the purpose of their investigation, and left. I had a taste in my mouth that could be soothed only by strong drink. Just the fact of the investigation had felt like a violation.

But the interrogators' visit came later. In the meantime I was having a delightful time with Alicia. Expecting a long wait, I was pleased to find her waiting for me in the lobby for our dinner date that night. I do not recall too much about the meal, but I do remember that Alicia prodded me for tales about my adventures, as she called them, in the space racket, as she called it. I told her some, but not all, of my experiences with the mist on Coolidge. She found it odd to be almost done in by something the consistency of a mild fog—although, she added, she had spent some time in Los Angeles a few years ago and, with the consistency of the atmosphere there, she could almost believe my story. I finally got her off the subject of my travels by initiating a string of reminiscences about ourselves. She astonished me by recalling those days at the beach better than I. I was also impressed by how often the child Alicia had seen through me. I thought that, with the advantage of my advanced years, I had fooled her in so many ways. I hadn't seen that she had, indeed, toyed with me.

After the dinner, under the influence of an overdose of wine, I found myself holding her hand and, ridiculously, could not think of a polite way to let it go. Certainly I did not want her to see the act as a fumbling attempt to initiate seduction—worse, I dreaded having to tell her why seduction would be impossible. For nights afterward, in my foolish way, I dreamed about holding her hand in the erotic way that a young man might dream of more physical things. Later that evening, when I was not holding her hand, Alicia disappeared again. Walked out on me without saying goodbye. And of course came back the next morning apologizing for leaving the night before without saying goodbye. From then on, I came to think of holding her hand as a spell preventing her sudden disappearance.

That day she took me off shopping with her, and made me buy a dreadful skintight suit. Three pieces, but they fit so close when the suit was on, it looked like a one-piece jumpsuit. I wore it in the outside world one night, watching people watch me (if the tightness were not enough, the fact that it was bright blue, her color choice, was enough to draw such attention), and, even though it eventually became a popular fashion of that odd time, I never could wear the suit again. Alicia noted its absence on several occasions, knowing of course that I did not intend to wear it any more. I think I told her once that it reminded me too much of the skintight jumpsuit I had to wear while "adventuring in the space racket," and that anyway I preferred loose clothing. She nodded agreement and told me I must wear it the next time. I don't remember now how I got away with not wearing it then.

We spent many of the subsequent evenings together. Besides restaurants and shopping, there was an array of cultural diversions. The plays, ballets, operas, concerts, puppet shows. Alicia had a taste for the offbeat, and I endured a few horrors she dragged me to. One of the street theater companies we attended was strikingly similar to the one I had seen in my visit to Hough. Their play was also unstructured, and they were also proud of that feature. An actress who looked nothing like Bru reminded me of her, and I felt sad the rest of the evening. Alicia was disturbed by my sadness but asked no questions. We went on long walks in dark streets that were not supposed to be safe, but we encountered no trouble. Walked through parks, with no care that we might be serving up our lives to anyone with a weapon. Saw nothing in those first couple of weeks that would have bothered anyone's maiden aunt. Nothing violent, anyway.

At some point during this period, on one afternoon when Alicia was away on one of her mysterious trips for her job (or so she said), came the second attack of an assassination team. It was very much like the first attack, except that the trio of killers stayed within buildings and fired out of windows. Stacy and I had taken to the carrying of our own weapons, guns adapted to the needs of the spacer, instruments more powerful and sophisticated than the makeshift guns of the squads.

We took little time disposing of the attackers, killed two of them. They apparently had not expected us to be ready for them. The receiving officers were not too happy with our work (the two bodies had definitely been rendered unusable) and probably wished that the next insurgent squad ambushing us would be more successful.

After finishing with the cops, we went directly to Ben's office. I told June what had happened and she went with us into Ben's inner sanctum. She forgot that he had been absorbing, and had neglected to set the time-lock on his door. He did not notice us burst in. June gestured us to a pair of chairs and we all waited patiently for Ben to finish his absorber-session. Rapt in intellection, the bulky absorb-helmet like an aura around his head, Ben looked quite angelic. When he was through and had set the headset aside, he turned to us as if he had known we were there all the time.

"And what can I do for a pair of degenerates like you? Who, by the way, had better stop putting dangerous ideas into my pretty assistant's pretty head."

June smiled, I was not sure at what.

I told Ben about the new attack and asked what were the odds on such a thing happening again.

"Pretty good odds but uncomputable. Most of these attacks in the past have been well planned. A few have been random, but most of them have been worked out by masterminds who know what they want. Like this Gorman Triplett who—"

"I'm not sure I understand, Ben. You're saying they're out to get me? To get me specifically?"

"Exactly. I don't know why, but I can hazard a good guess."

"Go ahead and hazard because I'm sure I haven't the ghost of an idea why anyone'd want to—"

"Voss, you don't seem aware of the fact that you're something of a celebrity. In these colorless times, celebrities are rarer than you might think. Even a minor one like you, whose fame is relatively fleeting, a lead human-interest story is all, and don't look so pained about it. I suspect that story about you had more impact than you might imagine. Especially among the rejects, for whom your risking of somebody else's body is something of a sin. If not a sin, at least a misuse of property."

"I don't get you. Why would they care that I risked this body? I should think they would see that as a worthy occupation."

"Ah, it is. And they might even have admired you, if you had managed to get yourself killed outside the possibility of any revival. But you did not, and you are here, and you are something of a symbol. A hero to the convinced retread, who can see your experience as a microcosm of his own."

"Ben, how is that—"

"Be patient. I am usually slower at getting to a point after I've spent an hour with the absorber. Okay, the average retread looks at a life like yours and says to himself: say, that's exactly what we all do with the *entirety* of our lives. We all have prospects of eternity, but continually risk those prospects with the mere act of moving about."

"What kind of a risk is that?"

"Not much a one, I'll admit. But the generalization is the kind of simplification that, by missing the point, hits it right on the mark. The risk of unreversible death turns some retreads into a particular kind of coward, the type of alchemist who turns his trivial day-to-day acts into heroism. He thinks, God Almighty, I could be killed, damaged beyond repair, at any minute. My eternity could go up in smoke. I know about this, Voss, I've been there. Anyway, okay, the retread deals not only with the ordinary risks of life but now he has to cope with the greater dangers of mad killers who *want* him to die, want him to be deprived of his precious immortality. So here's this guy, this mad-dog spacer, Voss whoever-he-is, and he puts his body on the line more times in fourteen years than the average retread in his normal lifespan. Now *that's* really something. Makes me proud to be a retread, he thinks. Then, *then,* how do you think that seems to certain rejects, who perceive that that is exactly how people are reacting to the heroic epic of Vossilyev Geraghty in outer space?"

"They want to kill me just to show up the people they hate."

"Well, that plus you're *also* one of the people they hate."

"I know, but it's a symbolic killing nevertheless."

"Yes. It's to their advantage to kill you now. It wouldn't be just an assassination, it'd be a victory."

June whispered an obscenity. Stacy watched her as if he were more interested in her expletives than in what Ben was saying.

"What should I do, Ben?" I asked.

"Wish I knew. It's difficult to become inconspicuous, but that'd be the best thing if you could do it."

"Yeah, I'll just shrivel up and hide in small spaces."

"If you have a place where you can hole up, do it."

"Now just where—"

"It's not all that hard to get out of sight. City government's not functioning well, what with the police strike and all; the world government doesn't care about internal politics, except where it affects the number of bodies. I don't know what they're worried about, they've got two complete retread chamber setups in their main headquarters. There's a good argument against government for you. Our retreaded leaders, who we can't get rid of because they won't die. If only those damn killer teams'd point their weapons at those people, then . . . then I suppose we'd get rid of the killer teams, because they'd be caught before they got within twenty feet of any of our noble leaders. Well, anyway—Voss, you should be able to find someplace more secret than that goddamned luxury hotel."

"Been meaning to move out of there anyway."

"Then do it. What about this new lady friend of yours I've heard about?"

As he said that, June turned away.

"Alicia, you mean?" I said.

"I believe that's her name."

"How the hell did you know about her?"

"I have sources."

"I told him," June said.

"Then how did you know?"

"Saw you with her, at the hotel."

"See?" Ben said. "I told you how conspicuous you make yourself by staying there."

"I was intrigued," June continued. "It was pretty easy to find out who she was. Alicia Reynal, social worker, et cetera. She's some pretty girl, Voss."

June praised her as if what she really meant was that she was not beautiful and Alicia was. I wanted to tell June that she was pretty, but realized that she would understand the unspoken addendum, but not as pretty as Alicia. Instead, I said:

"Well, yes, Alicia is a friend. I knew her as a child. But I don't know her well enough to hide me out."

"I don't know about that, Voss." June said.

"Why do you say that?"

"I don't know. Something in her eyes when she looks at you. Something in your eyes when you look at her."

I almost laughed aloud. June clearly had not just observed us, she had watched us for some time, spied on us. Then, translating what she saw into the clichés of romantic fiction—whether out of jealousy or a sentimental turn of mind or a little bit of both—she had turned what she had observed into a love story instead of the odd little comedy that it was.

Ben, scowling, suggested that June take Stacy to the outer

office for coffee while we had a private talk. June seemed content to go. Stacy followed her out.

"What's so secret?" I asked Ben.

"This is not so much secrecy as caution. I'm trying to figure a way to help you. Those killer groups are like all fanatics. They'll keep trying, and I don't know if they can be stopped that easily."

"Yes, well, maybe if I do get out of sight for a while, they'll find some new targets."

"Maybe. I'd have you come to my place but, besides being too small for any kind of reasonable cohabitation, I'm being watched and I don't know by whom, or even if there're watchers from many sides."

"Why are they–"

"I don't want to get into that but there are reasons. Anyway, it's possible that you'd be in just as much danger staying with me. But I might be able to help in other ways."

"How?"

"I have some . . . lines into the reject underground. They're tenuous but they might be useful. If I can get through to the right people, perhaps I can get the dogs called off."

"Don't do anything dangerous just for–"

"Why not? Why the hell not? Goddamn it, Voss, you're some asshole to be telling somebody else not to do anything dangerous. I might risk my life, my chance for a fourth lifetime. Does that offend you?"

"Just because I–"

"Oh, shut up. Boy, if assholes had to be stoppered, you'd go broke buying cork."

I laughed but it was an uneasy laugh, and so was the silence that followed it. Ben shuffled some papers on his desk before speaking again:

"I'll see what I can do. Maybe nothing. So you stay less visible for a while. Go away now. Contrary to popular belief, I do have a few bits and pieces of work to get through before I can go home for the day."

I stood up, held out a hand to Ben.

"I'm sorry. I really–anyway, thanks."

Ben looked at my hand but did not extend his.

"Right, sure. Keep in touch. Call June once in a while, she'll relay messages, okay?"

"Okay."

As I left his offices, disturbed by his irritation, I wondered what set of memories I had tapped. Something more than my stubbornness had keyed his annoyance. He might have remembered something about my father, or me. Or perhaps it was what it had seemed to be: he just did not like having his courage questioned. I wanted to tell him that recklessness was not courage, but this was not the time, and I did not have the courage.

10

The next days were chaotic, what with checking out of the hotel, finding out-of-the-way quarters for Stacy and me, feeling myself looking uncomfortably into every set of shadows I passed, trying to keep up with Alicia on our treks around the city.

At first I told her nothing about the dangers, then realized I must tell her, for her own safety. Even then I was reluctant, fearful that she might use my predicament as an excuse to keep away from me, pull her vanishing act permanently. When I did tell her about the assassination attempts, during dinner at the hotel restaurant the night before I moved out of the Conplaz, she seemed distressed and angry. A response which, I confess, pleased me.

"This shouldn't happen," she said. "It makes no sense, even according to the logic of the radical groups."

"I agree it makes no logical sense, but then I'm the target."

"I know a few people. Through my job. Maybe there's something I can do, somebody I can get to some—what are you smiling about?"

"It seems everybody I know has some connections within the reject factions, has somebody or other they can talk to, to take my name off the list."

"Oh? Who else?"

I told her about Ben. Her reaction surprised me.

"You know Ben Blounte then?"

"Yes, of course. Do you?"

"No. But I know something about him. A, um, a couple of friends of mine admire him."

"For what?"

"I'm sure, well, I don't think I remember, but his name has come up."

I had a definite feeling she knew more about Ben than she was admitting. Even I was beginning to get somewhat suspicious of him. There was something different about him this time around, something that was not easily explained away by the challenges of a new lifetime, the challenges he had said had made him finally opt for a new retreading. He was keeping more to himself, not saying everything that was on his mind, as he had done before. There were subjects he did not want to bring up.

I was going to ask her more of what she knew about Ben, but she shoved that thought right out of my mind when she asked if Stacy and I were homosexual partners. I thought I had heard her incorrectly, the question had come so suddenly, so far out of left field, and I asked her what she had said.

"It's been on my mind for days and I expected you to bring the subject up. Since you haven't, I thought I'd ask. No harm intended. Don't answer. Please don't, if you don't want to."

"No, it's not that, I'd tell you if it were so. I—well, it's never occurred to me that—although there was a time on Coolidge when somebody else came to the same conclusion, said it in passing, in a way. But I'd forgotten about that—"

I'd also forgotten Jack Branovich, whose face and not Stacy's appeared to me at the moment of Alicia's question. Branny was a colleague on the Coolidge research team. After Stacy left Coolidge for his new assignment, Branny started hanging around me. He had always been an uncertain ally among my enemies. He was short and chubby, the kind of man whose arms appear not to hang lower than his belt. His face might have been properly jolly had it not been for the weariness in his eyes, the sourness around his mouth. He was beginning to lose his hair, another oddity since baldness is so rarely seen any more. Also, he was a most energetic gossip. Like many gossips, especially those who perform that duty with some humor, he was well liked. He needed to talk so much that, when there was no one around to share his gossip, he talked to himself.

Branny took to showing up at my quarters with a bottle. We got drunk together several times. He compared our duty on Coolidge to a dried-up pile of dog manure. "You know it's lost its odorous properties but still you are not about to put your foot upon it." We had many good times together.

At our last drinking siege Branny drank more than I, but I did my share. I think his hand was caressing my back a long time before I realized it. When I did realize it, he moved closer to me. His intentions were so unmistakable, and the situation so highly comic, I had to laugh. First he took the laughter as a sign of willing participation, and he made his desires more direct. For some reason I laughed again. This laughter he took as an offense and drunkenly called me a couple of names. I don't know how I talked him out of his wishes for a liaison, the combination of alcoholic haze and the absurdity of the moment muddles the event in my memory. When he finally knew I was rejecting his advances, he recovered himself and tried to make light of it, saying that I obviously was "not inclined that way," especially on our puritan gossipy little planet, especially with the way the camp's females kept throwing themselves at me. I just said it was impossible, about as close as I ever came to telling anyone on Coolidge about my physical condition. He took a long swig of his drink and said: "There was somebody once who didn't find me romantically repulsive. He was among the original assignees here. But the powers-that-be spotted him immediately, spotted me for that matter, and arranged for his transfer to the orbiting satellite, then away from Coolidge altogether. My luck, I guess. But those sons of bitches, whenever I relate a really juicy story at the supper table, you know who listens most attentively? Drools it up? Asks for more information? They do, naturally, the sons of—ah, the hell with it. I think we're out of booze. You got any more?" I said we had used up my rations some time ago. "I got another. Be right back." He bumped his ample form against the doorframe as he went out, and didn't come back that night.

How simple it would have been for me to satisfy, at least partially, his simple need, instead of maintaining my pose. Branny was still on Coolidge when I left there.

My denial of homosexuality made me feel ridiculous. Alicia seemed disturbed by my confusion.

"So you're not, Voss. It's okay."

"Except for Ben Blounte, Stacy is the closest friend I've ever had."

"I'd like to meet Ben Blounte someday."

"I'll arrange it."

"Do. I'm sorry about my habit of asking personal questions. It's more than curiosity. Some things have to be known. I don't know why. I had a sort of homosexual encounter once. I was fourteen, the other girl maybe a year older. She initiated it, but I encouraged it. I don't think I'm right in characterizing it as a genuine homosexual encounter. There was some licking and a little probing, but all very tentative and not very successful."

"You don't have to—"

"I'm trying to tell you that I'd answer any question you asked about me. You may be direct with me."

"There's no reason to explore pasts, when it—"

"Oh, but I intend to. Explore pasts, I mean. I want to know about you. I'm going to ask more questions. I want to know everything, you see. Nothing to be frightened of, you just have to bare your soul to me. As I would to you."

"I'm not sure that's even a fair arrangement."

"Oh, it isn't. It definitely is not. It is designed to satisfy my obscene curiosity."

"Alicia, there's no reason for this. I don't want to know your deep dark secrets any more than I want you to know mine, I—"

"Ah-ha, then you have some. That's a start."

"It's not necessary for us to—"

"But it is, Voss, it is."

"Why?"

"Well, I didn't want that question to come up yet, but under the new rules I have to answer you." She held a glass of wine to her lips and tipped it slightly, imbibing very little of the liquid, then said: "I love you, Voss, that's why. Another question?"

Even though she was trying to be honest, she was being deceptive at the same time. While declaring her love, she watched me intently, and a bit impishly, for my reaction. Only years of dealing with the direct statements of others prepared me to keep a stone face before her.

"All right, we'll retreat," she said, after a long silence. "Back up a few feet, come at the subject a different way at a different time. Fire when ready, Gallstone. Would you pour me some more wine?"

Her glass was still nearly full. She was irritated, and even more, disconcerted. Our relationship was at a new stage. I did not want to deal with anger, yet at the same time I was angry myself. I liked things as they were, and felt irked at her for daring to change them. Pouring the wine, my hand shook and spilled some on the tablecloth. A waiter appeared almost immediately to help us wipe it up. She did not want his help, and interfered with his efforts. He remained aloof, as he placed a cloth napkin over the stain.

"Jesus Christ and St. Ethel!" Alicia said under her breath as the waiter walked away.

"What was that all about?"

"That man. He shouldn't have to serve and he shouldn't have to wipe up the debris of clumsy or drunken customers."

"Which one was I?"

"Which one were you what?"

"Drunken or clumsy."

"God, Voss, I didn't mean you specifically. I meant me as much as you or anybody. It's why I don't like to go to restaurants, or any place where the workers are primarily rejects. I don't like for them to have to serve us. The symbology is uncomfortable, especially with everything else they have to—"

She stopped talking suddenly, put down her wine glass abruptly, spilling some more wine onto the cloth napkin that covered the first stain, gazed at the result as if it were a breakthrough in abstract art, then stood up, saying:

"Bathroom."

She turned and walked away from the table without once looking back at me. I watched her progress across the room, was conscious of the firm line of her shoulders, the stiffness of her back. I found myself imagining the body beneath the tightly fitting material of her clothing. And thinking of her loving me. Was touched by the absurdity of it. Amused at the sadness of it. Felt foolish about my own stiff-upper-lip attitude, disgusted that I had played the drama out so far, and so unfairly.

I resolved that, when she came back, I would tell her all about myself, if only to discourage her love while there would be no harm. But she did not come back.

11

"On the other hand, maybe I don't love you."

"Alicia! What are you doing here?"

"Waiting for you. In intense discomfort, I might add. If this lobby is any indication of the looks of the rest of the place, I shudder to think what your rooms must be like. Where's Stacy?"

"I don't know. I never know. He has his own interests, his own—"

"I saw him the other night. Did he tell you?"

"No, he didn't. How—"

"I'm not altogether sure he saw me. It seemed like he looked me right in the eyes, then again it might have been a glazed look. His attention was clearly elsewhere."

"Where did all this happen?"

"In a bar uptown, East Side. A place that caters to, shall we say, *strange* people. It's a hangout for actors, spies, homosexuals . . ."

"Alicia, you're not going to suggest that again. Stacy is—"

"I know, he has his own interests, to quote you. No, he had a quite pretty brunette on his arm. A nice meaty young lady. I could use some of her dimensions."

"Well, your dimensions are—"

"Please, Voss, I was not begging. I should, probably. I'm a little off my rocker for not allowing you to say such things. I should feel I'm making progress. Anyway, so Stacy keeps a part of his life away from you."

"You might say that."

"And do you do the same for him?"

"Maybe."

"And am I telling tales out of school by telling about seeing him last night?"

"Not at all. What Stacy does with his free time isn't—"

"Where are you going now?"

"Over to Ben's."

"Hey, good. I'll come along then."

"I didn't invite you, young lady."

"Don't be so avuncular, uncle. I'm not nine years old any more. I want to meet Ben. Don't worry, I'll wait outside while you have your secret conference."

"We're not having a secret conference. You're obsessed with secrecy."

"I have secrets. I was going to tell them to you, now I'm not."

"That's okay. Anyway, I'm only meeting him for lunch."

"Good, I'm starved. Haven't had a good meal since I walked out on you last week."

"About that, I—"

"Don't want to talk about it. If you're going to someplace expensive, you can pay. This minute I almost qualify for vagrancy charges."

"I'll be glad to pay for once."

"Terrific. Take my arm at least."

"Okay, but why?"

"Jesus Christ and St. Ethel, do you have to be told everything?"

12

June looked up from her viewer, in which she had been reading *Retreads All,* a book Alicia called the *Mein Kampf* of contemporary thought. June stared at Alicia as if she were one of the diseases Ben would be consulted on. Alicia misinterpreted her stare as interest, and smiled serenely at her, then with some impishness at me. In her best professional voice, June said she would see if the doctor would see us. Never before had she been so crisp with me, and I was mildly irritated. She announced us to Ben. He told her to send us in. As we passed through the door, Alicia whispered:

"That woman at the desk, that's the one Stacy was with."

"You look shocked," Ben said as he came toward us. "What have you two just been whispering about? Hello, I'm Ben Blounte. You must be Alicia."

"I must be. Pleased to meet you."

Ben held onto her hand long after shaking it. Or Alicia held onto his. He ranted for a full minute, it seemed, over how lovely she was. Then we all sat down for about thirty seconds of silence. Alicia and Ben appeared self-satisfied. I don't know what I looked like. Ben spoke first:

"Alicia, will you marry me?"

"Look, I have some irons in the fire. One of them doesn't come through, we can talk about it."

She looked slyly at me. I am sure Ben caught the look. There was a little pain in his eyes, concern, when he next looked at me, although he continued to smile.

"Shall we go to lunch now?" I said.

"In a minute," Ben said. "Voss said you had connections in some way with the rejects."

She hesitated, some anger in her eyes that I had betrayed a confidence. When she spoke, her voice was controlled.

"I deal with rejects in my work. I'm assigned by the government to investigate social problems. I've lately been working most closely with a branch of the St. Ethel group."

"That's where some of the most intense radical activity is going on, I'm told."

"There's been some speculation in that direction, yes, but I don't–"

"You know more than you're saying. I've done some traveling in reject circles where the name of St. Ethel has been invoked often, and not always for religious reasons. A couple of St. Ethelites I met are probably on a killer team. What's the matter, dear, you seem troubled by something."

"It's, it's just you're kind of reckless in–"

"I speak out, yes. Don't worry. I'm protected. Ask Voss."

"I don't know that, Ben, and you know I don't."

"Just thought I'd lie. I remember times when you could lie most expeditiously. Well, you two bring out the reckless in me. Maybe it's time for lunch. One thing, Alicia, this restaurant we're going to–"

"Yes?"

"I want you to be sure to sit quite close to me there. A few people I know and hate'll undoubtedly be there. It's my club, you see."

"I don't understand."

"Well, you sit close and I'll be the envy of them. *They* never get to sit next to such a vision of beauty."

"You're quite insipid in your flattery, doctor."

"Certainly. But just sit next to me."

"Well, certainly."

He offered his arm to leave the office, and she took it. I felt for a moment like a fifth wheel, every spoke of it. Especially after Ben asked June to accompany us. With a glare, June took my insincerely offered arm. The touch of her seemed to burn my skin through several layers of clothing.

I wonder if Alicia felt the tension of that meal at Ben's club. June, quite obviously sullen, barely responding even when spoken to. Me, jittery, worried about each of the others. Even Ben was not quite himself. He spoke too energetically and, God, he could not get off the subject of himself. Usually secretive Ben told Alicia a solid portion of his life story. I became aware of chemical flavorings in certain items of food, started feeling waves of nausea, excused myself and went to a men's room. The waves subsided almost as soon as I left the table. I returned. Ben was still talking. June stared at something on the other side of the room. Alicia started telling Ben about how we had met at the Atlantica Spa, painting a funny picture of my newly retreaded awkwardness. June laughed, a bit too hard. My nausea returned. I got up from the table, excused myself, left Ben's club without waiting for answers.

13

Anger that had accumulated during my walk back from Ben's club made me throw open the door of the hotel suite Stacy and I shared with more force than normal. The suite's outer room was in disarray. Clothing had been flung over pieces of furniture, three or four bottles were scattered around. The bedroom door was open, and I could not stop myself from looking in. Stacy sat up in bed, looked out at me. Beside him a woman stirred. I turned around and walked out, walked the streets again for an hour. When I returned, I passed the woman, or a reasonable facsimile of her, in the lobby. She did not recognize me, did not even look my way. She had a gentle face, an ample busty body. Although she looked nothing like her, she reminded me of Mary, the prostitute who had betrayed me in the Hough District so long ago. Probably it was more the similarity of profession and status than an actual physical resemblance.

Stacy was straightening the outer room when I re-entered the suite. He had dressed. His color for the day was brown, and the suit was tailored.

"I'm not upset or angry or—" I said.

"Didn't say you were."

"I wouldn't have come in like that if I'd—"

"Right. Thought you were gone for the afternoon myself."

"I was. Something happened. I cut the engagement short. I saw June Albright today."

"You usually do when you go to Blounte's office."

"Yes. I don't know why I said that. Yes, I do. I wanted to see if you'd show any reaction, although why I'd expect anything like that's beyond me."

"It appears so."

"Have you ever brought June up here when I've been away?"

"No."

"Don't you wonder how I know about you and her?"

"No."

"Doesn't it bother you one of your secrets has been discovered?"

"No."

"No, it wouldn't. Have you been seeing a lot of her?"

"Some."

"I hope you're treating her well. Are you?"

A slight hesitation before his response.

"Can't judge. Well enough, I expect."

"I hope so. She's not like that whore who just left, she's got—I mean, you can't treat—it's—"

I fumbled for the words because I suddenly realized I was being prissy, acting like an outraged lover in June's stead.

"Thought you said you weren't angry or upset," Stacy said.

"I am."

"Sorry."

"I don't even know what I'm angry about. It's the mess of the room, that woman, she's a shortlifer, I could tell by the look, she's—"

"Don't worry about her. She's got some angles figured."

"I don't know. Something went wrong today. Began long before I came home here. Began before I got to Ben's office. Something small, but it grew."

Stacy poured me a drink, handed it to me. The offering reminded me of our time together on Coolidge when he often handed me things before I knew I needed them.

14

"You should've stayed for the dessert, Voss. Apple cake, simply delicious, and so artificial there wasn't a single calorie in it."

"Hello, Alicia."

"Hmmm, that was a pretty flat greeting. Hello, Alicia. Crawl in a hole, Alicia. Listen, I don't wait on streetcorners like this for just anybody. I could get knocked off by one of the nut squads."

"Sorry, Alicia."

"Oh, great. Sorry, Alicia. Explode, Alicia. Why did you walk out on us?"

"Funny you should ask that, what with all the times you've disappeared on me."

"It's all right if I do it. But you upset people."

"You don't, I suppose."

"I have an idea I don't, really."

"You upset me."

"Yes, but you're always going to forgive me for it."

"Maybe not."

"If not, not. I do talk compromises, habit of my job. Anyway, Ben was genuinely upset when you took off so unceremoniously."

"How do you know that?"

"I asked him."

"And he told you he was upset."

"Actually, he didn't. He said it was all right. I told him to shut up, of course he was upset. I said anyone could see that. I turned to that woman, what's her name, you know, Stacy's wench . . ."

"June Albright."

"Right. Right, Albright. I turned to Right June Albright, who seemed pretty upset herself about it all—is she in love with you, too; answer that in a minute—anyhow, I asked the wench if she saw that Ben was upset, and she said she was sure she didn't know whether or not Ben was upset, and I turned to Ben and said—see? So there. But he was upset all right, and I have a hunch it was about more than just old buddy Vossilyev making a rude exit."

"I didn't mean to be rude."

" 'Course you did, else why do it? Remember, I'm the expert on the subject. Is she, Right June Albright, in love with you?"

"You saw her with Stacy."

"Stacy might be a route to you."

"If so, it's a dangerous one."

"Oh? Tell me more."

"Get off it, Alicia."

"Jesus Christ, but you're testy. Anyway, c'mon."

"Where to?"

"You're going out on call with me. I have to visit a St. Ethel settlement. St. Ethel Camp, it's sometimes called. Be something different for you, maybe convert you."

"Is it far from here?"

"Other side of the river. New Jersey, as we continue to call the area, in spite of all dictates against it. Do you recall New Jersey? It was pretty ravaged during some war or revolution or something. Anyway, we'll take a boat across the sludge of the river, and then a mudsled for the rest of the way."

"Mudsled? What's a mudsled?"

"Exactly what you think it is. Things are a bit more primitive on the other side of the river. The grass certainly isn't greener, 'cause there ain't no grass. You'll see."

15

She had not exaggerated the primitive conditions. Parts of the state had turned into a swamp—the result, Alicia said, of the place being uninhabited for so long during the dangerous radioactive period. I dimly recalled living in New York City for a while in my youth, and the protective force-field dome that sheltered the city. I could not remember at what time the air content had improved so much that the dome was discontinued.

There were no cushions in the mudsled. Although it had side windows, they turned out to be insufficient protection against the reverse splattering of mud. It was lucky I wore an old suit. Later I discovered what seemed thousands of small brown specks all over the dark garment. But the mudsled had power if not beauty and it plowed through the frequent areas of murky swamplike ground just as its winter counterparts slid across snow. And with some speed.

In some of the ruined areas I saw, sticking out from the mud, the remains of old buildings, old houses, a sign or two. I asked Alicia about the general condition of the ground. She said it had once been good land and she didn't know how it had become such a swamp. The tableland had been flooded in some way. Nevertheless, it had been like this for many years.

The St. Ethel Village itself was a surprise. Surrounded by a gigantic muddy area, it rested on dry ground. Alicia said the land had been reclaimed. Big machines, draining equipment, had been brought in and cleared the bog away. When viewed from a distance, the village was stark–looking something like an Old West town, although better constructed and more richly colored. It spread across the landscape, covering quite a bit of territory. No building seemed more than three stories high, which had a pleasant effect in this age when even the small cities were studded with skyscrapers. The mud in front of us gradually formed a road, and we found ourselves on harder terrain for our approach to the village.

"I don't quite understand the reason for this village, or camp as you called it," I said to Alicia.

"It's called both. It's just an area where rejects can live together, in more comfort than the ugly sections they are allotted in most cities. Some politico long ago decided they had the right to their own areas, and he and his brethren made damn sure the rejects were given areas in the middle of nowhere, places where tabs can easily be kept. The arrangement works out well for both sides, actually. Rejects get something of a normal life during their few years, and the powers that be have a better system for keeping track of them than in the cities, where anyone who wants can frequently go to ground for some red-tape-consuming time. The officials don't like that sort of busy work."

"Good project, I guess. Still, way out here and in such primitive–"

"Primitive because they want it that way. The rejects, I mean. They have been offered all kinds of luxuries and've vetoed many of them. The Ethel people tend toward spareness. But they're not fools, so some amenities are accepted."

The Village Commissioner briefed Alicia on village troubles. Nothing special, just isolated incidents that made farmed-out bureaucrats like him a bit nervous. Smiling, she said she'd see what she could do.

As we walked through the old-fashioned tree-lined streets of the village, I could see nothing that looked even remotely like trouble. People moved busily but without urgency. Street sounds blended together musically into a pleasant hum. There was plenty of space to move around in. One could be less conscious of the usual swiveling and twisting involved in getting through city crowds. Where sometimes the city smelled like bad meat, the village had about it the faint aroma of flowers. I mentioned the flower odor to Alicia. "Piped in," she said. She halted us in front of a statue. A plaque beneath the statue indicated that this crudely executed and bizarre construction was intended to represent St. Ethel. I tried to see something beyond reverence in the off-balance face that the sculptor had furnished. The statue's hand was held out, evidently to suggest hope, although the effect was more like panhandling. Queer symbols were painted onto various areas of the representation.

"What're those?" I said, pointing to the strange symbols.

"That's one of the small crimes the commissioner spoke about. A common one within reject circles, actually. To him it's defacement, though I don't know why the hell he cares about what happens to a St. Ethel statue. What they really are, are symbols of the rejects' rebellion written in a special coded calligraphy."

"What do they say?"

"Oh, they're little prayers, little messages about the coming time when bodies will no longer be sacrificed to the greed of mankind."

"Greed? Why do you call it that?"

"Isn't that what it is, greed? Greed for more years, a much more spendable commodity than money."

"You really sympathize with them, these radicals, don't you?"

"I don't trust you enough to answer that question, Voss."

"I thought you were considering loving me."

"Not the same as trust. Emotions aren't links in a chain. Jesus and Ethel, now you've got me spouting folk wisdom, reject maxims. I'm sure I don't love you."

"That'd be better, probably."

She did not like my saying that, and she glared at me as if I were a defacer of statues or had written obscene prayers all over her body. We walked further. The streets no longer seemed so pleasant. People rushing by us seemed on unhealthy errands. She interviewed a storeowner who had been robbed, a woman whose apartment had been vandalized. The rationale for the crimes seemed to be a vendetta against rejects who accepted their lives. The storeowner and the woman were frightened creatures ready to do whatever Alicia told them. At each of the crime scenes, the criminals had left something scrawled in the code writing behind them. Alicia would not translate the messages for me.

On the way to another place where a crime required her investigation, she decided to take a shortcut through an alley. I trailed behind her. A bit sullenly, I'm afraid–which might explain my lapse in alertness. I did not become aware of the two young men jumping at me until too late. One came from a doorway to my right, the other from behind a pile of boxes. At the same time, a tall woman appeared from nowhere, it seemed, and walked toward Alicia. Involuntarily Alicia took a step backward, while I struggled against being pinned to a wall by my two assailants. The woman said:

"Good to see you again, Alicia."

"Hello, Rosalie. I wondered when you'd come out of the woodwork."

Rosalie had high cheekbones and violet eyes that seemed focused on something else. A scar on her cheek disfigured what would have been, at best, an ordinary and quite plain face. Scars were always an intriguing sight, a hint of the romantic, since they always suggested wounds so severe they would not respond to skin-healing treatments, or that had been left untreated by the victim for personal and usually bizarre reasons.

"Look," Rosalie said, "we already know we don't like each other, dear. We don't have to dramatize it each time we meet. Who is your friend?"

"His name is Voss Geraghty. You probably already know that. Could you tell your two uglies to let him go, he won't—"

"Pleased to meet you, Mr. Geraghty. I am Rosalie. I am the local St. Ethel priest. Tom, Stan, let him go."

Tom and Stan released their grips, in immediate and disciplined response to Rosalie's command. While addressing Alicia, Rosalie stared intently at me. I felt as if I were still pinned to the wall.

"I have a new HQ, since they burned out the last one. Shall we repair there and talk?"

"Fine with me. There's a lot to be done."

"Sure. Can we trust your friend?"

Alicia looked over her shoulder at me.

"No. No, I don't think we can."

"Well, we'll find someone to amuse him then. Take him around, bring him by the church later. Sorry to inconvenience you, Mr. Geraghty, but our meeting will be short, and we will see you later. Stan, show our guest the sights."

Rosalie led Alicia down the alley in one direction, while Stan turned me around and escorted me back the way we had come. The one named Tom accompanied us to the entrance of the alleyway and then, without speaking, walked off in a different direction.

Stan did not seem particularly interested in showing me the sights. We walked silently along several streets for some time. Passersby seemed to know my protector well. They gave him a wide berth, sometimes crossed the street when they saw him coming. Their reactions seemed odd to me, since Stan did not have a threatening appearance, nor was he especially muscular. He had just enough meanness in his face to make people want to avoid him. Eventually we stopped at a ramshackle building that had a huge cross painted in several rainbow colors across its facade.

"In here," Stan said.

"The church, I presume."

"Correct."

He gave my shoulder a light shove, which I resisted. As we entered the building, Stan made what looked like a ritualistic touch of the circular fake stained-glass windows in the middle of each of the double doors.

16

The inside of the church was a large bare room. A few chairs were thrown haphazardly around and not many of them seemed directed toward the big St. Ethel altar in a corner. The altar's centerpiece statue of the venerated saint did not appear to be in any better repair than the one we had examined in the town square, nor was it better made. The only windows in the room were placed high on the walls, and there wasn't much decoration anywhere else. Wherever a design was suggested, a closer inspection of the surface showed it had merely been a deception caused by shadows. Alicia and Rosalie entered the room through a door cleverly concealed next to the altar.

"Stan been treating you all right?" Rosalie asked as they approached.

"Just fine. I didn't think one person could know so much about the customs and mores of his hometown."

Rosalie scowled at Stan, then at me, then laughed quite heartily. The bellow sounded occult in the way it erupted from somewhere deep within her rail-like body.

"Alicia told me who you are, Geraghty," she said. "If I had known you'd crippled two of our assassination squads, we might not have been so gentle with you in the alley today."

Trying to ignore Stan's hateful glare added to my discomfort. Rosalie continued:

"But, St. Ethel and Christ! I can't blame you for defending yourself, I guess, even though we can't afford to keep losing trios of good men that way. Alicia has convinced me you are potentially salvageable. I sent out a few messages."

Rosalie, taking a folding chair and flinging it under her body as if she did not care whether it was placed properly, sat down next to me. Alicia slid a chair across the floor and sat across from me. Stan walked around me in circles. I felt hemmed in.

"My friend," Rosalie said, leaning in toward me, her eyes an opaque violet now, "I hear you are so tough you shit stone turds."

"Uh, look," I said.

"I hear you are so tough you drink crushed glass through a straw."

"What are you–"

"Hear you are so tough you–"

"Okay, okay, but I'm not so tough I can't get nauseous at this kind of ritual."

Rosalie laughed.

"Right," she said. "Just testing."

"I don't like being–"

"Look, Geraghty, I am sure that, when I get to know you better, I will find you just as offensive as you find me. But for the moment I just want to talk."

She was interrupted by the opening of the main door. A young man, shabbily dressed, looking as if he were about to fall down in the throes of a final illness, entered. He stood just inside the doorway, obviously wondering if it was proper for him to come into the room at just that time. Rosalie stood up and strode toward him. Her voice, when she spoke to him, was different from the way she had addressed me. Softer in tone, warmer in inflection. It took a moment before I realized what it was. Piety.

"Hello, Martin. It is good to see you agàin, son. Will you pray with me?"

Martin nodded and Rosalie walked to the corner altar. The man's shoulders heaved. He was obviously crying. Rosalie embraced him, whispered to him, kissed his forehead. Gradually she calmed him, and they turned together toward the altar. Rosalie touched something with her foot and a gentle lighting created a kind of aura around the St. Ethel statue. I couldn't hear what she and the newcomer whispered, but it was clearly praying of some sort. When they turned away from the altar, the young man's face was at peace, and he walked out of the church with some briskness in his step. Whatever Rosalie had done, it had had its effect. She watched him leave. Her eyes gleamed, she'd been crying. There was more of a bluish cast to her eyes now, as if the color had come into them as part of the religious ceremony. Religious nobility, assumed or not, made her more attractive. Even the jagged scar on her cheek, standing out more in the healthy redness of her skin, seemed to take on a deeper meaning.

"Saved a soul?" I asked when she returned to us. Alicia glared at me, clearly annoyed by my flippancy. Rosalie, however, remained calm.

"You might say that," she said, as she took her seat again. "Martin is faced with his date with the retread chamber. He is scheduled to report for transport there tomorrow. He needed spiritual help to give him the courage to keep the appointment."

"You advised him to keep the appointment then?"

"Yes, of course."

"Why not advise him to run away? Many do, after all."

"True, but that course of action was not for him. Those who are committed to the message of St. Ethel, who have decided to sacrifice their lives to her, must make the trip to the charnel house."

"Even when they're scared stiff, like him?"

"Cowardice is not an unsaintly trait. Before she joined the charnel house line, St. Ethel admitted her fear."

"So he comes to you for the treatment of his cowardice."

"It is normal to seek the comfort of priests the night before one's execution. One needs to be assured that his soul will be preserved when his body is ultimately destroyed."

"And you believe that? In the soul's survival through the body's retreading?"

Rosalie smiled. Her priestlike smile.

"You understand the principles of our religion better than most."

"I, uh, I was instructed in them once."

"Very good. About your question: No, I am not always certain of the soul's survival after the charnel house, after retreading, after the eventual death of the body. It is a part of St. Ethel's teaching, yet I am not always sure that she was really a saint. Still, the struggle with my belief seems worth my shortlifer time. That's what priests have always done for people, after all—struggled with the beliefs so that others may have the freedom to ignore them."

"Rosalie," Alicia said, "this sort of discussion may be very informative but we have—"

"We'll get around to that, dear. I have to know about your man here before I can make my decision."

"What decision?" I asked.

"About whether to ask that you join us."

"Join you? In what? In preaching the doctrines of St.—"

"Not exactly. Although, in a way, yes. We need your expertise, could use your experience if you chose to throw in with us."

As Rosalie spoke, the brusqueness which I had heard earlier pushed the saintliness out of her voice.

"My expertise. In what? I have no talents at all, I—"

"Alicia implied that you were not, well, not entirely perceptive. That's all right. It is a good trait in a hero. And, simply, we could use the services of a hero."

"Don't make a joke out of it," Alicia said. "This isn't the time for that."

I had never seen Alicia so tense before. Her fingers kept touching objects or parts of her body or furniture, and never seemed to stop for rest. Rosalie, on the other hand, maintained a steady calm.

"I'm not making jokes, dear. We have a lot of brave men and women in our cause, many who welcome death, many who actively seek it, but we are short on heroes, especially those with enough understanding of the retread personality, psychology, philosophy to make the kind of plans that are more than sporadically effective. To put it simply, Mr. Geraghty, not many of your kind involve themselves with the treatment of rejects. A few, but not many."

"Normal enough."

"Normal? Not the word I would have used."

"Perhaps. But retreads—and now you've got me saying the word as if I weren't one of them—retreads deeply believe that the system is right. The preservation of humanity's best characteristics by—"

"We know the justifications, Mr. Geraghty. Did you think we could not understand them? You believe in your way. We believe ours is the right way."

"You speak like a priest. I can see why you've chosen the profession."

"Priest is only my slot in society. I am a priest so I can find efficient ways to kill."

"Am I to dispute that paradox?"

"What a fucking sophist you are, Geraghty."

"You don't talk like a priest sometimes."

"You don't talk like a hero most of the time."

"Your point. What's this all about?"

"We need more people who can move freely among your kind. We have a few, mostly intellectuals or professional people. Hardly men or women of action like you, Geraghty. There are certain, well, deeds—missions, if you like—that we cannot do efficiently without the help of someone like you. There is reason to believe, I am told, that you might be willing to join us."

"Reason?"

"I cannot say for sure, but I think it has something to do with a certain recklessness with which you treat your life. There are reports from various sources, not just Alicia here, that you—"

"Where would you get information about me?"

"As I said, sources. I cannot even be sure of their points of origination myself. I receive orders, as does Alicia. Such orders forced her to bring you here for this discussion. But I am not privy to all the discussion and reasoning that led to that decision."

I looked over at Alicia, who was avoiding eye contact with me.

"So this isn't just a pleasant little excursion, after all."

"No, it isn't," Alicia said softly. "Sorry."

"No need to be. All right, Rosalie, I'm here. For what it's worth, you don't have to worry about betrayal by me." Alicia cringed slightly at the word betrayal. "I'd never do anything that might endanger Alicia, I'd—"

"That is comforting. But I only provide comfort, I do not accept it from other quarters, and I don't quite believe you. Let's get down to basics. What do you think about helping us?"

There was a long pause as Rosalie stared at me, I stared at Alicia, and Alicia stared at the farthest wall. Finally, I said: "Why should I help you?"

Rosalie leaned back in her chair, appeared thoughtful for a moment.

"Well," she said, "I was going to give you the argument that we would put your whole future in jeopardy by putting your dead body in storage so that it could not be recovered for retreading, but something tells me that might not be an especially effective argument with you."

"Not by much."

"No, I thought not. That same something tells me you might have pretty good incentive for joining us. An urge toward death tends to motivate many of us, especially since we have few alternatives anyway. And, beyond that, we understand there are reasons you just might want to—"

"Rosalie," Alicia interrupted, "not now!"

"No? Just when we have him on the hook? Alicia, I think—"

"Not now!"

"When then?"

I felt like a member of an audience watching their conversation, and was disconcerted by the pause following Rosalie's question. Alicia did not seem to know what to answer. Night had fallen rapidly outside, and nobody inside the room had bothered to turn on a light. The room was illuminated by the still-connected aura around the St. Ethel statue, a dim wall light, and the little street lighting that could get through the small windows.

"Well?" Rosalie said.

"I need time to think. Could, could I be alone with Voss someplace? The room, the room I use when I stay overnight?"

Rosalie considered that for a moment.

"Okay," she said. "Adjournment for the time being. Send me a message when you are ready to talk again. I will see you soon."

Rosalie stood abruptly, turned, and strode back to the door by the altar, where she turned and said:

"I will be conducting some services in two hours. Come down and join us if you wish."

She spoke these words in her priestlike voice.

17

"I never expected a plush room like this in the back of a church. Not very ascetic, priestlike—"

"Rosalie likes her comforts. You should see *her* quarters."

"The church pays well these days."

"Not the church. Rosalie just takes what she wants. Try sitting on the bed. It's quite soft."

"Hmmm, it certainly is. Reminds me of being a kid, when the most energetic pleasure you could find indoors was bouncing on a bed. All the more enjoyable because it was forbidden."

"Know what you mean."

"How did you meet the, uh, renegade priest?"

"Too long a story. Mainly, I just let it be known when I was first sent to this village that I had, well, some sympathy with the cause. Rosalie greeted me one day in an alley, much the same way she confronted us today. It took a while, but I was finally recruited, and—"

"A while, but I thought you—"

"I did, but they didn't trust me at first. I had to perform a couple of missions."

"Missions? What kind of missions?"

"You don't want to know."

"But—"

"No, I am sure you don't want to know. Just, I did the missions, and they were pleased, and I have been, oh, useful ever since."

"I gathered."

"Please don't be sarcastic, Voss."

"Sorry, but I'm a little tense from the scene downstairs."

"Don't be. Rosalie just talks big."

"Did you ever go out on a mission with one of those special squads? The killers? Well, did you?"

"Not as a killer, if that's what you're probing to find out, damn you. You really want to know about my missions, don't you?"

"Well, since they're trying to recruit me for the—"

"All right, all right. I've been along, as a lookout. Nothing very glamorous, just sitting on a rooftop or in a café and staring at streetcorners and doorways. Simple straightforward reconnaissance. Only once did it turn out to be a killing. Okay? Is that all right? Answer, damn you!"

"It's, it's fine. I realize . . ."

"You realize what?"

"That there're reasons for what you—that you—hell, I don't know what I think. I never figured you would—hell, forget it."

"I shouldn't but I will. We have different things to talk about here, things of matter and weight, about how you're going to join up and why and what you're—"

"Slow down now. I don't know if I—"

"Am I really pretty, Voss?"

"What does that have to do with—"

"A lot. You said once, more than once, that I was beautiful. I'll settle for pretty, if I can convince myself. Am I pretty?"

"Of course. But coyness isn't your specialty, what are you—"

"Don't try to form coherent thoughts, just respond. What's pretty about me? My face, say?"

"Yes."

"Why?"

"It's—look, Alicia, this is silly, I—"

"My face is silly?"

"No, I didn't mean that. I just think there're other things to talk—"

"What about my goddamned face?"

"It's a beautiful goddamned face. A goddamned beautiful face. A—"

"Nice eyes?"

"Yes, of course, but—"

"They're blue. Some of the time anyway."

"I know that!"

"What kind of blue? Could you give me a metaphor for them?"

"I—look, I'm not adept with words, I—"

"Off it, Voss, we know you're *adept* with *words.* Something simple'll do. Blue as the evening sky, mysterious dark blue, that sort of thing."

"Okay, I agree. Evening blue, mysterious."

"Jesus, that's not the way they look to me. Anyway, my mouth?"

"A, uh, lovely, uh, healthy—"

"Is it sensuous?"

"Yes, of course. Good."

"My body? A nice body?"

"It's, it's quite lovely. Alicia, will you—"

"Well-proportioned? Tits as nice as ass?"

"This is—you have quite lovely, a quite lovely—you have a very attractive figure."

"Very attractive, eh? I can see that. Can you do better?"

"I don't—"

"Globes, pears, rounded curves, alabaster, ivory, any of those?"

"I don't think I—"

"But how can you tell? You've never really seen me. My clothes fit well enough, I'm sure they're quite provocative, at least suggestive, but how can you tell?"

"You are quite prettily shaped, the bloom of youth is upon you, is that all right? Now can we–"

"No. I want a proper evaluation of my body. Wait a second, till I get out of these raiments. Like that word, raiments?"

"Alicia, can you–this is not–it's not *necessary,* what are you laughing at?"

"Nothing. Nothing at all. Do you like watching a woman undress?"

"Not–"

"I'm sure I look awkward. I never could master the art of delicate striptease. Too many accessories jam, stick, slip out of my fingers. There, so much for that. Now this, and we can have the full beautiful display. Is the lighting subtle enough for you?"

"Alicia, will you stop? This–"

"No. Just a second. There. *Voilà!* No, this is a terrible pose. How about this? Examine. Don't look away. Examine me. Am I pretty or not? Voss, I will have to conclude that I am not. What are you laughing about?"

"Noth–I can't say, I can't–"

"Yes, you can! You better, in fact."

"No, it's not–"

"Come closer. No? Then I'll just move in on you. Swoop. There. Touch me. Touch me right there. Let me prop it up for you, as it were. What a silly time to be saying as it were. How does that look? Touch me there, damn it! Here, let me."

"Alicia, please stop. Look, let me just get out of here for a minute."

"Where can you go? Here, please. God, you back from my fingers as if they were poisoned blades. Here, let–Christ and Ethel, you're jumpy. You know what this is like? A Victorian seduction, with the roles reversed. Don't you think–"

"No, I don't think. I don't think that–"

"Will you defend your manhood? Speaking of your manhood–"

"We'll have to, damn it."

"I know. Let me hold you. Don't back away, goddamn it. Please, Voss, let me hold you. Hold me. I need you. I love you. I don't know of any way to prove it to you. I don't even know why I love you. I don't even care if you love me, damn it to hell. You have no responsibilities in that direction. Hold me tighter."

"Alicia, it's not a matter of love, it's . . ."

"It's what?"

"Alicia, I can't—I mean, it's not possible for us to . . ."

"For us to what? C'mon, darling, you *can* tell me. For us to what?"

"For us, us to make, to make love. Physically."

"Darling, I know that. I've always known that."

"But—"

"I just had to make you admit it. I'm sorry, but I just—"

"You bitch!"

"Yes, I'm afraid so."

18

We stayed in the back room of the church for three or four hours. Alicia, demure in a flannel nightgown she had earlier stored in a closet, frequently touched me with her fingertips, with the back of her hand. Her touch was delicate, as if she were handling lettuce leaves or damask cloth—an unlikely pair of images, I'll admit. I felt almost catatonic, as emotionally lethargic as I was physically. I could not help thinking one of us should not be there.

Somewhere along the way, I told Alicia I loved her.

Strange, I cannot remember what happened just before or just after saying it.

Later, she took my hand and pressed it against her body, forced it to caress her. I kissed her impulsively, enjoyed the kiss as a sort of scientific experiment, tried to find in my body some other reaction than that of the slight pain on my mouth—felt miserable that no such reaction developed, but wanted to kiss her again. She opened her nightgown and for a long time I fondled, then kissed, the erect nipple of her breast. But I could not help thinking how stupid it was that it was erect and I was not. She asked me the cause of my laughter, and I could not tell her. She taught my hand to caress her sexually, whispered when I had touched her clitoris. Remembering some of the form of passion from my previous life, I tried to increase my attentions, tried to excite her. I could not, however, stop thinking about Selena and realizing that our lovemaking had been some kind of parody of passion. Alicia sensed my discomfiture, said it was all right. Closing her eyes, she tried to get some pleasure out of my caresses. Finally she said:

"All right, let's stop. No use. My fault, not yours. I suspected there'd be nothing for me in half a love-life. I don't know what . . . you know, there's a new kind of dildo, it's brought to erection realistically by the way the man fondles a cushion in his hand. A cushion, can you imagine? The cushion sends out electronic signals to the dildo which cause in it a simulation of engorgement, then it—shit, I don't even like to describe it. Forget it. I wouldn't like that, either. I'd hate it. I guess there's . . ."

She did not finish the sentence. We stopped pressing against each other. We lay back on our own sides of the bed, and only our hands touched. Lightly touched. She was sad for a while, then abruptly started talking again:

"You know, I decided to love you fourteen years ago. Isn't that ridiculous? I told my father about it. He of course said nothing. So I pressed the issue, really dogged him about it. He finally said that you were a good man and he'd be happy if, when I grew up, I found a man like you. Not like him, I said, *him!* My father said he doubted you were a good bet, but it was all right for me to go ahead with it if I wanted. Maybe he had some foresight, prescience. Maybe he had a flash of the future, seeing us here, seeing—"

"I'm sorry this is making you so—"

"Don't say it. I'm all right really. Happy really. I am . . . delighted just to be with you. Say, maybe we can become dream lovers, you know, like Peter Ibbetson and whats-her-name. Somewhere in one of the pleasure-seeking groups there must be a device that makes sexual illusions come to pass. Don't you think so?"

"Probably there is. But I don't think I'd like that."

"No, me either. I guess we're stuck with platonic love. George Bernard Shaw and Ellen Terry. Dante and Beatrice. Plato and whoever. Do you think we can be together for a while anyway?"

"I don't know, Alicia."

"Don't you want to, damn it?"

"Yes, I do."

"All right, then. We will."

She paused.

"May I take some lovers then?"

My turn to pause, but lacking her good timing.

"Of course."

"I don't think I want to."

"How romantic."

"Ah, would it were. Do you like would it were? Better than as it were, I mean."

"I don't know."

"No, how could anybody? I don't do too well with men."

"I can't believe that. Unless you mean it with special irony."

"Special irony? What do–you mean you? Oh, Jesus, I'm not that cruel. No, I meant what I said. I don't do well with men. They don't like me."

"Why not?"

"Beats me. If I'm demure, they yawn and wander over to some aggressive type. If I lead the way, they get bugeyed and flee. If I'm polite, they're rude. If I'm rude, they politely make an exit. I think I just don't attract men."

"That's stupid."

"Or women, for that matter. What I do attract think they have to reshape me to some illusion known only to them. That's why I think they don't like me either. If they liked me, they wouldn't have to change me, would they?"

"Perhaps not, but I don't think I can advise on this particular subject."

"No, I didn't intend that. I'm just trying to tell you why I'll probably remain faithful—Jesus, is that right? Faithful. Whatever anyway, I won't be taking lovers. Loyal, that's it. I'll be loyal. That sounds good and dreadfully romantic, I think. Do you want to know how many lovers I've had already?"

"No."

"It's embarrassing to me. You have to know, if only to use it against me."

"I don't want to use it ag—"

"Two. That's all. Two men. And long ago at that. I've struck out mostly since. I could lie on my back in the middle of—"

"All right. But try for three."

"No, I won't. Well, we'll see anyway. Do you want to know about the two men?"

"What two men?"

"My lovers. My previous lovers. My lovers before you. Was that sentimental enough for you? Yes, I see it was. But don't worry, the pain will pass."

She did eventually tell me about her lovers. In some detail. I have deliberately forgotten most of it. But we laughed a lot. And I do recall some of the mean things she said about the two men.

"I wonder . . ." I said later.

"What?"

"I wonder if I'm not glad about my, what to call it, my affliction."

"Why on earth do you say that?"

"Well, by not being your lover, I am denied the humiliation of being your ex-lover and—"

"You son of a bitch!"

"Well, as you describe them, it is something like being impaled for viewing on the point of a pin."

She hit me, then kissed me. Again I did not feel the reaction I wished for. And I started to cry. Without asking the reason for them, Alicia kissed away the tears, and said that at least we were beginning to collect things to be sentimental about.

19

We watched Rosalie's service through a small window hidden behind a bureau. The window, which overlooked the main room, was of one-way glass, so the congregants could not see us. Rosalie, in a flowing red robe, walked among her people, some of whom were seated on straightback chairs while others knelt or lay prostrate on the wooden floor. She touched them lightly, often just skimming her hand across the tops of their heads, and spoke softly to them. At one point in the proceedings she made a long sermon about St. Ethel in heaven, where she sought out those reject souls which had completed their long journey to heaven, and with them she mourned the souls still confined to Earth because their bodies still lived.

"You seem rapt," Alicia whispered.

"I have an outsider's interest in religious matters. I used to be a Catholic. We never really give up."

"I was a Catholic for a couple of days."

"Only a couple of days?"

"It was summer and the air was rotten and they had the most comfortable hideaway in town. You could sit back and lean against cushions. Not very ascetic, but I could almost endure a religion that provided cushions."

"I don't recall cushions from my Catholic boyhood."

"Well, I think this was a kind of offshoot Catholicism, breathing new life into a dying religion, that sort—"

"They always claim Catholicism is dying. That's one of the ways they keep it going."

"Maybe, but this one almost converted me. I think the cushions may have been treated—sending off rays of belief or penitence, whatever was necessary—like theater was for a while."

"I went to one of those plays."

Rosalie alternately dispensed miracles and bullied her congregation. At one point she beat and kicked two church members whom others had pushed to the floor. They seemed grateful for the beating. The service ended with a softening of the room lights and increased light from the St. Ethel statue. From hidden loudspeakers came some vigorous music. It was not exactly melodic, nor was it evenly rhythmic, but it was stirring, uplifting. A march without a heavy beat, a hymn without insipid inspiration. With Rosalie moving among them, the congregation stood, relaxed but motionless. I could not imagine the discipline that kept them still while hearing such rousing music. After the service the people seemed reluctant to leave. They were arranged around Rosalie, leaning her way bodily. Slowly she surveyed the room. My impression was that she looked briefly at each person. Her thin smile was beatific. Gradually the people drifted out of the room in twos and threes. Rosalie did not move from her position until the last one had left. Then her body stiffened and she moved briskly toward the altar, giving directions to invisible assistants to disconnect this and do something else a different way the next time.

20

"You're not going to help us, are you?" Alicia asked. She was in her streetclothes again, looking very efficient and businesslike.

"I don't know. But I don't see why you need *my* help."

"It isn't just *your* help, although you do have abilities that are in short supply these days. But we need any help we can get to crush a system that—"

She was interrupted by a noise downstairs, and recognized the sound as threatening before I did. She rushed to the little window, muttering under her breath.

"What's wrong?" I asked.

"Just the village police. Routine harassment."

I looked out the window. Two official-looking men were trying to intimidate Rosalie, who stood straight and looked as if she might be intimidating them.

"We should get out of here," Alicia said.

"Why?"

"It wouldn't help if I was discovered here, unless of course they already know where I am."

"I don't understand. I thought you were supposed to be working with rejects and—"

"True, but nonetheless they won't take too kindly to my being with Rosalie. They've never been able to catch her at anything, but their spy systems are elaborate and effective. They know a great deal about her work. Anyway, it won't do my social work image any good to be discovered in a back room with you. A back room of a church, for that matter. C'mon, I know a way out."

We descended a set of stairs and slipped out a side door that looked more like it would lead to a closet than to a sidestreet. The night was dark, a bit misty. Someone nearby was cooking something I could not quite identify, but it made me realize how hungry I was. Alicia led me through a maze of streets to a square where a celebration was going on. Some people danced, others strolled about arm in arm. More food odors, in greater abundance, made me dizzy.

"What is this?" I asked.

"I don't really know. Some kind of festival, perhaps without a reason. They do a lot of this sort of thing at St. Ethel Camp. Some say it is based on old customs, others that it represents a programming, one of the many to make rejects forget what they have to look forward to. I make you shudder, why?"

"Everywhere I go, I get the feeling that there's a great conspiracy to make me feel guilty."

"Or perhaps to draw out the guilt that's already there. I don't know of any conspiracy, but I'd certainly like to make you feel guiltier than you presently seem to feel. The kind of murder that you—"

"Please don't drag out all the old arguments. I get them from Ben often enough."

"Maybe there's a lesson there."

"What possible kind of lesson could—"

"The people who love you, really love you, are concerned for you. People who take pains to convince you to think like them may be the most compassionate people around."

"Or the most fanatic."

A woman nearby had removed some clothes and was dancing bare-breasted through the crowd. Some things never change.

"All right, I may get tendentious in my single-minded purpose, but look through my eyes: at the mountain of stolidity that you are. How can I continue to love you and know that you're against everything I believe in?"

"I'm not *against* you, I just—" I could not think of what to say, I did not know what I meant. "Let's get something to eat, I can't argue and starve at the same time."

"I sense strategy, but I'm hungry, too. Let's go."

We found a booth dispensing a flat pastry, thin with intriguing spices upon it. It was delicious, and we washed it down with a yellowish liquid that had a delicate sweet underflavor. I asked the vendor what the food and drink were called, what cuisine they represented. The disappointing answers were that the pastry was simply called Ethel-cake and the drink altar-wine. The spicing of religion added to the food's ingredients made my subsequent bites and sips less satisfying. We found a bench at the edge of the square and sat in silence for a long while.

Alicia would not look at me. She watched people in the square, dancers and strollers, fools who bowed to her as they passed, children who weaved in and around legs. I touched her hand and, for a long time, she did not seem to notice it. Finally I said:

"I'm sorry."

"God, Voss, let's not get into that kind of mood. Sorry, sorry about what, just sorry, sorry if I hurt you, sorry if, all that kind of crap. You're not so much sorry as you want me to say something soothing to you."

"Anything wrong with that?"

"Yes. A lot. But don't ask me what. The explanation is as much a trap as the saying of I'm sorry."

She continued to look at things she did not seem to be seeing. I wanted to hold her.

"I didn't have any *traps* in mind. And I'm genuinely sorry, if at nothing else but that fact that I am unable to make love to you. That alone—"

"There's—there's no point in talking about that any more. I'm sorry about your impotence, too. I'm—"

"Impotence isn't quite the right word. It's not, after all, a physical dysfunction that developed from a complex series of emotional or bodily disorders. One of your precious rejects took time out to sabotage this body, to get it sabotaged, anyway. Not something calculated to make me join your oh-so-lovely cause, my dear."

I don't know why I made such a fuss at that moment, why I cared so for semantics. What was there in my background that made *impotence* such a dangerous word? When Alicia said it, spoke it aloud, I felt upset. I felt that I had really failed her. It was one thing not to be able to fuck successfully, for whatever reason, it was another to be accused of impotence for that sexual failure. The anger caused by the accusation led, I suppose, to the petulance of my attack on my saboteur. Up to that moment, I had not allowed the previous possessor of the body much identity in my mind. Once good old Ernie became the *saboteur,* he seemed something more. At the very least he was the man who had doomed me to my present frustrated-romantic helplessness. That was sufficient reason for my hatred, especially as I looked into Alicia's lovely face. I could really hate the man, as I reconstructed him in my mind. More than that, the reconstruction was so damned simple since he looked like me.

Alicia remained silent for more than a minute, resisting, I think, what she wanted to say. Finally, she spoke in a low whisper:

"I was not just talking about your physical impotence. I can accept that, I could even live with it the rest of my life. The rest of my never-to-be-retreaded life. It is a minor thing, Voss. As you said, a mere physical dysfunction. Sad, but no more threatening to me than if you'd lost an arm or a kidney, than if you had to wear false teeth. But don't you see, you are impotent on every important level. You're socially impotent, you don't fit in anywhere. You can function with people only if you adopt one of your poses—of which galactic hero is one of the most tedious, by the way. And what about your impotence as a human being? You stay outside of everything, Voss. You toy with me, you engage in feeble sophistry with Ben, you can't even talk straight with Stacy, whom you are forever claiming as your great and good friend. Jesus and Ethel, if you cannot deal with us in any kind of direct and incisive way, how can I expect you to take up a goddamned cause? They can give you all the lives they want, you'll still stay outside of things, still refuse to really touch any of us. If you can construct a good case for retreading out of that, you're welcome to it. In spite of all that, you will always be a great man, Voss. I mean that, a really great man. One who, so long as his life is properly circumscribed, by a scientific laboratory or a mission on some distant planet, will function quite heroically, with efficiency and for the good of mankind in its most limited sense. Mankind as an abstract mob who requires the beneficial acts of such great men. Oh, shit, Voss, stop me! I don't want to attack you. God, I feel so sorry and I'm the one who said we're not supposed to use I'm sorry as a ploy, but that's exactly how I want to use it. I have to leave."

She walked across the square. The crowd seemed to part instinctively to allow her passage. She was all the way to the other side of the square before they closed in and I lost sight of her. When I tried, much too late, to follow her, the crowd seemed conspiratorial in the way it closed ranks so that I could not easily pass.

21

I wandered through the strangely busy streets of St. Ethel Camp for a long time before it dawned on me that Alicia did not intend to come back to me that night, that I had been left stranded without even a place to sleep. There was only one place to go, Rosalie's church.

The interior was dark. What light did come in from the small windows created shadows that did not resemble anything I had previously seen in the main room. A faint odor of candlesmoke passed by me. Metallic sounds came from one of the back rooms behind the altar, somebody working on something. After I had walked a few steps, I had lost my bearings completely. I turned a circle trying to locate the door that I thought I had left open when I had entered. Suddenly the lights around the St. Ethel statue came on. Without supporting illumination from other parts of the room, the statue looked mysterious. Shadows within it could almost seem like movements, as if the venerated saint had chosen this moment to return to life and start her campaign of conversion with me.

"I didn't expect you, Mr. Geraghty."

I was startled. For a moment I thought the statue had, after all, spoken. But I recognized the voice as Rosalie's.

"I thought Alicia might be here," I said, not sure in what direction to speak.

"She might be here," Rosalie said. "Or, rather, might have been here. She isn't now."

"Where did she go?"

"I can't say, Mr. Geraghty."

"Is she on a mission, some kind of assignment for you?"

A trace of laughter in Rosalie's voice:

"I cannot tell you about that either."

"She does do missions for you, doesn't she?"

Even though I still had no idea where Rosalie was, I felt her eyes upon me as she considered her response.

"Let's say that she does the church's work from time to time."

"Is she a killer, ever been a killer?"

"You continue to ask me questions I am not delegated to answer, Mr. Geraghty."

"And you continue to imply answers deliberately."

"No, I do not. Believe me about that. I am not tricking you. I am just not talking."

Another long silence. I could have sworn that the St. Ethel statue smiled. Then Rosalie said:

"She left you alone, walked away from you?"

"Yes."

"She does that. She is not entirely stable."

"Are you some kind of psychologist, too, Rosalie?"

"It comes with the territory. She may be quite stable, I cannot always tell. She is at the very least unreliable."

"Oh, I see. She doesn't always do what you people order her to, that seems to be what you're saying."

"Are you some kind of psychologist, too, Mr. Geraghty?"

"Look, I don't want to banter with you. In the meantime, is there any place, any hotel, where I can spend the night?"

"Go to the commissioner. He'll find you a place. I believe they maintain a guest house or something. Normally I would offer you a room here at the church but tonight that will be impossible."

"It's all right. Thanks."

I turned to leave.

"I conclude that you are not joining us," Rosalie said.

"Did you believe I would?"

"Not really. I was not among your supporters."

"Supporters?"

"Alicia, naturally. She wanted you to join. And there were others. Others who still advise me to wait and see."

"I'm not worth your time."

"Precisely what I thought. But your friends, adherents, believe otherwise. I almost wish you would join us. I could use you right now."

"Why just now?"

"We are about to be attacked. I don't think we can win. If you are as good as they say, we might win."

"I don't believe any of that."

"Well, wait and see."

"I will."

"There's a park across the street. With benches. Stay and watch. Goodbye, it was pleasant meeting you, hero. Maybe we'll meet again."

"You never can tell."

"No, you can't. Oh, the next time you see Alicia . . ."

"Yes?"

"Tell her I had no options."

I started toward the door, then stopped and said:

"There are always options, Rosalie."

"For you, maybe, hero."

I shrugged and nodded, positive she could see both actions even though I stood in a dark area of the room. Without looking back toward the statue, I left Rosalie's church and found the bench she had told me about. As I sat down, I saw that the bench had messages carved in it, in the rejects' coded symbology.

This late at night, nobody seemed to be using the park. Logical perhaps, since the night was cold and I found myself shivering underneath what should have been seasonable clothing. I had a long wait for anything to happen. I began to wonder if anything would happen. Then I noticed there had been no pedestrians on the street for some time, a half-hour or more. Almost as soon as I realized that, a man walked around a far corner. He walked along the street slowly, with the nervous casualness of one who is striving to appear inconspicuous. He noticed me sitting on the bench and briefly studied me. I thought he was going to walk over and shoo me away from my front-row-center seat. But apparently everything was too scheduled for that severe an interruption and he continued on, passing Rosalie's church without looking at it. That, too, was suspicious, since he had furtively examined every other building on the street. He turned the opposite corner and was out of sight for a while. Yet I knew he was still there. He had not gone around that corner with the intention of continuing a stroll. A few minutes later he returned with some other people. They composed a squad of about ten members. The majority were men; at least three looked like women. A couple of vehicles came around the corner from which the man had first appeared. They were ordinary nuclear-powered cars but even in the dark I could see they had been reconstructed with several new features, battle attachments. The pedestrians picked up their pace as they neared the church. The cars stopped just outside the building.

They gave no warning, simply entered the church (whose doors were unlocked, anyway). Nobody got out of the vehicles, which made the whole scene even more ominous. I wanted to run past the vehicles and see what was happening inside. For a long time I heard nothing. Then the battle began. First there were a couple of shots which seemed too distant, too powerless. Something from one of the vehicles cranked out of an opening and pointed toward the church doorway. The faint noises were followed by several louder ones. Nothing extravagant or explosive, just threatening. An attacker returned to the doorway, made an incomprehensible gesture toward the vehicles. As far as I could see, the personnel in the cars could not understand the gesture any better than I could, for they did nothing after the attacker had returned to the church interior. After two more flurries of shots, the church became silent. The attackers began filing out the front entrance. Not as many of the squad as had entered, so I assumed others left by different exits. Two of them, a man and a woman, were evidently hurt superficially. Another pair carried out a corpse who looked, from my distance, like Stan. The last man out was the first I had seen. He led Rosalie, pulled her roughly out the door. She interrupted her strident criticism of her captor to look briefly over at me and, I think, smile. He put her into a new vehicle, an ordinary car which had come around the corner when I was not looking. The two remaining vehicles then methodically, with artillery and explosives, destroyed the church. Its demolishing was accomplished quickly, without even a scar of damage to neighboring buildings. Quite efficient. The car containing Rosalie and her captor remained nearby, apparently to allow her to watch the destruction of the church. When the building was almost leveled, the car started suddenly and drove past me to the opposite corner. Rosalie was looking straight ahead. I never saw her again, although once I thought I saw her retreaded and somewhat older new self from a distance on a city street.

PART IV

1

When I returned to New York from St. Ethel Camp, the city seemed more repellent than ever. Something had gone wrong within the ranks of the weather control people, a strike in their midst or one of those big supervisory failures that occur from time to time, and an unprecedented spell of heat and humidity had descended upon the city. Streets and pathways at all levels were crowded with people who looked as if it would take only a small provocation for them to do each other in. I began to notice how parts of the city were showing definite signs of decay. A facade peeling away here, a crack appearing there. I thought of what I had been told about the city in the old days, when it had been one of the worst strongholds of overpopulation, before it had been rebuilt and revamped according to more advanced municipal theories that rearranged and relocated the mobs, and I wondered if history was repeating itself. Whatever, there always seemed to be too many people around now.

Returning to the hotel suite, I found that Stacy was not inhabiting it. He had left a brief note indicating that he had gone off somewhere else, implying that it was out of town, and he did not know when he would be back. With Stacy, you could never know. He might show up soon, or it could be years. Stacy would be around when he wanted to, that was that. Still, I was disturbed that he had left no trace of himself around any of the rooms of the suite.

I tried to contact Ben but he was out of town, too. On some government business, according to June. I asked June out to dinner. She seemed reluctant, but also unable to think up a good excuse. Because of a dock strike and some bad planning on the part of restaurateurs, there was almost nothing of any appeal available from the menu of the place where we went. We had to settle for some laboratory-devised nutritive stuff that tasted like sautéed masonry. There was a jazz revival festival going on somewhere downtown, and I offered to take her to it, but she said jazz made her nervous, and it was becoming impossible to find a cabbie willing to attempt a downtown trip, and anyway she'd rather not. When she saw that I was trying to think of something else to do (and probably perceived that I was searching for the event merely to occupy time and not her), she said she was particularly tired and had better go home. Before I could talk her out of it, she hailed a taxi, told me I did not have to see her to her door, and rode off.

I decided to return to the hotel, resenting the fact that everyone I knew was out of town or might as well be. A crowd had gathered in the street I usually took to the hotel. The route was impassable. I asked a person on the outskirts what had happened. She told me there had been a massive assassination-squad ambush. Three or four squads had converged, killing a large number of people on the street. Most of the dead were apparently part of a group of Third or Fourth Lifetimers on their way home from a get-together. Not enough ambulances had arrived to cart away the bodies, and there was some chance a few of the undamaged dead would not become Fourth or Fifth Lifetimers.

I thought Alicia would reappear at any time, as she so often had in the past. In the ensuing days I kept watching for her, especially when the air felt odd, but she did not show up. I took longer walks, hoping to run into her, and made a couple of unsuccessful attempts to locate her. A pleasant-sounding man working at her agency said they never knew where she was, but that she had popped in a couple of times in the past week. I left a message for her.

I meditated a lot about our trip to St. Ethel Camp, sometimes regretting all that had happened there, sometimes regretting only a part of it, always regretting those last moments when I saw Rosalie taken away. With nothing better to do, I tried to contact someone who might be able to tell me what had happened to Rosalie. I quickly found out there was no way to ferret out such information. Nobody official ever told me the information was classified, but clearly it was. I was especially apprehensive about the way the person in charge would ask me who I was and why was I possibly interested in a legal matter regarding a reject. Once I asked if she had been sent to the retread chamber. My listener seemed to regard the question as an insult, a subject that polite people did not bring up with each other. It was an attitude I had encountered before.

I might have investigated Rosalie's disappearance more thoroughly but, with the entrance of Pierre Madling into my life, my world turned upside down.

2

Pierre Madling was interesting to look at in that way that especially unattractive people are interesting. He was short, narrow-shouldered, and thin-chested above an incongruous pot-belly and stubby legs. Pear-shaped they might have called him in days when pears had been more abundant. Still, with that body he might have been cute if his face had not been truly repulsive. Eyes that seemed always tearful floated beneath heavy clouds of thick black eyebrows. His nose suggested alcoholism, a nearly extinct illness, with its tinge of redness and shape like a slightly deflated balloon. His mouth was thin-lipped when everything else about his face demanded that it be fleshy. There was an odd patch of white at the point of his chin that suggested clown makeup but was apparently some kind of skin condition. His hair was usually unkempt and, though real, often looked like a wig. He was in his fifties and, in contrast to most people in today's world, he looked it.

I had been sitting in a street café, drinking a kind of bitter concoction that they claimed reproduced the taste of *espresso.* Suddenly I became aware of this short fat man standing next to my table.

"I will join you, sir," he said. "Your permission?"

I pointed to the chair beside me.

"Thank you," he said, seating himself. "Never order the *espresso.*"

For some reason I felt I had to lie to him:

"Why not? I rather like it."

"Of course you cannot. It tastes like the urination of an aged monkey. Let me order you something else."

He took my demitasse and, with a cavalier gesture, poured its contents into the earth of a nearby plant. I expected to see leaves droop immediately. He gave me back the cup and, even though I hated the coffee, I resented his interference. As he gestured toward a waiter, with that kind of elan that demands immediate attendance, he said:

"I am Pierre Madling. I do nothing useful in this life, having—after an active initial two lifetimes—opted to spend my third lifespan in leisure. As it may be my last, I wish to have everything I've always wanted and selfishly deprived myself of."

"You're expecting to request elimination from the program?" I asked him. Elimination from the program, like "suicide," was a general term describing the refusal by a retread or natural to accept a new lifetime.

"Oh, no, hardly that!" Pierre protested. "I want as many lifetimes as I can get. I'm not one of your namby-pamby types who feel qualms about taking on somebody else's body. Hardly, hardly. I merely do not expect another chance, according to the odds."

"The odds?"

"My sense of history, which has evolved well over my two and a half centuries on this good earth, tells me that forces beyond my control are rushing onward on a collision course whose eventual explosive meeting may substantially reduce my chances, and indeed the chances of many of us, for another lifetime. Don't stand there fidgeting, Oswald, you know what I require at this time of day, and bring a glass for my new friend here."

This last declaration was addressed to a waiter, who did seem quite agitated. He strode away from us, clearly thinking something very subversive for the world of service. I could understand his mood. I resolved that, if I did not like Pierre's "usual," I would pour it into the earth of the same plant he had used for my *espresso.*

"I'm Vossilyev Geraghty," I said.

"I know who you are. Your exploits were well covered several weeks ago. I made an attempt to see you then, but some rude young man said you were not available."

"That'd be Stacy."

"What would be Stacy?"

"The rude young man. As you called him."

"I hope that you never bring him along to see me."

"What makes you so sure I'll be coming to see you at all?"

"Conviction, dear chap. I always convince myself that what I require to happen will occur. And it generally does."

I was tempted to say, fat chance, but decided to hold my judgment.

"I don't quite understand how your sense of history informs you that you'll be robbed of another lifetime."

"In good time. Let us enjoy ourselves first. I will pour, Oswald."

The waiter had brought us a liter of Courvoisier, together with two rather large brandy snifters. Madling opened and poured with extreme care, while still talking:

"From my private stock, some of which I have had to place in the unsure hands of this café because I have no storage room of my own. It is a pleasant brandy, not so good as some others that have unfortunately become nonexistent in our times, but a good example of the art in its time. Cheers, dear chap, although I've always found a toast over brandy redundant."

He timed his sip of brandy so that it would coincide with mine, looking over the edge of his snifter at me with his watery swinish eyes. I had to admit to myself that the Courvoisier was good and could think of no reason to waste it on the plant.

"A second toast, because it occurred to me too late for the first," he said, holding up the snifter again. "Roll the liquid around your tongue more this time. The toast: I sincerely hope that you have a third lifetime, and that it be richly abundant with either purpose or luxury, whatever you desire."

I nodded a thank you and sipped again, this time following his instructions. As the aroma of Courvoisier gently invaded my nasal passages, I felt myself beginning to get high from the fumes.

"You have doubts about my third lifetime also," I said.

"About everyone's. Or perhaps I should say everyone except those in the higher echelons of privilege, wealth, and power. And/or, I might say. I shall explain."

"Please."

"First, our chances are somewhat diminished by circumstances. There has always been the slim chance of an accident from which one could not be saved in time by the retread chamber rescuers—the recurrent retread nightmare, as it's sometimes called. Not all of us are fortunate enough to die in bed as I was able to in both of my lifetimes. I always had a proper death, flowers by the bedside, the relative I most wished to put through the anguish of waiting for my forgiveness next to the bed. Oh, I can say that death has always been an enjoyable experience for me."

"I think you're straying from the point a bit."

"I always do. You must put up with that. Everything that is artful strays from the point just, as you say, a bit. But, about our odds: In addition to normal accident or any kind of death that, for any reason, prevents a successful retreading, there are those deaths caused by the current social turmoil."

"The reject killer squads."

"Exactly. As their fervor grows, their success ratio seems to increase proportionately. Not only that, they are, more and more, planning their killings, punishing certain of us for sins perhaps known only to the killers or planners. I notice myself looking over my shoulder often these days."

"You think you might be slated for extermination?"

"It's possible. I talk too much, and may have expressed an undesirable opinion in the wrong quarters. I am careless also. You did not protest when I said I talked too much."

"I prefer not to interfere with other people's opinions of themselves."

"Your point, dear chap. I see your impatience and rush back to my main topic. As you know, bodies are at a premium. If you or I should meet our final reward today, and were rushed to the retread chamber in time, these mysterious bits of matter which they extract from our brain, souls as they so disgustingly call them, would have to survive in the preserved brain-case in one of the storage areas for what we so inelegantly call a period of darkness. And that period of darkness will last even longer than we suspect now. It could be ages before revival."

"That doesn't surprise me."

"But you've not really thought about it, I can tell. You take things as they come, and time doesn't frighten you the way it does the rest of us."

"Maybe."

"Well, you may evade. But think about this: Something must be done about the shortage of bodies. After all, those at the top, those with money, power, prestige, don't especially like to face long periods of darkness. They try to arrange shortcuts but the retread chamber administrations are notoriously stubborn about keeping to schedule, and they rarely allow advantaged people any advantages. Deals can be made here and there, but mostly the rich and powerful must wait about as long as the poor and powerless rest of us. They don't like that. They are retreaded and find that others have become richer and more powerful in the interim. They resent all the laws that obstruct them from earning substantial interest and dividends during their periods of darkness. They have to scrabble their way to the top again, use their resources to purchase advantage that should have been theirs automatically. Those people, although the rest of us hardly ever see them, are too comfortable in their expensive sinecures, and they want to get back and enjoy them all the more. So they're cooking up new plans."

The more Pierre Madling got into a subject, the more he involved his body in the conversation. He did not so much move his arms and hands, as most of us do when talking excitedly (although he did gesture with them often enough), as move his body and bounce his legs. He leaned forward and backward, revolved his body, crossed and uncrossed his legs at the ankles, tapped his foot on the cement floor. When he was thoughtful, he pulled at the folds of his neck or scratched a cheek with his unnaturally long but well-manicured fingernails.

"What kind of new plans?" I asked.

"The rumor is, at least according to certain friends whose sources are (I think) unimpeachable, although of course sometimes false sources are provided for whatever nugatory purpose the government might have, but the rumor I have heard in several discrete places is that there is presently being concocted at the highest levels a plan, a new set of procedures intended to govern the entire practice of retreading. In some dark and dank office in some deep underground level, plots are being hatched to tighten the selectivity requirements for all of us who are currently in the retread state."

"I'm not sure I follow you, Mr. Madling."

"Call me Pierre, please. I'm very fond of the name. My favorite grandfather was named Pierre, and it was my father's middle name, and in the rare times in this world when I have met another person bearing the name, he has always been an exemplary individual, someone easy to admire . . ."

"In other words, you never met a Pierre you didn't like."

Especially yourself, I thought but did not say.

"What a nice turn of phrase. It is so piquant in fact that I suspect you didn't invent it."

"Not exactly. There is another version of it in our history."

"Explain, please."

"I'd rather not now." I tried not to appear too exasperated. "For the moment I'd rather hear about the new procedures you were telling me about."

"You will call me Pierre?"

"Interminably."

"May I call you Voss?"

"You can call me collect if you want."

"Call you collect? I don't understand."

"Just a bad old joke. They seem to be coming back to me in droves today. Go on with what you had to say. Please. Pierre."

He twisted in his chair and looked over his shoulder as if he expected to see someone there. His jacket had an old-fashioned collar on it. I wondered if collars were coming back into fashion. As he returned his attention to me, he started to run a chubby hand along the collar and I realized it was not a new fashion development. People like Madling needed a plenitude of decoration on their clothing, in order that they could finger it nervously.

"The laws governing retreading may be changed in such a way that many of us will no longer be eligible to be passed along to new bodies. That's all. It is as if those of us who've already qualified for the retread privilege and who, incidentally, were assured that the retreading privilege was not revocable, are suddenly being plunged back to the beginning where we will have to prove ourselves anew. Not only that, but the new regulations will be more restrictive, stiffer was the term one of my informants used, so that many of us will suddenly become, as it were, rejects. We'll find ourselves in our very last lifetime. Think of that, Voss, think of that."

I thought of it. It was like dying right at that moment, as if this strange fat man had reached casually over the table and buried a knife in my heart. Years ago, I had not exactly passed the qualifying tests with flying colors. A few months ago I would not have cared. But in between I had met Alicia. With Pierre's piece of secret news, my one slim hope, my vision of myself in a new and efficient body, overcoming Alicia's silly biases about retreading, seemed to recede to impossibility, as if it had been exploded in front of me. But there had to be a way, a way I could have Alicia and not be confronted with the total absurdity of a physical and social situation that I did not wish. For a moment I wanted to destroy everything—this contumelious man in front of me, the city, myself.

None of what I was thinking was evident on my face. I took it with a calm that apparently surprised even Pierre Madling.

"You don't wish to comment?" he said.

"I don't wish."

"Ah, you are still too young. When you get older, you will care about your next lifetime. I guarantee it."

"You may be right, Pierre."

"I have an appointment soon and must leave," he said. "Perhaps you'd wish to accompany me. I am to be shown a collection of late-twentieth-century sculpture. It is quite nice, all bold and made of the most unlikely materials."

"I don't think so, but thank you."

"I comprehend. It's not an especially important period for sculpture, lacking somewhat in inspiration. Nonetheless, I enjoy the energy and find a certain sententious beauty in it. Then you will dine with me tonight. I insist."

"Really, Pierre, I don't know if—"

"You mustn't argue with conviction, Voss. I'll have an extra-special meal for you, I promise. Meet me here at, say, seven. I require it. Until then."

He had left and was waddling down the street before I could say goodbye to him. I remained at the café for some time, wondering how such an apparently blasé individual like Pierre could cause such despondency in me. Fortunately, he had left behind the brandy and I took some pleasure in killing half the remaining supply.

3

I felt dizzy when I got up from my chair. When I stepped into the street, I decided to take a long walk, in order to clear my head.

The crowds on the street gave me a claustrophobic feeling. The spaces in which they allowed me passage were—to me—like tiny rooms whose proportions kept shifting. With each tiny room my phobia grew. I knew I must get to some out-of-the-way area. Following instinct and some vague memories of the general neighborhood, I found some side streets in which the flow of humanity gradually diminished to a small stream.

The area in which I now walked was a commercial center. Vehicles were parked at entrances and unhappy-looking men carried cartons through large doorways. Littered paper was not being sucked up by the clogged street vents. Pedestrians displayed clear purpose in their walks. There were no children anywhere to be seen. Many of the buildings facing the street were now windowless. On some of them were hung business signs that must have been authentic relics of past eras.

"The next doorway, Geraghty," said a voice behind me. I had not even felt the presence of anyone that close.

"What?" I said, glancing over my shoulder. The man, slightly taller than I and walking slightly to my right, did not return my look.

"You're to go into the next doorway."

"Who are you?"

"Doesn't matter."

"You're going to force me into the doorway."

"There're three weapons pointed at your head right this minute. Any one of them could make you nonexistent above the neck. This doorway here."

He spoke politely. Just a man making a simple logical request of another.

Somebody I could not see held the door open. We went through the doorway into a long narrow corridor, where wallpaper peeled and rotting boards inside the walls were on exhibit.

"All the way to the end," said my guide.

The last door had glass in it, plus some lettering which said, MANAGER. Manager of what was not clear. This door, too, was opened by somebody on the inside. We entered a large airy room, the living room of a once-plush apartment that looked and smelled as if it were no longer inhabited on a regular basis. An odor of dampness seemed to pervade everything, as if the walls and furniture were regularly watered down like plants. The furniture, and there was plenty of it scattered around the room, looked comfortable. In spite of its plushness, the two men who awaited me had chosen to sit on a pair of straightbacked chairs whose legs seemed to bend outward with their weight. They were pleasant average-looking men.

"We meet again, Mr. Geraghty," said the man on the left. I looked him over, tried to recall where I could possibly have met him before.

"Did we?"

"At Rosalie's church. I was there, you looked directly at me a couple of times. I guess you could say we didn't exactly meet."

"I don't remember you."

"Sit down."

I selected a well-padded chair near them, and regretted my choice. Its cushions were soft enough but the musty damp odor was particularly heavy in it. Its fumes revived my drunken state. My head felt woozy and my stomach nauseous. If these people were planning to kill me, I hoped they would do it before I really got sick.

"I was wondering," the man on the left said, "if you had changed your mind about things. If you had decided to join us."

"Join you in what? I'm not very good at cards and I'm afraid I—"

"You needn't joke with us, Mr. Geraghty. None of us amuse

easily, and certainly not at a style of humor that must date from your first lifetime."

"Earlier than that, probably. Much of my attempts at humor have solid historical roots."

The other man shifted in his straightbacked chair. He evidently did not care for me, but thought it was not time yet to show his disdain.

"Rosalie asked you to join us. Your answer seemed to me tentative."

"I did not realize that the negative could be tentative. I'm sorry—I said no, which I took to mean refusal."

"I see. We were not able to reach your sympathies."

"And you won't with little heart-tugging remarks like that either."

"I apologize, Mr. Geraghty. I sometimes let my feelings get the better of me."

He did not sound like a man who was much guided by his emotions, nor did I sense much commitment in his voice. He also looked too old to be playing this game.

"Where is Rosalie?" I asked.

He glanced at his companion, who appeared impatient.

"We don't know," he said. "She was taken away."

"I saw that."

"Did you? Without getting your heart tugged then either?"

"What's this all about? Why have you forced me in here?"

"Discussion. Perhaps we'll kill you. We could. Kill you, store your body somewhere until it became decayed, useless. Hand you a complete blank of an eternity."

"You guys don't look much like a killer squad."

"That's right, you've seen a couple of our teams, haven't you?"

"Up close. They didn't do too well trying to get rid of me. I suppose you think you can do better?"

"We have somewhat improved our methods. The books show a higher rate of success lately."

"You keep books on assassinations?"

"Progress must be measured."

"And death is progress?"

"In this society, yes. But we don't intend to kill you. Not now. You still may be useful to us, may experience some epiphany that'll turn you around, make you come to us."

"In the meantime," said the other man, speaking for the first time, "we just want to remind you that we're here. And that, if we get tired of waiting for you, or should see a political advantage in doing it, we can still become a killer squad meant for your elimination."

"I'll keep an eye out. May I go now?"

"Yes," said the first man. "I've been looking forward to speaking with you. Perhaps we'll talk again sometime."

"I'd say over my dead body, but then you'd tell me you could arrange that, and I don't much care for ritual."

I walked to the door. I glanced back at the seated pair, who watched me impassively. There was something odd about the way they sat, looked. Something too calm, too lacking in the revolutionary spirit. They seemed to be acting. But for whose benefit? It was hard to believe that they had only wanted to talk to me, especially to such pointless effect. Maybe they only wanted to look me over, test me in some way. But why?

4

I would have liked to skip the dinner engagement, jilt Pierre the way Alicia enjoyed walking out on me, instead I met Pierre at the café. He got up from his table abruptly and led me out, back to the street.

"Where we going?" I asked him, as I tried to keep up with his remarkably fast pace. It was amazing how much distance he covered with each stride of his short legs.

"I have reserved a private room at L'Etre, the only really fine restaurant left on this continent. L'Etre is exquisite, but cannot match some competitors across the seas."

"You're something of a gourmet then?"

His face made a moue of sadness—perhaps, even, of despair.

"Unfortunately, no. In all my lives I've had a pronounced distaste for certain foods that form the basis of haute cuisine. I cannot abide fish, either shell or natural, and therefore miss out on many elegant dishes. Veal, also. But I strive to do my best within my culinary limitations. The art of preparing so many of the really fine dishes has, alas, been lost. Even our best chefs cannot reproduce them with the best of instructions, sometimes not even with newly unearthed authentic recipes. The materials with which they have to work are just not up to par. But a certain middle level is maintained and at L'Etre we perhaps have something akin to what was considered topflight cooking in the past. What I have planned for us this time originally came, like many of the snobbiest dishes, from a peasant cuisine."

L'Etre was well hidden. Looking at the front of the wretched building that housed the restaurant, no one would have suspected that any example of finery was concealed within it. The building was in an old part of the city, a barely inhabited section whose edifices were old-style, whose streets were straight and right-angled (I recalled my impressions of Cleveland so many years ago). A few seedy individuals loitered here and there.

"How can a restaurant survive in such desolation?" I asked.

Pierre shrugged.

"It doesn't worry about the desolation. The proprietors *prefer* not to draw attention to themselves, since their services are somewhat limited, anyway, and expensive. It's definitely more efficient to provide service only for those who know about L'Etre. More than anything else, they fear government interference."

"This place is secret? An underground gourmet restaurant?"

He laughed.

"Of course it's not secret. Many in the government know of its existence. We're lucky that a qualification for government service continues to be a tendency toward boorishness. They simply don't care about food and, in fact, tend to favor the kind of chemical pigslop that is served to them daily in plastic cafeterias. Let's go in."

Pierre had a key to the place, a beige key with a purple velvet handle. Inside, we crossed a dark, tenement-smelling lobby to an elevator by which a man slept precariously on a tall stool. We awakened the attendant, who did not seem at all glad to see us, and convinced him to take us to the fourth floor. The doors opened onto a view of elegance so surprising that, despite the fact that the decor was accomplished in soft and dark colors, and the lighting was subdued, my eyes hurt, dazzled by the contrast with the world outside. Historic-appearing furniture was arranged neatly around the room. The few tables were covered with rich maroon tablecloths. The paintings on the wall were in Renaissance style, or perhaps—considering the number of authentic works of art on the black market—they were genuine Renaissance.

A formally dressed maître d', who obviously recognized Pierre, came over to us and greeted him warmly. Pierre introduced me. The man scrutinized me, approved, then greeted me just as warmly. He said our room was ready and led us across the restaurant's main room. I tried not to look as self-important as Pierre and his maître d'.

Our private dining room was a smaller version of the main room. The two paintings on its cloth-covered walls derived from a much later era. One portrayed bathers on a turn-of-the-twentieth-century beach. They wore striped and frilled bathing suits that covered most of their bodies. This picture, appealing in its sedate blues and soft greens, fit the mood of dining in L'Etre. Across from it was a long portrait of a dandy, done in very dark colors. Although there was an aloof look to the man, as if he questioned our right to dine in the same room with him, he seemed an appropriate representative of the clientele.

As we sat down, I realized that the room's pleasant odor came from red and yellow flowers set on our table in a Greek-design vase, whose raised surface depicted scantily dressed people in pursuit of each other. Flowers were such an expensive rarity, grown by fiat only in authorized element-controlled greenhouses around the world, that I wondered how the management of the restaurant could possibly afford to provide them and still feed us. I also regretted not knowing what kind of flowers these were. I mentioned this to Pierre, but he merely sniffed them for a moment, then said he had never much cared for flowers. Thinking of their expense led me to wonder just how much Pierre was going to pay for the forthcoming meal. He probably could afford it, I thought. He might be a rich man, probably had an unlimited credit shield.

"Not as rich as I look," Pierre said.

"You read my mind."

"A trick of intuition, naturally, but I'm quite good at it. No, I have accumulated and earned sufficient quantities of income in my time, but I've always felt that highly placed people will someday change our economy structure and render wealth worthless, especially as too many old retreads enter the extremely wealthy category, in spite of the laws designed to prevent the accumulation of wealth between lifetimes. However, so far the economy has remained stable for decades, and the newly rich have done little to disturb it. It's to their advantage not to. At any rate, I think that those in power have worked at it—to convince us that most of what we want from wealth and power is not worth our getting, philosophically discouraging us from entering their domain where we would find, indeed, most of everything we would've thought we wanted if they'd not convinced us not to want it. What are you smiling about?"

"Cynicism. I often think of myself as cynical but at this point I'm willing to concede you the game."

"Hmmm, bizarre."

"What's bizarre?"

"I'll tell you in a minute, old chap, let me signal our waiter. Timothy."

I wondered if he made a point of knowing waiters' first names. Timothy acknowledged Pierre's officious gesture and left the small dining room.

"I hope you don't mind, but I feel that corrupting the palate with a before-dinner cocktail spoils the impact of certain portions of the meal."

"I don't object. The brandy this afternoon kind of killed my taste for any drink."

"Really? How unfortunate. Here, dear chap, take this."

He handed me a small colorless capsule.

"What's this?"

"Never mind. It cures hangover, and that's all you need to know."

I swallowed the capsule. A wave soon passed through my head. I could no longer discover even a trace of headache or, for that matter, unease in my stomach or anywhere else in my body.

"Why did you think I was bizarre before?"

"Did I? Really? Let me see. Oh, no, not you exactly, Voss. Hardly, hardly. Well, you, in a way. You see, you called me cynical as if I were perhaps the most cynical being you'd ever come across."

"I meant something like that."

"And I was thinking, how bizarre. That you should call me the height of cynicism when it's you who have no respect for your life."

I wished I had not changed the subject. Why did everyone seem to agree about my reckless attitude about my own life?

"Well," I said, "I only meant that your attitude toward this world seems cynical. I can see that you have respect for your life."

"Your point, Voss. I'll explain, but first let us enjoy this."

Timothy set before each of us a greenish melon with a scoop of what appeared to be raspberry sherbet upon it.

"Both are real, dear chap. That is to say, the melon is real and was grown who knows how many decades ago, then preserved. I arranged for its preservation, as I did for all the items of this meal, during my last lifetime—as I did for as much real food as I could get rights to. I don't recall exactly when I purchased the consignment of melons. You see, that's where my money went. I invested in food, Voss. In food. The most fortunate business insight of my entire professional career. I have stored here at L'Etre, and other selected places whose personnel I can trust, sufficient real food to allow me a meal like this once a week for the rest of this life, plus a good segment of my next. I suggest you do similarly. It'll bring you much more satisfaction than any amount of money you put away, or any amount of material possessions you collect for the future. A diamond is no good with mornay sauce, Voss. Invest in food. If you can find any. There're cartels now that're cornering the market. The cartels were interested in other commodities in my day. Eat, your sherbet will melt."

Pierre saw I was pleased with the melon and sherbet and, in the manner of a man whose hobby has just been validated, he beamed with delight. He ate much slower than I, seemingly savoring each mouthful. I reduced my rhythm to match his.

"Each time I sit down to one of my special meals," he said, "I'm happy that the cryogenic process for humans could not be developed. I'm regretful that food was not given more attention in my day, especially by me. I was a bit of a radical then, too much willing to protest the conditions of my time. Things seemed so much simpler then. Theory covered everything."

Mediating for a moment, he licked sherbet from the underside of his spoon.

"I used to watch TV in the old days, more so than anyone does now. We used to think TV was too commercialized. Prophets thought later periods would become dominated by TV, that we'd never leave our homes but instead use TV to accomplish everything—while we became mindless. I'm sure they did not envision TV's lack of importance in our time. They thought, for example, that three-dimensional television would be in every home. Well, so they developed it and it didn't go over. I mean, it's here and we use it, but it's only part of a service that we occasionally use. There's cassette recordings of almost anything we wish to watch in flat or 3D TV. Tri-D they sometimes called it in my day, although no one ever used the term after it was actually developed. But we have so much time, lifetimes, we can reduce our interest in TV. That's the paradox. When our lives were short, we used TV to schedule our time. We were so afraid of unscheduled time. Now we have lifetimes at our disposal, and we think more about how we're going to spend each *life,* rather than each day or week. TV is a small part of a life which first-death has taught us must be filled with useful activity, or the events and emotions that we have been missing out on, or whatever. There's just too much to concern us."

I wondered how many of us could be as self-satisfied and optimistic about our lives as Pierre was. I started to tell him that, but I had allowed the pause to go on too long, and really long pauses did not seem possible in Pierre's company.

"There's a movie I used to watch years and years ago, in another lifetime. *Gone With the Wind,* made in 1939 but about the Civil War period in American history. Did you study American history, or did they discourage you from it in your school days?"

"Well, it wasn't popular, but I delved into it a bit."

"Not important. The tragedy is, you can't see *Gone With the Wind* any more, not unless you can locate some old collector with an old print or cassette of it. The government suppresses the film now, they don't want it seen."

"Why would it be suppressed?"

"Maybe they don't like us dwelling on our past, looking back. We're a very progressive world, even though very little has changed over the last two or three centuries. I think—but let's get to that later. I wanted to talk about the movie. Ah, Timothy."

Timothy served us salads. It had been years since I had had a salad that had not tasted like it was made of cardboard with machine oil poured over it. This one was crisp and had a pink dressing on it.

"That's merely Russian dressing," Pierre said. "Not considered all that exceptional in its time, though quite popular. This is a pretty good example of it, from a batch concocted by a ritzy twenty-first-century supper club. There's better salads available to me, but I fancied this one today. Do you like it?"

"Very much."

"I won't bother you with the plot of the movie, but it's clear that the moviemakers found a certain beauty in the antebellum period. Something relaxed and sane about the quality of life then. Men were gentlemen. Ladies, ladies. Good folks were good folks, even bad folks were bad folks. You felt while you watched that you could have lived then, even though your sensible reconstructed mind told you it wasn't as marvelous as the film suggested and, besides, there were slaves. One point in the film a character, the sensitive one who's faced with all manner of postwar crassness, longs for the beauty of the prewar time. And you almost wish for it with him. Funny thing is, the emotion I feel, the wish for an uncomplicated time, is quite stronger in me for the time that I watched the movie, my own first lifetime, than it is for the antebellum period. I don't so much want to recapture the feeling of the movie as I want to recapture the feeling of myself watching it. That's union lettuce, by the way."

"Why do you say that?"

"I don't know. It used to be important once. But, about our unprogressive time—I don't know how far back you remember."

"Pretty far."

"How much of the general state of your life then is different from what it is now?"

"I'm not sure I follow."

"Yes, that's an unfair question, forces you to create the context. What I mean is: as far back as I can remember, to the earliest stages of my first life, I can dredge up memories that're only variations on things that are only slightly different now. Take a category—say, transportation. In my childhood we traveled short distances by car, longer distances by train. When there was money around the household, we often took trips by aircraft. Well, how do we get around today? We take cars and taxis, the monorails and the few aboveground trains and subways that survive, hop an air-shuttle, take flight in one of the giant airplanes where you only know you're moving when you look out a window, maybe take a spaceship to another planet. What's really different?"

"A lot, I think. Other planets, for one. Why—"

"Few of us wish to take, as you did, the risk of leaving Earth, so—"

"Well then, the cars are—"

"It doesn't make an iota of difference what the cars are, what new harmless fuels power some of them, what tiny little additions allow better functioning and comfort. Makes no difference that aircraft reach astonishing speeds and are shaped differently and utilize different methods of power. Same for the other landcraft. Even the moving sidewalks, where you can find them working, are not substantially different than they once were. You see, appearances may change, inner workings may change. But they are still cars, planes, trains. Nothing in transportation has changed importantly since my first childhood. All of the progress we claim in each of the individual categories of transportation is illusory. At heart every method of transportation is the same as it has been for centuries."

"Well, you could also say that the car is simply an extension of the horse and buggy or stagecoach, go back to the Roman chariot—"

"Perhaps we could, but I don't think we are then talking about progress in the same sense. I'm referring to the progress that's brought about by science and technology. I'm just saying, for example, that the car has remained essentially the same since the development of the internal-combustion engine. Car engines today are tinier and not based on the internal-combustion principle, but they are still engines. I don't care for extensions or any other metaphoric comparison you might make. The only real change we made in the history of the car was when we banned them from the roads for so many years."

"Too cynical for me, Pierre, I—"

"Well, I don't pretend to logic. I so long for the kind of road they tried to develop, where the road was more important than the vehicle upon it. We would've just hooked onto beams and been guided to our destinations. What happened to that project?"

"The principle is in use in some underground enclaves but I'm afraid I don't recall anything about a network of roads operated by such beams."

"Hardly anybody does any more. Those who do, seem amused by it. I don't—telephones, remember that telephones were supposed to be combined with television so we could see the people we talked with. They came out with them but people didn't want them. Didn't want them! Notice how rarely you see them now, years later. People turned out to be ostriches, they preferred to hide behind the sound of their voices. Businessmen couldn't put up with the high-resolution work of the cameras. Pic-phones couldn't substitute for intimacy and privacy. Not only them, other inventions too, so many we looked forward to, expected to have them revolutionize our lives. And, when they came, they were disappointing, just more things to clog up a room with. You seem puzzled, dear Voss, why's that?"

I swished the last piece of lettuce around the bottom of the black wooden, or simulated wood, salad bowl to catch what was left of the dressing.

"I'm not sure what puzzles me. This afternoon you seemed to love life, to be quite satisfied with your lot."

"I am changeable, nothing unusual in that. Sunny afternoons make me romantic. Nostalgia sometimes leads me to a harsher outlook. I'm happy, I suppose. Survival makes me happy. We must have the first wine, to clear our palates. Timothy."

Timothy removed our salad plates and set them on a sideboard that was covered in a blue fleur-de-lys-patterned cloth. The wine had been awaiting us there, open in order to allow it to breathe. After Pierre had taken the first sip of the wine, a harmless burgundy, he pronounced it adequate. Uninspired but utile.

"There should be some progression to the use of wine in such a meal, but I tend to choose different wines according to my mood, and not according to the ingredients of the meal or the proper rules. I apologize for the lack of a fish course, but I never indulge. I've chosen a rather pleasant main course. A dish that allegedly originated in the Hunan province of China, although its origin is sometimes disputed, and it is sometimes claimed as an American invention. Such things are clouded in history, and would be even if our culture had any interest in history. Anyway, it is an Orange Beef, consisting of small pieces of beef, again meat preserved from my second lifetime, in a delicate but spicy sauce, together with crisp pieces of orange rind. I think you'll find it pleasant, and I mention it now so that you may anticipate it through the next of the preceding courses."

He sipped at his wine and became strangely thoughtful. Perhaps he was organizing his next set of speeches, correlating them with the food courses. At times I had the impression he merely said things whose idea, and even syntax, he had formulated long ago. Perhaps speeches, like food collecting, were a hobby with him. New friends were courted merely so that he could run through his voluminous and varied collections of opinions. But I didn't mind, the food and wine were helping me to enjoy his company more.

"All I'm really saying, Voss, is—"

His new oration was interrupted by a loud explosion outside the building. He jumped. The noise startled me, also. After a moment of confusion, I wondered why L'Etre, with its plush walls and remoteness, was not better soundproofed.

"What was that?" Pierre said.

Timothy, walking no faster than he did in normal service, walked around our table to the door of the room. I stood up and looked over his shoulder just as he opened the door. Some of the diners in the main room had rushed to windows and pulled back their velvet green curtains. As soon as they leaned forward to look out, there was another loud sound, much louder now that the cushion of the curtains was gone. The viewers sprang backward, almost as a unit. There was a shattering sound. A windowpane had been struck and a gunshot pattern of spidery lines instantly formed. Stepping around Timothy to look closer, I crossed the main dining area. The maître d', who had been watching from the center of the room, came to my side.

"We are safe, do not worry," he said.

"What's going on?"

"Merely an attack."

An attack from heartburn might have caused greater anxiety in the man than did one from artillery.

"An attack? They're attacking a restaurant? A *restaurant?* Who?"

Although he clearly would have preferred not to tell me, he responded:

"It is a killer squad. They sometimes harass us by firing a few artillery volleys at the building. But we are safe, they are merely threatening. The police will come, they have been alerted."

I looked out a window. Whoever it had been, they were already scattering. One disappeared around a corner, another scampered over a fragile-looking old wood fence.

"See?" the maître d' said, "they are gone now." Then he addressed the crowd: "It is all right, ladies and gentlemen. They have gone, and they will not come back."

"How do you know that?" I whispered.

"They never strike twice in the same day, nor do they linger around for the purpose of ambush. Now that the police strike has been settled, we get adequate protection. At least after one of these attacks. Please return to your meal, sir."

"No. I want to know why in hell they'd mount a futile attack on this place. On a restaurant, for God's sake."

The man sighed, as if he had had to answer that question frequently, and hoped never to again.

"They try to discourage our clientele by it. They do not care for the implications of what they term an outdated luxury, the kind, that is, that L'Etre provides its customers. By attacking us, they remind us they are there. Our business declines. I can tell you no more. Please accept a complimentary bottle of champagne for the conclusion of your meal."

I returned to the private dining room, where Pierre was sipping contemplatively at a fresh glass of burgundy. Timothy had delivered a new course, a cold pork in ginger sauce. Pierre said it came from a similar cuisine as our entree's. Perhaps my stomach had been agitated by the suddenness of the artillery attack, or perhaps I was just not ready for this kind of dish, but the pork was not to my taste. The meat was too chewy, the sauce was harsh. I thought I might like it better warm. For Pierre's benefit I pretended it was a flavorful delicacy. He seemed pleased.

"That's the third time this place has been attacked while I've been dining here," he said. "Perhaps I should find a new restaurant."

"The maître d' tells me part of the reason for the attacks is to discourage the clientele."

"I am discouraged. This, after all, is an important pleasure in my life. I don't like it disturbed by harassment from dissatisfied groups."

He took a slow sip of wine.

"Of course, they may be harassing me directly, or people like me, and not so much the restaurant."

"I don't understand."

"I have a unique distinction, Voss. I'd planned to tell you but had hoped to wait for dessert for the revelation. To satisfy my sense of drama."

"With the size of the portions here, I may not survive until dessert."

He smiled.

"All right." He took another wine sip. I suspected this one was also calculated for dramatic effect. "It has been speculated that I am the longest surviving retread from the initial experimentation with the process almost three centuries ago."

He let that sink in, smiled enigmatically, poured himself another glass of wine. He was drinking about two glassfuls to each of mine.

"You were one of the originals?"

"No. Interestingly enough, they seem to be all gone now. The experimentees, the first to allow themselves to be passed on to other bodies, seem to have joined the first donors in heaven, so to speak. Which leads us to the unpleasant conclusion that so far no one has actually been assured of eternal life through retreading."

"I wasn't aware of that. Is there something in the process that prevents an accumulation of lifetimes?"

"Hardly, hardly. There's no reason why, through retreading, we cannot go on forever. As a romantic, it is my intention to go on forever. I may seem relaxed in this lifetime, but I do have future plans, much that I have to do, intend to do. My nightmares are that I'll be prevented from this. I have this one strange dream that makes no sense to me, at least according to the lore of dream experiences. I dream I've been in the period of darkness but am removed and placed in a new body, and it does not take. It is as if I wake up to nothing. How is that possible? If a retreading did not take, I'd never know of it—how can I know of it in my dream? Everything tells me even while I'm dreaming that it's impossible to be aware of my own nothingness but I am. Do you ever dream anything like that?"

"No. I usually dream of a woman."

"Ah, the normal."

"Not exactly. You'd appreciate the irony if I could tell you, but I can't. In this case I dream of the same woman nightly."

"And she rejects you."

"No, generally she accepts me. With some cruelty, but also with some love."

"Then it's not a bad dream."

"It's a very bad dream."

"I see. Riddles. Ah, well, I prefer my own problems to yours, if you don't mind."

He toasted me with a freshly refilled glass.

"What's happened to all of the originals?" I asked.

"A variety of fates. Some have not gone on to successful retreadings, some've had accidents in their later lifetimes that were too serious or they were brought to the retread chamber too late. And there were those who achieved some kind of satisfaction with their extra years and opted for natural deaths, as the law allows. But, even with all those logical eventualities, a few of the originals should've easily survived into our time. In fact, there were quite a few around until recent years."

"What's happened?"

"About fifteen years ago someone broke into a government office that housed some official records pertaining to retreading. Among the documents stolen were some files that gave complete histories not only of the famous original group of retreads, but of all the pioneers who followed them in the early decades of the project. Since that time killer squads have been working systematically at finding and thoroughly assassinating those retreads whose records were in the early files. I've been informed that everyone left from the original group has been located by killer squads and eliminated. The jobs seem to be performed by specialists, killers who form an elite brigade within the entire assassination setup, the *crème de la crème* of murderers. Their methods are so refined that most of the kills are not committed in normal killer-squad fashion. They are much more devious, have to be because their main purpose is to ensure that the victim will not survive into another retreading. The last I've heard, they have finished off all the people listed in the first set of files—that is, the originals and those immediately subsequent to them—and now they've proceeded to the next oldest file. My record, dear chap, is in the next oldest file."

Pierre's dull eyes had been ignited. He savored the theatricality of his little monologue just as much as he savored the wine.

"And you think they'll be after you soon?" I asked.

"I believe they may be stalking me already."

The morbid undertone of Pierre's statements was beginning to make sense to me. His fear that he would be denied a future lifetime were based on his fear of the elite reject killer squads. As the old saying went, they had his number. For that matter, they had all his numbers—file digits and ID's. Even in the over-crowded conditions of our world, there were probably few places to hide from such dedicated pursuers. Also, his physical appearance was too much a giveaway. There were not, after all, many potbellied spindly-legged watery-eyed people around any more. His decades of third-lifetime self-indulgence had made him an easy target.

The Orange Beef finally arrived. I enjoyed the flowing orange flavor of the rind mixing with the tender pieces of beef. Pierre, after leaning over his dish quite a long time, sniffing at the entree, apologized for introducing a downbeat note when he should have saved such talk for a later moment. He approved of the way I devoured my hearty portion of Orange Beef.

As we ate, he became abnormally silent, making only a few brief comments about the food. Accompanying the entree was warm saki, another marvelous taste I had never encountered before. It went down smoothly, and each of us had a second serving of the delicate Japanese wine served in the delicate small white bottles. At one point Pierre was unreasonably amused by the difficulty I had fitting my large hand around one of the minuscule saki cups. He said I did not look especially dainty. After Timothy had cleared the main course dishes off the table, he served the complimentary bottle of champagne, the one the maître d' had promised me. Pierre was ecstatic because, he said, it was usually impossible to get L'Etre to part with champagne *gratis.* He said it would enhance the dessert. I said I didn't know if I could eat a dessert, I was already so satisfied and full. He said to wait and see. The dessert turned out to be a Mexican dish, *cajeta,* a puddinglike candy that had a rich and exquisitely elusive flavor.

"It is probably forbidden to mix cuisines so radically like this, but I do adore *cajeta,*" Pierre said. "Reminds me a bit of butterscotch. Delicious. I think, if those vile people succeed in assassinating me, I'll regret most not having consumed all the food I so laboriously had preserved and stored away during my last lifetime. Perhaps I could will those future meals to you."

"Don't be gloomy, Pierre. You may be wrong about all of this, misinformed."

"Oh, I'd dearly love to be wrong, but my sources are unimpeachable. Some of the killers' methods are known, even their identities. But none of that does any good. When someone desires to kill you, and is monomaniacal about it, there's not one hell of a lot that can be done to deter them. I begged to be retreaded ahead of time, a new body could be a perfect hideout. But the laws are so strict against retiring a body that hasn't been, so to speak, sufficiently used up. Unless of course you're in the government, where you can arrange a new retreading any time it suits you. Anyway, since they refused me, I've been trying to use up this body as fast as possible, as you can see, but I'm afraid I can't ruin it in time, not before the killers finally make their move."

We ended the meal, improbably, with Irish Coffee, which I might have enjoyed if I had not already had so much to drink. Too late Pierre noticed my condition and supplied me another capsule of the anti-hangover medicine. My head cleared immediately but by that time the coffee had become lukewarm and the whiskey in it had a too strong and oppressive flavor.

"After you returned," he said, "from all your wonderful exploits in outer space, I became fascinated with all the stories about you that came out. Envied you, in a way. Previously I had not felt even the slightest urge to try space duty for any part of my lifetime. I couldn't have faced the dangers, the risk that I might lose out on retreading. Until it occurred to me that the possibility of space duty was about to be taken away from me by the murderers. Suddenly–fat, weak, and unresilient–I had this absurd urge to sign up for the next ship out. It's probably lucky for the space service that I'm so out of condition."

"I doubt you would've liked it out there."

"Oh? Why?"

"I don't think it would've suited you even if you were fit. Sensibilities are not too refined in the space service."

"Oh, I know that. No, I'm adaptable. Remember, I *chose* to devote this lifetime to the pursuits of pleasure. If I'd chosen something more rugged, I'd've looked and become more rugged. The bodies we inherit are our tools. We can do with them what we will, hone them in any way. Reason I sought you out, Voss, is I wanted to see a hero for myself, try to get a feeling–by osmosis, if necessary–what makes a man take such infernal risks with his life. The funny thing is–what I've learned from talking to you and observing you is that you're not much different from me."

"You're right. I'm no hero. That's just the exaggeration of those accounts you read."

"Maybe, maybe not. I doubt that many of our historical heroes usually went around thinking of themselves as heroes. Perhaps the word was more significant to the failures, the General Custers and such who pretended to be heroes when they weren't. Ah, but this conversation is, in spite of the sobering-up pills, getting too wine-drenched and foolish. Shall we leave, take a walk?"

"Fine with me."

He tipped both Timothy and the maître d' generously, and left some instructions for his next visit. As we left the main dining area of L'Etre, I noticed a bigger crowd of diners. There was a general air of calm. Artillery attacks apparently did little to diminish appetite.

5

With the coming of darkness and the turning on of streetlights, the area outside the ancient building had become more active. The air was pleasantly cool. I detected a faint odor of water-drenched wood. We had to be near a river, I thought. A man, muttering to himself, wandered along the edge of the sidewalk. He picked up bits of loose paper, stuffed them into a pocket that was already bulging with trash. A self-appointed streetcleaner, he scoured areas where trash-vents did not exist or were broken.

Feeling tired, I rubbed my eyes. When I reopened them, Alicia was coming toward me.

"I was *not* looking for you," she said, without any other greeting.

"Magic," I said.

"What can you possibly mean?"

"A minute ago you were nowhere in sight. I just rubbed my eyes a moment and suddenly there you are."

"You might have even better luck if you'd be more conventional, rub a magic lamp. How have you been?"

"More to the point, *where* have you been?"

"You're not to ask me that. Would you introduce me to your friend?"

I made the introduction properly and formally. Pierre immediately turned on charm for her. They plunged into a discussion of twenty-first-century sculpture, the last period of art to utilize holography. I had never been much interested in the visual arts, at least as a topic for conversation, and so I strolled along beside them, frustrated that because of Pierre's presence I could not talk to Alicia about the matters that had been on my mind for days.

Soon we had progressed to a more populous district. Pierre suggested we go to a place he knew nearby. Tired of being with Pierre in "places," I tried to decline. Both Alicia and Pierre ignored my reluctance. We all hopped on a free electric bus that toured the area. The bus, a slightly smaller replica of the old London double-decker buses, was abysmally crowded. All such buses were mobbed regularly because special zoning laws allowed only buses to use the roads of certain districts, like this one, in the evening. The vehicle's historicity prodded Pierre to present Alicia with his opinions about all things progressing while remaining the same. Since he used some of the phrases he had earlier spoken to me over our meal, I became further convinced that many of his ideas were memorized set-pieces.

We disembarked from the bus in front of a wide-based pyramidal building. Wavelike undulations appeared to go up its sides. At the peak of many of these undulations was a window.

"What kind of architectural style is this?" I said.

"Nightmare-commercial," Pierre said.

"Are you joking?"

"No. Hardly, hardly. Nightmare-commercial is an actual style, although that was not the name originally attached to it. It flourished briefly, oh, a few decades ago."

"It's hideous."

"If you think this is hideous, you should see its manifestations in the other arts."

We were going, Pierre explained, to America, a rooftop club in the nightmare building. We passed through doors whose borders also had a wavelike shape and into a conventional lobby that was dominated by an enormous holomural depicting early American history.

We ascended to the rooftop club in a lift inside a glass-enclosed tube that rose from the center of the lobby. As the elevator made its slow climb, we were invited by a voice from a speaker to admire the figures on the outside of the balconies that encircled us at each floor. They were, the voice informed us, the last remains of such decorations from earlier periods of New York architecture, preserved here after being rescued from junkpiles and crumbled buildings. They were an interesting assortment. Ugly monks reading books, gargoyles poised for flight, masks that seemed about to speak. Alicia said that one of them, a dragonlike monster who seemed about to spring at the elevator, sent shivers up and down her spine. I was fascinated by the wattled design of its head and body. Pierre had, of course, an opinion on the history of architectural flourishes, but I shut off my mind to it and don't even recall whether it was approving or disapproving.

The elevator stopped at America. A neon sign, activated by the arrival of the elevator, started flashing. The speaker-voice invited us to cast our minds back on the nearly three-century history of the United States of America, of the ideals and beauty that had been lost when the country had been dissolved in order to form and join the world government. The voice briefly invoked the usual incantations about the sacrifice of a great country for the greater good, words I had heard ever since I was a child—the time when, in fact, these events had occurred.

As the elevator door opened, concealed lighting was triggered. We saw before us a gangway leading to a partial reconstruction of the side of a ship. A large paddlewheel revolved slowly beside the end of the gangway. An illusion of water, performed with the lighting, rippled at our feet. However, just beyond the edge of the illusion I could see the more-than-fifty-story drop back to the lobby, along with the menacing figures that hung along the more than fifty balconies. I felt grateful for the high transparent side of the gangway. Patriotic background music softly accompanied our walk up the gangway. As we reached the "deck," a man in colonial garb met us and asked for our choice of location. Pierre requested the Gramercy Room. The man nodded and led us there.

The Gramercy Room was ornate, overly so. Dominated by a many-faceted chandelier that sparkled annoyingly as it revolved, the room had too many elegant tables and plush tablecloths, too many fussily decorated pieces of furniture, too much depth in the carpeting. Too much of everything, perhaps, including people. A faint cigar-smoke odor was all the more irritating because nobody appeared to be smoking. Pierre requested a private dining room. A waiter led us to one of the doors set neatly into the red velvet walls, and we entered a smaller version of the main room. I felt quite uncomfortable. So did Alicia, apparently.

"It feels musty," she said to Pierre.

"Part of its charm, child."

"You're the child, Pierre."

"I'm sorry, Alicia, didn't mean to be condescending."

"Certainly you did."

"You are much too direct."

"There is no such thing."

"I wonder, my dear, if you'd grow less charming with more contact."

"Ask Voss. He'd know better than most."

"Well?"

Pierre switched on an impish gleam for my benefit.

"Charming," I said, "is not exactly a word I'd use to describe Alicia. But, on the other hand, I knew her best when she was nine years old and a scamp of the first order. It's difficult to perceive the present charm in a woman when you knew her at nine."

Alicia laughed.

"Voss," she said, "I think you were trying to be diplomatic in some way, and failing. Or trying to be epigrammatic, and failing. Either way, I'll keep my old stories about you to myself."

"Please don't, my dear," Pierre said. "I love to hear anything that has the slightest tinge of gossip to it."

"I think maybe you're succumbing to the period feel of this room."

"No, I merely have a talent for decadence. Voss has already seen it in operation.

I nodded agreement.

"Well," Pierre said, "speaking of decadence, what kind of indulgence shall we experiment with here?"

"If you don't mind," I said, "I think I'd rather not. I've been drunk twice today, sobered up by your pills twice, I don't think I can suffer through that experience a third time."

"No need to. You mistake the ambience here. While drinking is, naturally, possible, historical service is the main objective. Anything from the period that we might enjoy can be provided, if available. There's a guidebook."

After some discussion we decided on popcorn (called popped corn in the guidebook) and sarsparilla—which, of course, were favorites of Pierre, items he regularly ordered when in the Gramercy Room. As rarities they were both terribly expensive. It might, in fact, have been interesting to sample them. But they did not arrive before the killer squad attacked.

6

Pierre enthusiastically started to lecture us about New York City politics during the late nineteenth century, the period our room imitated, but Alicia kept interrupting him to correct his facts. Amazed at the possibility that Pierre could be misinformed about anything, I said to Alicia:

"How do you know about this period of history?"

"Voss, darling, I'm educated beyond your suspicions, I am—"

The door of the room was thrown open and three men entered quickly, holding their guns high so that we'd be sure to see them.

The killer squad had entered America as legitimate customers, three young men on the town who wanted to dine nineteenth-century style. They took a table near our private dining room and went through the motions of ordering a meal. Then, as if they all required the rest room in concert, the three arose from the table and walked to our door. Diners were too busy to notice that they drew weapons before entering. Only an approaching waiter, who knew something about killer-squad methods, spotted the weaponry. If frightened him, but he turned around and went to the manager's office.

Alicia saw the door opening first. I followed her gaze to the doorway and recognized what the three men must be immediately. At first I thought they were after me. I started to stand up. Alicia touched my arm, whispered, "Wait." The leader of the group ordered me, in a surprisingly soft voice, to sit down again. I sat. Pierre was still laughing as he turned around and saw the intruders. He seemed to sink in his seat as he obviously realized what they were.

"What are you—" he said.

"Quiet, Madling," the leader said, touching Pierre's cheek with the barrel of an old-fashioned looking pistol. Its barrel was almost rifle length and its sides decorated in delicate filigree. "This is to be a very orderly procedure. Everyone keep their hands in sight."

"God, even your clichés are shopworn," Pierre said, a nastiness in his voice that I had not heard before.

"I said quiet!"

"Voss, can't you do something?" Pierre said. His voice was pleading, his eyes scared. "I mean, you're the one who specializes in this sort of—"

"Shut up, Madling," the leader said.

"Shoot now," Pierre said. "I'd rather you did, than kowtow to the demands of a puny—"

"You'd like for us to do it now, wouldn't you? Here? So there's a better chance they can come and patch you up and feed you into a new body? You'd like that. He'd like that, wouldn't he, Richard?"

Richard, the large man standing directly behind Pierre, grunted affirmatively.

"But that's not what we intend," the leader said. "Stand up, Madling."

"Then—" I began. The leader seemed to read my mind.

"No, we're not here for you, Geraghty."

So they did know who I was.

"I'd like a shot at you," the man said, "but it's against orders. Unless of course you get in our way. In that case, it would be a pleasure. So just keep your hands to yourself and be calm and we'll just be out of here in a few minutes, taking this nice little pig with us."

He gestured toward Richard, who put an enormous hand on Pierre's shoulder and pushed him roughly sideways. Pierre fell off the chair, to his knees—which seemed to disappear into the red carpet of the floor.

"You bastards'll get what you deserve for this," Pierre said, breathing heavily.

"What can you possibly do to us, Madling? What can any of you do to us? Kill us off? I'd rather die than let you have one more useless lifetime. Get up and come with us."

"I won't do—"

"Pick him up, Richard."

Richard put both his enormous hands on Pierre's body and lifted him straight to his feet, a considerable achievement considering Pierre's weight. Pierre squirmed in the man's grasp. He looked quite foolish. A flushed, homely fat man whose stomach moved up and down the frame of his body with each attempt to squeeze out of his captor's grasp. The third member of the squad, who had been watching the regular customers and employees from the doorway, gave the big man a hand. The two of them started dragging their prize toward the door.

"Voss," Pierre shouted, "don't just sit there. You can take these guys. You've done it before. You can—"

"Muzzle him," the leader said. Richard's hand made a more than ample muzzle, although Pierre managed louder throat noises than might have been expected. I stood up, started rounding the table. The leader raised his long-barreled weapon and smiled at me. Alicia shouted:

"No, Voss, let it go."

"I can't. It's not—"

"You'll just get yourself killed, hero. Listen to her advice. She's wise."

His pistol aimed at my head was a convincing argument. I just stood there, without an idea of what to do, wishing Stacy were there.

"He's not worth it, Voss," Alicia said. "He's just an ugly, self-indulgent little—"

"It doesn't make any difference what he is, he doesn't deserve—"

"Sorry I can't stay around for the debate," the leader said. Pierre was being dragged by Richard through the doorway. A path had been formed behind him, apparently from the threats of the squad's third man. It led to the elevator gangway. The leader backed through the doorway just after Pierre's expensive shoes.

"Always wanted to meet you, Geraghty," the leader said. "I've heard a lot about you. My name's Gorman Triplett. I look forward to seeing you again."

His words were a promise, he meant to see me again.

Richard had dragged Pierre halfway across the large main dining area. If I did not do anything soon, I would not be doing anything. Triplett closed the door behind him. Previously I had not been aware of the room's soundproofing, now its silence was terrifying.

"I was so afraid you'd do something," Alicia said, in a near-whisper. "They would've—what are you—"

I had the door reopened and was diving through the doorway before I had located anything to dive at. Triplett, sure of my submission, had turned his back on our room and was speaking to the passive crowd. Richard saw me and started to cry out, but I was clinging to Triplett's back by that time. Surprise gave me leverage. I pushed Triplett forward. He fell onto an adjoining table, his face in a bowl of some food item with a steaming sauce. He screamed and squirmed sideways. Turning, he tried to bring his pistol around, but its long barrel was trapped under his body, and his hand slipped off the ornate stock. I remembered a martial arts chop I had been taught in Space Service training, and I aimed it at his neck. Apparently Triplett had been similarly trained. He reacted away from the blow. It caught a part of his neck anyway and he rolled sideways, temporarily stunned. Knowing he was incapacitated for at least half a minute, I looked toward the gangway. Richard and the third member of the squad had reached the gangway entrance. They stood by the still-revolving paddlewheel. Richard's hand still grasped Pierre's collar. Both squad members seemed unsure of what to do without Triplett to order them. I took advantage of their momentary uncertainty to make a mad rush toward them, another Space Service tactic, especially when a horrible scream accompanied the move. The smaller man reacted quickly and brought up his weapon. He might have got me, but the manager of the place, alerted by the waiter and entering the area from the squad's blind side, threw a large cleaver at my potential assassin. He had picked up the weapon on his run through the kitchen. The cleaver was not especially well aimed, but it grazed the arm of my attacker just as he was about to shoot. The shot was deflected, leaving a deep rutted burn in the deep carpeting at my feet. I jumped over the burned patch and rushed the man before he could get off another shot, pushing him back against the railing beside the gangway. A kick to the groin doubled him up, and I turned my attention to Richard, who was dragging the screaming Pierre toward the gangway. He looked appropriately like a pirate dragging an unwilling victim to a gangplank destiny.

"You can't make it, Richard," I shouted. While the message of my imprecation was clearly good common sense, the shout was also intended to make him hesitate as I positioned myself for attack. Since he did have Pierre in his hands, he had an advantage which I could not allow him to realize. But of course he realized it quickly enough.

"Good for you, Voss," Pierre said, his words coming out between gasps. How he talked at all I don't know, since Richard had a massive arm clamped around his throat. "These lowlifes haven't got the wits to—"

"Shut up, you stupid bastard," Richard said, while squeezing Pierre's neck even harder. Pierre grimaced but was determined to continue taunting him. When he could speak again, he whispered:

"You haven't got the brains of a crawling insect. That's all you—"

"Don't, Pierre," I said. "Richard, everything's okay. So far nobody's hurt much, just let—"

"We've never failed a mission yet," Richard said, and that was all the explanation he gave for his next act. Just as I was about to spring at him, he picked Pierre up over his head and contemptuously turned away from me. I lunged at his back. My timing was off by only a fraction of a second, enough time for him to gather full force of his weight and heave Pierre over the high railing. With a shriek of anger, and hysterical strength, I threw Richard to the floor and jumped on him, hitting him about the head with all the power I had. At the same time I listened to Pierre's scream as it faded away down the fifty stories he fell, heard after what seemed an eternity the impact of his body hitting the lobby floor. At the moment of impact, Richard's eyes closed in unconsciousness.

I can still hear the descending scream, feel in my body the impact as if it had sent tremors all the way, fifty floors and how many years, back.

If I had not been so intent on demolishing Pierre's murderer, I might have sensed the escape of Gorman Triplett and the other member of his squad. When I looked up and saw them rush past me—Triplett hesitating a moment, perhaps contemplating the rescue of Richard, perhaps considering my annihilation—I could just barely move off Richard's chest to pursue them. As I, after what seemed like many heavy steps, reached the end of the gangway, I saw them enter the elevator, which a fourth confederate had been holding for them. The doors closed behind them. Triplett looked back at me over his shoulder, with what could have been a look of either victory or pain, I could not tell, as the door shut off my view. I ran halfway down the gangway, even though the elevator was already descending—as if I could somehow chase the elevator down the transparent shaft. Then I fell to my knees. I had forgotten that the floor of the gangway was also transparent. Looking through it, through the fake illusion of rippling water, I saw a gathering crowd, could not even see

Pierre's body. They seemed to hover over him, some of them looking upward. At me, it seemed, as if they suspected me as the murderer. Triplett and the two other squad members ran out of the elevator, tiny sliding figures passing the crowd casually, ignoring the lobby disturbance as a matter beneath their important worldly concerns. I started to shout out to the people below me to go after them, but realized I could not be heard and stopped. Kneeling on the transparent floor, I merely watched them casually walk to the front entrance and go out. I felt a hand on my shoulder. Alicia's. She was crying. So, I realized suddenly, was I.

7

Authorities came, questioned us and other America customers, took Richard away. Richard, pleased with himself, smiled through the bruises of his face. The manager offered us the run of his establishment. An empty offer, since we wanted to leave and he wanted to close up. Riding down in the roomy elevator, I felt severely claustrophobic. Alicia held on to me.

We passed cautiously through the lobby, circling the area where Pierre's body had been. Or where we thought it had been, since efficient cleanup crews had erased all traces of the event.

"Is there anyplace we could go, recuperate?" I asked Alicia.

She hesitated.

"Well, I suppose my place is as good as any."

"All right. I've never been there, I'd like to. When I wanted to see you, I couldn't find anybody who could tell me where you lived. I called—"

"I keep it a secret. I don't like to be visited and need a place disconnected from all the other parts of my life. So I can think without any of the idiots who pass through my life pulling at my sleeve."

"Am I one of the, um, idiots in your life?"

She smiled. I had not realized how much I missed her smile.

"No, just a figure of speech. I try not to think of anybody as idiots, that'd be succumbing too much to the prevailing social philosophies. But, I don't know, sometimes I get so annoyed, feel so helpless, everybody around me seems to be drooling at the mouth and waving a machete. Let's not talk about it for a while. My place is only a few blocks from here. We can be there in a few minutes."

Her place turned out to be in a rather fashionable section of the city near the East River. Newly built townhouses, recalling other eras, dotted the street on which she lived. Her own building was more modern and functional, living units piled on living units without any particular flair for architecture. What always disturbed me about that kind of building was the then-current fashion for concealed windows. Not a single window was evident from the street. The glass, opaque on the outside, was treated to look like stone so that outside observers could not discern the borderlines between window and building material. Inside, of course, the windows were normal, allowing for a wide and excellent view and with the controlled-tint function that lent so many appearances to the living unit itself. Alicia's could also be programmed for other views and, in fact, happened to be set for Swiss Alps when we first entered the apartment. It was quite disconcerting and distracted my attention from the apartment itself, since the mountain scene was bright daylight, and we had just come in from a bleak dark night. When my eyes became adjusted, I saw that Alicia's living unit betrayed its essential functionality of design in spite of her efforts to remove the effect. She had put up a whole wallful of mirrors to give depth to the single room, but the depth only doubled the room's barrenness. Several vinelike plants arranged with obvious care just emphasized the mechanical bleakness of the decor. Her prints and paintings seemed drained of their color. Her furniture looked (and was) rock-hard in a much too tasteful way. There was just not much one could do to hide the sterility of a slightly rectangular living unit whose walls contained or secreted the basic necessities, whose ceiling was not high enough, whose walls seemed to move in at you if you stared at them.

"Sit down," she said. "I have to be in the bathroom for the next hour or so. No, I'll be right back, I just need—"

She let the sentence trail off, slid back a bathroom door from what looked like a wall cabinet (it was also fashionable then to conceal bathroom and closet doors), and I got a glimpse of a peach-colored bathroom wall as she slid the door shut behind her. The door seams were so artfully hidden, I wondered for a moment if Alicia had been in the room at all.

She was not gone long. During that time I watched a skier weave his way down one of the closer mountains in the window-view. The tape loop ended before he reached the bottom border of the window, and I wondered if he made it finally and how long it would be before he would appear again on the upper slopes of the mountain. Alicia had changed into a loose tuniclike robe whose azure color seemed designed to fit in with the blue skies above the mountain scene. Apparently she did not intend to be color coded, for she put her hand on the switch governing the window-scene, asked me if I minded her shutting it off. I said I didn't, although a concern for that skier did pass through my mind. She restored the natural view of the city. The sky was now the wrong blue, the blue of night. It made Alicia appear paler, and I wanted to suggest a further change of clothes.

"I should've offered you something before leaving you adrift in here," she said. "Why didn't you sit down?"

"One of the chairs bit me."

"What?"

"I don't know, I just forgot to sit down. I will now, okay?"

"You seem edgy."

"Surprised?"

"No. Would you like something calming?"

"I drank so—"

"I wasn't thinking of a drink. I have a library full of pills."

"Never use them."

"I don't use much either."

"Why have so many?"

"You never know. I think I will take something, now that I've asked me."

She made a cabinet appear near the concealed bathroom door. I paid no attention to what she removed from it. Pill-taking always seemed a private matter to me, a hangover from the period when there was some stigma attached to the act.

I sat in a white oddly contoured chair whose curvature seemed meant for a much shorter man. After I sat in it, I felt it readjust for me. Alicia sat on the floor on the other side of the room. As she sat, the tunic billowed around her, and was a long time settling, as if it perhaps was maintained by air currents. She brushed back a lock of hair with her hand, tried to pat it into place.

"I should've combed it or something while I was in there. I have a temporary hair styler, accent on temporary, it'll set my hair into any of several different styles. The set seems to disintegrate at the wrong times, though. Embarrassing."

"Your hair is lovely enough as it is."

"Mussed? Frazzled? You're so polite, Voss, such a gentleman. Goes with all the other levels of your deceit."

"Deceit?"

"I don't want to talk about that." She spread her arms sideways; it looked as if she were playing airplane. "Ah, that's better. I feel better. It's working, the pill. Or I'm trying like hell to convince myself it's working."

She moved her hands into pockets of her robe, then took her left hand out again almost immediately. She began to finger the light cloth of her robe, creating a row of wrinkles in the smooth fabric.

"Our silence together is annoying. I don't like it. We should talk, bubble, make love. Sorry about that last, still somewhat bitter."

"There's nothing–"

"We maintain quite a distance. Spatially, I mean. Otherwise, too, I suppose. Maybe we have to. I thought so, until I saw you again. I mean, I knew I missed you, what I didn't know was that I wanted to see you again."

"I wanted to see you again. I tried."

"I know. I'm aware of most of your attempts. You don't try hard enough."

"How hard could I—"

"I don't know. Send roses, wait crouching in doorways, hire mercenaries. How the hell should I know? When I saw you again on the street today, I was so happy I—no, shouldn't talk about that."

She smoothed out the wrinkles, started them all over again in a new pattern. The other hand came out of its pocket but could not seem to find an occupation. It returned to the pocket like a person seeking shade. She looked directly at me for the first time since she had sat down, said:

"How can you be so calm?"

"I don't think I am."

"You don't think you are. Terrific. What I—no, calm's not the word. Detached. That's the word, detached. Your voice is separated from your body and speaks from a distance about two feet above your head. Just above your halo. In the middle of your aura. Why don't you tell me to stop this and come and hold me?"

I acceded to both her requests. We sat together on the floor, my arm around her shoulders, for some time, in a silence that was not annoying.

"You know something?" she finally said.

"What?"

"I feel womanly. I mean here, like this. Always used to think I'd hate feeling womanly. Maybe there's something to the idea of basics. Basic man-woman stuff. I'd like to just walk back into the eighteenth century, wear hoop skirts, run down garden pathways, go—"

"I think hoop skirts were nineteenth century."

"Don't kill it. I'm just talking about romantic love. We'd be a great combination for that. We'd never have to worry about your abilities, or lack of them. Sorry, keep forgetting you might be sensitive."

"I'm not."

"Right, that is definitely a problem. I told you to shut me up. Kiss me, you can do that."

"Seems a harmless revenge."

After the kiss, she said:

"I closed my eyes and saw you all in lacy sleeves and upturned collar, myself in hoop skirts, anachronistic or not."

"There're places you could go and play at history."

"Not the same thing. They're for the real escapists. I can only accept momentary escape. Brief dreams. I couldn't live without harsh realities."

"Really?"

"Harsher the better."

"And that's why you love me."

She whistled.

"Right through the heart with that one. Maybe I love you because you're so much like me. If only I could strangle you, throw you into a window-view of the Alps."

Another silence. She started creating wrinkle patterns in her clothing again.

"I keep waiting for you to ask me specific questions," she finally said.

"About what?"

She pulled away from me slightly. Still in my arms, but with more points of separation.

"Maybe you don't know the questions. Maybe you're not thinking them."

"I'm not, apparently."

"Well, we should leave it at that."

"Let's."

"Unfortunately we can't. I'm going to hear the questions whether you ask them or not. I should instruct you in the catechism."

"Why don't you just rest? Let the pill work, be calm."

"That's just it, I can't be calm. I keep hearing you blame me—it's a jump into the future of this conversation, but I can hear it. I must reach that point in the future, get it over with."

"What on earth should I blame you for?"

"That's not the right first question. First, you have to ask me—"

"Stop, Alicia, this is—"

"Hold my hand, please. Please!"

The ensuing silence was, in contrast to the previous silences, neither annoying nor comforting. It seemed to have a sound of its own, incessantly reminding us that it was silence.

"What was I doing, just so coincidentally, on the street outside of L'Etre?" She squeezed my hand, a signal. "Go ahead, ask me that."

"No, I'm not playing this—"

"Okay, don't ask. The answer is, I was sent there. I suppose they sent me because they were afraid of you. I don't know why, it was just an order. Notice how now I'm supplying the answers without even stating the questions."

I tried to settle her back into my arms, hold her tighter. She pulled away farther. Something went wrong with a lamp or with power in the building. Whatever caused it, there was an irritating series of flickers, which created a combination of harsh shadows and metallic glints on the opposite wall. Alicia waited for the flickering to stop before speaking again:

"The point is, I didn't know you were going to be there until I saw you leave the building with Pierre. They had just told me to be there, to either contact or merely follow Madling. The area was too dangerous for most of their regular people, was their excuse. They'd made too many raids in that general district and might be spotted. I thought it was all routine. Routine? you ask. Well, yes. You see, it's not unusual to set up a hit in such devious fashion. Pretty young lady like me to distract a difficult target, lead him to an area where he'll be more vulnerable, paint a bull's-eye on him, so to speak, dazzle the—why aren't you saying anything?"

She pulled her hand out of mine, moved her body a few inches away from me. I reached out to her, but she half turned away, brought her knees close to her chin, hugged them.

"I can't think of what to say."

"God damn it, Voss, this is no fucking exercise! Not some ritual I'm putting you through."

"I know that, just don't expect me to respond in the way you have planned. I really don't know how to, what I should say. There's no reason for me to hear any of this, you could've—"

"No reason? Are you insane? Do you think we can crawl into a cocoon and not bother with—or maybe, maybe we should just the two of us go back to that precious enclave you speak of so lovingly, maybe the three of us—you and me and, what was her name, Serena, we can—"

"Selena."

"Good. Selena. Sellleeennna. The three of us can live together in a torture chamber with black painted-over glass all around, and do our work—oh, do our work for the good of the enclave and, with any luck, society—and be blocked off from any outside disturbances. You'd like that, would you?"

"No, I wouldn't. Look, Alicia, I know you feel guilty and there's some sort of purging need that you're—"

"That's good. A purging need. That's what I've got all right. Good title for a chapter of my autobiography. A Purging Need. Don't look at me like that. I have a purging need for ridicule of myself. If I could duplicate myself, and get a whip, then—"

"Okay, calm down. I don't—"

"All right, I'm sorry. But you're wrong about one thing. I don't really feel guilty, I—"

"Alicia, Pierre was murdered, and you—"

"And I had something to do with it. You're catching on. Slow as usual, but catching on. I am, what do they call it, an accessory. That's no big deal. I have been an accessory before."

"That's what you do during your disappearances. I thought—"

"No, damn it, that's not what I do during disappearances. Not often, anyway. I also have a legitimate job, as you might recall. I'm also not especially trusted, I don't get many missions. This one today was the closest—"

"Maybe I should leave. We can talk about this tomorrow when you've had some sleep, when—"

"No, now! I have to say these things, make you understand, if you can ever understand. Just listen to me. All right?"

She ran a hand along her shin, just below the hemline of her robe. She was either rubbing out imaginary dirt or pulling at hairs that depilatory treatments had eliminated long ago.

"Will you listen?"

"Of course I will."

"Of course you will—such nobility in your voice. Sorry, I don't mean to—attacking's become a habit with me. All right. So I was there, down in that street. In a doorway, actually. I'd been shown a picture of Pierre Madling, been told—well, I told you what I was told. Follow him or distract him. All right. Triplett said there was somebody with Madling, it might be helpful if I could get that somebody out of the way. In the way he could prove to be dangerous. Triplett was prophetic, as you so bravely demonstrated. He's a very cautious man, Triplett is, and has been the best of the assassins. To prove it—he is nearly ten years past his scheduled date with the charnel house. As far as we know, no other reject has avoided the fate for that long, although it's said that some disappear forever. Anyway, Triplett must've known who you were, and that I knew you, else he wouldn't ever have sent me out on this kind of mission."

"Did he have something to do with the attack on the restaurant earlier?"

"Don't know anything about an attack on the restaurant. Maybe it was some kind of diversionary activity. Check your nerves or something like that. Most likely, it was just a coincidence."

"There were a couple of men who questioned me earlier today, before I went to L'Etre with Pierre. They have anything to do with Triplett?"

"Look, Voss, I'm not privy to all the secrets of the organization. They don't tell me much of anything. I am not a reject, and therefore suspect. All naturals or retreads who've joined the underground are suspect. You have to do something mighty to earn their trust. I haven't had a chance, though today may get me a few points."

"Points? Is that what this is to you, a game? Playacting, like you did today, crying over Pierre's death, is that—"

"The crying was, it was—ah, hell with it. I can't explain that now. Maybe later. Let me stay chronological. And it's not a game, believe that, it's not a game. I know it's hard not to scream at me, but just listen."

I nodded. By this time I had to listen. She waited a long time before speaking again. The trouble with the flickering light reappeared briefly, then stopped, but something must have burned out, for the room had become darker. Out the window I could see the satellite moon, which was rarely visible any more, hanging over a building as if balanced there.

"Chronological," she said. "To be chronological I should've started earlier. How I was recruited, the missions I went on. Hell with it. All I can think of right now is how I felt when I saw it was you with Pierre. I kept telling myself it was not possible, it could not be you. I would not allow it to be you. I could not perform my part of the mission with you there. It was not fair to me. The bastard Triplett was behind it, I wanted to go kill him. I thought about just returning, not making the contact. I could hardly move anyway. It was like I was clamped to the sides of the doorway, that I'd have to push at its sides, that the building would collapse on top of me, and that'd be good, the building collapsing. But there you were, love, and you kept coming toward me, and I so much wanted to see you again, talk to you. It'd taken extraordinary willpower to avoid you for so long. I wanted to see you dozens of times, but I had so much willpower I stuck to my guns. I was proud of it, the willpower. Then fate and Triplett and I don't know what conspired against me, put you literally into my path, or at least my path if I chose to emerge from that doorway. Triplett of course doesn't realize the—the depths—no—the levels of my affection for you. He thought, well, he could just send me out and it'd all be very natural, casual—but that doesn't make much sense or he'd've told me you were going to be there. No, he must've known what he was doing, the bastard. How stupid I was, I should've just stood in the shadows and watched you walk by. That bastard! They would've gotten

Madling anyway, I didn't have to be involved in it. In a way I wasn't much. I'm sure Triplett will complain I was more obstruction than help. Especially since Richard got caught and is no doubt well on his way to an instant trip to the charnel house. Triplett and Richard've been a team for years, some say they were lovers once—though, heaven knows, they don't show each other much affection any more. Would you like anything? Something to drink? A pleasant person to talk to? You look awful."

"I'm sorry. I'm all right. Really. Talk."

"Sure, I can reach all-new levels of self-destruction. I don't want to go on with this. I've told you the important points, you know all about my killer instincts. Damn it, Voss, I hate you! I'm right. *We're* right. Assholes like Triplett and me, the others, we're killing people, we're robbing bastards like Pierre Madling of their immortality, they deserve it, we have every right to kill them. They're the real killers, accepting bodies as if retread chambers were tailor shops and they were just buying a new suit. Madling had nearly three hundred years of existence, three hundred *years* of forcing his smug intellectuality on the world around him. He's no loss."

"You cried."

"Sure I did. I've never actually seen them kill anybody before. If you hadn't risen to the occasion, I wouldn't've this time. I've seen aftermath but never the actual killing, and never up close. I've been part of missions, but never in at a kill. I've—"

"I suppose that made it all right, not having to watch the actual death of your victims, not—"

"Of course it did, damn it! I didn't have to get to know the son of a bitch first, spend some time with him, get to know him, experience his charm."

"You said you didn't like Madling."

"No, I didn't say that at all. I said his death was not important, to be specific no loss, I—"

"You think Pierre *deserved* to die?"

She sighed.

"No, at least not in the sense that he'd earned it because of his overall character or something. I'm saying that he was one of the oldest surviving retreads. His death isn't important simply because he had had so many lifetimes as it was. It's as if you quietly put to death the oldest surviving member of your tribe, where the ancient man even puts in a vote for his own death."

"Pierre didn't want to die."

"Okay, pick on the analogies. I—look, okay, Pierre didn't cast a vote for his own murder, perhaps he even believed he deserved to live, in order to drop stale *bon mots* into more boring conversations, or to inflict upon people opinions that had not changed in two hundred years. Look, I don't want to have to judge his worth, his—"

"I see. His value as a human being might interfere with your belief he had to die, right? The indivualized death is more horrendous than the dying of a figure, an object, an assignment in an assassination plot?"

Alicia, already at the end of the couch, tried to press herself further into its hard corner. I didn't know whether the hate in her eyes was for herself or for me.

"Have it your way," she said.

"No, Alicia! *You* tell me. You started all this. Tell me more. Explain it. Who knows, some day you might have to finger *me* for one of Triplett's squads to—"

"God damn it, that's not fair!"

I took a deep breath, tried to push control into my body. My arms felt as if they wanted to flail out, my legs needed to collapse beneath me. There was so much pain in my head I could not find a particular headache to concentrate on.

"No, it isn't fair. I'm sorry. I'm trying to understand, see from your side what looks like murder from mine. I—I love you and I want to—"

She laughed suddenly, a harsh penetrating laugh that had more attack in it than any of her words.

"Great," she said. "Terrific. Finally, in the middle of discussing my merits and demerits as a murderer, you tell me you love me. How neat and romantic of you. Would you like to share the vial of poison or are we doing this *al fresco?* Can we—"

"I'm sorry, I was just trying to—I wanted you to see what—I don't know what I wanted. I said I love you so you would know I wasn't accusing you, wasn't—"

"You were just saying you loved me. You don't and you were just saying it."

"No, that's not true. But maybe it is. In a way. Maybe—"

"You don't love me, you do, what?"

"I do. I shouldn't, but—"

"Of course you should, you can, you may. You may take three giant steps and you may love me. I want you to love me, have wanted it since, since I don't know when. Don't say anything, don't qualify, don't argue the shades of meaning. Hold me, that's best, hold me."

Her push away from the arm of the couch reminded me of a swimmer pushing off the side of a pool. I held her a long time before we spoke again.

"I can't explain how I felt today," she said, "while we were in that horrible place, that ugly overdecorated room that Pierre seemed to love so. Even when I was thinking how screwed up everything was, and how was I going to get you and me out of all of it, how could I get to Triplett and make him stop whatever he was planning so I could feel conveniently guiltless and uninvolved—thinking of all of that, my mind kept returning to the question of how was it possible that Pierre could adore such an ugly room, such an ugly place. I've been to L'Etre and I hated that, too. How could he devote a life, or part of a life, to such dim trivialities?"

"From his point of view they weren't trivial. In his eyes the rebellion you're so fond of was the trivial thing."

"I suppose. I don't hate him for that, surprisingly. He was used up. There was nothing left of him inside. Oh, I don't mean he didn't have character, didn't allow himself a few feelings. I mean erosion. He, and so many others, have eroded from the inside, taken what they like to refer to as a 'shell' and spent a good part of each of their lifetimes eroding it into more of a shell."

"That's what you think I'll do."

"Maybe. Wouldn't be surprised. If you'd stayed on Earth,

instead of doing all that frolicking offplanet, maybe that's what you'd be now, an eroded shell."

"Then we wouldn't be together."

"Forgive my unsentimental attitude, but maybe that'd be a blessing."

"Maybe."

"God, you're so enigmatic."

"Let's not fight."

"Sorry, didn't mean those as fighting words. You'll have to learn to perceive my levels of affection, that's all."

"I'll try."

"Good."

With her body so close to me, pressing against me, I found myself wanting her, even felt excited as if my body were suddenly cured because of my love. A medieval miracle, the lifting of a curse. For the first time in years I could clearly recall how my body had felt in my first lifetime when it had been stimulated sexually. I could feel phantom desires, phantom arousals.

But it was, of course, the illusory feel of a cripple for a paralyzed or amputated limb.

"So anyway there I was in that stupid historical-restaurant," she said, "wondering how I could get us out, not knowing that Triplett was planning his own invasion of America. I wanted to screw up the mission but couldn't figure out how. I thought the squad would probably wait for us on the street, follow us to a less-populated area. That was my safety factor, population, I thought. Sometimes they'll pull what they call a hit-and-run in a crowded street, but Triplett generally doesn't care to work that way. He's been on this pursuit-assassination *shtick* for so long he—"

"Pursuit-assassination?"

"That's his particular mission. What he calls it, anyway. Obsession, really. He and his team've been tracking down the first-generation retreads and killing them, pretty much in the order of when they first submitted themselves to the retreading process. Those in this general area, anyway. It's as if he wants to kill every retread on Earth, one by one, in the order of their appearance. A bit overambitious, perhaps. You see, he broke into these files and—"

"I know about that."

"Do you?"

"Don't look at me like that. Pierre knew, too. He told me about it. I thought he was obsessed and more suspicious than necessary. He seemed to know he would be killed, and it's possible he was acting on a premonition it would happen soon."

"Hmmm, intriguing. I didn't know how well known Triplett's squad and mission were. Means he's really put the fear of God into aging retreads. I know you don't approve, but it *is* a hopeful sign."

"Maybe."

"Well, we won't dispute the point. Triplett's shown considerable skill. He's especially famous for devising on-the-spot strategies when some planned aspect of his mission goes wrong or turns sour. Which is what he must've done today. Perhaps he sensed I was deliberately stalling the mission until I could get things straightened out in my own mind. He's perceptive, might've seen that for himself. So he decided to do a kidnapping job, right from a crowded restaurant. So I never had a chance to rescue us. He didn't want to give me that chance. Sensible of him. He's admirable even if he is repulsive. He wants me, you know—pardon the aside."

"You want him?"

"Hardly."

"Then perhaps it's not worth an aside."

"Okay. So I guess there's not much more to tell you. I was sitting there trying to figure a way out, you were sitting there looking very pleasant and handsome, Pierre was sitting there struggling to be impressive. And Triplett catches us all out. A neat plan, perhaps, in his case. Except that, unlike his usual style, he didn't exercise enough caution about you. That was strange. God, I can still see Richard throwing poor Pierre over that barrier. If only you hadn't interfered."

"Interfered. I should've sat back, let them kidnap Pierre, let—"

"I'm sorry I said that. I wasn't trying to make you responsible for Pierre or anything like that. I just am going to be haunted by that memory, by the—"

"Wait. When they took him away, if they had taken him away, they were not, I assume, planning gentle treatment."

"No, wherever they took him, they'd've killed him."

"Then what difference does it make that I interfered? I might have saved him, after all."

"And they'd've killed him later, someplace else. But you're right. And maybe it was good I saw the killing. We shouldn't think of our victims as ciphers, as targets on an operations map or whatever. Perhaps it's good to watch the death itself, to—"

"Please stop, Alicia. All this talk about it is too cold, too detached for me."

"Cold and detached, eh? Well, that's a switch, you accusing me of being cold and detached. I didn't mean to be. It's—um—it's part of the job, I guess."

"What job?"

"The job of being a killer, a member of a killer squad anyway. A detached attitude toward the victim combined with a deepfelt emotional commitment to the cause is a basic requirement. God, Voss, don't look at me like that. I'm not a maniacal mass murderer. I don't like killing, I don't salivate at a victim's death. In our meetings I've even argued against these individual killings. They don't make a dent, their value to the overall cause is debatable. They're just needless terror when perhaps more insidious measures need to be taken. Nobody sides with me, except a couple of the others, and it doesn't do any—"

"Does it excuse you, to apply reason, to argue, then go out and help out in the killing anyway?"

"That's a point that has to be made, I suppose, and I should hate you for making it. No, it doesn't excuse me. Not at all. I have to help them, or else I won't be able to accomplish anything. Inroads need to be made, harm must be done. I—did you ever think how good reasonable argument would be to a society of retreads who've convinced themselves they need their series of futures? Bargaining table, Voss? Would you sit around a table for bargaining with us, sign away your retread right?"

"Maybe."

She laughed.

"Well, hell, maybe you would. But you're rare and you know that. Anyway, we've reached the impasse. Extra lifetimes at small cost, or everybody getting a fair deal. I need to rest, very tired, quiet please."

She leaned her head against my shoulder and fell asleep. Immediately, it seemed. Her breathing, light but audible, was rhythmic, content. She slept for about a half-hour, which gave me ample time to think. I knew I would hate spending the next few years in a relationship with Alicia that would turn out, eventually, to be valueless and futile. Whatever an analyst might speculate, tenderness was not enough, emotional outbursts of platonic affection were not enough. I thought about leaving her, signing up to go offplanet again. But, no, I had taken that escape already and discovered only that escape was a relative term. I had to stay on Earth, I had to stay near Alicia. I wouldn't be able to stand the pain of being apart from her, I had learned that much already. I could not leave her; staying would only lead to a bitterness that would become rigid. The thought that kept coming back to me as I held Alicia in my arms was that I had to do something. I would do something.

She awoke suddenly, pretended not to have slept.

"And so," she said, "life is beautiful, there are daisies growing over nuclear-waste depositories, the sun shines on the city every day it's scheduled, the ugly satellite moon is almost dead, and we here trapped within the sunken *Titanic* don't mind missing a damn bit of it. What can I get you?"

"Nothing. But I should go."

"No, that you should not do. Stay."

"I was just thinking the opposite."

"Hell you were. Just stop it."

"Not so easy."

"Okay, don't stay forever. Just stay tonight, how's that?"

"Couple more hours maybe."

"Terrific. What, you've got an appointment or something?"

"Something. You have anything that resembles coffee?"

"Close enough."

"Strong coffee?"

"My coffee reduces spoons to molten silver."

"Exactly the way I like it."

"Terrific."

We drank coffee, talked very little. Alicia fell asleep again. I found a light blanket to cover her with, and left.

8

Although it was still early morning, Ben's outer-office door was unlatched. June was not at her perch in front of Ben's doorway, so I knocked lightly on the inner door. Following a rustle of sound inside, Ben came to the door. He opened it a crack to check who his intruder was, looked at me as if I might be somebody official and unwelcome, then brightened to see it was only good old Voss. When he opened the door wide, I was surprised at the lines in his young face, the darkness encircling his eyes. The eyes themselves were different. Even though he smiled and greeted me with his usual warmth, the eyes remained blank, as if he had suddenly become blind and was trying to bluff it through.

"Where's June?" I said.

"I don't know. She hasn't been here for days, didn't give me any notice."

I wondered if she was with Stacy somewhere, but didn't want to broach that subject with Ben.

"Last I was here, you were out of town."

"I was. Out of the office, at least."

"Government business, June said."

"No, I told her to say that, but that wasn't it."

"What was it then?"

He studied me with those vapid eyes, grimaced slightly, finally said:

"Come in. Lot I want to talk to you about."

He set the time-lock of the office door at one hour. Sitting behind his desk (which resembled a Ben-desk from his previous lifetime, with papers and other paraphernalia scattered around its top), he told me to sit anywhere I pleased. I pulled a chair to a position directly across from him. We each waited for the other to begin speaking. Ben finally broke the silence.

"How've you been?"

"Asking as a friend or as a doctor?"

"Both. Either. Have you been well?"

Why was he stalling, I wondered—or did such questions merely come out of his mouth automatically, as if he had to sound medical each time he took up position behind his desk.

"In a way I haven't been well. Which is to say, I've been physically fit but not well."

"I've no appointments for a while. I'm supposed to be working on a government project that is so thoroughly worthless I can talk my part of it into a voicetyper between bites at lunch today and still make it sound like I've been sweating it out. So, tell me what you want me to tell me, and do it slowly, take your time."

Methodically, because I had rehearsed it during my walk through the streets, I told Ben everything that had happened to me since I had last seen him. Of my trip to St. Ethel Camp, my experiences with Pierre, his death, and—mostly—everything about Alicia. Strangely, I found that when I talked about her and my feelings for her, my voice choked up and I could not always hold back tears. I looked at Ben to see if he disapproved of my sentimentality. His eyes remained as unemotional as they had been when I had entered the office. He rarely interrupted, and then only for clarification. After I had finished, we leaned back in our chairs and neither of us said anything. Ben spoke first.

"And what do you want from me?"

"I'm not sure, Ben. A solution, a miracle, a revelation that this has all been a practical joke and you can fix me with one turn of a magic medical dial. A way out."

"Anything more specific than that?"

I put a hand on his desk, began shuffling some of the papers there, rearranging them as if they were my own. Ben did not seem to mind, but he watched where I put each sheet of paper.

"Well, since the *specific* problem is this body I've been blessed with, I thought about ways of acquiring a new one. A deliberate suicide, for example."

"And you know better than that. Except under the most special circumstances, an obvious suicide's body may not be retreaded, you know the law. People who are useful to the society or, on a lesser plane, useful to the government are often retreaded after suicide. Some government officials get away with it. There's even a remote chance for you, since you're a minor celebrity. But the odds aren't with you."

"So the obvious suicide, as you call it, is out. How about one less obvious?"

"Very difficult to do. Accidents are too dangerous, since the corpse may not be retreadable. Or you might screw it up and become a worse invalid than you are. Body-tracer devices have pretty much discouraged the use of formerly untraceable poisons, although sometimes I suppose you can slip one by if nobody knows to look for it. Again, the odds. The way things are, most attempted suicides are returned to life in their present bodies through all our advanced medical and surgical techniques."

"How about faking a natural death? Make my heart stop or shoot me full of cancer or some–"

"Cancer's curable at all but the very last stages, and nobody's going to believe you reached that point without it being detected. Same applies for any other disease. Again, our advanced techniques tend to foul up your plan. Heart attacks cannot be induced that easily, at least not without leaving clues to the–if I may use the word–sabotage. I have to say, though, that I find a neat irony in answering your sabotage with further sabotage. Wish it could work. Anyway, with your luck, they'd get you to a hospital in time and have one of their fancy mechanical hearts ready. And a mechanical heart'll add years to your life, which you clearly don't need at this point. Too bad there's no such thing as a mechanical–"

"I see, but there must–"

"You might take the risk, but I don't recommend it. And, if

you plan on me performing such an operation, get the thought out of your mind. I won't do it, not even for an ancient friendship like ours."

I felt surprised, and a shade disappointed, by the tone of finality in his voice.

"I'm sorry, Ben, I wouldn't violate your medical ethics. There—"

His laugh was so loud and sudden it startled me.

"Medical ethics! If it were simply a matter of ethics standing in our way, I'd just reach across the desk here and murder you. Voss, there's much more involved. As much as I love you, I cannot risk, can't risk, well, certain things in my life, for the mundane reason that you need a new body so you can make it with your young lady. I'd like to reduce my beliefs to the simple matter of placing my value to a friend above my value to, well, other things, things I can't talk about here. Maybe later, when I get rid of my current obsessions, maybe then I can find a way to help you. But not now."

"More dark hints. I wish you felt free to tell me about your obsessions, as you call them."

"I will, I promise."

"I knew all the way here that this was a wild-goose chase. I guess it's hopeless."

I felt like a supplicant whose particular spiritual guide had been found wanting in faith. Ben stared at me as if he could fluoroscopically examine my insides from his chair.

"It is hopeless, isn't it, Ben?"

"Nothing's hopeless. I've never found a really good reason for despair, and that's after centuries of dealing with despairing people. Sententious of me to say that, I suppose. But I believe it. It's among the thousand or so worthless ideas I live by."

I began to feel weary, remembered I had not slept all night. I started to stand up, sensing a tone of dismissal in Ben's voice.

"Well," I said, "I won't bother you any longer. I'll just—"

"Sit down. I'n not through."

I sat.

"Okay, Voss, one thing: there may be something I can do, a

way in which I can fit your problem to my obsessions actually. I can't be sure but there might—"

"What? Tell me, Ben, what?"

"Can't tell you all right now. And before I can even consider starting the process, a few things need to be said. Number one, I've known you a long time, my friend, and one aspect of your character seems consistent to me. You're an intelligent, educated, personable sort whose friendship remains dear to me, but you're also the most incredibly naive individual I know."

Not, of course, what I wanted to hear.

"Naive? Why naive?"

"Too many reasons to catalogue. Let's just take the present situation. Okay, you feel you need a new body or some such solution."

"Of course. What's—"

"You've always gone after simple solutions. Sometimes there's an almost appealing romanticism in them but, God, are they simple-minded! Maybe that's due to the way you plunge so recklessly away from what are generally the main issues. Life is not lived the way you like it, so you retreat with a pleasant young woman into an underground enclave, emerging only occasionally to verify your suspicion that the world has not changed, it still doesn't suit your needs. So you get to your next life, something goes wrong with the retreading. Okay, so it wasn't fixable, so it was a minor disaster. What do you do? Confront it with that reservoir of courage that's made you a minor celebrity? No, you run off to the stars, battle tenebrous beings, cement an image of yourself that has no relationship to reality. Again, you try to resolve what is no more than a dissatisfaction with the way things've worked out for you, by altering the circumstances so that the problem is no longer a problem—changing the context, perhaps, as a way of not accepting the infirmity, controlling your life as a comic melodrama—"

"Ben—"

"All right, that was extreme. I get carried away. Okay, you come back here, encounter Alicia, build your love up to dramatic proportions, then come to me asking for a new body, or the means to a new body. Naive? It's almost childish, Voss."

"That may be, but what do you—"

"Shut up. Okay, let's say I come up with a new body for you, what's it going to do, aside from allowing you to indulge your appetites with your precious love? If she'll let you. Remember her feelings about the retreading process, her beliefs."

"How do you know so damn much about Alicia, how—"

"I may know her somewhat better than you suspect, my friend. Be that as it may, think about her. Think about Alicia for a change. Are you going to be so marvelous in your new body, one that you'll not be able to choose, remember—so marvelous that she'll just fall all over you, grateful to receive into her life and bed one whole, undamaged, virile, earnest, and romantic young Vossilyev? Answer that."

There was more anger in his voice than I was accustomed to. What he said kept getting mixed up in my mind with what Alicia had said at St. Ethel Camp, as if what she called my psychological and social impotence was now being clarified for me by Ben's attack on me as a *naif.* What he was saying couldn't be true. I was too intelligent, too aware of consequences, too much in command of my mind. I suddenly realized what a naive thought *that* was.

"Maybe you're right, Ben," I said. "Maybe it *is* the wrong idea, a new body. But I'm desperate."

"Voss, I don't mean to be unkind. Maybe you are so wonderful that you can reconquer Alicia in your shiny new body, I don't know. There seems to be a touch of romanticism in her, too. Anything may happen—including, you might consider, the fact that, even if one of your plots is successful, the intervening period of darkness could be quite long. When you come out in your spanking new body, Alicia might be an old crone. Thought of that?"

"Nobody ever becomes an old crone nowadays, you know that, Ben."

"All right, the beautiful but *old* Alicia greets the beautiful but young Voss at the retread chamber door. Red sunsets take on an especial glow just for them, they wave their fingers at the outer barrenness and trees magically spring from the ground, the retread chamber implodes because true immortality has been discovered, probably by the two of you, and there'll be no more need for bodies. That romantic enough for you? So get your new body and stop bothering me with your plight. Love will conquer all."

Ben swiveled his chair sideways, found something to stare at in the nearest wall.

"All right, Ben, I'm not sensible. I won't argue that. But what should I do?"

He did not answer for a long while, then he swiveled his chair back, looked at me.

"You want to know what I think?"

"Of course."

"I think you shouldn't do anything. Go back to your Alicia and make whatever kind of good life you can. Exchange tendernesses, have fun, take trips, make whatever kind of love you can, satisfactory or unsatisfactory, or don't make love and find other ways to express your deeper feelings."

My turn not to look at him. I found shadow-patterns in the same blank wall he had just stared at.

"Do whatever we can, you mean, within the limits we have."

"Exactly. You want what selfish people tend to want, a miracle. I hope miracles come to unselfish people, they probably don't. Anyway, I think you and Alicia should make whatever kind of pleasant, happy, terrific or mediocre life you can, for as long as you can. Life doesn't have to be forever, neither does love–that pithy enough for you? Maybe you can work out a full lifetime together, maybe not, what's the difference? Maybe when you come to the end of life's highway or orbit or footbridge, you can convince her to join you at the charnel house and the two of you can be reborn into stolen new bodies, and make up for your absurd deficiencies here."

"Alicia's against retreading herself, you said so yourself, she'll never–"

"I know. I'm partly punishing you, partly saying who knows what she'll want to do when she's eighty and doddering? It's a risk and you pride yourself on your skills at risk-taking. Anyway, that's my advice. And you don't look too happy about it."

"Ben, I'd like to be as cynical as you, just accept—"

He hit his fist on the desk, sending papers sideways and making me, startled, swivel back in my chair.

"Damn it, Voss, that's just like you, call me cynical and shrug me off. Okay, have it your way. I've given my advice, my cynical advice, and you can act on it as you will. So you're too melancholy to take the kindest way."

"Kindest?"

"Kindest to Alicia, and kindest to yourself, if you'd see it. Okay, it probably wouldn't work anyway. If I read Alicia right. She's not likely to become the kind of sedentary gal a tough guy like you requires. Nor will she be especially satisified with a life of tenderness. But you can have a few days, months even, take them!"

"No. I can't. It's not fair to her, not fair to—"

"Not fair to *you,* that's the operative phrase, my friend. Okay, it's not fair. You want more, she'll even want more. Something's got to be done, in your view. Well, shit, maybe something can be."

He chose this moment for another siege of looking off into space. I longed for his crisp professional manner. I was not used to the jitteriness, the inefficiency of the retreaded Ben.

"Damn it," I finally said. "What? What can be done?"

"I said maybe, remember. But there might be an operation possible."

"An operation? I thought you said—"

"Yes, I remember telling you that operation was out of the question. That was years ago, when we were just seeing sabotage for the first time. We know more about the technicalities, the surgical techniques involved, repairs that can be—"

"You've *known?* All the time since I've been back and you haven't mentioned it once?"

"Back off. I've thought about it, weighed the dangers—and

there are dangers—and I kept putting off telling you, waiting for a better time. Which, you must admit, this is."

"Still, Ben—"

"I know. You prefer to make your own decisions. Okay, there's more to this than you know. First, the danger. The chances of success in the operations involved, and there're more than one, maybe several, are less than fifty-fifty, and—"

"I can accept those odds."

"One of your weaknesses, you always accept less than even odds. So, okay. Now, your body—more than fourteen years have elapsed since you inherited that Apollo's delight of a body, fourteen years for who knows what to happen to the results of the sabotage. There may be deterioration, atrophy, types of conditions that you wouldn't know about or understand, any of which could make your problem inoperable."

"I realize, but what's the risk in that?"

"Not much. We can open you up, see what the chances are, take them or not, close you up again, heal the scar, and nothing would be essentially changed. If we do this operation, it's fairly intricate but your chances of survival are much better than for the success of the surgery. But other operations may be necessary, operations infinitely more dangerous. See, when I first checked you out with my less-than-perfect diagnostic equipment, I discovered only the sabotage performed on your body. No reason even to look for more than that. Your last checkup, after you'd returned from space, was more thorough. With all that government money, I've been able to get better equipment. Anyway, a further problem showed up on the current printout. I wouldn't even've thought to check for it. Okay, it's this—whoever did the job on you was more of a master than I'd previously thought, more malicious and more thorough. I can't give you all the details, I don't even know them, but what he did was an intricate operation on your brain. He's affected, destroyed actually, matter in your hypothalamus."

"My hypo-what?"

"Hypothalamus. It's a part of the brain, located near the top of the brain stem and by the pituitary gland. Controlling the pituitary gland is its main, but not only, function. It also exerts control over the more primitive human drives. Hunger, thirst, pleasure, temperature, aggression, and the area of your concern, sex. Each function is located in a different area of the hypothalamus. And our master doctor zeroed in on the region that affects the sexual drive. Don't know how he did it yet, but we may be able to find out. Might have used some kind of laser-adaptation. Whatever, there are signs of definite lesions there, and in no other part of your hypothalamus. If his aim had been bad, to the left, say, he might've destroyed your hunger drive—something that, judging by the gluttonous way you put away food, mightn't've hurt you much. Okay, what he's done is damage, perhaps render inoperable, the sexual-drive region of the hypothalamus. If I guess right, what he's done may severely interfere with your sexual success even if the operation on the body is successful. Your brain may not be able to send out messages to your body that'd successfully initiate the sexual process no matter what condition the rest of your sexual network is in. One of the hypothalamic functions affected, for example, is the secretion of LHRH—luteinizing hormone-releasing factor. LHRH governs the release of sex hormones in the body, controls ovulation in the female, sperm formation in the male. Right now you are deprived of LHRH secretion. So, you see, there may be countless blocks to your sex drive. On the other hand, considering the mysteries of the brain and the miracles of hormones, the doctor's tampering with the hypothalamus may not have all that much effect on your abilities. I really don't know. I have a feeling that this doctor knew exactly what he was doing, and that his work is going to cause you trouble."

"It doesn't make sense to me. I mean, you're saying that the damage may render me incapable of desire, yet when I've been with Alicia, even in my sabotaged condition—and with other women, for that matter—I've had desire for them, I know I have."

"You think you have. Mysteries of the brain again. The man did nothing to your intellection process. Think of it this way—you can think the message, but that part of the brain whose job it is to send out is unable to transmit."

"You're making my body sound like a telegraph. Lines have goddamn fallen or something."

"An inept metaphor but apt. Anyway, if the first operations fail, and the brain operation is necessary, and I believe there's a good chance it might be, we can attempt to work on your brain. Like all brain operations, it would be dangerous, especially so since the hypothalamus is set so deeply within the brain, it's not easily reachable. Still, there is a device. A sort of microsurgic thing that not only drills through the brain but is able to do certain things once it reaches its destination. Under the best conditions I can't guarantee a high degree of success and it's worse here since we don't know how the sabotage-doctor performed his work or what he meant to achieve by it. Therefore, it's difficult to guess what we should do as corrective surgery. But we can try, and the risk is great, and you can die."

"Well, if I die, then just ship me to the retread chamber and—"

Ben looked as if he might kill me right at that moment. When he spoke again, it was in a hoarse whisper:

"I won't send you to a charnel house in *any* case, even off an operating table."

We both turned away from each other, found our own particular blank wall spots to stare at.

"Anyway," Ben finally said, "I have to find out more about our possibilities. We can talk again someplace else. I'll contact you."

"I'm willing to take the risk on that operation."

"I already assumed that. But it's all not going to be as simple as you think. I'm not acting out of any misplaced medical compassion, I've got something else on my mind. You may have to do something for me."

"What?"

"That I'll tell you later, after I've talked with some—certain people. Check with them to see if my overall plan is feasible or desirable."

"So long as I can have the operation, I'll do anything."

"That's it, rush right in. Okay, it's not going to be easy, pal. What I'm going to ask from you, you may not be too keen on. We'll see. And I can't promise the operation just yet, remember that. I'm not sure I can even perform it. And, under the circumstances, I can't go consult my favorite brain surgeon. That's another handicap, the secrecy of the operation. It will be illegal."

"I don't understand. Why does it have to be—"

"It has to be. Don't ask questions. I'll explain later. Now, the time I allotted for you is up. Go. I'll contact you when I can."

"I'm not used to your acting so mysterious."

"It comes with the job. Get out."

Behind me the time-lock clicked. Not knowing what to think, I left Ben's office.

9

I tried to call Alicia from an outdoor phone kiosk, but there was no answer. Figuring that she had gone to her odd little social-worker job, I racked my brain for the name of the agency, finally came up with it, and called there. No, a pleasant voice told me, Alicia was not scheduled in that day and was, in fact, on an indefinite leave of absence, we'll leave a message for her.

I walked the streets a long time, trying to straighten out the confusion in my mind. Finally, it was clear that I was getting too tired to think straight. I needed sleep, a soft bed, my own soft bed. Nothing to do but head for home, such as it was.

When I opened the door of the suite, I was too sleepy to be cautious. So it was a moment before I saw a figure standing across from me, another moment before I realized there was something familiar about him, still another moment before I recognized the man as Gorman Triplett, the leader of the team that had killed Pierre Madling. He was not paying a social call. He raised his long-barrelled handgun and aimed it at my head, and I jumped sideways, my shoulder against the door. Caroming off the door and crouching, I wondered if I was still physically able to perform the forward flip over the couch that I was contemplating. As I started to roll into it, the shot went over my head. My coordination was off and I flipped a bit sideways instead of forward. I expected that mistake to be fatal, to feel the next bullet penetrate as I regained balance. However, dizzy and disoriented, I looked up to see that Triplett was no longer aiming at me. He was struggling with someone else. Since they were out of the light, beyond the aura which the lamp cast, I could not tell who was who or exactly what was happening. I pulled myself out of the awkward twisted position into which I had fallen, and moved toward the scuffle. I had hurt something in my ankle and I slipped as I came down too hard on it. Jumping up, favoring the ankle, I saw that the two fighters were grappling on the floor. A table was falling over. An unlit lamp slid off it and performed a forward flip much more stylish and coordinated than the one I had attempted. A foot lunged out and knocked against the lamp that was working, sending it rolling a short space across the floor, creating a wavering and flashing illumination. I still could not tell which of the battlers was Triplett, so I could not exactly jump into the fray. I came closer, in a circling movement.

"Get out of the light!" a voice hollered. That's Stacy's voice, I said to myself. Damn it, that's Stacy's voice, he's my rescuer. Of course. He was on top of Triplett now, and the chop he delivered to Triplett's neck looked like it might kill him.

"Don't Stacy, don't kill—"

As the blow connected, I could tell that Stacy had pulled it just enough. Triplett's body went limp, but it was clear he was not dead. Satisfied that Triplett was all right, Stacy eased himself off the man. He moved with an unnecessary caution, or so it seemed to me, as if he expected his victim to come to at any minute.

"I wanted to kill him," Stacy said, as he stood up. "Couldn't. My weakness, I guess."

"Not killing is a weakness?"

"Maybe. With Triplett."

"He's a son of a bitch, but he's a brave man."

"He was going to kill you."

"I saw the gun."

"Pointed at your head. He wanted to make your death untreadable."

"Well, that's his normal style."

"Excuse him then."

"What's the matter, Stacy?"

"Nothing."

"I think you saved my life again."

"All those acrobatics of yours certainly had nothing to do with it."

"So, thanks."

"Don't bother."

I sat down, waited for the pain to seep out of my ankle. Stacy produced a rope from a drawer, began to tie Triplett's hands behind his back.

"Maybe we should get him out of here?" I said.

"We will."

"Any suggestions?"

"I'll call somebody."

"Not the police."

"No, couldn't stomach that. But there's somebody."

"Okay, you say so. I just don't want to give him another chance at me today."

"He'll keep trying."

"Well, I'll deal with that when it comes."

"One of us may have to kill him."

"Perhaps. Maybe if he comes to before your somebody gets here, we can talk him out of it."

Stacy laughed. A brief but extraordinary event.

"You don't think Triplett'll respond to reason?" I said.

"He has a reputation for tenacity, and he wants revenge."

"How do you know so much about him?"

"Let's say I'm acquainted with the man."

"You're a friend of his."

"Didn't say that."

The knots in the rope with which he'd tied Triplett were more than enough by far.

"Well, anyway," I said, "I'm sure glad you were here. Lucky for me you returned just in time to foil his attempt."

As soon as I said that, I was aware that the assumption didn't fit the set of actions it described.

"I came here with him," Stacy said, jumping a whole series of my questions.

"Do you work with Triplett?" I said, jumping a series of assumptions.

"In a way."

"Were you on a mission with him today? At the elevator maybe?"

Stacy laughed again. Phenomenal.

"No. Much, much too ironic."

"But you've been on missions with him?"

"Never. I'm not sent on killing missions."

For some reason, I was relieved by that answer.

"But you do work with his—with his group."

"Not with his section at all. I'm against the killing, and they accept that."

"You're involved in other kinds of—duties?"

"How many times are you going to ask me before you believe it?"

"Several. Just what do you do for them?"

"Can't say."

"You people are so damn secretive and self-important."

"Maybe. I should call somebody."

"It'll wait. All right, you won't tell me what you do."

"No. Would you?"

"I guess not. How did you come to be with Triplett, if you weren't one of his associates?"

"I knew he was coming here to kill you. Nobody could stop him. The only way I knew to keep control of the proceedings was to accompany him. He returned to headquarters hopping mad.

He said first off he was going to get that bastard Geraghty if it was the last—"

"Why was he so angry at me? His mission was successful."

The question was deliberately naive. I was not yet ready to tell Stacy how much I already knew about Triplett. Not this new Stacy, whom I wasn't yet used to. At the same time, I was more than a little frightened. When Triplett sent Alicia to me, he already knew me by reputation. It was uncomfortable to know that, in a way, I had been in Triplett's sights for so long. Harrowing. What could you do when men like him decided to activate their weapons, pull their triggers, throw their bombs?

"The mission wasn't successful in his terms," Stacy said. "The man he killed today, seems he'd had him set up for some time, but had trouble nailing him. He said he wanted this one especially, it was a special kill."

"I think I understand. The victim was arrogant beyond the average. So—I fouled up the design of his kill, and he wanted to punish me for it."

"Something like that."

"But more."

"Yes. He wanted your death in exchange for the disposal of Richard. He made a try at rescuing Richard. He gunned down a couple of cops, but missed out. He got away but returned again to watch Richard being delivered to the charnel house."

"Quick justice."

"They've been after him, both of them, for some time."

"So I understand. I almost sympathize with Triplett's cue for passion. On the other hand, I have a few new reasons for wanting to stay alive."

"Glad to hear it."

"Are you? Are you really?"

"Stuff it."

"Only surprised to hear you say it. But what happened after Triplett came storming in mad?"

"He said he'd refuse any further missions until he got you. They tried to talk him out of it but—"

"They? Never mind. I know, you can't say. Go on."

"He got even angrier when he didn't get any support from any of them, so I told him he had every right to want to kill you and I'd help him. He bought it. He told me to come along."

"How'd he know to come here?"

"Beats me. He zeroed in on the place. I think maybe he's been stalking you for a longer time than you might imagine."

"Perhaps. Perhaps he was in on one of the earlier attempts on us."

"It's possible, though that makes us pretty lucky. He rarely misses, takes a double-crosser with him to make that happen."

"So you deflected his aim when I came into the room."

"Right. I was almost unable to. He has a stronger arm and more coordination than I'd thought, and was almost able to get off a good shot with me hanging off his arm. I better make that call."

"Sure. Go ahead. I need time to think."

He went into the bedroom to phone. I sat for a long time, staring at the peacefully recumbent Triplett. Stacy returned, sat in a chair which he turned slightly so he could observe Triplett better.

"They'll be here any minute," he said.

"Who?"

"Colleagues of Triplett's."

"And yours."

"And mine."

"Weren't they disturbed at your double-cross?"

"No, they approved of it, actually."

Triplett stirred. His body jerked convulsively, but he could not quite awaken.

"How long've you been doing this, this undercover work?"

"I was contacted soon after that first attack on us."

"How'd they know enough to contact you?"

"Their information's not bad. They've got files, dossiers."

"Some of them stolen."

"Some of them. They've got their own information-gathering network, too. It's efficient."

"Still, they *knew* you'd be receptive when they contacted you. How?"

"A good guess on somebody's part. Naturals who are also rejects are anomalies in this society, a peculiar kind of misfit. We enjoy a proper span of years but aren't eligible for retreading. Anomalies and rarities."

"Then your category made you a good prospect?"

"An excellent one. Naturals tend to feel guilty because we dodged our assigned fate, defected from our own people."

"So they had good reason to suspect you were ripe for revolution?"

"Something like that."

"And you're running off everywhere doing good."

"Bullshit," said a deep voice that at first did not seem to come from Triplett. We watched him slowly open his eyes. His eyes were dark and intense, full of hate. None of us spoke for a long time. Stacy and I stared at Triplett, each of us perhaps considering ways of warding off the man's evil eye. Triplett's glare at us gradually faded and he became quite pleasant looking. He arched his neck as if reaching for stored reserves of power. Then, assessing his situation correctly, he relaxed his body, shifted it a bit in order to regard Stacy and me, and smiled. The smile was more of a shock than I was prepared for; I think I recoiled from it more than I had from his weapon pointing at me. Although thick in his body and impressively muscled, he had an amazingly aesthetic cast to his face. His skin was pale and his eyes, nearly black in color, had an avuncular wisdom in them, even in hatred. His lips were full and added to the effect of his smile. The delicate angles of his face, culminating in a sharply pointed chin, made him look like an overmuscled poet.

"Where's my gun?" he said to Stacy.

"Got it."

"You better return it later, you son of a bitch. It's valuable, an antique. Nobody tools a gun as well as the old gunsmiths."

"You'll get it back, don't fret."

"Oh, I won't *fret.* Just anxious to get ahold of it again."

He turned his head toward me.

"You guys are a pair, huh?"

"In a way."

"What the hell you mean, in a way? In a way what?"

"Well, we worked together offplanet, teamed—"

"You're a pair of jerks. You got to be lovers, correct?"

"Not correct."

"Don't shit me." He looked back at Stacy, said: "Well, maybe you're not. Who could love this bastard, this double-crossing turncoat son of a bitch? No, I believe you. You're straight. It's me, I just think that way, whenever I see a couple of guys together. Experience."

"What do you mean?" I said.

His anger erupted suddenly.

"You bastard, don't play me! I miss Richard. You know that, you bastard. I'll kill you, you bastard!"

"Sorry. I did know something about you and Richard, about your being lovers."

"Once. That was true once. Not later. We couldn't work together so well, we found out. So we split up, it was better for the team. But, Jesus fuck you all, I miss that fat son of a bitch. I'll kill you. You be ready, I'll ambush you. I'd kill both of you, if they'd let me."

"Let you?"

"They'd have my ass if I made a cadaver of your buddy here. Even I have enough presence of mind to leave *him* alone. But I'd like to blow his cowardly traitorous head off. Richard wouldn't've let you off, Stacy, no matter what they said to him. He'da thrown you down fifty stories just like he did that stupid oaf today. I can still see the scared face of that louse, still see it when he realized he was going to be heaved over that barrier. I'll bet he started fouling his trousers right then. I bet he was shitting all the way down fifty stories."

He stopped talking abruptly. His charming smile had returned as he invoked the memory of Pierre's death. I did not want to have this man smiling over my mutilated body. I could not let him get me, not now, not after what Ben had told me about the operations. And yet I could not kill him.

That night he said nothing more to me. Stacy's "somebody" came, actually a man and a woman who took Triplett gently between them and led him away, presumably to a waiting vehicle. Stacy gave one of the attendants Triplett's gun at the door. After they left, he looked toward me as if he expected me to grill him further. Suddenly I felt much too tired.

"I've got to get some sleep right now," I said.

"Good idea. They're taking Triplett to a place some distance from here. It's not likely he'll return this way for a while, but I'll keep watch anyway."

My dreams were full of threat and ambush, but Triplett did not appear in any of them. None I could remember, anyway. I kept waking up, seeing people in shadowy corners, but not caring and falling right back to sleep. My nerves felt like they were working their way out of my skin.

Suddenly Stacy was gently rocking me awake.

"Wha—what's up?"

"Ben. He's on the phone."

"Oh, good."

I stared at the extension beside the bed for a long time before pressing the transmitter button and leaning back on a pillow.

"Hello, Ben."

"You sound terrible."

"Well, it's been an event-filled day so far, and I've been asleep."

"Are you awake enough to think clearly?"

"Enough."

"Your judgment of enough may not be enough. I can call back."

"No, it's all right."

"Okay, it's short and sweet, anyway. I think your mind'll get it all right. It's about the subject we talked about earlier."

"The op—"

"I don't care to mention specific details on the phone."

"Sure, Ben."

"What I suggested to you may be possible. Still, a deal has to be made. We have to meet some place safe."

"You name it."

"I intend to. Your girlfriend's apartment. You know where it is, I know where it is. Try to get there without being followed. I'll see you tonight, I don't know what time. You wait for me. If you're rude enough to be later than me, I'll wait for you. Got it?"

"Sure."

"See you then."

He hung up.

10

Stacy insisted on accompanying me. When we reached the street outside the hotel I saw two familiar forms who, when they realized I was staring at them, each started walking in a different direction. I told Stacy about my previous encounter with the two odd men, how they had pulled me in off the street and interrogated me to no apparent purpose.

"Seems like they're connected with Triplett's group," I said.

"Not to my knowledge. Never saw them before."

"Do you know the people in the underground network all that well?"

"Don't know everybody naturally."

"Then it makes sense. Though why Triplett sicked them on me, I can't figure. Would've been better if I'd been left—"

"Not Triplett's style. He's too cunning, an ambusher."

"Then perhaps they're from another part of the organization."

"Doubt it."

"Why?"

"They don't look right. They don't move right. They don't even stalk right."

"But if they're not part of Triplett's—"

"Don't know who they are. Right now I don't want to know. But we better take the long way to wherever you're going."

"You think they were lying to me about being a killer squad."

"Possibly."

We walked for a while, ascertaining that the first one of them was behind us. Then he was joined by his partner. We hailed a series of cabs, dodged in and out of a few places. They were damn hard to shake off but, after a time, we finally did it.

Stacy stayed outside Alicia's building while I went in, to keep watch. Alicia, answering the door of her apartment, looked especially vibrant. The smile she gave me was the one I had been thinking about while standing outside her door.

"Good," she said. "I was beginning to get anxious, waiting for you."

"You knew I was coming then?"

"I was told. Ben called."

"I didn't realize the two of you were such good friends."

"You almost sound jealous."

"I meant something else. It's just surprising to me how closely everybody who means something to me is linked in a conspiracy I've been kept out of."

"Not exactly a conspiracy. And it's not as natural as you might think. Anyway, you don't seem as glad to see me as I am to see you."

"Of course I am. I just—"

"Then kiss me, touch me, doff a hat at me, I'll get you a hat—"

"I'm sorry."

I kissed her lightly on the cheek, touched her briefly on the arm, pantomimed the doffing of a hat. She smiled.

"I get more intimacy from my aunt, but okay."

"I think I remember your aunt. From the spa."

"Sure, she came there once. I remember she was withered and wrinkled. You should see her now. She's got a face like a goddess and a body that's considered illegal in some countries. Of course she hates me. I mean, considering she looked terrible in two previous lifetimes, she's not ready to join any anti-retreading bandwagon. Ben should be here in a few minutes."

"Where do you know Ben from?"

"You introduced us, remember?"

"No, not that. You know what I mean. There's something going on about you two beyond my knowledge. Why else would he have us meet here?"

"You got me. Let's see when he gets here."

"You're evading."

"Damn right, chum."

"All right, be evasive. But I'll tell you what I know."

We sat together and I described what Ben had told me in his office. I was surprised by her antagonism toward the operations.

"I don't understand, Alicia, if they're successful we can have some kind of life together."

"Sure, *if* successful. What if they aren't?"

"That's a risk I can take."

"Is it a risk I care to take? Did you think about that?"

"No. Frankly, I didn't. And I don't intend to now."

"I can see that. Well, have the bloody things. Die. I'll get through the years. You'll become a blurry memory."

"Perhaps that's better."

"Perhaps that's better. . . . God. you're so noble. Sacrificing yourself. Facing death with such courage."

"It's not that."

"What is it then?"

Her window-scene was still the same, although it pictured a different time of day. A morning sun had created different scenic patterns on the mountainsides, clouds were drifting and disappearing into the window-frame.

"I don't know. It's more than just correcting something physical. Or even wanting a normal life with you."

"No such thing as a normal life with me."

"I don't want isolation any more. No more enclaves. Or feeling in between. Or not really understanding the words of the ideas that're important to others—to you and Ben—something with sense to—"

"Sense? Lot of people would say Ben and I are crazy."

"Well, I'd like to perceive that if it's true."

"Thanks a lot."

"I didn't say it *was* true, just that I'd like to know."

"Are you sure you aren't saying something abysmally simple, like you only want something to have faith in?"

"Maybe. But I don't think that's it, not all of it anyway. Perhaps an object or person worthy of faith would be a solution, but maybe all I want is to understand what I see in some organized perspective."

"I don't see how any damn operations are going to do that, Voss."

"Neither do I. It's just a suspicion. Maybe it's not the operations. Maybe it's you. If we can—"

"Look, you keep saying we, but your assumptions don't really include me. You've just got this fanciful idea in your head that, made compatible sexually through the wonders of medicine, we can have some sort of idealized relationship. But you forget *my* life, my life as it is when you're not around, treat it as if it's just a fantasy I indulge from time to time. It's *real,* darling, real. There is no reason for me to *expect* to see old age, Voss, share it with you. I may only have years, weeks, days. I could be killed as part of a mission, or I could be caught, sentenced to death. At least death for me, if not for my precious body."

"We have to escape from all that."

"No! No, that's the only thing I won't do. I won't escape, and you have no right to ask me that."

"But it's the two of us that's important, not some out-of-date, inept, killer underground that's—"

"Stop, Voss, stop right there. Let's not argue dialectics, rationales, anything. And operations, let's forget about them. Look, I'm not unsympathetic—it's terrible to be haunted so many years by a foolish and cruel act of sabotage. But I don't want you going through this ordeal for some mad belief that I feel my life will be made glorious by it. Okay?"

"All right, Alicia. And you may be right. I may be out of my head to want the surgery."

"Have it. Whatever happens, as the saying goes, I won't stop loving you. In the meantime, rub my neck."

We did not talk for a long time, as if we were both afraid that anything we said might grow into another fight. Still exhausted by all I had been through, I had almost fallen asleep when the buzzer rang.

"Ben," Alicia said. "I'll let him in."

11

Ben, looking less drawn, strode energetically into the room and asked immediately for a drink. Alicia went off to her cubbyhole of a kitchen to prepare it.

"Understand you had a run-in with Triplett," he said, sitting across from me.

"How could you possibly know about that?"

"Run-in with Triplett?" Alicia said, walking back into the room, a half-prepared drink in her hand. "Why the hell didn't you tell me?"

"I didn't want to alarm you."

"You didn't want to alarm me, how noble. What happened?"

I told them. Irritated, Alicia returned to the kitchen to finish making Ben's drink. Again I asked Ben how he knew about Triplett.

"Grapevine, mostly. Some people I know. First reports were only vague, but I got the real dope from Stacy on the way in just now."

"You son of a bitch! I knew you were connected with all this insurgency garbage!"

Ben laughed.

"Voss," he said, "sometimes I think I'll put you through hell, correct your mechanical defect only for the pleasure of giving you afterwards a kick in the balls that'd have some meaning."

"Seconds on the kick," Alicia said, handing Ben his drink.

Ben smiled at her, clearly savoring the psychological implications of her offer.

"Ben," I said, "you have more than just some lines into this so-called underground, more than just casual connections, don't you?"

"Yes. I am, as you say, deeply involved. That bother you at all?"

"A little. It's, well, disconcerting to find that everybody around you, everybody you care about anyway, is blissfully dedicated to a suicidal project."

"What can I say, Voss? It's necessary, that's all."

"Damn right," Alicia said.

Amused, they both stared at me, no fanaticism in their eyes. Ben looked like the cheerful handsome uncle who'd been off traveling and had hundreds of innocuous yarns to spin. Alicia seemed like a young lady who'd be more at home as the hostess of a lively party. Both were attractive people, impressive representatives of our attractive society.

"Which way is the rabbit-hole?" I said.

"The directions for you are a bit more complicated than they were for Alicia," Ben said.

"Get to the point, Ben, please," Alicia said.

"That I won't do. It's not time for that yet. It's just time to glance at my pocket watch and lead my friend here in circles to a bottle that says drink me."

"Christ," Alicia said, "stop being coy. I hate coyness."

"She's right, Ben. I don't want to be toyed with. What's this all about? What've you found out about the surgery? What—"

"Give me time. Okay, the operations. They can be performed. I've contacted the right people, those who can do them and—"

"I thought *you* would be—"

"The easy part, maybe, but I'd rather leave such things as brain-drilling to someone more qualified."

"And where do you find—"

"Among my colleagues, my suicidal project colleagues. I'll explain, just let me be more organized. If a brain operation's necessary, we'll go in with a microsurgical laser drill. It can do the job in your head. Maybe. The surgeon drills in and, through the use of miniaturized devices at the tip of the drill, is able to manipulate within the brain as if the devices were microscopic hands—or, better, microscopic hands of a surgeon. And they're guided by a genuine brain surgeon. Okay? As he watches on magnifiying screens, he uses the drill hands to replace, reconnect, whatever's necessary. That's a simplified view of the way the whole thing works, but I wanted you to know what it involved right off."

Ben's voice caught on a couple of words. Nervousness. It wasn't like Ben to be nervous. Alicia sat beside me, put a hand on my arm.

"Okay," Ben said, "what you should know. When you first came back to Earth, you silly bastard, you asked me how I had had the gall to allow myself to be passed on to a new body. At the time I handed you a gobbledygook excuse. I could not have coped with all the hardheadedness that's always been your response to whatever you didn't sufficiently understand."

He shifted uneasily in his chair.

"I had also fed you a number of lies in Cleveland, right after your retreading. Voss, even at that time I was one of the doctors working on sabotaging."

"You, Ben? You mean you could have—"

"Don't look at me like that. No, I didn't do the job on you. I wasn't skilled enough for that. Your doc was some sort of genius."

I did not appreciate Ben's obvious admiration of my saboteur.

"When I got to my own approaching demise, I asked to revoke my retreading agreement—to suicide, as it is in the vernacular. Knowing I had so little time left, I worked even more furiously with the underground, medically and in other kinds of missions where an enfeebled senior citizen was not a handicap. I came to be relied on within the resistance for certain key decisions. In some way I did not like to perceive I had become part of the hierarchy, a factor that made me all the more happy I was shedding the old mortal coils. So when I was ordered to retread and found I couldn't argue myself out of it, I was even a bit pissed off at being deprived of the treat of death."

"Ordered? How could anybody order you to—"

"Well, I'm gilding the lily in order to make my decision more logical. I was not exactly *ordered.* They told me I was too valuable to be allowed the luxury of death now. They needed me and, if there must be retreading, then they could be happy with the idea of sacrifice for a receptor like myself, who would then continue to dedicate himself to the cause. Subconsciously I may have wanted just such an excuse to go on, who knows? Anyway, the trade was better than even—I took one body, later would get rid of many. I enjoyed that part of the idea, too. So I revoked my revocation of retreading, took back my suicide. Nobody in governmental circles objected, since I was equally valuable to them, and I died and they gave me this quite functional young body. Using my government connections, I looked up the file on the reject whose body I'd inherited, a pleasant young man apparently adjusted to his fate. He opted for an insurance agreement and spent the last year and a half of his life as a world traveler in one of those luxury shuttles, the kind equipped with all the entertainment features."

He took a sip of his drink. Until that moment he had just held the glass as if unaware of it.

"After my renewal period, my old rebel friends contacted me. They had big plans for me, they said. No more sabotaging, the vogue was on its way out. It hadn't accomplished much in the long run."

I grunted. Ben smiled.

"A damn lot of inconvenience, to be sure, but little else. I was now to be in the forefront of a larger-scaled assault upon society. At first it was just sitting on committees, injecting an occasional dose of lovable reason into the more obviously asinine of their plans."

Ben's fingers kept wiping moisture away from the sides of his glass.

"Then an old friend, one from your father's time, Voss,

contacted me. He plopped himself down on an easy chair as if it had not been over a century since we'd last talked, and told me how valuable I was to be to the government. To the government! Somehow my underground activities had passed unnoticed officially. All my friend wanted to tell me about were my achievements, my abilities, my scores on all the new tests I had taken for recertification in my profession. Ironically the bulk of my new knowledge came from my subversive medical work. My rebel connections were, of course, delighted, saw it as a chance for them to obtain information useful to them. A comic situation, in some respects."

"But still dangerous, Ben," I said.

"So what's a little danger when you're on your third charmed life?"

"I'd be pleased with a little more danger in *my* life," Alicia said.

"But they could be on to you. Ben. Keeping watch over—"

"It wouldn't make much difference. Still, you might be right. Okay, say somebody's got his back up, and you knew it. What'd you do?"

"I suppose, try to find out where the trouble lies and deal with it."

"Reckless behavior, typical of you. Voss, this ain't some second-rate tyranny, some open dictatorship where you can be sure who your targets should be. We have thousands of people to deal with, thousands of monster-bureaucrats struggling for power, angling for more advantage, copping whatever they can for more undeserved luxury. There's not one single individual you could remove that would in any way change the basic situation. We're run by tiny little people whose main ambition is to climb as high as possible, then be retreaded and climb again and who knows what unless you're in the middle of it. They're Lilliputians who're holding the mass of the rest of us down with millions of tiny little ropes attached to tiny little pegs. They can hide in our hair, trim our moustaches, explore our nostrils, it makes no difference, we can't even swat at them. There's nothing we can do. Nothing. Do you have any trouble with that concept? It's nothing. We could attack en masse, slice about us left and right with our sharpened sabers, let off nuclear warhead bombs from our cannons, step among their dead bodies and try to fend off the next wave, and the next, and the next. They have found that power is quite adequate in small bite-size chunks, they want to keep their chunks. No matter what ingenious form of rebellion—sabotage, murder, bureaucratic inflíltrations, general terrorism—no matter what you try, retreading continues. Sure, it's hampered a bit, periods of darkness lengthen, but that's about it. A few individuals are eliminated, we cut off the excesses of someone like your buddy Pierre, but killing them on a one-by-one basis is just stepping on an occasional bug while the rest sit smug in cracks of the sidewalk. But, God, I can no longer be just *satisfied* with small victories. If that's all there is, sometimes I think I'd rather quit, devote myself to useless activity."

"I can't imagine you lounging around a beach, Ben," I said.

"Can't you? Beaches are fake today. I could be."

"That one's too much for me," Alicia said. "Your ice is melted. Want me to refresh your drink?"

"No, it's got a nice mellowness to it now."

"I suspect that's you and not the drink. I agree with you, Ben, about the uselessness, but what *can* we do?"

"Wish I knew. There's one thing we could try. It's an idea that's kept me going for months, and it's also where you come in, Voss."

"You want me to, what is it, do something for your cause?"

"You could say that. I have a bargain, might be better to call it a pact. A Faust-Mephistopheles pact. You need a service I can deliver, I can use your abilities. It's a deal I'm not sure I'd take if I were in your position."

Wanting that statement to register, Ben lapsed into silence. Alicia sighed, said:

"This reminds me of a wrestling match, man-alien, I saw years ago on some kind of three-dimensional TV. The alien seemed to be made of gelatin and the man, as you may imagine, had some trouble grabbing him. And the alien couldn't figure what to do with the man. What you two are doing is the same kind of sparring, moving for position, grabbing at parts you can't hold."

"It's necessary," Ben said. "Especially with someone as slippery as Voss. How did that match come out, I vaguely remember it."

"I don't know. The man won, I think. Maybe he ate the alien. Anybody hungry?"

"Not me. Not after that story."

"Voss?"

"No, thanks, Alicia."

"I'm starved. You two go on. I'll listen from the kitchen."

In the cubbyhole kitchen she rattled some packages, but Ben remained silent. I did not know what to say. Alicia said:

"I'm not hearing anything."

It was up to me to break the silence.

"Okay, Ben, the pact. What's it all about?"

He shifted in his seat. I had never seen him so reticent.

"Okay, the pact. You want that operation badly, right?"

"Yes."

"Badly enough to do something for me?"

"What?"

"A mission, one that might even do the kind of important damage I've been looking for, better than our usual hit-and-miss tactics."

"What makes me so important to you? Why can't one of your trained terrorists do it?"

He leaned forward, lowered the volume of his voice. Alicia came out of the kitchen to listen. She held a box of sea crackers in her hand, nibbled at one.

"My plan," he said, "derives from an odd set of circumstances that've come about because of my dual capacity as government employee and spy for the rejects. See, I happened to be told, as a friend of yours I suppose, that the government has some plans for you. Or one of its agencies, at least."

"Agency? Which agency?"

"It's called Public Liaison, just a form of publicity or public relations department. It's part of the overall administration of retread chambers. The Public Liaison goal is to enhance the concept of retreading at all levels. They try to make retreading acceptable to rejects, they disseminate information about new developments within the retread chambers."

"Then—" Alicia said and stopped talking suddenly.

"Then what?" I said.

"Nothing," she said. "Go on, Ben."

They exchanged smiles, so smugly I could have choked them together.

"Public Liaison," Ben said. "Typical PR agency, no matter how you slice it. And they're interested in you."

"Why on earth would they be interested in me?"

"You keep forgetting you're a celebrity of sorts. There's been a certain romance about the write-ups that reporter did on you. It's appealing in this day and age, where genuine heroes are rare and heroic tactics are being used primarily by terrorists. One of Public Liaison's jobs is to devise ways to connect celebrites with the retread chambers in publicity releases and on the media, that sort of thing. You're to be the star attraction of their next publicity tour."

"Star attraction? That's pretty far-fetched, even if those articles—"

"They had more impact than you imagine. In reject circles they made you a prime target until I put the stopper on that particular—"

"You? You stopped them from—"

"I did. They would've killed you for sure. Third attempt or thirteenth, they're persistent. You've seen Triplett."

I nodded, agreeing.

"Okay, the junket," Ben said. "According to my sources, they'll be contacting you in the next few days. You'll accept, of course."

"Ben, I don't want to make a tour of a charnel house. I don't want to see how they operate, don't want to see one up close."

"That may be, but accepting the invitation is a part of our pact."

"Why in hell do you want me to go on a tour that's nothing but a booster for what you're against?"

Ben laughed. A short, abrupt laugh that contained as much malice as amusement.

"If things work out my way," he said, "there's no amount of PR advantage that will make up for the results of this junket. And this is where the pact comes in, Voss. You perform the mission I haven't told you about yet, I'll see that you get your body worked on and maybe you two can find your happiness in the proverbial better society, if the mission creates the chain of events I expect."

Alicia picked up a cushion and arranged it next to Ben's chair. She sat down on it and looked up at him, excitement in her eyes.

"This is getting intriguing," she said. "Not just for your mysterious hints, but because I'm to be part of this mission, aren't I?"

Ben smiled.

"As it's turned out, your position is advantageous."

"Come on," I said. "What's going on here? You son of a bitch, one minute you're talking about my happy future with Alicia so long as I go on some two-bit mission that you seem to find so orgiastic—the next minute, I find Alicia's part of the setup. Well, damn it, I won't buy that part of it!"

Alicia turned toward me, angry.

"Try and keep me out of it!" she said.

"I will!"

"It's necessary, Voss," Ben said. "Alicia won't be in appreciable danger, she—"

"*Appreciable* danger? What's that? Just a little bit of danger, a tiny iota, a bullet or two, nothing to worry—"

"God damn it, Voss," Alicia said. "Listen to him, I have to be—"

"No! If I do this goddamned mission, it's for you, it's not to—"

"Forget it! You want me waiting anxiously for you, the goddamned hero, to return. Maybe I should dress in white, wear a lace shawl. I'm not going to back out of this just for you, just for your—"

"You may have to, my darling. I may make that part of the—of what Ben so felicitously calls *the pact.*"

"You bastard! Look, I'll be part of this mission or whatever it is because I *have* to be. Not only that, I *want* to be. It's an important part of my life. What's your life, your connection with all this, your value? You're a mercenary, that's all, a hired gun who happens to have the abilities to–"

"All right, that's enough!" Ben said. "You two squabble on your own time. Okay. Alicia's going to be part of it and, if you want to put it in these terms, that's part of the pact also."

"Faust had it easier. Not so many clauses."

"True. Just listen. We have to use Alicia. She's the only person from our immediate operation whom we've been able to use to infiltrate the administrative staff of a retread chamber."

Alicia nodded, said:

"That's how I knew right away I was included. Thanks, Ben."

"I don't get it," I said. "I thought you worked with some social agency, dealt with St. Ethel Camp rejects and other–"

"That's true, darling. But, like Ben, I've managed a dual identity. Never suspected *that,* did you? See, at the charnel house I have a separate identity. Very difficult to arrange, even these days when it's so difficult to keep track of people. And, my darling, my job there is as an agent of, get this, the Public Liaison Department. A pretty colleague of mine is busy these days arranging your tour, although she hasn't told me that you're invited yet, the bitch. How do you like them apples?"

"Not much."

"Didn't think you would. You're going to be hell to work with, you know that?"

"Hold on. I haven't agreed–"

"We realize that, Voss," Ben said. "Okay, the junket. According to my information, Stacy will also be invited on the tour. He–"

"Stacy, too. That's too–"

"Take it easy. Stacy's been part of the write-ups too, remember, though not the star attraction of course. But they want him. The trip is set for the Washington, D.C., retread chamber. It's the one they most want to show off. More advances and refinements in retreading are made there. Also, more important people–government types, artists, scientists, you-name-it–are stored in the recesses of the Washington retread chamber than any other one on the American continent. So it has that mystique of prestige about it, too. In a way that's what pleases me about its becoming our target, that it has that pres—"

"Wait. You said target. Target for what? If you think three of us can go in there and destroy the place, then you're out of your—"

"No, it's not that. We found out a long time ago there's no way we can smuggle explosives or weapons or any destructive material into a retread chamber. If you could get a bomb near one, which is impossible, it'd hardly make a dent since the place is constructed of materials a high-grade bomb could hardly dent. All the controls on nuclear materials make it impossible to get ahold of a worthwhile bomb these days. We've tried. So explosives and conventional weaponry are out. They'd be detected by security people at the outer entrance or any of the many checkpoints inside the facility. You can't even carry a gun in."

"I can't even steal one from inside," Alicia said. "I've checked that out. It'd be too risky if I tried."

"Agreed. You gave to go in without weapons."

"If I didn't know you better, Ben," I said, "I'd think you were setting me up for a deathtrap."

"Don't discount that possibility. I think this'll work but am painfully aware it might not."

"That certainly gives me confidence."

"I understand. Okay, because of the security we can smuggle nothing that's detectable into a retread chamber."

"Check. What do you have, something microscopic?"

"Good guess. The material I want you and Stacy to carry can be made part of your clothes, disguised as buttons, inner lining sewing, that sort of thing. It can be made to appear clothlike or like harder substances, makes no difference."

"Material. Disguised. You're so damn mysterious, Ben. What material?"

"Well, it's a synthesis. I don't know much about it myself, it was developed in another sector of underground research. They haven't even foreseen the use of it. The synthetic material itself has been called micronium. It has a slang name, micro-dust. It's made partly of Earth elements—some potassium, I think, is part of it. But the key ingredient is an element that goes by the name of Sheibel-43. The element comes from the planet Sheibel, named after its founder, I believe. When certain of its properties were discovered, it was decided to forbid its importation back to Earth. I came across a mention of it in an unknown report back in my previous lifetime, was able to put through a suggestion that we get some of it, although at that time I had different plans for it. You see, it had been discovered, probably when someone with an open cut handled it, that it dissolved human blood. Its original victim probably just got a few drops of the stuff upon his or her cut and was completely out of blood in an hour. Anyway, on Sheibel it worked that fast."

"Sounds like some kind of alien vampire."

"In a way. Originally no one saw any value to the substance, and it was written off as an undesirable element of a soon-to-be-abandoned planet. I thought its blood-dissolving action might be of some use in a sabotaging technique, especially if it could be placed in the body in some kind of time-release capsule."

"That's a vicious idea, Ben."

"Perhaps, Voss. The death would've been painless."

"That excuses it, of course."

"Stop sneering and listen. Okay, as it turned out I died before any Sheibel-43 was smuggled back to Earth. By the time I was retreaded, both underground scientists and government labs were doing some research on it. It's been used in a limited way in assassination attempts but has been less effective in Earth atmospheric conditions and just doesn't have the same destructive properties here. Dissolves some blood, lowers red corpuscle count, but doesn't kill. It displayed some side-effects on nutrients in the blood but nothing apparently useful to us. Couple people died, but their deaths were no good to us since the bodies were left retreadable. So Sheibel-43 has remained in the experimental stage for some time. Well, I got some ideas about it and set up a couple of labs working separately, experimenting with various compounds utilizing Sheibel-43. One of the labs came up with micro-dust, and tested the substance on some animal brains. My data indicate the miconium has a devastating effect when fed directly into the brain. In effect, it slowly and gradually burns the brain out. Methodically destroys cell after cell until there is nothing but dead tissue left, deprives it of oxygen and nourishment, does so many destructive things that, once it enters the brain, it is extremely difficult to reverse its corrosive attack. Our study of its effect on animal brains made me speculate on its possibilities."

"What possibilities?"

"I'll get to them. But first I want you oriented on the mission itself. Alicia's job, part of it, will be to arrange some sort of diversion that will allow you and Stacy to separate from the tour group. Perhaps we can arrange a power failure, throw an area into darkness. We've infiltrated a few people at the technician level, so it's possible. Whatever, Alicia will slip you and Stacy retread chamber clothing so that you'll appear to be part of the staff, and you'll be able to proceed on the mission."

"Won't they miss us back at the tour?"

"Of course they will. Later you'll claim to have wandered off."

"Oh, sure. That's a bloody likely story. Better refine that part of the plan, Ben."

"I'll leave it to you. After separating from the tour, you will make your way to the main storage and sustenance area in the depths of the chamber. Your objective'll be—"

"Wait a minute. I know something about retread chambers. They're labyrinthine. They are also well protected, populous, and filled with security checkpoints. How the hell do you expect us to get anywhere? We'll only get a few feet and—"

"Easier than you think, Voss. During the mission you'll know every inch of the Washington chamber, where everything is located, all the circuits and the—"

"Hold on. How? I realize I'm exceedingly able, even intelligent, but that's—"

"Very easy, as a matter of fact. You'll make use of the absorbing process. You know something about it."

It took a moment for me to remember.

"Oh, yes. You were doing that, absorbing, that first day I saw you at your office, and I've read about it. Absorbing information, right?"

"Exactly. Anything you need to know, especially on a temporary basis, can be imprinted on your mind in precise detail. Before the tour, I can—with the use of the absorber—feed you everything you need to know about the Washington chamber."

"But those places are protected, the plans'd be secret."

"Not so secret, actually, if you have the proper connections. Through my friends in government I've obtained *all* the available plans, layouts, details of procedure. Almost everything you'll need. And Alicia's been able to supply certain other information, the kind of details that aren't necessarily contained in files and documents."

"At Public Liaison," Alicia said, "we can always find excuses to ask questions."

"I noticed you said *almost* everything," I said.

Ben smiled.

"There're always potential obstacles, questions we forgot to ask, documents we didn't know about. But you and Stacy'll know every inch of the place. Look, right near the objective there's an especially difficult laser protection system. It was set up long ago because of budget considerations, when a manpower survey showed too many guards stationed around the soul-storage area. Now they have a number of beams that seem to switch randomly so that only someone with the proper key to shut them off temporarily can get through the barrier. As far as we can tell, there's no way we can cop a key for you without it being missed. But, because of the absorber, you won't need a key. That's the beauty of it. You and Stacy'll know exactly how the laser beam pattern works. One look and you'll know what stage of the programmed pattern the setup has reached. Then you can easily avoid the beams."

"Easily?"

"Well, at least you'll have the information allowing passage. The absorber will provide details about all the security devices, all the working schedules, all the details about retreading that apply to the mission's objective. You two will go in knowing more about what goes on in that retread chamber than any single employee or executive of the place. Whatever information we may have missed will presumably be detectable because the information you possess will give you points of orientation from which to make on-the-spot decisions. Another reason, by the way, why we need you and Stacy."

"Because we're so super at on-the-spot decisions."

"Exactly. That's why we have no one else for the mission, why we have to take this opportunity. Not many people like you two in the movement, frankly. Most of us'd freeze up at the first snafu, the first detail that didn't fit with the master plan. You and Stacy won't. Something is off, you'll find a way around it."

"You make it sound like a war mission."

"And this's a war where few people on either side have the instincts of a soldier. You do, you and Stacy, that's all I'm saying."

"Soldiers are fodder, automatons sent over the rim of trenches to function as targets. Not much *instinct* in that."

"Well, don't think of yourself as a soldier then, just—"

"No, I'm a soldier, have been for the last fourteen years. I just don't like it. If I agree to do this mission for you, it is the *only* mission I will ever do for you."

Ben nodded, said:

"This is strictly a business deal. You do your job, I'll do mine. Mephistopheles always pays off, no matter what kind of double-cross Faust tries to pull. That's why Mephistopheles is the good guy. Okay, we've got you past all the barriers, into the main storage rooms at the deepest point of the retread chamber. This, of course, is where the *souls,* as they so delightfully call them, are kept. How much do you know about how retreading is done within the chamber?"

"Damn little."

"I'm not especially well versed on the subject either, few of us are. They don't want us to know, of course. The less we know about retreading and how it's accomplished, the more protection they have. But security's not one hundred percent. Only technicians, certain surgeons, the combination of both they call mechsurgeons (mekdoks, sometimes)—only they have anything like considerable knowledge of the process. Sufficient security leakage has occurred to allow us to accumulate some information over the years. Bits and pieces have combined into some sense."

He took the last sip of his drink, shook the glass in a circular motion to see it was really empty. Alicia interpreted this gesture as a wish for a refill and took the glass out of his hand. He muttered thanks. She held the glass toward me, a signal to ask if I'd like one. I nodded yes.

"The hardest part about retreading to accept," Ben said, "has always been the idea that there *is* something like a soul within us. My God, the theological arguments I've heard about that one since I was a pup. Or since you were a pup, really, since I was already grownup when the development of retreading was announced, mysteriously and cautiously. Even then the party line was that the soul of an individual which was extracted during retreading process was definitely not the soul so hallowed in religions. But who could believe that? For that matter, I doubt they wanted anybody to believe it. The disclaimer was just to protect their scientific asses. Why else introduce the word soul into it at all? Sure, they wanted everybody to believe it was *exactly* that kind of soul. Christianity has always been a solid ally of the retreaders. So, the great news spread through organized religions, not to mention the thousands of disorganized ones. The *soul* had been discovered! It actually existed! Terrific. Well, you were around for the lustiest times of religious revival."

"I have some vague memories. Mainly of an aunt who was thrilled by the idea that she could consecrate her soul to God over and over and over, *ad infinitum.* Only trouble with this aunt, she never qualified for retreading. Then she became bitter, godless even."

Alicia took a couple of steps into the room.

"I like hearing ugly stories about people's ancestors," she said.

"Anyway," Ben said, "even when the religious crap subsided, the belief about the soul remained in something of an undertone. Naturally, we who were intelligent enough to qualify for retreading tended not to believe in a literal soul. Still, the idea of the soul was a big help in distracting our attention from the business of the retread chamber. Kept the retreaders' little enclave enclosed, their little pocket of knowledge to themselves. The more knowledge is spread, the more danger to it can grow. When people like me get ahold of some useful knowledge, look at the disasters we can bring about."

Alicia brought us drinks. Pulling a chair across the room, she placed it near me, sat. Behind her the window-view was sunny. Alicia's eyes seemed dark, moody, as if no sun could illuminate them.

"So okay, back to the *souls,"* Ben said. "What it is they extract from us and call soul is the focus of great controversy. Maybe there is cell matter, as some people believe so firmly, that in some way contains that essence of ourselves that we so fondly call soul. If we can have genetic blueprints there, then why not souls? There always seemed to be something the genetic studies missed, something that all the impersonal theories about DNA and RNA left out. So all our genetic abilities were clinging to that old DNA helix, so all right. We just couldn't be accretions of matter motivated by essentially unmysterious forces. There had to be *something* supernal, something beyond the pale, something to explain the life-force we all felt inside us. The idea it could be extracted through a new secret process was at first incredible, but of course we had to believe it. Then further credence was given the belief in soul extraction as the source of retreading when we were informed that the soul, or whatever, was transferred from us to a new body by being extracted from the brain, which was preserved during the period of darkness. Of course! From our mind, where the soul *had* to be! I know it's all absurd when we talk of it like this, but it is the way retreading works. When the force was isolated by Bandiello and his research team—who were, incidentally, actually studying the possibility of astral projection as part of the parapsychology research at Duke University—they thought they had something else, actually interpreted it as some sort of ectoplasmic nonsense that fit what they were looking for. But others intervened and immediately saw the possibility of being able to capture the soul. Think of that for a moment, a bunch of scientists and logicians scampering around looking for the bell jar that would contain the ethereal! Anyway, over years of experimentation, they developed the series of processes that led to retreading. Many human beings died as part of many pilot projects, but the devices to remove the soul were finally developed and retreading became possible. The means to it came, I understand, when they discovered that the astral-soul, as they were calling it at that time, actually could not survive outside the body for a long time. Then came the concept that the brain of an individual, from which the astral-soul emerged, could be maintained for indefinite periods. The first retreadings, you see, were performed only at the moment of the original subject's death, when the body, though dead clinically, was still functioning. Quite a game at that time. Somebody's brain failed, its soul was rapidly scoured out, the receptor-body was hooked up to the man whose body was dying, all the connections were made, and, zap, the dying man found his consciousness again in the new, and fit, body. All very miraculous, all very mysterious. After they discovered how to comfortably preserve the dying man's brain until the new brain was ready, it wasn't too much longer until the idea of recruiting bodies to accept the preserved centers of consciousness occurred to some genius in one of the early retread chambers, though they weren't called that then because the words retread and reject had not yet crept into our marvelously flexible language."

"You said recruited," Alicia said. "I didn't know anything about that."

"Well, it was in the old days and the custom didn't last long. But it's the source of all the insurance plans you do know about nowadays. See, it turned out there were people around at that time with perfectly normal bodies who no longer cared to live out their despairing existences. Psychologists and psychiatrists, who for so many decades had operated with the idea that suicide prevention was a worthy ideal, suddenly had the convenient insight that perhaps people who had been brought so low that they could not be prevented from killing themselves should be spared all the pain and bodily mutilation that generally accompanied the act. Secretly, and with some interest in the psychological factors of retreading, they began working with the scientists and technicians of the retread centers, providing the bodies of desperate people who, either for reasons of their own or for considerations provided by the retreaders, agreed to die by donating their bodies to the retreaders. So—"

"Ben," Alicia asked, "what do you mean by considerations?"

"That's the primitive form of the insurance. A lot of what drove people to suicide was basically financial. They had families or people they loved whom they could not provide for, or for whom they wanted better lives. The retreaders offered generous financial rewards to the beneficiaries of the suicide. Any deal seemed suitable if a body could be obtained out of it. Of course, suicides with physical defects were not treated as generously as those in good condition, but that, after all, was business. The researchers no doubt had breeding for beauty in the backs of their minds as a desirable subsidiary goal. Those suicides without beneficiaries were convinced to allow money to be donated to some cause, often a cause that supplied money for the further research necessary for retreading. Quite a neat trick on the part of our financially conscious pioneers. I mean, there was a lot of grant money floating around but, since they were for the time being keeping their project relatively secret, they had to perform some excruciating documentary maneuverings to obtain it. Nevertheless, despite all the difficulties, a number of bodies came their way. Loads of proof piled up that people could, after all, be retreaded. Psychological effects were minimal, mostly positive. I mean, it was strange to be in a new body, but it was pretty good, too, right? No physical aftereffects. Everything was hunky-dory. There definitely were souls, and they could be manipulated by men. They were no harder to manipulate or direct than microwaves. Easier, actually. A jump in evolution!"

"God," Alicia said, "it's revolting. How could intelligent men do it? How could they think like that? How could—"

"Now wait a minute, my dear, don't let hindsight obscure the wonder of the discovery. Those men were extremely optimistic.

Think of it, they had passed beyond the boundary of genetic manipulation, of bodily healing, of psychological adaptation. All of the sunny theories they applied to retreading at that time would amaze you. It was glorious to those men working on the project. Realize, Alicia, people like that usually don't see beyond the borders of their working areas. Voss here can give you some insights into that style of thinking, from his first life. Right, Voss?"

"True. There were times when the thought of leaving the enclave actually terrified me."

"The developers of retreading," Ben continued, "never foresaw the uses to which it would be put, or that it would become the basis for a whole social system. If they had remained gleefully working at their centers, giving new life to a few selected people, taking hated life away from others—and all in isolation—they might have been able to provide a useful little service to humanity, in the optimistic parameters they had formulated. The trouble was, they were afflicted with generosity. And, I suppose, retreading was the kind of secret you could never keep. How, for instance, could you prevent the new retreads from praising the miracle-workers who'd given them years of additional life? Too many complications, you see. The optimists in the retread centers wanted to present the gift of retreading to the public. A few farsighted types foresaw consequences, but the good guys believed those speculations to be absurd and dismally futurological. *Wise* use of retreading would be magnificent, they thought. The doomsayers just enjoyed exploring the worst of possibilities. Look at transplants, they said. The transplant concept went through some negative times, but now it was a routine procedure. (There was little trouble about transplants then, you see.) So retreading, they decided, should be presented to the public. They didn't realize it was just too good for people."

"Too *good!*" Alicia said. "Now, Ben, that's—"

"Okay, maybe I was being pompous. But you have to understand—I, too, believe that retreading could've been marvelous. The idea of preserving certain people, those whose presence among us improves and enlightens us, is acceptable to me. If there were any possible sensible way of controlling it. Even the providing of bodies—if it were accomplished through willing suicides—is not repulsive. But the fact is, we are not retreading our gods and the bodies are shanghaied, and perhaps there never was an idealistic way of achieving immortality. Maybe all immortality concepts are doomed because they involve the immortality of people, and not gods. Who knows? It's just another subject for debate from the days of my youth. In reality we have to try to destroy it. When the early developers of retreading, the followers of Bandiello and Emont, generously presented the gift of immortality to the world—at that moment, the corruption began. Instead of retreading the occasional great man or woman, the powerful people just wanted to retread the elite. The elite, as discovered through such inhuman devices as standardized intelligence tests and manipulated achievement ratings. It was the old genetic engineering shit all over again. Improve the race, breed only for those genes that met public approval. Eliminate all unsocial characteristics. Damn, there were so many people gleefully working away at scientific fascism in those days. Before retreading, we had the genetic engineers. Before the genetic engineers, we had the behavior modificationists. Before them we had, I don't know, Nazis and evangelists. Always the improvement of the race, no matter who claimed the need for it—it was the excuse for the perpetuation of oneself. All of these theories, workable and seemingly ideal though some of them may have been in their purest states, helped to create the social mood for the introduction of retreading. It came to the people as a kind of miracle. Since the early methods of separating the potential retread from the potential reject were so insidious, and so prepared for through astute use of the media of the times, there was not even much complaint from the people at large, so few of whom were among the early rejects anyway. The process of increasing the reject-supply necessarily took time and, by the time more of the population was necessary as shells for the new immortals, an aura of magic had accrued to the project so that those who were not necessarily enthusiastic about heading for the charnel house had no way of circumventing it. Oh, they could be strident, they could try to escape, they could kick at their captors' legs, but they were brought to the chambers. Gradually more and more of the 'elite' were retreaded. Since powerful people fancied themselves as elite, no matter what their intelligence or contributions to society, the tests and requirements were rigged further. And, well, you know the rest. Somehow we have fewer godlike types to retread—general contributions to the welfare of mankind, you may have noticed, have diminished considerably since retreading's introduction—and there are more and more retreads. There is no elite, there're only greedy immortals. We wanted the continuations of Albert Einsteins and Salvatore Bandiellos, Shelleys and Rembrandts—what we got were thousands and millions of Pierre Madlings and Ben Blountes and—"

"And Vossilyev Geraghtys," I said.

"I suppose," Ben said. "Although there are times when I think I detect a molecule of authentic worth in you. What time is it, Alicia?"

She checked a clock on a nearby table.

"Almost three."

"God, I've got an appointment at three. Well, they can wait. I've made them wait before. Okay, the mission. You and Stacy work your way down to the center of the retread chamber storage area. In this massive room—room, hell, it's an underground cave half as large as Manhattan Island—are stored the brains of future retreads, all in their various periods of darkness. Some say that the whole brain needn't be preserved, a smaller area might nevertheless yield the soul. Still, the soul has always been extracted from the brain, so that's what's preserved. During the period of darkness, a nutrient flow is fed through the brain in order to keep it alive. Alive, but not actually functioning. Essentially, each brain is preserved in a near-cryogenic fashion. Not in the old-fashioned method of freezing—no, the new process would be better described as numbing. That's why the feeding remains necessary. The liquid in which each brain floats keeps it perfectly preserved in the numbed state while feeding and caring for it. The brain itself, the actual physical lump of matter that we call the brain, is primarily the housing for the soul. By keeping the brain alive, the nutrient flow preserves the soul also. When the time of revival comes, the liquid is the conductor through which the psychic matter of the soul is so mysteriously extracted. I don't really know how it's done. I can only make the microwave analogy. Even then, to me it is just as mysterious as the early theories of Tesla and Lodge must've been to their peers. I just know that when the retreading devices are attached to the container holding the brain at one end and the new body at the other end, the so-called soul is passed out of the original brain and into the brain of the new body (which has, of course, already had its soul extracted and disposed of). At this point science, to me, becomes magic, especially since we've been unable to obtain certain significant details of the retreading technology. I don't know, perhaps magic *is* what it is. I do know that some cells from certain parts of the original brain are medically implanted within the new brain *before* the actual magical transmission of soul, but've never been able to figure out how they blend in with cells of different genetic makeup. In some way, the cell transference makes the soul's adaptation to the new body possible. After the transmission, a team of technicians, surgeons, and mekdoks works furiously on the new body, and doesn't stop until the body and brain are clearly functioning in concert. Then the new retread is born, or reborn, or whatever the hell it is. That's about as much as I can tell you. You don't even need to know it. But I want your awareness so you can see the sense of your goal, especially since your real problems begin when you've reached that storage cavern. That's where you could lose out, and there's no way I can assure you that you'll succeed, it's the area of greatest risk."

"What exactly are we to do when we reach this goal? For that matter, what's the goal?"

Ben held his glass against the side of his leg, twisted it to the left a half-turn, then to the right, as if he were trying to bore a hole through his skin with it. Then he stared at me and leaned forward.

"That's the hardest part. The conducting and nutrient-flow liquid is circulated among the brain-storage containers by a vast network of intricate tubes and piping. It seems that it must circulate in order to be effective. All a neat setup really, little waste. Additional nutrients and other substances are fed into the network through conduits. As you'd suspect, all this material functions much like blood flowing through our bodies, even though its composition differs somewhat, and the cavern itself is like a vast underground body. Theoretically, the efficiency of this network can be affected by the introduction into it of a neutralizing or poisonous agent, just as we can be harmed or killed by the injection of similar agents into our bloodstream."

He paused, started to take a sip of his drink, then seemed to think better of the idea. He put the glass down on a nearby table.

"There are numerous checkpoints along the network where technicians can make tests to determine whether the composition of the liquid is being maintained properly or whether some adjustment should be made. Very rarely does anything have to be done, a point in our favor, but the checks have been made for centuries and still go on. The absorber-imprinting given you and Stacy will let you know the location of these checkpoints. You will go to certain selected ones and, in the disguise of technicians, introduce small doses of the micronium substance into the outlet."

"I don't quite—"

"The substance, which you remove as buttons, lining threads, and decoration of both the clothing you wear into the chamber and the labcoats which Alicia will supply you, is easily pressed into powder with the firm pressure of your fingers. Very small amounts of it are necessary for each outlet in your mission. Not only that, once in the conducting liquid it divides and grows, In a very short time the substance will be conducted through much, perhaps all, of the network. With any luck, it will be introduced into each container where a brain is being kept living."

"And then what?"

"Are you naive, Voss, or just avoiding the obvious truth? All right, face it, it's exactly what you think. The introduction of the micro-dust will, in effect, neutralize the liquid, poisoning its nutrient flow and burning the goddamned soul out of the brain. There will be no retreading for these souls, in theory they will no longer exist. Because of the slow action of the micro-dust, its harm won't be detected right away. By the time the technicians realize what's happening, there'll be little they can do about it. It would be a miracle for them to come up with an antidote quickly to a substance they've never seen before, have no right to expect to find. Before they can make any technical changes, shut off parts of the network, or engage an alternate nutrient flow, anything to prevent the flow of the poison to other areas of the storage chamber, thousands, maybe millions, of brains will be affected. Thousands or millions of future retreadings will be prevented. With real luck, if they are as inefficient as I expect, we may wipe out the entire room, send an uncountable number of waiting retreads into the eternal period of darkness. With any luck—"

"Luck? God, Ben, you talk about this so—you're so—"

"Detached?"

"I wouldn't've chosen that mild a word."

"Come off it, Voss. You're the publicized hero, the soldier, you know what deaths in war are all about. Of course I'm detached. This is the best chance ever to strike back against the charnel houses. Think of it, we—"

"Ben, we're not talking about abstract deaths in a battle, statistics. This is genocide."

"Exactly the word I'd've used eventually."

"I'm just getting the impact of it," Alicia said. "Ben, it's brilliant. It'll set them back about—"

"Stop it! Alicia, it's inhuman."

"Retreading's inhuman."

"You say that with all the love of formulaic slogan of a revolutionary."

"Damn it, Voss, that's what I am. I want to be part of this. If I could, I'd go down to the depths and help you with the job."

"But the human lives—"

"*What* human lives, damn it, what human lives?"

In anger, Alicia's eyes glowed brightly. They would have seemed quite lovely if we had been talking on a less insane subject.

I let some time pass before speaking again:

"We're not talking here about occasional targets on an assassination mission, dead bodies in the street. You heard Ben, there are millions of people who may be killed by this, millions—"

"That's where you're wrong, Voss," Alicia said. "You keep thinking of them as people. Human lives. But they're not, don't you see. They are the remains of corpses that've long gone to dust. They've had their *lives,* some of them have had more than one life, you know that. It's not the same as murder or genocide. These—call them individuals if you like, anything but people or lives—all of them are waiting in their period of darkness for someone else to be *murdered* so they may inherit the bodies. Talk about murder and genocide! They're the murderers, each and every one of them. The genocide is not what *you* do to *them,* it's the annihilation of every reject who's been slaughtered so they may seize a paltry additional five or seven decades of life. It's not murder, Voss, there's no way you can make me see the elimination of a million individual murderers as some kind of philosophical mass murder."

"You don't understand, you—"

"Of course I understand. I'm just trying to make you see—"

"It's not even that. I—there's no—I can't—"

I stopped talking, could not find anything more to say. I could not even look at Ben or Alicia. When I finally did, I was astonished to see that no seething anger, no rebellious hostility showed in their faces. They looked at me with kindness, in what was probably sympathy. I felt that I was in a witness box, and the jury was on my side but was still going to vote against me.

"Voss," Ben said in a professional dutch-uncle manner, "I know what you're thinking. It's the same for me. It goes against all my beliefs, my medical ethics. I curse the fact that the word *soul* had come into vogue instead of a more sensible one like psyche or anima. But psyche or anima could not have carried the same emotional weight. They knew what they were doing, not encouraging such terms. There is no alternative to genocide, and I don't mind using that word for it. I *prefer* to think of the matter within those containers as people, as lives. I want to kill them. I don't want to think about the future lives, the possible contributions to humanity that might be produced by these extra-special retreads if I didn't snuff out their existence, I'd just be falling into the ideological traps that've justified retreading through the years. The few valuable retreads *must* be sacrificed in order to restore value to humanity as a whole. Not only value but hope and achievement. We have to do the best with the single lives allowed us—or, in the case of some of us, the last life allowed us. I know that I am, to a large degree, employing facile rhetorical tactics just to convince myself. Not you, Voss, but *myself.* But things tend to reduce themselves to insanely simple ideological propositions."

He laughed softly to himself.

"There's an old, I don't know what to call it, riddle or conundrum that could be adapted. If you were on a rowboat, or a falling starship, or an about-to-explode planet—and you had the power of salvation through the use of two buttons—and one would save only a small group of Einsteins and Beethovens and various saints and philosophers, all of whom were still producing some works and tasks of value—and the other button would save the entire rest of humanity, but destroy the Einsteins, Beethovens, saints and philosophers—which button would you push? Would you save the small number of people of worth, and hope to set up a future containing all the marvelous heredity, with all the descendants of the Einsteins, Beethovens, saints, and philosophers—a world that'd take centuries of subsequent generations before it came close to the level of your present-day population? Or would you press the button that'd merely free the rest of humanity, saving millions and billions more lives? And, for that matter (so that the example of Beethovens, et cetera, will not stand alone representing people of worth), saving millions of people and their descendants in whom the human potential is always there, with the result that there'd be just as much chance for great works and ideas coming from the mass of people you save with your button?"

"But neither answer is satisfactory."

"Not exactly, Voss, not exactly. Do you know which button you'd choose, Alicia?"

She clearly did not want to be asked. She rearranged items on a table next to Ben's chair. Finally she said:

"I guess I'd press the one saving millions, but I'm not sure why."

Ben nodded.

"Obviously it's the same one I'd press. See, Voss, it depends on your orientation, right? If you strive for objectivity or you're compassionate, then you're stumped by the riddle. What you really want to do is press both buttons, save *all* of humanity, Beethoven and the common mix. The dilemma, naturally, is that's a solution that the riddle does not allow. Remember, it is just as difficult for the cynic or the misanthrope, who doesn't want to press either button—that choice is not allowed either. No, you *must* press one or the other. Hold your hand above the buttons. Paralyzing, isn't it? Which? Which? The hand must come down, must depress one piece of rounded plastic. Crash, one group is saved."

Ben's half-smile was one of the more irritating smirks I had ever seen.

"Drop it, Ben," I said. "It's not the time for clever riddles, not after what you've asked of me, after what you've—"

"You may be right, but I have the compulsion to explain my choice, Voss. See, in my mind, twisted and deranged though it may be, I'd be making a definite mistake in saving the Einstein/Beethoven crowd. And the mistake is exactly the same benevolent one made by the early retreaders when they saw their new process as some kind of salvation for mankind, the preservation of its best traits, et cetera. They isolated the elite in just the same way as the presser of the special-group button would, set off the Beethovens and Einsteins for special treatment because of their achievements."

"Well, why in hell shouldn't they?"

"Because their achievements are accomplished. See, what I've done if I press that button instead of the one saving the millions and billions, is individualize members of the smaller group. Forget that I've given them ancient names, but think how I've put them into groups. Scholars, teachers, philosophers, artists, scientists—all of that. The presser of that button has elevated these members of the groups, the top echelon according to general judgment, into a special category worthy of salvation over the entire rest of the human race. Right?"

"Well, sure, but—"

"But nothing. It's exactly what I've done, it's exactly what the retreaders did in categorizing the human race. All the retreads are, in theory (and, for the riddle, we needn't consider practice), the top echelon. They are salvageable, by that view. The rest of the race is garbage. Don't choose their button, don't press it, let them blow up. Great, the top guys are saved, all that's best in the human race may be continued. Forget the dross that now lie in fragments of skin and bone about you. But okay, think of it my way for a second. Let me select the other button. Okay, what've I done? Blown up a few of the top echelon. Well, damn it, Voss, we are proud of their achievements, but, as I said, they—most of them anyway—are already accomplished. They deserve our praise, but the deeds are mostly past. How few are left to them in their individual futures? And who's to say what their descendants, because of their marvelous genes, are going to achieve? Or whether those achievements would somehow be better than those of the entire, and larger body, of the human race whom I'd prefer to save? No, Voss, there's more reason to believe that there is potential quantitatively in the lesser people whose lives are governed by the other button. Talk about mute Miltons, unheard Mozarts, whatever! Talk about rejects who, at 27 or 39 or 66, or whatever age that is now kept from them, might create music the equal of Beethoven's, or develop a theory the equal of Einstein's! They, or *their* descendants. Again, who's to say? Are you? Am I? Which one of us should be given the duty of pressing the button, how about that? Now look, Voss, I don't really want that either group should have to be killed. I'm like you in that respect. I've just as much compassion for humanity by pressing one button or the other. I just believe, for whatever warped logic you want to accuse me of, that we have to act for the so-called greater good. And, if that means disposing of a million or three million about-to-be-retreads in an act that just possibly might lead to the elimination of retreading, or would at least force into the consciousness of people like you that retreading must be stopped, then I think the 'death,' if you want to think of it as such, of the potential retreads who'd be destroyed in this mission is worth it."

Ben stood up, walked toward the window-view, examined the hoarfrost that was magically collecting around the edges of the window, looking like the real thing and not a reproduction. He placed a hand on a pane of glass tentatively, then drew it back as if he had really encountered winter coldness.

"Well, Voss," he said, "that's about it. The mission can be performed. You have the abilities to do it. Either you do it or you don't. The parameters are clear as far as the mission itself is concerned, but I can't give you any genuine reasons to do it. Not even the goddamned surgery. It may be your reward for doing the job, but it's not a reason to agree to the mission, and I think you know that."

Alicia reached toward me, touched my hand. I already knew she did not want me to have the operations only for her. I was no longer sure if I wanted them, their importance had faded in the last few minutes. Ben turned away from the window, looked at me as if making a diagnosis. I shifted in my chair, squirmed under the gazes of both of them. I felt dreamlike, my mind did not seem to be my own. I was back in the mist of Coolidge again, the light-creature was inside me. The pain was the same. I wondered if Alicia or Ben would be affected or impressed or frightened if I ran hysterically around the room, as I had emerged from the mist that day and chased Stacy around the forest. I tried to imagine what they would have thought if they had been there. I could not imagine it. I would not have wanted them there. In a way, I did not want them *here,* complicating my life. If only I had been able to maintain isolation, had managed to avoid both Ben and Alicia, I could have been just a spacer on leave, enjoying the offerings of the ports of Earth. But no, that could not have been, either. I would have had to watch Pierre Madling die, or someone like him, or someone. Why was that individualized death, that horrendous memory of Pierre's fading scream and the overhead view of his crumpled body and the mob crowding around it, so much more painful, so much more vivid, than this abstraction of murder that Ben proposed? He was talking about the philosophically arguable demise of a million, two million, more—souls, psyches, animas, life-forces, life principles. But not, somehow, *people.* When I tried to think of these millions of life-sustained brains in sterile containers surrounded by life-giving liquids, I could not see them as more than objects, just as Alicia said I should. The death of Pierre kept coming back to me instead. Of course I was only thinking *their* way, forcing myself to think that way so that I could more easily consider the mission. As I thought that, I was appalled that I was doing just exactly that, *considering the mission.* I might do the mission. I might sprinkle the magic micro-dust into various openings in a network of machinery. Be a murderous sandman bringing a restful sleep, a painless death, to the millions who, by Ben's involved reasoning, deserved to have the light of their souls snuffed out. When I realized that I could think of what Ben so coldly called "the mission," I knew there was a chance I could do it. A chance. I did not want to do it. But there was a chance. The air around me seemed oppressive, as if I had been placed in a mortuary in order to lend the correct mood and atmosphere to my decision-making process. I could die, that'd thwart Ben's convenient little plans. They could ship me to a retread chamber, maybe the Washington retread chamber (was that possible, was I enough of a celebrity to get special shipment there?) where I could become one of the cared-for brains that would be disposed of by whomever Ben finally did convince to go on his precious suicidal mission. The thought was comforting. I almost told it to Ben. Instead I said:

"I don't know, Ben."

He nodded, said:

"Reasonable. No reason to decide yet. The tour's not even set, won't probably come off for a month. So, I've told you, and I've got appointments for which I'm characteristically late. Okay, so you give it some thought. I'll be in touch. We can go to supper at my club." He started for the door. "And, hell, if you decide against it, and enough time passes, maybe I can still arrange that surgery for you. Ain't that a crock? See you."

He made an actor's kind of exit. For a long time after he had left, I seemed to feel him crouching in the wings.

12

"Well, what do I do now?"

"You could have some jasmine tea."

"Jasmine tea?"

"Only kind I've got here. But it's authentic. They've tended to avoid artful substitutions in the Orient. I can brew some."

"Not right now. What's wrong with this room?"

"Wrong how? The decoration, the—"

"The air. It's so close."

"Oh, that. Something's gone off in the air purification unit. Does it regularly. Some outside air's creeping in. I hear they're developing an adaptation-pack breathing device for Earth. You know, you must know, the kind that—why are you smiling?"

"Nothing. Just a memory. Are you wearing makeup or something?"

"No. Never do. Why do you say that?"

"Your eyes look different."

"They change color according to mood. They're probably greenish now."

"More gray actually."

"I never see them as gray. Other people do at times, but they never look gray to me. Stacy's eyes are gray all the time, have you noticed?"

"I think he planned it that way. Gray is the color for distance. He'll go on Ben's mission, he—"

"It's not *Ben's* mission. You make it sound like some kind of selfish power-play that he's using for—"

"I'm not sure that isn't what it is. I'm beginning to feel I don't know him, haven't known him for some time. Everybody around me's suddenly become about as comprehensible as Stacy, including you."

"Listen, you don't have to do this mission if you don't want to."

"Sure. I'll just leave and we've had a nice chat, all of us, a nice long chat, had a lot of fun kicking some hot topics around, but that's it. Ben'll just go on, you'll never mention it again, the—"

"I won't. I promise you that."

"And nothing will change. Everything will be the same as before."

"No, that I can't promise you. I couldn't under any circumstances."

"I'm probably going to do it."

"All right."

"Is that your absolute best response? All right?"

"I could say I love you, but it doesn't seem to fit right here. The air *is* terrible in here, now you mention it—let me check the unit."

"You swagger when you walk. I never noticed that before."

"And you can keep your observations to yourself."

"God damn it, Alicia!"

"I'm sorry—don't keep your observations to yourself then."

"Not what I mean. I mean we're sitting here, having just decided almost casually to destroy a half million, a million, three million souls, and we fuss about the staleness of the air or we make banal observations."

"What do you want?"

"I don't know. Just to—just to arrive at the decision through a number of logical stages, then to empower it with bursts of emotional energy. Not for me to say I think I'll do it and you to say all right."

"Can't help you there, darling. I'm glad you decided yes, I would have, what more can I say? I'm genuinely sorry you're suffering, I'd suffer, too. Moral issues are like toothaches."

"Why, pray, are they like toothaches?"

"I don't know. The image just occurred to me, that's all. Are you sure I can't get you something? Some tea or something? It'd give your hands something to do."

"Look at that. Look at how much it's shaking."

"Let me hold it. Of course you tremble. I would—"

"I know. You would, too."

"I would. I am."

"I'm not so sure of that."

"That's cruel."

"I think I'd better go."

"No. Stay."

"Stacy's waiting downstairs. He'd been there some time."

"So what? Send him away."

"I could try, but he probably won't go. He'll just go on watching. That sort of thing's become habit to him."

"You do use him terribly. Why does that make you laugh?"

"Nobody ever *uses* Stacy. No matter how it might look to you, he does exactly what he wants."

"Let him stand in the doorway there then, if that's exactly what he wants. I don't want you to leave yet."

"Well, maybe I can stay a little longer."

"That's good, then we can—oh, damn it to hell!"

"What's wrong?"

"Just realized how late it was. Ben said it was late, but it didn't penetrate. I've got an appointment."

"Break it."

"Can't. It's for my job, my real job, at the agency."

"I thought you were on leave."

"I am, but I promised to return to clear up this one case. It's very important."

"How important can it be?"

"Things work out right, it'll help a lot of people, a lot of rejects."

"And why's that—"

"Let's not fight over it. I have to go. I'm sorry, I don't want to. But I have to. I can't afford to miss the chance to achieve something with this meeting and, beyond that, I can't afford to blow my cover at the agency. I'm supposed to be on leave doing a goddamned study for the project that's the subject of this meeting, I'm not supposed to be moonlighting at the Washington retread chamber under another name."

"The chamber—I just realized, that's where you've been disappearing to so suddenly all those times."

"Not all the time, but often. It's a neat job because I have control over my hours. I've got to go back there tomorrow, so I guess we won't be seeing much of each other for the next few days."

"I'm sorry about that, I need—"

"Don't say it. I'm sorry, too. We're not going to be too much in control of our time for a while, either of us."

"Time's not going to be much of a problem for me. Aside from straightening out the flaws in Ben's plan, I can just sit on my ass until I get the official call, I don't—"

"Then you can anticipate your future—"

"I don't want to think too much about that, not about the mission."

"Think of beyond the mission, the surgery, your new—"

"I thought you said the surgery wasn't important."

"Yes. And that's true."

"Then why do you recommend my anticipating the results with fervor?"

"Well, all I said was that the surgery wasn't necessary, that it shouldn't be the goal for endangering your life. But I didn't say that, once it was over, I wouldn't like it."

"I'd better leave."
"Yes. But kiss me first. Goodbye, darling."
"If there weren't so—"
"Goodbye."
"Goodbye, Alicia."

PART V

1

Stacy guided me through a quite circuitous route in the first stages of our return to our quarters. When I brought up the subject of the mission, he refused to discuss it with me. All he would say was that if I was going to do it, he was going to do it.

It was a bright afternoon, with one of those intense doses of sun that even the weather-control people could not plan for. As we stopped at a corner because Stacy sensed a tracker and had to scan all four directions to check out the suspicion, I noticed a new gauntness in his face, a hollow in his cheeks that preserved shadow even against the intense sunlight. There was a gray cast to his skin that seemed to blend with, even absorb, the grayness of his eyes. His clothing, all green, seemed wrinkled in places that had previously been smooth due to a tight fit. I suggested we have a big meal somewhere, he said he wasn't hungry.

We returned to the rundown hotel that housed our rundown suite by a direct route. One of the men I'd encountered in that seedy room a few days earlier sat on a lobby couch, trying—almost successfully—to look inconspicuous. I sat down next to him and searched his bland face for clues as to which of the two interrogators this one was. I could not tell. They had been so alike, they were not separately recognizable.

"Hello again," I said.

He did not respond. There was, perhaps, a just perceptible nod.

"You've been trailing me," I said. "I wanted to know why."

"Merely an assignment."

His voice was flat, businesslike. He did not take his eyes off me when he spoke, but he looked away after speaking.

"An assignment from whom?"

"I'm not allowed to say."

"You're just a paid shadow then, a flunkey, a thug, one of the court's household drafted as spy. I know you're not who you pretended to be the first time we met."

"We needed to know where you stood on the subject of rejects. Your presence in the church at St. Ethel Camp caused some concern."

"Some concern with whom?"

"It is not my business—"

"I know, you don't intend to say. Did I pass muster with whomever it was?"

"For that moment, yes, as a matter of fact, but . . ."

"But what?"

"Your presence at the killing of Mr. Madling caused further concern."

"I tried to save him, God damn it!"

"That has been taken into account."

"But you and your buddy're going to be following me a while longer."

"That's right."

"Your privilege. I just wanted to say hello. If you ever get cold or bored or want to come in for refreshment, just ring up. See you later."

"So long."

So long? I thought. For a moment there he sounded just like an old friend. I could not recall what his face was like the minute I turned away from him. On several occasions over the next two weeks I noticed one or the other of the two men staying a comfortable distance to the rear of me. When I told Ben about them, he knew of their existence already from his government sources. Chances were, he said, that they weren't especially dangerous, and probably posed no threat to our mission. They came from an investigative arm of the government and were on my tail as much to offer protection as to keep track of my comings, goings, and associations with criminal elements. Their reports were being routinely filed away. Ben said he was followed from time to time and had learned to think nothing of it. However, we both decided that it would be necessary to shake my two shadows just before the Washington trip.

2

Ben, who was of course delighted by my acceptance of the mission, put me through a series of grueling physical conditioning tests and exercises. He shouted with glee each time I failed, sulked when I demanded rest periods. He made Stacy submit to some of the same rituals, but pronounced him in generally better shape and excused him from several sessions. The favoring of Stacy naturally angered me and made me press harder.

Every third day, the minimum interim suggested for absorber use, Ben supervised Stacy and me in two-to-four-hour sessions with the absorber. I had never experienced knowledge-absorption before and so was unprepared for its mystical side. When I had placed the absorb-helmet on my head and experienced the initial period during which my mental activity was forcibly relaxed, and the following period of almost lethargic meditation, I felt what seemed like a strange union between myself and a god in which I did not believe. My false god was comforting. I rather liked his easy crotchetyness, and my own mocking worship. In my memory now, that god seems more and more like Ben, so perhaps I imposed his persona upon my god-figure. When the brain was properly relaxed and in a receptive mood, the information—programmed beforehand by Ben—started seeping into it. At first it seemed to come slowly. (Once I was inside the absorb-helmet, my time-sense was valueless.) Little bits and pieces of data, apparently unrelated, would slip to the surface of my mind. Then the process gradually accelerated. Soon the information was like a sky of falling stars, isolated areas of knowledge entering my mind in swoops and curves. At a later time, these apparently discrepant pieces of information would come together, and—as my pattern of knowledge formed—I would realize the relationship of different items. While this occurred, I began to understand levels of subtlety that were an incorporated part of the growing mass of data. If, for example, the absorber was supplying me information about the layout of the Washington retread chamber, I perceived this data not only as a blueprint, a floor plan which gave me accurate outlines, but I also received correct images of what the place looked like, including such details as pictures on the walls and the precise location of wall switches. Further, the raw data was subject to subtle analyses that suggested to me various possibilities of how the area might be used if certain alternatives had to brought into the mission plan. There were such small frightening details as which areas afforded the most risks, which corridors provided the most efficient escape routes, which inefficiencies within the personnel might be used to advantage, et cetera. I gradually apprehended the workings of a number of devices and systems that could have no probable use to the mission—all just in case a situation arose in which they *might* come in handy. I was provided history, philosophical implications, literary selections that in strange ways related to the overall purpose. I would learn everything about a particular sector, then in the next session go through the same process about another area. Eventually I was convinced that nothing relating to the mission had been left out. Other sessions gave me all the known information about how the process of retreading worked, what the psychological quirks of the security force were, the menu plans for a month of the three cafeterias strategically placed throughout the retread chamber.

I asked Ben why such things as menu plans. He said it was all part of the guise in which Stacy and I would be walking the corridors of the chamber. Somebody might comment on the day's luncheon. It was important to know what had been served, so that an innocent-appearing response could be used.

Unsurprisingly, I soon felt I knew much more than was necessary about the Washington chamber, its surrounding area, retreading, and all the facets of the mission. When I told Ben that, he said:

"Don't get overconfident, chum. Information is only just that, information. *You* still have to perform the mission. The human factor can screw the whole thing up, it's an old adage."

"I know, I know. I'm just complaining because I'm eager to get on with it, get it over. And I'm resisting the absorber. I don't really want to go under that helmet again."

"Nobody does, after a while. There's a druglike effect to the accumulation of knowledge, no matter what kind. First it's exciting and you want more and more of it. Then it begins to drag you down. You either start seeking its limits or want to swear off. I have to take vacations from the absorber regularly."

"Another thing, while I'm in a complaining mood—I've noticed that several bits of propagandistic stuff about rejects and their cause have been creeping into and among the data. I don't like that."

"How come?"

"Oh, Ben, you know how come. I don't want to be conditioned, damn it, I've agreed to the mission, let's just leave it at that. I don't want to be *forced* into the belief that what I'm doing is somehow justified. At least I don't want that belief programmed into me. Whatever the beliefs, if I'm going to have them, I'd like to arrive at them on my own."

Ben steepled his fingers and muttered:

"Interesting."

"What's interesting about it?"

"I told you that the absorber would provide information, and that was the truth. I provided the materials about the history and philosophy of the reject cause so that you could see the mission in perspective. I didn't do it to slip in some insidious propaganda. What's interesting is that you want to resist it so much that you see it as conditioning, which it is not."

"Wish I could be sure of that."

"But you don't trust me."

"Not entirely."

"That's probably wise. Even with you, I'm not entirely trustworthy, and I feel more comfortable with you realizing that. Still, it's true about the absorber. It is not a conditioning device. Something in your head is transforming the reject data into propaganda. Nevertheless, I'll revise accordingly."

"Kind of you."

"Don't mention. Let's do some pushups."

"C'mon, Ben. I'm physically ready, you know that. I'll return to the exercise program when I get the tour invitation."

"You'll continue now."

"Ben, I'm worn out."

"Not according to my information."

"Damn it, I'm not a printout."

"Get to it."

I could usually do more pushups when I was angry at Ben.

3

"Have you been waiting for me long, Voss?"

"No longer than usual."

"Don't be testy. I tried to reach you. There wasn't any answer at your rooms."

"No wonder. Ben's had me and Stacy on a treadmill since dawn."

"Poor thing. But you do look better. The whites of your eyes gleam."

"Alicia—"

"I know, it's a silly way to put it. But it's true, sort of. Your eyes used to be dullish. You know, mysterious and dark. Now you look eager. Even a bit fanatical, pardon the expression."

"Let's walk somewhere. I don't sit still too well anymore."

"No, neither do I. I'd like to dance or something."

"Sure, but I'm out of practice."

"No matter, I'm essentially unrhythmic. I know a place near the river. We'll go there."

"What job have you been on this time?"

"You must already know."

"No. I don't."

"The Washington job. I've been toiling away at PR releases designed to sway the reject mind. I'm getting good at it. I may actually be bringing more rejects to the retread side of things than vice versa. Damn."

"I wouldn't be able to manage a double identity myself."

"Ah, it's easy. In spite of our worst suspicions, nobody's really keeping much track of anybody else these days. Those agencies with the good occasional piece of secret information generally don't know what to do with it or whom to forward it to. Information is dormant, the system is composed of bulges all pulling down at one another. Listen, Voss, what we're planning, we wouldn't've been able to do twenty, even ten, years ago. Something's happening. It's as if the time is ripe for the destruction of the organism and everybody senses it, as if the organization itself desires its own destruction and is paving the way for us."

"That's a bit too romantic for me."

"Well, your kind does better if he expects danger around every corner. Ooops, nothing at this corner, unless you count that—"

"I don't think I like the tone of that. What do you mean by *my kind?*"

"Just what you think I mean. The adventurer, the risk-taker, the hero, however you want to call yourself."

"I don't like to be categorized."

"Nobody does. But we're all too willing to do it to others. I'm sorry, didn't mean to categorize you. All I meant was—"

"Forget it. Have you fixed the coffeemaker in your office yet?"

"No. There's nobody in the entire goddamn chamber who knows how to—wait a minute. How did you know the coffeemaker was on the blink?"

"The absorber is quite thorough. I know all kinds of minor details about your office, and many others. There are more details in my mind about some rooms than others, depends on the efficiency of the observers and interpreters of documents, I guess. Your office isn't even part of the overall plan, doesn't even figure into an escape route."

"Spooky. You make me feel spied upon."

"That's it exactly. But at least it's being spied upon by our own side."

"I still don't like it, even though I'm one of the spies. What does it tell you about me?"

"Depends. My assumption has been that you're Nancy Donner and not Cheryl Hidalgo in your secret identity."

"That's correct. God! How could you ever confuse me with Cheryl Hidalgo, she's got tits out to here."

"Well, I admit that's one of the reasons I assumed you to be Nancy Donner, although it occurred to me that my information on your chest size might be incorrect or was part of your disguise."

"Why didn't the absorber just give you pictures?"

"It did. They were fuzzy. In a fuzzy picture you and Cheryl Hidalgo look something alike."

"Thanks a lot. I won't be able to look at Cheryl again."

"According to her record, she wrote and published several novels in her previous lifetime, under her original name, Cheryl Simpson. She's taken up the custom of accepting the name of her husband, as people used to. Anyway, as Simpson she wrote one novel that's still being read today, a classic."

"Don't tell me any more. No wonder she writes better copy than I do. But why is she writing crap now? Why settle for doing PR copy when you've been a first-rate novelist?"

"Who knows? According to her dossier, she's in some club called Retreads Forever. What it is, she's probably a dedicated retread who wants to be, in some important way, contributing to the cause instead of idling her time away writing novels."

"Maybe. I always thought she was kind of dimwitted. Well, why are we speculating about Cheryl Hidalgo?"

"Absorber-knowledge fascinates me. Any detail I want about any phase of the subject can be called up so easily. I could speculate about anybody in Washington chamber like we just did about Cheryl Hidalgo. And odd details like disappearing watercolors, one of which has been co-opted by your fifteenth-level janitors, by the way. But the hell of it is what I *really* need to know is not so specific. The deeper you go down into the Washington chamber, the fuzzier my information about it is. I know more about your Public Liaison office than I do about the area where souls are stored—where, after all, the main part of the mission is to take place. We're lucky we have some blueprints or we'd know next to nothing."

"At least you know where you have to go."

"Sure. But I'd like to know more. What the place actually looks like, what it feels like, where the demons live. It's absolutely frustrating to encounter dark areas of information. You get nervous, you feel you *have* to know what's in the dark areas. worry that you'll be somehow incomplete if you don't find out."

"Hmmm. Like Pandora's box or Bluebeard's locked door."

"Precisely. The only thing that makes me happy is that the whole body of information can be erased after the mission."

"That sounds horrifying."

"Not as bad as it sounds. The absorber merely triggers a mechanism in the brain that cancels the need-to-know impulses. I'd go crazy carrying around such mundane details in my mind for decades after. It's frustrating to have such an abiding concern for them *now.* I'm getting impatient—I find myself desiring the mission to take place, can't get to sleep at night without thinking about it for hours."

"Well, you can begin to rest easy. Way I hear it, you'll be getting your invitation to tour the charnel house any day now."

"Good. I'm glad the waiting period's over."

"None too soon."

"Why do you say that?"

"Triplett's escaped. I'm afraid he might try to get you."

"That's comforting. Well, I've dealt with him before, right?"

"Don't be so flip, Voss. He's dangerous, he really is."

"I'll be cautious. God, what's with this drizzly rain? I thought weather control had eliminated this kind of—"

"The weather-control people are still striking. Two hours a day. Any two hours they feel like."

"Are the police still out, too?"

"Part of the time."

"You still feel like dancing?"

"Not much."

"Anything you'd like to do?"

"Well, there's a ballet . . ."

"No."

"Nothing then."

"Maybe we could—"

"I love you, Voss."

"What brought that up?"

"I don't know. The sheer dullness of the moment, I suppose. Look, we're both too concerned about the mission, can't settle down. Come to my place, lie beside me, *just* lie beside me."

"I don't know if it's—?"

"It is. Come on. We'll listen to Mahler's first."

"His first what?"

"I'll ignore that. But you really do put a strain on my affection."

"You look beautiful."

"With rain dripping off my chin. What with dumb jokes and silly remarks, you're really terrific to be with, Voss."

"You, too."

"That sounds sarcastic. Let's go back to the part where I say I love you."

"I love you, too."

"Somehow I don't think we're communicating. Let's try walking in silence through the drizzle. And you keep your mouth shut."

4

Washington, although no longer the capital of a nation, retained much of its former majesty as a center for records and culture. A century before, a historical preservation association had vowed to restore the former capital by rebuilding the decaying city and transforming it into a living museum. Different sectors of the city represented it as it had appeared in different historical eras. The downtown area, where Stacy and I were housed in a quite ugly hotel, was basically twentieth century. Actors represented governmental figures—there was a president, vice president, an entire Supreme Court which re-enacted Important Judicial Decisions of the Ages. Less than half a Congress was represented—because, one of the actors told me, only about half the senators and congressmen normally attended any given session.

Since some unexpected red tape forced Stacy and me to wait four days before the tour began, I started exploring the city's various historical neighborhoods. Stacy stayed behind at the hotel, fascinated with its carefully preserved twentieth-century artificial luxury. For some reason he liked bad television and ice machines. Myself, I liked the colonial period and spent much of my time strolling through its preserved image, soothing my eyes with red bricks and white borders, sculptured trees and even gardens, men and women walking around in authentic clothing, some of them in blackface.

During my last day of touring, I crossed the border from the colonial park into one that represented late-nineteeth-century America, especially the flourishing of industry. It reminded me of the restaurant where Pierre had been killed. I almost choked on simulated cigar smoke and the faint odors of inefficient plumbing. The researchers for the industrial area had been almost too thorough. I almost could not enjoy the place, especially when I had to daintily step around the carefully arranged piles of horse manure in the street. The manure was fake but looked so real I would have felt the need to bathe immediately if I had accidentally touched it. Anyway, many piles may have been real, no matter what the brochure said, since genuine horses were used to draw carriages through some of the streets.

From behind a horse-drawn milk wagon, Gorman Triplett stepped suddenly into my path.

"I've been looking for you," he said.

I might have jumped out of the way or tensed myself for battle, except that Triplett's body was so relaxed I did not sense any threat from him. He smiled at me, reading my thoughts on my all-too-expressive face.

"No," he said, "I've been ordered to lay off you, and I tend to follow orders. At least I will for the moment. I might've disobeyed, but they told me you were on a mission of such magnitude that I mustn't interfere. I'd hate to ruin a mission of *magnitude.*"

He lounged against a corner of the milk wagon. It rocked slightly in reaction to his weight. The horse looked back as if it were assigned to keep tabs on him. Triplett stared at me without speaking further. He was in period clothing, looked like a historical reconstruction of a village tough. A dirty checkered shirt, nearly hidden by the massive corduroy overalls, a floppy cap on his head.

"Wanted to look at you again," he finally said. "Get an in-tight look at a real hero."

"Damn you, Triplett, I'd like to—"

"Don't get angry, Geraghty."

"I'm just sick and tired of the way you and your friends toss the word hero at me."

"Aren't you a hero? I mean, isn't that your type?"

"No, of course not."

"You were written up as one. Everybody tells me you're one. I think you're one. Why else would you draw a mission of magnitude? Oh, you're the type, that's true. Ready to save anybody with deeds of derring-do, making big-mouth declarations, I can see all that."

"Whatever you say. I don't care to argue with you, anyway."

"Am I that much below you? On your private social scale?"

"Look, Triplett, it doesn't matter to me what you think. Or how you're planning your revenge."

"Who said anything about revenge?"

"You implied it. And I've a definite impression that there's nothing like an all-is-forgiven tone in your voice and manner."

"In my voice and manner? You speak so goddamned carefully sometimes, I don't know what the hell you are, Geraghty. Or if you're real. Hell with it, I just wanted to look you over again, remind you of my presence."

"Good. I'm reminded. See you around."

I walked past him. The horse, who'd continued to watch us, turned his head away as if he no longer gave a damn either.

"Wait, Geraghty," Triplett said.

I stopped walking but preferred not to turn around, face Triplett again. I could hear him take a couple of steps toward me.

"After I got away," he said, "escaped from those turncoat assholes who were watching me, I checked some records—I have sources—and found where they'd taken Richard. You remember Richard, don't you, Geraghty? You beat his face in, remember?"

I nodded, said:

"After he'd thrown someone down fifty stories."

"Someone. How delicate. Why can't you say his name? Pierre Madling. He was your friend."

"I'd just met him that day. He was hardly my friend. I didn't even . . ."

"Didn't even what? Didn't even like him? I wonder. You looked like you were cut out of the same cloth, you two, but no matter. I want to tell you about Richard."

"Maybe I don't want to hear about Richard."

"Maybe I want to disobey my orders and kill you anyway. One

way or another, I'm going to tell you about Richard, you might as well listen now. How about relaxing on that Park bench over there?"

We both chose an opposing end of the green bench without looking at each other. Triplett stared at the park behind us as he talked. I only glanced at him a couple of times as I listened.

"Richard's body's been inherited by a rich bastard, name of Harry Longwood. Nice classy name, what? Well, this Longwood chose the Louisville Readjustment Center for his renewal period. That, as you may know, is the ritzy place, the rich-bitch place where only the most privileged can go to get used to their new bodies, strengthen control over the fresh body, learn about the ways and mores of today's society—you know, learn the right slang, pick up on the new etiquette. A foul place, Louisville, but—on the other hand—an easy place to infiltrate. I forged credentials as a recreations specialist. A couple of days passed before I saw Longwood, although how he remained inconspicuous in that massive body I'll never know. He came to the door of my exercise room when my back was turned and I was working over some gawky slob of an especially stupid retread. I heard his voice say, 'Are you the famous George Thomas'—the name I was using—'who can teach especially clumsy people how to regain their muscle control?' Although the diction was elegant and the words pronounced precisely, I recognized the voice as Richard's. You retreads aren't probably aware of how your voice, during the early days of the renewal period, stays quite like the voice of a person whose body you've obtained. Later, your own habitual inflections tend to take over. I'd been told this, but'd never really heard it for myself until the day Longwood showed up in Richard's body. The stupid son of a bitch, I should have killed him. That would've been the proper revenge. Preserved Richard's body by not letting it be used by that stupid son of a bitch! Why didn't I kill him, can you tell me?"

Triplett hit the back of the bench with his hand. The wood threatened to split. Apparently he hurt the skin of the hand, and he sucked on the pained area for a second or so.

"Anyway, soon as I heard the voice, I turned around knowing

what I was gonna see. God, he almost filled the goddamned doorframe, he was so large. I'd forgotten already how large that body was. As it was, its new inhabitant was in a hopeless condition, his shoulders bobbing against each side of the doorframe. All you bastards have to struggle to get used to your new bodies, but when you've been dealt one as enormous as Richard's your difficulties are tripled. A guy like Longwood would normally have to spend much more time in the renewal period center than most. So they'd sent him to me for the most obvious reasons. I had already shown considerable skill in helping with bodily readjustment. Longwood was to be my test case to see if I was *really* as good at my job as I appeared to be. Most of my other cases were pretty far along, so I decided to dismiss them, spend all of my time on Longwood. I told him that, and he said he appreciated it.

"I never saw a retread so at war with the body he'd inherited. Longwood could hardly walk around my workroom. He had to reach out and cling to things, pull himself along, stare at his feet to make sure that the tentative steps he was taking were connecting properly with the floor. I nearly howled out loud watching him. Instead, I sat him down and pretended I had to take a history of him. There was no need for such a procedure, I just wanted to find out all I could about the bastard. Turns out Longwood was an architect, and he just sat on his ass for most of the previous lifetime making little lines on paper and computing figures. He said he'd never done much athletic and was a bit appalled, that's the word he used, *appalled* that he'd come up with such a large body this time around. What was he going to do with it? he asked me. Me! I felt sick to my stomach, but I suggested he might consider keeping it in condition, maybe choosing a more active profession this time. He looked hangdog about that, said he'd hoped to return to the firm. He had his own firm, the bastard, a very rich firm that'd rebuilt something like half of Seattle. And he wanted to go back there and go right on being what he'd already been for sixty or seventy years, the rich son-of-a-bitching bastard. I told him to do as he wished, but he'd still have to do something to keep the body in shape, otherwise it'd just go to flab. He said, so what? I said, if it went to flab it wouldn't be useful—not only that, it'd probably conk out years too soon. He'd have a heart attack or something. He just said so what again. I asked what did he mean. He said it might even be better to check out of this body earlier than normal, get one more suited to his life and work. Like a body was something stitched together by a tailor! He went on talking, something about how he didn't know how the retread chamber bureaucracy could've so fouled up. They had all the facts, he said, they should've known better than to connect him to such an unwieldy body. Their efficiency really was going downhill, he said, just like everybody claimed. He just went on chattering, not suspecting in the slightest the loathing I was building up for him. I would've liked to've slit his throat right there, get him his damn new body ahead of time. But it would've been too much like killing Richard, so I had to sit there and nod, pretend to agree with him that he'd been handed a dirty deal back at the charnel house, where they should've suited bodies to the type of soul being transferred. The son of a bitch, I kept thinking, couldn't he at least be likable?"

A well-corseted young lady passed by the bench, paused for a second, looked Triplett and me over. I knew she was an actress wondering whether to entertain us with her prepared spiel, and I was just as glad when she decided against it and walked on. Triplett never noticed her.

"So for the next three days I taught Harry Longwood how to use Richard's body. He was a quick study, but I went through agony. Every time he put an arm on my shoulders for me to steady him in his practice walks, I remembered Richard's arm on me in affection. There just wasn't that much difference in Longwood's putting the arm there as a help for balance, and Richard's way of hugging me. There certainly wasn't any difference with what I felt inside. I began to dread any touch from Longwood, hated any time he reached out for me. Sometimes when a part of my therapy had worked especially well, Longwood patted me on the shoulder. Then I really hated the son of a bitch. It was one thing to disregard a casual touch, another when the touch really meant an affection, albeit a casual affection. But, one way or another, I endured all of Longwood's touches. What I could not figure out was why I worked so hard for him to master the body. I knew the moment I saw him I couldn't kill him, why did I keep going? Why didn't I just slip away from the Louisville Center? I had seen Richard's body, after all, which was the reason I had come there in the first place. There was no reason to go on with it. But it became important to me that Longwood, if he was going to be stuck with Richard's body, learn to maneuver it properly, even though I knew in my heart that all my good work would go for naught. The bastard would return to Seattle, and let his flab fall all over his goddamned drawing board. But I did the job. And I did it well. In three days, much too short a time for a problem like Longwood, he was working the body very well. He had excellent control over all the motor processes and my superiors were impressed with the miracle I'd wrought, were telling me they had big plans for me in Louisville Center. Great, I could see myself pickled in this fake identity spending the rest of my life as a therapist, never getting caught, and getting myself retreaded in the bargain. Damn it, Geraghty, you know I was almost tempted? The only reason I could think of for not doing it was this overwhelming need to get out of there and kill you. I wanted to kill you so much, not even a life of paradise and good works could sway me from it. Impressed?"

"Not much."

"No, you wouldn't be. I'm shitting you, anyway. I was never really tempted. I could never work for retreads, become one, I think you know that."

"Let's say that it follows."

"It follows. Okay, it sure follows. So there I was, having been completely successful in the project of Harry Longwood. He was in complete control. The hell of it, he manipulated the body just like Richard did. I mean, he had the same walk, a lot of the same gestures. I got sick just watching him walk across the room. All kinds of memories about Richard coming to me out of nowhere. I could almost believe this was some kind of drama, that Harry Longwood *really* was Richard returned from the dead. I almost called him Richard a dozen times. I remembered the time when

Richard and I were actively lovers and wanted to return to it. At nights I had dreams about it, Geraghty, dreams.

"I resolved to get the hell out of Louisville at first opportunity. I'd seen enough of Harry Longwood, wanted to get the hell away from him. The split, I thought, was complete—I could now devote my time completely to tracking you down. Then, after what I'd planned as the last session, Longwood invited me to take a Turkish bath with him. Things like Turkish baths and saunas are very big at Louisville Adjustment Center. I liked Turkish baths and would encounter very few of them back on the outside, so I said to myself, what the hell, one last trip through the hot mists would do me good before I escaped. Well, Longwood and I were in the baths having a mild chat about things. He thanked me effusively for all I'd done for him, asked if there was anything he could do for me on the outside. I said no. He said, okay, but to check in with him any time I wanted, there'd always be a place for me, that kind of crap. Well, he said, I've had about enough of this hothouse, gotta leave. Apparently he wasn't in as much control of the body as both of us thought. As he stood up, he swayed and almost fell. The towel around his waist slipped away. He made a grab for it, but too late. He stared at me and I think his face went a deeper shade of red than the red from the heat of the Turkish bath. And he had a good reason. I looked down at his crotch and he had an a-number-one erection there, a firm hard-on like the one I'd seen so many times back with Richard. He was embarrassed for it, and he crouched over to retrieve the towel. What could I do? My reaction was natural, almost unthought out. I touched his thigh, began caressing, reaching for his cock, wanting to hold it, feel its firmness. Ah, shit, I don't want to tell you that part. Forget it, Geraghty. Suffice to say that Longwood did not respond to the advance. He pushed my arm away and took a couple of steps away from me. I don't know what went wrong inside my head, but I thought he was just playing it coy. He seemed to glance around the bath to make sure no one was watching. I don't know, I just had to touch him again. I reached for him, and that was my mistake. He grabbed my arm and practically pulled it out of its socket. I lost balance and skidded past him. I turned. The only thing I could think was how well I'd taught him. He had more coordination than I'd even thought, the way he tossed me around so easily. Next thing I knew, he was punching me in the gut. The kind of force behind that punch, I knew I'd been a good teacher. The fucker knocked me right out with one punch—the way Richard used to take out guys with a single well-placed blow. It was almost as if there was some muscular memory left in that body, an ability it would never forget no matter who was inhabiting it. Anyway, I came to and was alone in the room, my head against my own rolled-up towel. Longwood had, I guess, rolled up the goddamn towel and placed it under my head, then left. I don't know, Geraghty, I never felt so humiliated in my life. If I could just give you the feeling I had at that moment, I still have now, I'd be satisfied that I'd paid you back on equal terms. That's it anyway, what I wanted to tell you. I got right out of the Louisville Center, never even saw Longwood again, went back to New York, where the stupid bastards who rule me told me I couldn't lay a hand on you. They've tied me up good. But I'm going to keep track of you, hound you the way I did Richard's body. There'll be a time, hero, there'll be a time. And I'm patient. I can wait for it."

He became silent. I felt foolish, but I had to ask his permission to leave. He said it was all right with him. He remained seated on the park bench, staring at the park without, I suspect, seeing anything. After an abbreviated tour of the late-nineteenth-century park, I walked by the bench again, but he had left. A young tough lounging against the milk cart proved to be the actor cast for the role.

5

Back at the hotel, I found Stacy as deeply engrossed in another artifact of twentieth-century TV situation comedy.

"They called," he said abruptly, without looking up from the screen.

"Who called?"

"People at the charnel house."

"Careful, don't call it a charnel house among them. They don't particularly like the term, I'm told."

"Anyway, the charnel house people said the time of the tour's been moved up. Some personnel problem or other."

"It's not tomorrow anymore?"

"Nope. Today. In a couple of hours, matter of fact."

"Jesus Christ!"

All I could think was, I'm not ready, I'm not goddamn ready. But of course I knew I was. All the preparation under the absorber, all that psychological prepping from Ben—I was ready to move at a second's notice. I just wasn't sure I wanted to go, that was all.

"What're we supposed to do?" I asked Stacy.

"Just wait. Sit around."

"Till when?"

"They're sending a limo at three o'clock."

"That's less than an hour and a half away."

"Correct. Too bad."

"Why too bad?"

"Program at three o'clock."

"Stacy, are you aware of what we have to do today? At the chamber?"

"Sure."

"And you're not nervous, bothered, a little agitated?"

"Depends on how you measure it."

"Then you are a little bothered?"

"Didn't say that."

"Forget it. I'll, I don't know, I'll rest for a minute or something. I can't think of anything to do."

"Couple things I have to tell you."

"Something's gone wrong."

"No, I checked out the clothing we wear into the place. It's okay, the micro-dust is safely placed in the buttons and linings, everyplace it's supposed to be."

"I already checked that."

"Never hurts to recheck anything."

"Suppose you're right."

" 'Course."

Stacy turned away from the TV set. He had turned the sound down. All I could tell from the picture was that some man, apparently a husband, was furious with some woman, apparently his wife.

"While you were gone, I went for a walk," Stacy said.

"Great. You needed the exercise."

"I had a notion to try out cigarettes."

"Why in hell would you want to do that?"

"Something about the period, I guess. I saw all those people smoking on TV, wanted to try it out."

"Good reason as any, I suppose."

"Anyway, that part of it's not important. I didn't even like the cigarettes. Take getting used to, I guess. But, while I was buying them, I saw a familiar face on the other side of the store."

"Familiar?"

"Well, at first I couldn't place him. For good reason, since I hadn't seen much of him, and then only at a distance."

"Well, who was he?"

"I think it was the person who was tailing you. One of them."

"Damn, I thought we shook them the day we left New York."

"We should have. Maybe we did."

"Why do you say that?"

Stacy glanced back at the TV set, apparently to check whether or not he was missing anything important. It seemed to me now that the wife was screaming at the husband, with something of a look of triumph on her face.

"The man was buying something at another counter, didn't seem to be looking my way at all."

"That could've been his cover."

"Could've. But I took a long walk after I left the shop, acting like I was checking out the cigarettes, which I *was* doing, and I'm sure he didn't follow me."

"Maybe he didn't have to. Maybe he knows where we are, doesn't have to keep a tail on us."

"Thought of that. Might be true. But I felt you should know."

"Of course I should know. Ah, well, Ben said not to worry about them."

Until shortly before three o'clock, when we changed into our specially prepared clothing, we rested—Stacy watching another TV program that looked like the one I'd interrupted, me trying to rest on various pieces of furniture and bedding that did not seem designed for human use. Mentally, I went over all Ben's instructions. He had made the mission sound like an easy job, one that we could do in our sleep. Desperately I wanted to doze off and stay that way for the next few hours.

6

The limo sent by the Washington chamber, in keeping with the period of our sector, was a twentieth-century gas-powered type, complete with a chauffeur. Other VIPs, who'd been billeted in the same hotel but not integrated socially with Stacy and me, joined our party. Inside the vehicle we were an uncomfortably cozy little group. Stacy volunteered to open up some backseat space by sitting with the chauffeur, but the man would not allow such a breach of ancient etiquette. As a result, he got to sit up front in luxurious spaciousness while the rest of us were all squeezed together in back. It was, I supposed, the privilege of the oppressed servant class, even when impersonated by an unoppressed actor. I made this observation to a fellow passenger, a woman who looked at me as if I had violated more than her organs of hearing.

From what I could discern, based on conversations from which Stacy and I were pointedly excluded, most of the other guests were connected, in one way or another, with the government. There was a lot of talk of paperwork and the kind of red tape that caused tours like this one to occur at times other than originally scheduled.

We arrived at the Washington chamber almost before we realized we were anywhere near it. There was an early false alarm of expectation when we passed the building where the rejects entered for their bodily contribution. A small forlorn-looking line waited outside a doorway as our car zoomed past that entrance. From one of my absorber-sessions I knew that the reject entrance was a facade designed to hide from the general public the actual retread chamber entrances. Once inside, the doomed rejects were doped and driven to their actual embarkation point in underground vehicles. After the fake reject entrance, we passed through a few kilometers of barren countryside. Only Stacy and I among the limousine's passengers were prepared for the car's gradual stop in what seemed like the middle of nowhere. Although the absorber had fed me the place's approximate location, I had expected clues to where it was before we got there—signs, remarks from the chauffeur, some kind of building or shack to denote an entrance. When a passenger asked the chauffeur why the sudden stop, the man maintained his stolidity, told us to wait.

Out of the mists a building drifted toward us. A wide, domed building whose method of locomotion was not easily apparent. It halted a few feet from the car. A light flashed on in the car's dashboard and the chauffeur, moving with sudden alacrity, got out of the car, waved toward the building, and opened the passenger doors. With an imperial hand-wave, he directed us toward the building. We walked to it through the bleak mists.

The air was icy and damp, bits of it seemed to be attacking and clinging to my skin. As we neared the strange structure, I sensed what I can only describe as a scientific odor—the odor of a laboratory, a whiff of oily matter, suggestions of chemicals. My hands moved nervously over my clothing and I wondered why I was so fidgety. Then I realized the pattern of my agitated movements. I was touching all the places where the destructive micro-dust was concealed, checking uselessly to make sure they were still intact. A dumb move, I thought, a dead giveaway to anybody suspicious. I stopped my hands, tried to make them stay still at my sides. Then it occurred to me that the awkward look of my stiff arms would also catch the attention of anybody watching me. I must look natural, I said to myself. How the hell can one look natural when he's about to embark on a mission of murder? I tried to relax. Impossible.

The door of the building opened. The shaft of light that came from inside the building nearly blinded our mist-adjusted eyes.

"Welcome," said a soft voice. Someone standing in the doorway. "Welcome to the Washington Chamber for the Reprocessing of New Life. Enter, please."

We filed in. When we were all assembled in an office, the door snapped shut behind us and the soft-voiced woman spoke again:

"We at the Washington Chamber for the Reprocessing of New Life are happy to welcome you for this tour. We apologize for any inconveniences you may have suffered in coming out here, but certain procedures are necessary for security purposes. As you must sense, we are moving again. This building, as it appears to you, is actually an enclosed vehicle which will take us to our proper point of entry. Just relax, we'll be arriving there soon."

Our hostess was an amply proportioned young woman with large brown eyes on a cherubic face. Bright red hair was carefully combed into old-fashioned waves. It was the most carefully arranged hair I had seen in some time, perhaps since my childhood, when curls had a short vogue and my mother had had her hair restyled in that fashion. As I examined the face of our hostess, wondering what she was doing here in place of the male guide originally scheduled, I felt there was something familiar about her.

"My name is Cheryl Hidalgo," she said, "and I will be your guide for your tour of the chamber."

Cheryl Hidalgo! Alicia's officemate in the Public Liaison Office. Why had Cheryl Hidalgo taken over the tour? Our scheduled guide had been one William Tannenbaum, a man whose entire personality, it seemed, had been fed to me through the absorber. I knew Tannenbaum's style of presentation, his vital statistics, how much he loved a woman whom he kept out of sight in an unreconstructed sector of Washington, how likely he was to crack under pressure, what his tastes in art and music were. I became very uneasy. First the change in starting time, now this. It made me nervous that this big-chested young woman was not a reformed Jewish male with a hidden mistress.

As I had told Alicia, the data concerning Cheryl Hidalgo were vague and contradictory, especially the part about her being an important novelist in her previous lifetime. As if she knew I was thinking of her, Cheryl Hidalgo looked my way. Her shrewd brown eyes seemed so knowing, I was momentarily certain she must know of the plot, was here to prevent it. And, when she spoke, she seemed to be talking directly to me.

"Some of you may be wondering why Mr. Tannenbaum, your originally scheduled guide, is not here to meet you. Mr. Tannenbaum has unfortunately had a family crisis and cannot conduct any tours this week. As the selected alternate for his job in our command roster, I naturally took it over. I regret that you will not have his well-phrased insights into our operations here, but I will strive to do my best to please you."

She continued in this fashion for some time, presenting us a preliminary set of explanations about the various functions of the Washington retread chamber. Or, as she insisted on calling it, the Washington Chamber for the Reprocessing of New Life. Her preview was a bit coyly phrased, and I suspected it was merely part of the material written for the absent Tannenbaum, whose 'well-phrased insights' had been carefully assembled from a computer study of how to treat important visitors. That study had been a part of my absorber-input, so I was bored hearing it all over again. On the other hand, the repetition allowed my mind plenty of time to wander and to become adjusted to the unexpected change in the schedule. After all, what was one tour guide more or less?

I glanced at Stacy, who leaned casually against the corner of an information desk, thumbing through a brightly colored brochure. Apparently the change had not disturbed him, or perhaps did not activate in his mind that flood of absorber-knowledge. He looked sleepy.

When our guide announced that we had arrived at our destination, she led us through a door leading to another room, from which a stairway descended. This room, then, had been linked up to a chamber entranceway. Even with my understanding of the connecting process, I still could not tell where the fake-building stairway ended and the one descending into the chamber began. At one point I saw on a wall in stencil WRC-594-Q, and I felt some relief. This was the entrance we were originally scheduled to use. That part of the tour had not been changed, at least. I did not have to readjust my mental blueprint of the retread chamber layout to correspond with a change in accessways. The stairway descended only a few feet, and we soon found ourselves standing in a large lobby with a block of elevators in front of us. A lethargic old man, sitting at a reception desk, gestured toward a particular elevator. Cheryl greeted him by name, in a kind of phony office-cheerfulness that fitted her role, and herded us toward the designated elevator. Its door opened as she passed her hand over a side-panel light, and she herded us in. I lagged behind and was the last tourist to enter. Our guide followed me in. She told the group that it would only take a few minutes for our descent, and reeled off a bunch of data, some of it I knew to be inaccurate, deliberately so, about the depths and dimensions of the Washington chamber.

Abruptly she turned away from addressing the others and edged a little closer to me. I felt her breast against my arm, as she whispered:

"I've been looking forward to meeting you, Mr. Geraghty."

I did not like being singled out for her attention.

"You know me?" was all I could think of to say.

"Your reputation has preceded you. Normally I work out of the public liaison office here and we help plan these tours. That malarkey about being Tannenbaum's alternate was just some bullshit to set everybody at ease. When I saw your name on the guest list, I thought I'd figure a way to meet you. Then Tannenbaum's convenient little family mess came along so I didn't have to do any involved figuring. I said I'd be delighted to take over this tour and, what with our understaffed state, Billy was quite grateful . . ."

She turned away from me again and gave the others another set of facts and figures to occupy their minds during the dull descent. I noticed that most of these office-types nodded their heads particularly at numbers, the larger the better. Returning her attention to me, she said:

"During the supper break, I've arranged a private dining room for us. I hope you don't mind."

"Well, I don't think we should leave the others . . ."

"They could care less, believe me. They'll be busy comparing notes on technology. It'll be all right.

"Well, I don't think—"

"Don't be shy. It's an attractive quality in somebody of your accomplishments, but don't bother. It's all settled. I get what I want."

Gradually the elevator slowed. I searched my mind for some piece of absorber-data that would allow me to escape the clutches of our lovely tour guide. With all of the knowledge at my command, nothing came to mind. This contingency had not been provided for. Its solution would have to be one of those improvisations that Ben always harped about. Damned if I could think of anything at that moment. The elevator doors opened and we were faced with a small lobby, with several corridors leading away from it.

Some of my confusion must have shown on my face, or at least been evident to Stacy, for he touched my arm and gave it a reassuring squeeze as we left the elevator. It took a moment for me to realize the significance of the touch. We never touched, Stacy and I, at least not outside the necessities of business-as-usual. Perhaps this contact was business-as-usual then. Whatever it was, the touch seemed to suggest that we shouldn't worry yet—there was time.

Cheryl took up position at the center of the lobby, walking to it with the bouncy self-confidence of one who knew her body was pleasant to observe. I liked neither her arrogance nor her businesslike manner. As she went into her spiel, I was again disturbed by the falseness of it, the forced gaiety, the slickness, the giggle she would press into her voice to indicate when she was telling a traditional inside joke. I kept thinking of her past, the cold data about her provided by the absorber, the achievements of her bizarre previous lifetime. I saw now why Alicia had been agitated when I had detailed Cheryl's biography for her. Since I had talked with Alicia, I had located *Who Are the Manxmen?*, the novel Cheryl had written as Cheryl Simpson. I had read the book in one evening. It was an arresting piece and I felt that, given the time to mull over its implications for a few days, I would have been able to discern its endearing appeal. It was a strange story, the plot details never sufficiently clear, about a set of modern characters who, after being trapped on a rich man's desert island, suddenly find themselves thrust back in time to a primitive and uncivilized age, a time when life was rough and lifespans were quite short. A studied and detailed contrast was established between the denizens of the primitive time and their visitors from the future—and not just on a civilized versus uncivilized basis. Several of the moderns became appalled at the waste of a short life. Others were attracted to its less civilized aspects. In the course of the narrative some of the characters died. Eventually the survivors returned to the future just as mysteriously as they had left it. Underscoring their relief at the escape from the primitive time and their release from the mysterious rich man's island seemed to be the message that one should revel in all the extra years allotted him, greet new lifetimes with enthusiasm and energy, and always strive to achieve more with each valuable passing year, regarding luxury and leisure as the main sins of a retread's life. Still, there was some muddle, some aspiration to art, that obscured the message and I was never quite sure what Cheryl Hidalgo's book meant.

So here she was now, the great proselytizer for a life of achievement, conducting a worthless guided tour of a retread chamber, with all the phony requisite charm of the position. In her mind was she bettering the achievements of her first life, carrying on as her novel indicated a retread should? I wondered if she thought a job at a charnel house was more important to her because it was, in a general way, useful, and therefore better for her than the abstracted, and luxurious, life of art.

"Now I must ask you," Cheryl was saying, "to submit to a routine security scanning. While we were in the building above, you were given a preliminary scanning. We apologize for not making you aware of it when it was taking place but there are many fanatics around these days, some of them foolish enough to carry an unauthorized weapon into a high-security institution. Follow Mr. Arthur here please."

I wanted to consult Stacy about all the schedule changes, but Cheryl, who had stood aside while the others were ushered out, came to my side, took my arm, and led me down the well-lit, sterile corridor. I immediately knew the classification number of the corridor and what was ahead. If only, I thought, I knew what was ahead with the sexy young woman at my side.

"I put your name on the guest list in the first place," Cheryl said suddenly.

"Oh? Why was that?"

"Saw the writeups about you, became intrigued. In the Public Liaison Office the routine gets to you after a while. You do anything to pick up a day, even improve a few minutes."

"If it's so dull, why do you do it?"

"It's not dull really. Actually, my life levels out to what most people would consider an exciting pace. I just generally crave additional excitement."

"How do I fit into that?"

"Don't know. Exciting things seem to happen to you, thought some of it might rub off, I guess."

She inflected those words as if there were some sort of double entendre in them.

"My life's not all that exciting. It's been misrepresented."

"I'll bet. Well, I'll take my chances."

"Your chances on what?"

"That something exciting'll happen while we're together."

The whole success of our plan depended on Stacy and I being able to slip away from the tour group for about an hour. A power failure in one sector, arranged by Alicia, would give us the opportunity. During the failure, she was to slip us lab uniforms and ID badges, then Stacy and I would scurry down a particular corridor and be gone for the assigned hour, perhaps without our absences being noticed right away. That was the ideal projection. But we had not figured on the participation of Cheryl Hidalgo. What the hell, I thought, could I possibly do to get away from this woman? Maybe something disgusting. Pick my nose or fake an apoplectic fit. No—either of those was too exciting, no doubt, by her definition. Absurdly, I wondered what I could tell Ben, how explain it. The mission was called off on account of a pushy female. He'd love that.

The scanning room was exactly as the absorber had depicted. I was beginning to be annoyed that there were no architectural surprises. Cheryl handed me over to a scanning attendant with some delicacy. He seemed to accept me in the same spirit. She stood to the side while the scanners did their work and cleared me of carrying any secret material. The attendant waved me out of the scanning cubicle with some pride, looking toward Cheryl. I had passed the test, and her eyes seemed a deeper brown.

"What are you smiling about?" I asked her, after she had a look at my scanning charts.

"Nothing much. These just show that you're in prime physical condition, I like that."

"You seem to enjoy being direct with people."

"Comes with my PR job, I guess. Have to deal with so many people, I've found it best to lay it on the line at all times."

Again the strange sense of double entendre in her inflection.

"Well," I said, "direct people usually appreciate directness in return."

"It's not unusual, I guess, but—"

"I intend to be direct. I don't want to be separated from the group to enjoy a sexy little repast with sexy little you. I don't like special treatment, I—"

"Shut up. You didn't let me finish. While many people do, I suppose, appreciate directness in return for their own directness, I am not one of them. So I'll just forget what you said. Anyway, I didn't spend half my month's salary to pry a good side of prime ribs out of that corrupt stingy kitchen crew, just for you to tell me no. I want a sexy little repast, as you say. And, with sexy little *you.*"

For a moment I wondered if Ben would object if, at the beginning of our mission, I strangled the tour guide.

"I don't especially like women. I'm a—"

"That was implied in your dossier, too. But I don't believe it. You'll like me."

"You don't *choose* to believe it, that's what you mean."

"I think you're right. That *is* what I mean."

"You're some bitch, you know that?"

My heart beat faster, as I hoped that the insult would discourage Cheryl. But her smile showed clearly that being classed as a bitch was not exactly unpleasant to her.

"This dossier of mine, how detailed is it?" I said.

"In some areas, very. But so many departments make reports, it's hard to get a clear correlation, you know?"

"I don't much like the idea of a file of misinformation or incorrect interpretation."

"Me, either. None of us do. You know, one department's submitted a report on you which implies you might have sympathies with the reject cause."

I searched her face for a clue as to whether she was trying to let me know that I was under suspicion. Under her suspicion, particularly. But the remark had been tossed off as if it had equivalency with everything else she said. I tried to counter by agreeing:

"It's easy to have, as you say, sympathies with the reject cause."

"That's the truth. A lot of us do. Excuse me, I have a job to do, but stay close please."

Everybody else had passed through their scanners and were awaiting the tour's resumption. Cheryl delivered a short history, inaccurate in many details, of the development of retreading, and the gradual establishment of centers in which the miracles could take place.

"The Washington Center was one of the first three. It has become, through custom, the repository for very important people, people like yourselves"—a small titter from the group, most of whom had clearly fallen in love with their guide—"and housed here now, waiting for a reintroduction back into a world in which they may create anew, are some of the most prominent artists of recent years—their souls, of course. Not only artists, but philosophers and statesmen. Whenever the soul of a great man or woman can be moved here, that move is encouraged. We have a certain obvious pride here in the Washington Chamber for the Reprocessing of New Life, and I think you'll agree it's justified."

She received the warm approval she sought from her audience. I did not like being reminded, even in PR rhetoric, about all the great persons' souls housed in the Washington charnel house. I was already obsessed with the button-pushing riddle Ben had posed.

"Now," she continued, "about transportation in the—"

"Excuse me, Cheryl," said a fussy voice at the door. We all turned to see what appeared to be a fussy person, a man dressed neatly and a little too tightly. The look Cheryl gave him would have made me vanish from the doorway immediately.

"What is it, Jed?" Cheryl said, some exasperation in her voice.

"Two late arrivals for your tour. Sorry to interrupt. This way, gentlemen."

Cheryl switched to a friendly PR expression as the two men came through the portals. I don't know what kind of confused look I had on my face. The two men were my shadowers, the government agents who'd hounded me around New York. They did not look my way as they entered the room. I had never been aware of my heart beating so fast before. First, the switch in schedule, then the change in tour guides to Cheryl, now the appearance of enemies. I glanced toward Stacy, but could not detect his reaction. Perhaps he was recalling seeing one of the men in the cigarette store earlier that day. We probably were foolish thinking we had shaken them. What I could not figure: why were they openly joining the tour? What did they know, suspect?

There had been no instructions, either from Ben or through the absorber, about what conditions made the voluntary abortion of the mission allowable. Opportunities like this tour did not come along often, abortion did not seem programmed into the mission. We would have to continue to try, no matter how many Cheryl Hidalgos or enigmatic agents got in our way. Still, I wished I felt as confident at that moment about my abilities to perform the task as I had always felt after each session with the absorber.

7

The two men were quickly security-scanned, a redundant procedure I suppose, and they joined our happy little band. During this time Cheryl explained the transportation facilities within the chamber. Part of our tour would utilize four-seated open vehicles, linked together in line, and guided along by transportation beams. There would also be moving walkways above certain areas which would carry us from one side to another, enabling the tour to observe procedures without interfering with work. And some of it, as Cheryl brightly informed us, would be just plain good old-fashioned walking. Halfway through the tour we would adjourn to the cafeteria for what our guide termed as the best meal ever to be served on a plastic tray. She grinned my way. I wondered if the rest of the group would appreciate their best plastic-tray meal if they knew I was scheduled for special private-dining-room treatment.

Ascertaining that all of us were present and accounted for, Cheryl led us out of the scanner room and down a long hallway to the first of our modes of transportation. Parked in a row along the side of a large arched passageway were several of the four-seaters. Holding me back with her elbow, she assigned various of the people to their cars. At the end, five of us stood facing the last two cars. Stacy, Cheryl, the two shadowers, and me. She told the shadowers and Stacy to ride together, while I rode alone with her. She stressed the "all alone" coyly, while not hiding her joy that the mathematics had worked out so well in her favor. Or perhaps she had planned this outcome, like she had planned so much else so far. I tried to sit against the far side of the cushioned seat of the four-seater, but Cheryl then moved to the middle, against my side, and flicked on the switches that locked our car to the other cars and all of the vehicles into the transportation beam. The vehicle started smoothly, slipping out to the center of the passageway, then picking up speed.

"We're heading downward, aren't we?" I said, making conversation without even thinking that I was drawing the fact from my absorber data.

"You have a good sense of descent then," she responded. "Most people don't even notice, think we're traveling straight ahead. The slope is very gradual."

"I have a lot of experience with different gravities. Makes me more aware of that sort of thing."

"I can see where it would."

During the first phase of the tour we made several stops. I cannot even recall in what order they came, so desperately concerned was I over the obstacles to the mission. Every so often I would look up and notice one of the two shadowers *not* looking at me, trying to appear as an interested member of the tour. I couldn't tell the two men apart, a difficulty I had always had with them. I knew there were differences. One of them, for example, had a mole on his cheek, the other one had a habit of hitching his shoulders. But, unless I was staring, I could not remember which one had which characteristic, and sometimes I thought that the one with the mole was also the same one who hitched his shoulders or that they both had moles and both were afflicted with shoulder tics. There was something about their demeanor that made them blur even on close examination, even when you knew they were spying on you. I could sense them waiting for me to make my move. I had pictures of them, one on each side of me, clamping their well-muscled arms on me, dragging me away, tossing me in some kind of retreading vat.

Early phases of our tour took us to the areas involved with the reception of freshly dead, or about to die, people whose souls were to be extracted for the retreading. I recall thinking that some of these people, if their souls were shipped downstairs to the main storage vaults, would be some of my victims. Cheryl told us we would not be allowed to view the operating rooms where the soul-extraction took place. Security would not allow any viewing of any phase of retreading from which a spy could obtain valuable information about its workings. I sensed my shadowers looking my way, but refused to glance at them.

At another level we were shown some of the preparation of reject bodies before they were taken off to operating rooms, also forbidden to tourists, where the actual retreading transferral would be effected. I watched this part of the tour with a fascination that I could not attain during the other parts of it. Although the absorber had supplied me very detailed information about the treatment of the reject body, its scientific descriptions were not equal to the real thing. It was chilling to watch so many dead bodies pass through so many manipulative hands. Knowing exactly what I was viewing, in contrast to Cheryl's carefully modified official version, made my observation of it all the more painful. I resented the technicians at the beginning of the chain rubbing their damn chemical that served as a temporary em-balming agent into the skin. Their hand movements were so gentle, so like caresses. I could that minute have killed all the scanner-operators, who kneaded the body in order to evaluate its internal organs, propped it up for other phases of their examination, sketched in light-colored symbols as if they were seals of approval for unspoiled meat. I hated the haggard and gaunt man whose job it was to ensure that all traces of the body's previous inhabitant, all remnants of its soul, had been successfully removed from its housing. What would he do if he held that soul in his hands? Would he toss it into the air, like a bird being released to fly to the clouds? Or would he close his fingers into a fist? Further down the line were the mekdoks, the mechanic-surgeons making their minute incisions into the body, hooking up the nearly invisible wires, introducing cells from the brain of the about-to-be retread, cells suspended in a preserving liquid, cells to be introduced into the brain of the reject as advance scouts for the new inhabitant. It was theorized that the introduction of these cells altered the composition of the body itself. That seemed impossible to me, but I did not question theology any more. I don't know how many bodies I watched disappear from view into a cylindrical tubing that took them to the operating rooms, sterile and flawless places where the new being could be placed into and integrated with its new body. I was glad we were forbidden these rooms for viewing.

In one enormous room whose lines seemed to go on to infinity we were shown the computer banks that helped run everything, including the monitoring systems in operation throughout the facility. Everybody on the tour properly oohed and aahed. In our early discussions of the mission I had been most concerned about this complex monitoring system. I had asked both Ben and Alicia about how much of a threat to Stacy and me it was. What if, after our sabotage was discovered, someone in the security division decided to scan old tapes to attempt to discover irregularities in the scenes recorded by the intricate network of electronic sensory and video equipment? Ben said the odds in favor of an inspector shrewd enough to recognize us from the masses of tape and other recordings he would have to scan, covering much too long a period of time, were mathematically absurd. Since the equipment, when I did see it, looked impressive enough to read minds, I began to have more faith in Ben's mythical scanner-inspector, felt I should wave to him when I passed a monitor camera.

At another stage of the tour we attended several classes, in which training for retread chamber jobs was being conducted. Additionally, an elaborate public relations setup, unknown to the general public, was teaching students how to make the concepts of reject and retread more palatable to the masses. This training had originated as one of Cheryl Hidalgo's pet projects, and she was especially enthusiastic in describing it for our group.

"You see," she said, "a main problem in attaining a good balance between reject and retread has always been contained in the pejorative qualities of the words themselves. Well, we're stuck with those words for the time being, so I feel that every effort must be made to make the words more palatable to the public. Think of it this way—since most retreads get, oh, fifty to eighty years of the bodies we provide them, and the date at which a body is generally contributed is twenty-six, the allowable reject proportion of the population can slip as low as, say, twenty-five to thirty percent. As you all must know, at many periods it has unfortunately been below that level and the chamber is always working at a disadvantage to keep periods of darkness down to a reasonable time period, so that new retreads will have less disorientation upon their resurrections. Therefore, the reject class must be educated to accept their fates, to realize that what's important isn't the fact that they've been judged to be unworthy of immortality. That's one of the ideas that've caused a problem over the years. No, rejects must be inculcated with the belief that everyone who is a human being has his own personal worth."

She emphasized the last phrase, then studied the tour group for their responses to it.

"Rejects must be encouraged to live their lives to the fullest. It's so obvious, so vital, so humanistic. Such programs as the insurance-policy plans and the easy-life luxury programs have been useful in bringing many rejects to an adjustment to their personal and social situations. But more is needed. Desperately!

As you must know, the backlog of souls awaiting retreading must be diminished. My program is a step in that direction. It's aimed not so much at finding new solutions, new programs, to divert the reject's attentions, as it is to ameliorating their views of what already faces them. The recent, shall we say, fierceness of underground reject actions"—Cheryl glanced at me as she said this—"indicates to me the failure of earlier public relations programs which tended to underrate the intelligence of the reject class and presented information in much too simplistic a form. The newer programs, for which new salesmen and media representatives are being trained in the classrooms we just inspected, are designed to get to the reject youth at earlier stages, and provide special luxuries for that previously ignored age period. My theory is that if you train young people for the easy-out program, they will be less likely to rebel later. What some of my more reactionary colleagues have called radical in my plan is its insistence that the childhood of the reject be better, richer, than that of the children scheduled for retreading in what is, after all, the far future. Reject children must learn to deal, in contrast, with the *near* future, the time when they must contribute their bodies to the retread chamber."

She paused again, watching us for the effect of her words. Her spiel may have been one of the purposes for organizing the tour—to see how these ideas would set with a group of outsiders. Stacy and I might even be the control group, considering the frequency at which Cheryl sneaked glances our way. From what I could judge of the rest of the group, her words were going down well with them. Annoyingly, they kept nodding with approval.

"In the last classroom," Cheryl continued, "you saw a salesman-indoctrination session, in which one of our apprentices delivered a sales speech geared to the five-year-old mind. The five-year-old *reject* mind, that is. Since many of you have been away from childhood for a long time, you may not have been aware of how toys have progressed in recent years. Here we have on display an entire castle with miniature holographic representations, complete with programs that allow for romances, jousts, wars, anything a child can concoct with an active imagination. Watch."

She gestured toward an attendant, who put the toy through some of its paces. Watching it, I thought it would be pleasant to live in medieval times, in times when heroism could be as simple as a knight with a jousting pole, with a threat no more complicated than death.

"This castle is, in fact, one of the simpler toys, but good for the five-year-old mind. There are other toys, which we can offer to reject children, the use of which will introduce into their lives more excitement, more romance, more exhilarating play than does this primitive item. Think of it, with toys like these, why should the reject child even think of the troubles of the outside world? With new offerings at each age-level, the child will not be so easily tempted to join the underground when he or she is older. You have a question, Mr. Geraghty?"

I don't know why I interrupted at all. Perhaps I could not stomach any more of Cheryl's marvelous toys.

"Isn't there a possibility such a plan could backfire?" I asked.

Cheryl put on a face of interested concern, but she began to fidget with a notebook she was holding, and I guessed that she was irritated that anyone could object to such an immaculately idealized plan.

"I don't see what you mean, Mr. Geraghty."

"Well, such games could easily draw their players *into* the underground instead of away from it."

The others looked to me as a group, giving me as much rapt attention as their tour guide.

"How could that occur?" Cheryl asked.

"Well, the games set up romantic illusions, and the underground is equally romantic. It is, in fact, the *best* real-life analogy to their childhood. It might—"

She was so angry that she had to interrupt, an unguidelike action that I could tell irritated some members of the tour group.

"Studies have shown," she said, "that such toys comfort a child. Conclusions state that they are not likely to turn him into an instant rebel, as you suggest."

I shrugged, conceding her the point. No sense in drawing too much attention to myself. A man, a message-bearer, came out of a nearby corridor and presented Cheryl with a piece of paper.

She excused herself for a moment and read the communication. I used the interruption as an excuse to sidle over to Stacy and whisper:

"What do you think?"

"About what?"

"What we're supposed to do. What about the complications?"

"They don't seem too serious to me."

"What about this Cheryl Hidalgo?"

"What about her?"

"She's attached herself to me. I don't know how I'm going to get away from her."

"You'll think of a way."

"Ah, a vote of confidence. But she's like a leech."

"That's your problem, seems."

"Seems it is. And you've no ideas?"

"Nope."

"She wants me to dine with her during the supper break."

"I heard that."

"Prime ribs in a private dining room."

"Don't you like prime ribs?"

"And what about the two new additions to the tour who, incidentally, are watching us now and pretending not to."

"They don't seem too bright to me."

"And you're not worried."

"Not more than normal, no."

"What's normal?"

"Same as for you, I expect."

Cheryl announced that there had been a small transportation breakdown up ahead, but not to worry, there was a lounge nearby and we would all have a short rest there, with drinks and light snacks. She reminded us not to gorge ourselves on the snacks, for there would be a supper break immediately after the next phase of the tour.

The lounge was complete with a human bartender and velvety plush seats around the tables. I tried to edge Stacy and myself into a dark corner of the room, but Cheryl had not taken her eyes off me. She swept past Stacy and said:

"I'll take charge of your friend. There's a couple nice young ladies, Mr. Stacy, right over there, and they have been dying to meet you."

She nodded toward a pair of moderately attractive office-types, who did seem to be gazing at Stacy with interest. Perhaps gaunt types excited their libidos. With no change of expression he turned away from Cheryl and me, and ambled over to the two women. In the ensuing minutes, the two women frequently giggled with delight, and I wondered just what the enigmatic Stacy could be saying to amuse them.

As I sat down at the table, I glanced around the room, noticed that our two shadowers had split up, one sitting near Stacy, the other near me. Every nerve of my body seemed tense. What did these two men know? Were they just following us as a routine duty, or were they watching for us to initiate our mission? For that matter, was this interruption merely a delaying tactic against Stacy and me, while they gathered their forces?

I realized suddenly that Cheryl had been speaking to me. Somehow two odd-looking drinks had materialized in front of us. I did not recall ordering anything.

"You weren't listening to me," Cheryl said.

"No, I wasn't, I'm afraid. Sorry."

"I should be used to it, running a tour. Intelligent people, it seems, tend to shut out the company words of a tour guide."

"Were you saying company words to me just now?"

"No. I was saying that I don't much like your style, your game of elusiveness, might be called."

"To be frank, it's hardly a game. I *am* being elusive."

"What, it's going to hurt you to spend an hour with me over some authentic prime ribs?"

The way she emphasized the word *authentic* reminded me of the pride Pierre Madling had taken in the food he'd arranged for. So much in my life seemed to reduce to the question of how real was the food. There was just enough hurt in Cheryl's eyes to make me want to escape the mission for an hour and huddle in a private dining room with her.

"It's not that it's going to hurt me, Miss Hidalgo, I'd just prefer not to."

"Doesn't matter what you *prefer*. It's on the schedule. We do everything by schedules around here. So you might as well prepare yourself for it."

I was only complicating the situation by denying Cheryl her little pleasure. I had been told by Ben to improvise. Even though I did not like the idea of being physically separated from Stacy during any phase of the tour, the best solution was to give in to the beautiful Miss Hidalgo.

"All right," I said, "but my portion had better be cooked medium-rare."

"Depend on it. Try some of your drink."

I did not like the tone of victory in her voice.

"I'm not much of a drinker," I said.

"You're lying again. Remember, I've read your dossier. You are not a heavy drinker, neither are you one to deny yourself its pleasures."

"Perhaps. What is this drink anyway?"

"It's a special of the place. They call it Resurrection Cocktail—two sips and you're a new man, retread."

"I think I'll pass on it, thank you."

In addition to not wanting to have drink spoil my purposes within the deeper levels of the chamber, the idea of a retread-highball started a faint nausea in my stomach.

"Suit yourself, but it's delicious."

She took a sip, overdramatized her delight with it.

"We got off to a bad start, Mr. Geraghty, and I agree it's part my fault. I tend to attack. But it can be remedied. It's hard to explain, but I've been interested in you for some time. I knew something of your offplanet exploits even before you returned to Earth and there was all that publicity."

"How could you know about me?"

"Had a lover who worked in the space-service division. He was not sufficiently security-minded, and he liked to bring me home stories of extraterrestrial adventure. He thought it added spark to our sex life. Did, in a way. I sometimes fantasized him in the role of space hero, even while he was making love to me and pretending to be a space hero. I don't know—when I saw your picture and remembered what he had told me about you, I also saw that you looked very much like the man I used to fantasize about in the lovemaking. Quite an accident, I assure you, but there was a lot in your face that echoed in my mind. I knew I wanted to meet you, even tried to figure out a way to arrange it, perhaps on one of my trips north—then, magically, this tour came up and I put your name on the list. I was going to somehow join the tour and amble over to you, but then luck continued to be on my side and put the guide job in my lap for today. See, it was all destined, and your recalcitrance was only spoiling a dream."

Her tension gone, Cheryl had become pleasant. She went on to talk volubly about her job, her interests, and—curiously—a hope that her life would turn to adventure some day.

"Sounds funny, I suppose. I'd like to lead the kind of life you've led. You know, go off to the stars, do exciting things. I hate being earthbound."

"You don't have to be earthbound. You can go."

She smiled.

"No, can't. I'm too much of a coward. I have too many plans and getting myself killed forever won't help them. Odd, they never thought when they invented immortality for us it would turn us into a world of cowards."

"I read a book once with that theme in it. Something about manxmen in its title."

I tried to look as innocent and undevious as I could. Cheryl was not so expressionless. She was pleased, and a little excited, at having her book mentioned by someone who, she assumed, could not have known about her earlier identity.

"Think I read that book, too."

"It was a good book."

"Struck me that way, I think."

We might have talked more about her book, but we were interrupted by the same messenger who had stopped the tour earlier. Cheryl assembled the group, said the breakdown had been repaired, and we went forward on the tour.

I could not concentrate during the next half-hour. I have no idea of what we looked at, what we did. All I can recall is shuffling along with the group, watching the others to see what they looked at, then following their gaze so it would appear I was as much impressed as they. I kept going over our plans in my head. As scheduled now, the planned power breakdown would take place in the research laboratory sector. Research labs were, according to our reports, very busy—Stacy and I could blend into a crowd more easily there, our disguises would not be so easily noticed. It appeared now that the tour would hit the laboratory sector after the supper break in the cafeteria. In our original plan the laboratory tour would have taken place before lunch, giving Stacy and me time to wander back into the cafeteria, with our disappearance, perhaps, not being noticed at all.

As we neared the cafeteria locale I was surprised at how hungry I felt. The thought of prime ribs became more and more tempting. At the same time I was a bit disturbed that I could so ease into thoughts of food before the mission itself.

"I sent a message ahead about the medium-rare," Cheryl said, again standing next to me. The rest of the tour was grouped around an exhibit whose subject was hidden by their bodies.

"That's very considerate of you."

"Part of the service. I want everything to be just right so—Nancy, what are you doing here?"

In my fogginess the name did not register, and I was startled by the unexpected sight of Alicia standing in front of us. She had a businesslike false smile on her face, but I thought I detected a critical mischievous smile in her eyes.

"Hello, Cheryl," she said, ignoring me. I remembered then that, in these circumstances, she was of course Nancy Donner, an office-mate of my aggressive tour guide.

"What's up, Nanc?"

"I'm afraid I have to borrow two of your VIPs for a while. Geraghty and Stacy, which ones are they?"

She looked over her shoulder toward the group looking at the exhibit.

"For how long?" Cheryl said.

"How long what?"

"How long are you borrowing them? And what for?"

"I have an order to do an interview with them. You know, get their impressions about our facilities and so forth. The former spacer's point of view, earthly matters versus cosmic. It's part of *your* program, Cheryl."

I was as confused as Cheryl. Alicia was not scheduled to encounter the tour until just before the power failure. Reluctantly Cheryl introduced me to "Nancy Donner" and called Stacy over to us. As she talked, she held on to my arm as if she had no intention of letting me go for the interview. I saw Alicia glance curiously at her hold on my arm, but she exhibited no reaction to it.

"Make this interview short, Nancy," Cheryl said. "I want them back in the cafeteria for the supper break."

"Oh, that won't be necessary," Alicia said sweetly. Cheryl's grip on my arm tightened to viselike pressure. "I'll have somebody send some food and drink to us. It'll improve the interview, relax us and all."

"No!" Cheryl said.

"Don't worry, dear, I'll have them back to you in time for the start of the second half of the tour. Come with me, gentlemen."

It was becoming obvious, even to our fellow tourists, that the two women were struggling to maintain their professional politeness.

"Nancy, Mr. Geraghty and I are dining together in one of the private rooms."

Alicia again did not react.

"Well then, I'll try to return him to you if possible, Cheryl. In the meantime we are wasting time here by fussing about time. I'll see what I can do. In the meantime, gentlemen, my office is this way."

Cheryl's fingers slid along my upper arm as she finally released me. It seemed to me that, if she could have fought Alicia with me as the prize, she would have done so. But, so long as she was faced with official policy, even her plans would have to be altered. I almost felt sorry for her, especially as I looked back and realized that she intended to stare at us until we were finally around a corner and out of her sight.

8

Alicia set a fast pace through the hallways. Catching up to her, I whispered:

"What was that all about?"

"Change in plan."

"What change?"

"You're off, Voss. Now. After a brief and showy visit to my office, where I've hidden the lab coats and badges."

"Now? What about the power failure?"

"That's going to occur, too. While your tour group's in the cafeteria. Not too long after your dear friend Cheryl's been served her prime-rib entree, no doubt with tears flowing *au jus*."

"You know her plans?"

"I figured them out. Especially when one of the kitchen people called to inquire the order of courses for your little tryst in the private dining room. Sorry to deprive you of that, Voss, but . . ."

Tension in Alicia's shoulders.

"It's a silly time for you to be jealous," I said.

"Of course it is. And don't kid yourself, I'm not especially jealous. Merely observant. Christ and Ethel, I just hate that big-titted bitch, that's all. Remember, I've had to pretend to enjoy working with her all this time."

"I found her rather pleasant."

"You would. If you'd like to keep your dinner date, perhaps I could change your plans even further."

"Okay, okay, let's just get to it. I'm nervous enough without having to banter with you about Cheryl Hidalgo."

"You're right. Sorry. I'm jumpy, too."

"Is she on to us, do you think?"

"She might be. That's why I decided to change our method of attack. She's liable to've been assigned to spy on you."

"That might be overkill. There're already two spies in the tour group."

"What?"

I explained about our two shadowers.

"Damn, I wasn't informed about any last-minute additions to the tour. Everything's fall—well, no time to check it out. I'll try to assign somebody to keep an eye on them, make sure they don't leave the tour, but I don't know if—"

"You've other agents here?"

"Naturally. You don't think I can pull off the power failure all by my lonesome, do you?"

For our own security reasons, I had not been informed of the extent of underground infiltration within the retread chamber complex.

"Obviously you're going to have to be extra careful, Voss. In here."

She pointed to an office door that said, in big letters, Public Liaison Office. The names of Nancy Donner and Cheryl Hidalgo, along with four others, were in smaller letters in a corner of the glass. She held the door open for us and we passed through an empty outer office (the other personnel went to supper early, Alicia said) and into a smaller cubicle. She nodded toward the overhead monitoring camera, said:

"We'll have to look like a real interview for a few minutes. You're going to answer some questions in a good strong voice, both of you, then you can adjourn to the next cubicle, where the monitoring camera's temporarily inoperable, change into your chamber duds and follow the assigned route to the destination."

"All right. Let's start."

Alicia abruptly raised her voice and asked a series of rather dull questions. She spoke rapidly and efficiently, tapped me on the knee if my answer was becoming too long. Stacy's answers, were, of course, never too long.

"That should do it," she said loudly, then whispered, "I think I'm giving you more time than the original plan called for. Good—"

A door click outside made Alicia tense her body. She spoke again:

"And, Mr. Geraghty, about your impressions of our–"

A tap at the door. I looked up and saw Cheryl.

"Are you through with our friend here?" Cheryl said in her soft, all-business voice.

"Oh, not nearly," Alicia said. Cheryl, annoyed, held her body straighter. Standing in the narrow doorway, she looked statuesque and somewhat forbidding.

"Well, damn it, Nancy, can't you do the rest of the interview later? After, say, we've looked at the labs."

"That wouldn't be *proper,* dear. You know the routine. I'll send our two fine men to you as soon as I'm done."

Cheryl, clearly resisting the urge to insult her colleague, said instead:

"All right. I'll be awaiting you, Mr. Geraghty. I've given orders to wait for my signal to begin cooking the entree. If that's all right with you."

"Um, of course, it's okay with me."

"Good. I'll see you. Soon, I hope. Be quick, Nancy."

Cheryl slammed the outer door with some force.

"That bitch," Alicia muttered, while the echo of the slammed door receded. "It's like she's determined she's going to screw things up for us."

"Maybe I should keep the date. We could go ahead with the original–"

"No. Too late for that. This'll work better. Don't worry. I'll take care of things at this end."

"Alicia–"

"That's what I'm here for. And stop calling me Alicia, Mr. Geraghty, when Nancy will do just fine. You two–now, into the next cubicle. Oh, and there's some micro-dust under the collar of each lab coat, a bit extra I was able to smuggle in at Ben's request. Okay? Move."

I wanted to say more to her, but there was nothing to say. Stacy was already out the door. I followed him. Alicia came to the doorway, kept a check on the outer office while Stacy and I donned our lab uniforms, attached the security badges.

"Ready?" I said to Stacy, and he nodded. The uniforms fit us snugly, as if they'd been tailored for us. A good sign.

Alicia went to the outer-office door, propped it open a bit.

"Everything's okay," she said, returning to us. "After I return to my cubicle, you two leave this one and go out normally."

As she turned to leave, I took her arm, leaned forward and kissed her.

"That was pleasant," she said, and left.

Stacy and I waited half a minute, then left her office. Our absorber-knowledge informed us that, to get to where we were going, we had to turn left, go to the first intersecting corridor, then take a right.

9

The passage through the network of corridors was simpler than I had anticipated. At each intersection a bit of absorber-data clicked into place and we traveled correctly without even thinking about it. The briskness of our walk no doubt convinced other chamber employees that we were on a job-related task of some importance. Some of them nodded to us as we walked by. Occasionally I would notice the name on a passing badge, and that person's life-history would flash in front of my eyes.

We were able to procure a four-seater for a part of the descent, a bonus to our plan that we hadn't been able to count on. It seemed that, with each phase, the plan became simpler. We were, in fact, gaining time at all points. Checkpoints, which were scattered throughout the chamber, proved no problem. Guards merely glanced at our IDs. The deeper we went into the chamber, the less trouble we seemed to have. I remarked on this to Stacy.

"No surprise," he said.

"Isn't it?"

"I expected less trouble in these parts."

"Why's that?"

"No reason for them to be efficient here. All the real security's up above. They've probably never had a serious violation this deep down before."

"Maybe. I hope so. So far everything's too easy."

"Supposed to be."

"I don't care if it's supposed to be. I don't like it. And, look at this for luck, *another* four-seater just waiting for us."

We latched onto a transportation beam, penetrated the lower depths of the chamber even more. Other cars and people passed us. I realized why we were proceeding so well—everybody looked just like us. As long as we continued to look like them, there seemed no obstacle to our mission. We parked the vehicle where another of the transportation beams ran out. Checking our location, I knew we were now very close. Getting out of the car, I started walking fast. Stacy had to lay a hand on my arm to remind me to keep a natural pace.

Turning a corner, we saw one of our shadowers just ahead, talking with a technician, apparently interrogating him. The technician had his back pressed against a wall, the shadower leaned over him. Stacy and I found a reason to check an atmospheric-unit impaneled near us.

"What do we do now?" Stacy said.

"Not just walk past him, that's sure."

"There's an alternate route just back there, around the corner."

"Let's hit it."

Pretending our check was over, we made our way back around the corner, found the alternate route. I breathed a relieved sigh, as I stared at its relatively empty corridors.

"How much farther do you figure we have to go?" I asked Stacy.

"Not far. About five minutes to the security lock, couple minutes there—less than ten minutes, I'd say."

"I wonder if Cheryl is sweating it back in the private dining room."

"Ask for a raincheck."

"Very funny, Stacy. I'll—"

The other shadower, or maybe it was the same one, jumped out in front of us. Where he had been concealed was a mystery. He seemed to appear, a shadower out of the shadows. He held a mean-looking modern-looking weapon in his hand, and he waved it at our faces to make sure we noticed it.

"This is as far as our curiosity will allow us to let you go, mister," he said.

"Curiosity?" I said.

"We hoped we could ascertain what you were up to here. But this's as far as we can stretch it, Geraghty. It's the end of it."

"I'm sorry, but we were authorized for this secret inspection by higher-placed officials than your puny department. I don't know what idiotic affair you suspect, but—"

"Don't try to bluff it, Geraghty. I'm sorry. I'd like to get into your mind a little more, find out what makes a natural hero turn traitor, what turns him into—"

"Sir, I don't understand. Traitor?"

The man wanted to laugh at me. I would not have blamed him. My protests were too transparent a ruse. And a stupid way of biding time. Still, I did bide the time . . .

While I was thinking of how unfortunate it was to get this close to the retread-soul storage area and be caught, Stacy was pushing the man's weapon aside and dealing him a quick chop to the neck. I recovered quickly enough to take the weapon out of the man's hand and catch him as he fell.

"I think there's a—" I said.

"It's about three meters from here, on the other side."

We both had thought of this hallway's janitorial closet simultaneously. For the moment there were no other people in the vicinity, and we were able to drag our enemy to the closet and place him between a suction-mop and a water-purifier. I tried to hand Stacy the weapon.

"Maybe we should take it with us."

"Why on earth would–"

"His partner might show up any time."

"Still no reason to carry a weapon that'd get us into unnecessary trouble."

"What'll I do with it?"

"Shove it into the water-purifier."

"Okay, good idea."

We closed the door on the unconscious man just in time, for a pair of technicians strode around a corner. They looked at us in puzzlement for a moment. I pulled out a notebook from a jacket pocket and made a notation, convincing our observers that our duty was checking janitor's closets. They went on.

Now–along with being more watchful than ever–we had to cope with the implications of what our enemy had said. He had let us get this far in order to discern our purposes. That meant others knew we had left the tour group and were heading downward. His partner, at least. The important question was whether they were acting on their own or had alerted others. If so, how many others?

Ahead was the most complicated of the security blocks, an improvement on human guardians known as a laser-barrier–a set of a dozen laser beams that flashed across a relatively narrow passageway, set at an intensity to kill potential intruders. Those people cleared by security to enter the retread storage area, a small percentage of the chamber's entire personnel, could shut off the beams with a special key, then pass through the corridor before the lasers automatically reactivated. We had no key and the only way we could make our way through the maze was based on our knowledge, provided by the absorber, of where the laser projection-units were located. As we approached the passageway, and I saw the multiplicity of caution and danger signs that preceded it, I recalled the nightmares I had had about this phase of the mission.

The door to the passageway was locked but, among Stacy's skills, was a talent for lockpicking. (If only he could have done the same for the specially treated portal whose mechanisms turned off the laser beams, but we had no time for that series of locks.) He had the door open in seconds. We stared ahead, sensing the power of the laser beams we could not see.

For the first time since we had left Alicia's office, I felt relaxed. This was something I could handle, a problem without the threat of human interference. The absorber had fed us the current pattern of the laser barrier. As always, there were six beams running vertically, invisible pillars that we had to get around. Another six ran horizontally, at different levels, two of which were at floor level. So long as the pattern had not been altered in the last day or two, and it was not scheduled to be, we had a good chance of getting through the passageway unscathed.

I am sure that, if we were recorded slowly making our way through that maze, we must have presented a comic picture. First we had to crouch down to avoid a crossways mid-level beam, then ease our way by a horizontal beam halving the passageway.

"Everything seems in place," I whispered to Stacy.

"Don't talk."

"Touchy."

"Yes."

"Okay. But now we have to stand."

We daintily stepped over a floor-level beam, then quickly had to twist our shoulders to squeeze through a pair of horizontal beams. It was that way for the length of the passageway. Crouching down, stretching up, twisting sideways, crawling under. We managed to limbo under the last beam, which had been set at crotch level, and were at the other end of the corridor. Stacy let out a long loud breath.

"You seem shaken," I said to him.

"I am."

"Didn't think something like that'd scare you."

"Well, you were wrong."

"Why'd you worry? The absorber fed us—"

"Absorber's been wrong on some things."

"Maybe it has. Anyway, not to worry. We're here. That's the last hurdle. Down that hall and through that door—the old goal. C'mon."

10

As we stood on a balcony overlooking the massive storage room, my eyes could not adjust to the vistas in front of me. It had felt strange enough to open an innocent-looking door, pass through a normal doorway, and step into the phantasmagoric cavern in which more than a million "souls" were stored, nurtured, and—until our arrival, perhaps—protected.

My first impression was of a havoc wrought by a mad scientist that had been slyly put back together by an orderly, but just as mad, scientist. A Hieronymous Bosch painting reorganized into a precise but diabolical landscape. Everything was in lines and patterns, lighting was soft but normal, people moved casually and confidently up and down straight aisles. Perhaps it was my knowledge of the place that lent it the atmosphere of suppressed madness, but at my first viewing all I could see was insanity. There was insanity in the very normality of the massive room whose far side could not be seen even from our extraordinary vantage point. I am more inclined now to believe that the feeling I had at that moment of abnormality attacking me from all sides was a correct perception, the emanations of more than a million sleeping minds, all willing to kill me if they had known what I was there for. I don't know if I had the vision then, or it has come to me since—but I have a dream-memory of the millions of souls individualized into elongated shimmery beings with their hands outstretched to me, knives and guns in some of the hands. It was a sickening sight, that place, and it was a normal, efficiently functioning laboratory.

Stacy and I exchanged glances, but said nothing. There was nothing to do but proceed. Without a signal we each turned away from the other, and went off in separate directions, each with his own bit of territory to cover. As I reached the metal staircase I would use to descend into the laboratory, I looked back. I could not see Stacy. He apparently had reached his exit point earlier than I, and was on his way down. I thought I felt the stairway sway from side to side as I descended, but that might have been my imagination. The air seemed different as I reached the bottom of the stairway. Colder, as if hidden air currents were blowing in from underground caves. So damp that I could not help touching the nearest wall to see if it sweated. A nearby technician, who was checking a panel of dials and gauges, looked at me as if he were about to ask a dangerous question. It was time to look efficient. I nodded at the man in a professional way, and started down the nearest aisle.

From my knowledge of the general layout of the room, at least in blueprint form, I knew my first stop was only a few meters down the aisle, a few footsteps away. I began walking slower, in spite of my feeling of urgency to get the damn job done. Each side of the aisle, with its numerous shelves containing the blackened containers which housed the brains and souls of my prey, rose above me. I looked up and could not see the top. They looked to me like unscalable library stacks. Suddenly, without realizing it was even that close, I found myself at the foot of the small stairway leading to the first nutrient feeder-outlet. I hesitated, the toe of my shoe just brushing against the first step, ready to turn back of its own accord. Maybe I did not have to do anything, I thought. I could let Stacy perform his half of the mission, which would be sufficiently destructive, and nobody would know I had failed purposefully. It would look as if we both had done it, yet inside I would know that I was not guilty. Not guilty? No, impossible. If I did not drop in a grain of micro-dust, if I disposed of my entire supply in the nearest dustbin, I would still, of course, be guilty. I was here, wasn't I?

A hand on my arm startled me out of my thoughts. I looked into the face of a young woman. It was a scarred face. What looked like the result of two knife slashes crossed on one cheek. If she had not spoken first, I might have asked her if she, too, had inherited a sabotaged body.

"Is anything the matter, friend?" she asked. Her smile, although meant to be pleasant, seemed to imitate the shape of the knife-wound scars.

"Just a dizzy spell, I'm afraid," I said, searching her dull hazel eyes for a hint of suspicion.

"Touch of the jeebies."

"What?"

"The jeebies. You know. Or are you new here?"

"I've been here, uh, a short while."

She held a clipboard to her body as if it were a fighting shield. I realized that she stood atilt, and knew then that one of her legs was shorter than the other.

"Well, we all get dizzy once in a while. We call it the jeebies. It's the spooks. Superstition is all it is. The feeling that our wards here escape from their little houses and inhabit us momentarily. Possession by spirits, it's an old tradition. You've just had a touch of the jeebies. One of these souls has taken to you and has possessed you for a moment, that's all."

She was trying so hard to be friendly, comforting, that I felt ashamed to feel physical repulsion toward her. I could not figure out why. I had seen scars before, seen a cripple before, without flinching. Why was this particular woman so repellent to me? Then I took a careful look at her and saw why. Beneath the scars, she resembled Alicia. A vague resemblance, yes, but a resemblance. As if Alicia's best features had been somehow compressed and placed on a broader face, as if her hair had been redone primly, as if her body had been made stouter and twisted in one leg. And she was standing there and touching my arm and telling me everything was okay. Suddenly I wanted to take this gimpy scarred woman in my arms, hold her and tell her that, no, everything was not okay. But I just nodded and said:

"That must be what it is. The jeebies."

"Sure. Every profession has its nightmares, and that's ours."

"I'm all right now. I'll just, uh, go about my job."

"My name's Flo. R and D. Office next level up, drop by sometime. I got stuff strong enough to ward off the jeebies."

"Stuff?"

"Hard stuff, as it's sometimes called. See you around."

She patted my arm a couple of times before finally releasing it. I noticed, as she walked away from me, that she had compensated well for her bum leg. Her limp was barely noticeable. She wore a short skirt, as if proud of both her legs. The good one was shapely, the short one a little thick in the ankle.

I started up the steps. I saw my goal, the feeder-outlet, sooner than I wanted to. At a point in the tubing which connected the soul-containers, a triangular section led into a small enclosed vat. The vat had a funnel-like opening through which samples of the circulating liquid could be extracted for examination. From time to time, the balance of the circulating liquid was altered by the addition of various materials which revived fading ingredients and restored proper nutritive functions. Reaching the feeder-outlet, I stared into it, hoping to see something sensible in the active liquid. All it looked like was active liquid, I don't know what I expected. Like much of my absorber-information, this was exactly as I had been instructed.

I stood over it for a while, trying to look official, while I carefully removed my first object that contained the substance I was to introduce into the liquid. A button. As I held it between my fingers, I was astonished at how easily it crumbled. I had thought I would have to exert more pressure than that. It seemed that, in the earlier tests with the micronium, I had had to squeeze harder. Then I felt the tension in my fingers and knew why the button had become dust so easily. I stared into my hand. There it was, my weapon, all bits of dust clinging to my sweaty fingers. One big exhalation, and I could blow it all away. It seemed dark blue in the subdued lighting of the area. I curled up my fingers, hiding the micro-dust from casual view. As if testing the working of the funnel opening, I placed my hand along its rim, but not yet within the circle. My heart was racing. I seemed to feel one of the spirits which Flo had talked about, possessing me. No, not one spirit, several. Well, I said to myself—or to them—you'll just have to haunt me. I am going to kill you forever and finally, if killing is what this is.

Moving my hand off the rim, I unclenched my fist, and watched the dust fall into the liquid. Grains of it floated momentarily, then disappeared into the permanent swirl. Bits of dust clung to my index finger. I flicked them away, down into the funnel, with my thumb. Even though the finger was free of any remaining grains, I had to wipe it on my lab coat.

I tried to see if there were any change in the liquid, an alteration of color, a school of dust-grains swimming together. There was, of course, nothing. I had known that, known there would be no detectable aftermath, but I had to look for it. I wanted verification.

I turned away from the feeder-outlet, raced down the steps, rushed down the aisle even though I knew I had to look calm and businesslike. I tried not to notice the odd glances coming from the occasional passing worker. I was moving too fast for them to think out what I might be doing.

The next station was being attended by a technician. I loitered for a moment in front of one of the blackened containers, trying to see into it, pretending to examine it as a natural duty. Inside, I knew, was a brain, a mere housing for the soul or spirit or jeebie that would not, if I continued to be successful in the mission, ever leave it. I wished I could see through the opaque dark surface so that I would at least have more than a mental image of what I was destroying. I don't know what difference that made; it would have looked exactly as I expected, exactly as I saw it in my mind.

The technician left the station, strode past me without looking or questioning. I was grateful for that. If another one of them had stopped me, especially one as pleasant as Flo, I might not have been able to keep up my pretense, my disguise. I might have had to say, I'm an infiltrator, here to destroy your precious charges. Prevent it if you can, stop me. As soon as the man had passed, I ran up the stairs, duplicated my graceful moves over the top of the funnel opening there. Flicked my thumb again, wiped it on my lab coat again, raced down the stairs again.

In my memory, my feeding of the dust into the feeder-outlets is distorted. I see myself dancing balletically down aisles, stopping at the right points, lifting myself onto my toes, waving my hand and watching the sleep-dust, the gift of the mass-killing sandman, fall out of it, drift down the river of life, float away on its gently waving surface. Of course I was more efficient than that. Although I walked too fast, took the stairs too quickly, I did the job without grace and with a plodding efficiency. My mind, filled with absorber-knowledge, did not seem to be thinking beyond data, it merely functioned.

Or merely functioned until I turned a corner and saw the other shadower, or maybe the same one we'd so recently stored in a closet, standing in my way, holding onto Stacy, a weapon placed—rammed against—Stacy's neck. The weapon seemed to be the largest gun I had ever seen, massive, fuzzy in outline, I could not seem to fix on it.

"Just stand where you are," the man said to me. I had not thought of doing anything else. His face was twisted into an awesome stupidity.

"I can't figure out what the shit you guys are up to," he said. "But, whatever it is, this is the end of it."

Mentally I calculated how much of my part of the job I had accomplished. Most of it, I figured. If the poisonous substance worked as well as Ben claimed, I might have sprinkled enough micronium to annihilate more than half of the sleeping souls in the entire storage room. I could afford to appear self-satisfied in front of our enemy.

"We're missing the tour," I said. "Perhaps we should return. I did want to see the research labs."

The flippancy angered the man, and he tried to press his weapon deeper into Stacy's neck. A couple of workers in back of our shadower had stopped walking toward us and were silently watching. The room's subtle lighting seemed to alter, everything felt more dim. Our assailant did not know it, but death was all around him, swimming past us, minutely beginning to enlarge, multiply.

"You've done enough touring, Geraghty. Now it's our turn—to deal with you and your friend here."

"I'm sure you'll squeeze us dry. But we're willing to go with you, as meekly as you'd like. Why don't you ease off a bit, especially with that gun?"

He moved the weapon a little, and color returned to Stacy's cheeks. I decided to confuse the man further and said to Stacy:

"How far'd you get, Stacy?"

"Far enough."

"Good."

The cryptic exchange angered the man, as I'd expected, but instead of questioning it, he merely pushed Stacy ahead of him.

"Let's go," he said, and led us down a long aisle to a different exit. Stacy and I walked side by side, silent. Our assailant followed, reminding us a couple of times that he had a bead on us.

At the new exit, the pattern of its laser-barrier came into my mind. I was oddly pleased at the way our absorber-knowledge clicked into position at each juncture of the proceedings, even when it was not especially needed. Our captor told us to stand aside. He produced a key and inserted it into the lock that would turn off the laser-barrier. Before turning the key, he told Stacy and me to stand in front of him.

"We only have thirty seconds to get through the barrier safely, so don't pull anything, or you'll die, too. Okay, Geraghty, you go first. Your friend here'll be right behind you, and I'll be behind him, with this gun pointing at his back. Either of you try anything and you'll be dead. Okay."

He turned his key. I could hear the faint click of the laser system disengaging.

"C'mon, move," the man shouted.

I entered the passageway. Before I was aware of what was happening, I felt a foot kick me and I went sprawling on the floor. As I twisted around to look up, I realized that the kick had come from Stacy. He was now struggling with the man. Getting up, I started toward him.

"No!" he hollered. "Get to the other side!"

I hesitated for a moment, then turned away from him, ran forward. As I reached the other end of the passageway and plunged through the doorway to safety, I heard the system click on again. I looked back. Stacy and the man were still fighting, right at the edge of the passageway. The dimness of the light behind them obscured the details of the fight. I could not tell who was winning.

Suddenly the man caught Stacy a hard blow on the side of his head, and Stacy slumped against the open door. The man looked my way, shouted:

"You won't get away, Geraghty! Just wait there, where you are!"

He started to insert the key into the lock again, to shut down the laser-barrier, but Stacy suddenly jumped at him. The man, taken by surprise, fell backward, but managed to slam his weapon against the side of Stacy's face. Involuntarily I reached forward, as if I could affect the outcome of the battle, and, just as involuntarily, I drew my hand back before it came near a laser beam. One of the two fighters, I still don't know which one, dislodged them both from the doorway, forced them both to fall into the passageway. Their screams of pain mingled, until I could not tell which was the man screaming and which was Stacy.

11

I can recall little about my return through the retread chamber corridors to Alicia's office. I know I managed to appear businesslike, knowing where I was going, making connections mindlessly. I made the correct adjustments, followed the right routes, always knew which way to turn at each intersection.

When I reached the hallway that led to the Public Liaison Office, I had to stop and lean against a wall, no longer caring what passersby might think. I did not want to face Alicia, to tell her about Stacy, to try to figure what we should do now. The basic plan was no longer applicable. I could not just casually rejoin the tour group, flirt with Cheryl as if I had been absent only a short time, maybe keep a late date for those prime ribs. The bodies of Stacy and the government man were going to be found. And soon. There would be a search, an investigation, an official inquiry. The investigators would be led naturally to me, and probably to Alicia. All I could think was, we had to get out of the chamber, had to find someplace to hide. I felt better—at least I was being rational, trying to work out escape possibilities. I resisted feeling emotion, breaking down in the corridor. I had to resist that. I had to force out the memories of Stacy, the feeling that, when I had really needed to save his life, I had merely been an observer at the far end of a passageway.

When I had forced the important things out of my mind, I felt relieved. All that was left was the escape, I could deal with that. Escape. I pushed myself away from the corridor wall and went to the Public Liaison Office, entered it. The outer room was empty, as before. I went to Alicia's cubicle-office, whispered her name. No response. I wondered if she had not been able to wait, had had to leave, had been taken away. I went to the adjoining office, stashed the lab coat and badge. Returning to her office, I was surprised to find her there, sitting at her desk, slumped down, her head leaning back against the cushion of her chair. For a moment I thought she looked dead. Then I saw she was breathing. I walked to the chair, revolved it a bit, touched her shoulder. She did not stir.

"You needn't worry, she's all right," said a voice behind me. I turned, having already recognized the voice as Cheryl Hidalgo's.

"What happened?" I said.

"Had to hit her, that's all. I've had training. She'll be okay in a few minutes."

Alicia moaned.

"See?" Cheryl said. "She's coming around already. A remarkably resilient young lady, that Nancy Donner. If that's her real name."

"Why shouldn't it be?"

Cheryl laughed.

"You really take me for as naive as I act. The naivete's for public relations, I leave it here at the end of every working day.

But I am able to see, by the way you touch the young lady, that Nancy is not a stranger to you, that she—"

Alicia moaned again, this time opening her eyes.

"Cheryl!" she said, then looked at me. "Voss, what—"

Cheryl smiled.

"See?" she said. "Okay, what is this all about? I know there's been a disturbance at the lower levels, but nobody up this high knows what. They're certainly not ready to break their security for someone from the Public Liaison Office. But my guess is that you, both of you, have something to do with it. Am I right?"

"I don't know what you're—"

"Don't crap me, Geraghty. I know that our two newcomers to the tour were spying on you. They took off as soon as they saw you go, no explanation to me or anything. Tell me."

She looked from me to Alicia, back at me again. We were both silent.

"Don't tell me then. Doesn't make any difference, I suppose. There're more skilled interrogators around."

"Cheryl, I'll kill you," Alicia said softly. The timbre of her voice was unlike anything I had heard from her before.

Cheryl laughed.

"With what?" she said. "You don't have any weapons, I checked that. And I do."

She raised a hand, which had held a small handgun all during our little talk.

"I wouldn't want to lose all the points I'll get for capturing you two. I needed a chance to graduate to a higher job, this'll help, I'm sure. I'll just signal them upstairs and—"

"No, you won't!" Alicia said, standing, beginning to walk around the desk.

"Alicia!" I shouted.

Cheryl smiled, but backed off a couple of steps.

"Alicia, huh?" she said. "That should be a valuable piece of information for them to—don't come any closer, Nancy, Alicia, whatever your name—"

Alicia did not even hesitate at Cheryl's warning. I started moving toward both of them, not knowing exactly what I could do—push Alicia out of the way, jump at Cheryl, whatever seemed appropriate. Alicia, noticing my move, waved me away.

"Okay, that's enough," Cheryl said and raised the gun to eye level, taking aim.

"It's okay, shoot," Alicia said. "I don't care."

"Stop!" I shouted.

I jumped toward Alicia. Sensing my move, she eased out of my way. Cheryl was distracted and her shot went upward and away from either of us. Alicia ran at her, threw her off balance. The gun fell out of Cheryl's hand. Alicia saw it, but made no move toward it. Instead, she grabbed Cheryl and they began to struggle. I recovered my balance and picked up the gun, watched as they rolled around on the floor.

"Alicia," I said, "it's all right, I've got the gun. Get away from her, we can get out, we can—"

"No, Voss," Alicia whispered, and that was all she said. The battle between her and Cheryl went on in a strange silence, interrupted only by muffled sounds of shifting. Neither seemed able to counter the strength of the other. Gradually, Alicia broke Cheryl's hold on her arm, pushed her body away and grabbed her neck, began to squeeze. Cheryl tried to break out of her grip. The surprise on her face seemed divided between fear of death and astonishment at Alicia's strength.

"That's enough, Alicia," I hollered.

"No, Voss," she whispered again.

Before I could interfere, Cheryl's eyes closed and her body slumped. I may have heard something crack.

"Let go, Alicia," I said. "She's unconscious, we can go."

"No, Voss. No, Voss. No, Voss."

Her ritual incantation made me grab her by the shoulders, pull her off Cheryl. Cheryl's head rose with Alicia's hands. She would not break the grip. I had to hit Alicia in the arm to force one of her hands free. She let the other one go slowly, reluctantly. I did not need to check Cheryl for signs of life.

"Alicia, I—"

"Don't say anything, Voss."

She sat staring at the body for a full minute. I looked away, not so much in revulsion at the corpse of Cheryl but because I did not want to have to look at Alicia.

"It was necessary, Voss," Alicia finally said. "We still have something of a chance. If she were alive, we might—"

"What chance? They've got Stacy!"

"Stacy? They captured him?"

For a moment I could not speak, not wanting to tell her that he must be dead, too. Then I told her.

"I'm sorry, Voss. I'm sorry you couldn't tell me. But I was right, I think. We had to kill Cheryl. I don't mind. Don't think that I mind. No reason to—"

"Forget it. Let's get out of here. Like you say, we might have a chance."

Before we left the office, Alicia looked back at Cheryl's body, said:

"I hope they get to her in time."

"In time?"

"Well, it's convenient for her to die here. She can be retreaded and maybe go back to something sensible, writing novels or—"

"C'mon."

I did not remind her until later—until after we had run down corridors and through hatchways and snaked by checkpoints and found our way to the outside world and stolen a limousine and sped back to Washington and a fast flight to New York—that her hopes for Cheryl's retreading were based on a remote chance. She asked why, still dazed. I said that Stacy and I had been successful—very few retreads were going to emerge from the Washington Chamber for the Reprocessing of New Life for some time. Alicia had not included Cheryl in her mental tally of destroyed retreads. A momentary flash of horror was evident on her face, then she calmed. She said again not to think that she minded. She was sorry, but she didn't mind.

12

On the trip back I kept dozing off and seeing, in odd shapes and wavery lines, the souls that I had "killed." I reminded myself that they were not even dead yet, that they were still unconscious entities being cared for and preserved. But their death was coming. They would slowly burn out without awareness, meeting their appointment with eternity a lifetime or so early. Or late, depending on whose side you took. In each dream the souls seemed to suffer, to implore me to change everything back, let them live, give them just one more lifetime, one more chance to right wrongs and make miracles, one more lifetime, one more go at fouling up their minds, one more lifetime, one more go at finding the loves of their lives. I kept shaking myself awake. Alicia, concerned but wise enough not to ask, merely whispered comfort and asked me if I would like anything to eat or drink. I couldn't eat or drink.

Finally, when we were with Ben and he was being so goddamned cheerful, happy at the success of the mission, I had to say it:

"Ben, it was wrong."

"C'mon, Voss, don't get moral on me now. We had all that out. I know both sides of the issue, I—"

"No, that's not what I mean. I don't want a college bull session. I think I would die from another bull session about ethics and morality. I'm just—just saying it was wrong. I am sorry I did it."

"Forget it, Voss. It'll pass."

"You're wrong. I'm wrong. There was no need to kill them."

"You're just upset. I expected this, it's a natural reaction, logical—"

"Don't keep telling me about logical. Nothing's logical. Sending millions into ovens, bombing cities, blowing up populated asteroids, planting a ridiculous magical dust in a retread chamber. None of them are logical."

"I think you should rest, then—"

"I'm not even all that sure about the wrong of it. I'm just sorry. I wish that I hadn't done it, me, me alone. Anybody else, maybe I could pass a sound moral judgment, even give them credit for a job well done, but I wish to hell that I hadn't done it. Don't say anything more. I don't want to hear about anything making sense, or of the rights of the many over the few, or right against wrong."

Ben nodded, lapsed into the silence I demanded. Alicia said:

"I can't think of your million souls. I keep seeing Cheryl dead. Cheryl and Stacy, imagining Stacy. They're the only deaths that have meaning for me. The others . . ."

She didn't finish what she was saying. We were all silent, then I said:

"I feel foolish. I'm trying too hard to feel pain, and I feel pain, but it's receding. Just shut me up, or give me something to force me to sleep. Sleep without dreams, can you do that?"

Ben nodded.

The next day he checked me over, put me through the absorber-debriefing, said we could go ahead with the medical stuff any time. I had forgotten about the surgery, but said yes, let's get it over with. He said he would make arrangements.

He sent Alicia and me to an abandoned building that, as I realized upon our arrival, was very close to L'Etre. I almost suggested that we check into the restaurant for a gourmet dinner, but I didn't think either of us would appreciate it. On the fourth floor of the abandoned building of former offices was a fully furnished, and rather luxurious, apartment. There were many pictures hiding the walls, and sumptuous furniture, a circular bed in the bedroom, ornate decorations in the bathroom. I took a bath just to stare at horn-blowing cupids and gargoyles and pretty ladies and curlicues.

Ben came by and said the operations were arranged for, and later I would be guided to the secret hospital where they'd take place at the earliest safe time. I asked him about the apartment. He said that years ago it had belonged to a successful pimp. Someone with an interest in historical preservation had seen that it was kept up, even after the neighborhood had been declared unfit for revamping and the building had been abandoned. He left, saying there were many preparations to be seen to, he would return when all was ready. He gave me a gross of instructions about not eating or drinking and said he wondered how I'd look with my head shaven. He went out the door laughing. I was amazed that I did not hate him.

For a long time after his departure, Alicia wandered around the apartment, examining its artifacts, commenting lackadaisically on their historical value.

"Can I get you anything?" she said, as she passed my chair.

"What?"

"Something to eat, I don't know."

"Can't eat anything, Ben said so."

"Oh, right."

"Are you nervous about me, my surgery?"

"Shouldn't I be?"

"I suppose."

She picked up a game that was the centerpiece of an end table. It was some sort of old dice game, five dice enclosed in a plastic cube. She shook the cube, watched the numbers fall.

"Maybe I'd like to be a retread, after all," she said abruptly.

"Are you joking, or—"

"Partly. At least, partly. But there was a moment there when I thought I was going to die, back when I was struggling with Cheryl, and I've been thinking about it. That I wasn't quite ready to die, you know, the old stuff. I had things to do, I wanted to be with you more, the usual sentimental garbage."

"You can change your mind when the time comes. Be a retread."

"No. I can't. Not even if they never trace my identity."

"You think they will?"

"They might. I've been told there's a bulletin out on you. One on me, too, but in the name of Nancy Donner."

"Well, Ben says he can fix a new identity for me, we can fade away into the remaining wilds of this country."

"Sure. I'll look forward to it."

She put the dice game down.

"My father took me on a trip west once. I liked it, especially what used to be called Colorado. Maybe it's still called Colorado, not too many names are changed. The trip, it happened not long after you abandoned us at Cleveland."

"Abandoned?"

"I was mad at you. Mad at my Uncle Voss, for making me love him, then going off without looking back. I guess I knew that my real uncles didn't much care for me and that my father would never show his love. He never did. Except when he left, the day he took off for the stars, having brought his only daughter to a proper age. Funny how my two childhood images of the two people I've loved most deal with them leaving me—you at Cleveland, my father to outer space."

"How did he?"

"How did he what?"

"Show his love for you that day."

She stared at me for a long time.

"I don't want to tell you right now. I have to get out of here for a while. I'll be back soon."

She did not look back before leaving the room. I opened my mouth to tell her to stay, but I could not say it.

I dozed off almost immediately. I had been dozing a lot since the mission, falling off to sleep very briefly, waking with a start, trying to concentrate, then dozing off again.

When I woke up from a bad dream I don't remember, I thought I was just having another bad dream.

Gorman Triplett stood in front of me, the door open behind him. When I realized that it wasn't a dream, my first thought was why didn't Alicia lock the door?

"Nice place," Triplett said. "Not exactly what I expected, but quite nice."

"Glad you like it. Actually, the decor should fit your personality better than mine. Used to belong to a pimp."

"I'm beginning to get used to your dumb jokes."

"Maybe we're destined to be friends, Triplett."

"Fat chance. Actually, you want to know, I heard about your heroics and I wanted to congratulate you."

"Please don't."

"Okay, I won't. Also, it's time."

"Time for what?"

"The lid's off. You have been devalued within the underground. I'm here to kill you."

"Oh, come on, Triplett, nobody waltzes into a room and announces the kill before—"

"I do."

He had raised his hand and shown me the gun and fired it before I could even move out of the chair. I hardly felt the pain as my vision began to cloud. Alicia, at the doorway, screamed. Triplett was turning around and aiming the gun at her as the sight went completely out of my eyes and, the second before I died, I realized that I was going to die and could do nothing for Alicia. I think I also felt terribly stupid.

13

"What the hell are you doing here?" were my first words after being returned to consciousness. I was looking up into the face of one of the two men who had been shadowing Stacy and me for so long. As usual, I could not tell which one, although I was aware only one remained alive. I wondered if this one could be a third lookalike, an idea that was quickly dispelled by the man himself.

"I requested that I be present at your revival."

My mind was foggy. I had no sense of time. Because periods of darkness are not felt by the individual soul, I had no awareness that I had just passed through one. I am glad that I was not conscious during it. What I saw before my death would have been imprinted on my memory; I probably would have been insane by the time of my return to life. As it was, I thought it must be only a short time later, that Triplett's shot had not hit a vital organ, and I was still in my former body.

"Alicia!" I said. "How is she? Where is she? Is she all right?"

The man smiled, a smile that hinted he would dearly love to torture me, but he said:

"I'm sorry. I can't answer that question, I–"

"You have to! I must–"

"I was trying to say that I simply do not know. I am not even sure who Alicia is, or was. When we got to you, you were quite alone and quite dead."

"Then maybe she's all right. I have to go to her. I–"

I tried to move, but could not. My body would not respond. At first I thought that Triplett's shot had paralyzed me, then I looked down at my feet and thought, *those are not my feet.* They are too long, too wide, what the hell is that crooked toe doing there, what–and then of course I realized. As the man had said, I had been quite dead. What I looked down at now was a fresh, new, retreaded body.

I started to laugh. I could not help it.

My observer merely stood by, apparently sensing the reasons for my irrational laughter. When I calmed down, I said:

"Nobody else was there, in the apartment then?"

"Not in the apartment."

A pang of fear in my chest.

"I don't like the sound of that. Not in the apartment. Anywhere else?"

"There was a dead man out in the street, that's all. We've never known if he was connected with your death for certain."

"Gorman Triplett."

"Let me check." He looked into a folder which he had been holding all along. "That was the man's name, yes. A minor revolutionary, an assassin. Had quite a reputation at the time. There were some sighs of relief at higher levels."

"But no woman anywhere about, no woman dead?"

"No woman. That seems to please you. I'm not quite sure why

you are more concerned about this woman than you are with the oddity of the fact you've been retreaded, which I thought would occupy your attention primarily and—"

"Oh, shut up! I don't give a damn about that. You'll tell me, I'm sure."

"Then the woman was most important. The only woman's name that's prominent in your dossier is one Nancy Donner."

I became afraid again. Afraid this man was going to tell me something awful about Nancy Donner.

"Yes, Nancy," I said, trying to sound unemotional. "What happened to her then?"

"Beyond my knowledge, I'm afraid. No trace of her was ever found."

"She said you might not locate her."

"Well, we may . . . still."

He was deliberately trying to sound ominous. I chose to ignore him.

"Which one are you?" I said.

"What do you mean?"

"I'm so used to the two of you. Wondered about your partner, and who was who, since I could never tell you two apart."

Some pain in his eyes. I almost regretted my rudeness.

"You nailed him. You and *your* partner. He was killed in a struggle with your ally and could not be retreaded, due to your genocidal good work within the retread chamber."

"And Stacy, he was killed, too?"

"I think you know that."

My control over my new body was too weak, and I began to cry just as hysterically as I had laughed a few moments before.

14

The man's name was Michael. I still had trouble thinking of him as anything else but our shadower, I had thought of him that way for so long. He blamed me for the death of his partner, whose name he never mentioned, and I could understand his anger. I only had to think of myself and Stacy, or of Triplett and Richard. For a while I became obsessed with an odd theory about male pairs which I have since forgotten.

Michael had ordered my retreading, had gone through several channels to effect it. On that first day a long time passed before I finally looked closely at him. Saw the age in his eyes, the struggle to fake youthfulness around his mouth. I asked him how long I had been in the period of darkness. Eleven years, he told me. I was amazed at the tenacity with which he pursued his goal of getting me retreaded. When I thought of it, I was even more amazed that I had been stored away in the first place. When I asked Michael about that, he said:

"I had little to do with it. There were pressures. After you had been originally salvaged and placed in a Connecticut retread chamber, the evidence of your destruction in Washington came to the fore. There was some agitation to remove your soul from the chamber and do to it what you had done to more than a million others. But there were official complications. Something to do with your official status, the fact you were known as a hero, some such thing as that. Some of our noble leaders thought you should have a chance to defend yourself, that your preserved soul could not be adjudged guilty on the basis of circumstantial evidence. I hated that—my testimony being considered as merely circumstantial evidence. They shoved me into a closet, I hollered; they said that was circumstantial. Part of it's that nobody's been able to figure out how you did it, you and your friend. Official curiosity is still high, I'm authorized to tell you. Others argued that, if they revived you and you were found guilty, it might mean the waste of a body. It's been proven nearly impossible to submit a body twice to the retreading process. So the argument dragged on and it became clear that there could never be a trial, nor could they just destroy you. So, I came up with my plan."

"Your plan."

"You'll see. What I can tell you about it now, while you're still in your renewal period, is that I argued that, since neither trial nor destruction was possible according to existing laws and practices, that you be retreaded anyway. That you be given the full privileges of a new retread and be returned to the world."

"Returned?"

"But only after I was through with you."

"For what?"

"That's what I can't tell you."

I desperately wished to ask him about Ben, and to find out anything I could about Alicia. But, of course, I could not endanger them by such requests.

As it turned out, I might as well have asked.

15

When the renewal period was over, I learned the purpose of my retreading. There was one thing I *was* useful for, in Michael's reasoning, and that was information. He told me that as soon as I told him and his cohorts everything that had happened—who was involved, places, details, etc.—he would "return me to the world," and they would never bother me again, unless of course I transgressed. I laughed at him, said he was a fool. Of course I would tell him nothing, I would die again before I told him anything.

Michael just smiled and said that *of course* I would.

I did. They had methods. I told them everything. Every detail. I told them about the mission, about Ben's planning of it. I told them every detail I had at my command about the underground and how it worked. I told them about micro-dust and how it had destroyed the souls. And I told them about Alicia.

Michael was pleased with the information. I asked him why, aside from the fact that it justified his existence. He said the information I had given was valuable. I shouted, how could it be so damn valuable? For one thing, it was eleven years old. For another, I was not an integral member of the underground. For a third, it was information that they, with their methods, could have extracted from any other of the radicals whom they captured.

Michael flashed me his best enigmatic smile, a smile whose overpowering wisdom I had come to hate. All information is valuable, he told me, and particularly some of mine, certain bits that could *not* have been obtained from anybody else. He would not tell me which. He merely said now they knew some questions they had not known before. And—and he smiled viciously—a couple of names that had escaped their notice previously.

He smiled again when he announced they were through with me, that I was now healthy enough to return to society. I had never really believed that part of his spiel, and so was astonished to find out it had been true all along. My reward for giving them information whose value was puzzling to me was to be returned to the world, to be allowed still another lifetime in exchange for unspecified treasons.

"Has anything changed?" I asked, after I had raved futilely at Michael for more than an hour. It was a question that, even though it was the normal retread's first query, I had not thought to ask in the several preceding days.

"A bit. Nothing you won't adjust to. Most returnees have been in the period of darkness for much longer than you, have to adjust more. You'll be okay."

"I gather there still must be some reject activity, or you wouldn't have needed my information.

"Oh, you'll be happy to know there's even more than before. Regular insurrections all over the place. Nothing we can't handle, but it keeps us hopping. And happy."

"Happy?"

"My job. I enjoy social turmoil, gives me a purpose."

There was no talking with Michael. It had taken forever, it seemed, for me to learn that.

16

Michael was right about the world. There were no changes in it I couldn't handle. Anything can be faced if you don't care much about it.

I even managed to fake a normal sort of life. It was not too hard, what with my new body and all. *Especially* with my new body. They had treated me rather well in that department. Michael had arranged for a well-kept body, in better condition than either of my two previous bodies. It came from a fortyish reject revolutionary who had been captured in a raid. The body was older, the oldest one in stock apparently, because they did not want to waste a genuinely young and vigorous body on me. I was happier with the older body, I didn't have to pretend to the kind of youthfulness which most new retreads attempt as a matter of course. And besides, the body was an attractive specimen. Not too handsome in the face, but well lined. From the orginal intensity of the eyes, I guess that my predecessor in the body must have been some mean bastard, another Gorman Triplett. I go. a kick out of pretending that it really was Triplett's body I'd inherited. (I was mad for a while, but I don't want to go into that.) My hair was dark and curly, my eyes brown, my nose must have been broken at least three times. My mouth was fleshy and I never can quite get rid of the ignoble aspect it lends to my face. The body had apparently been wounded a couple of times, because I had a regular set of recurring chest pains and I had trouble throwing with my right arm. Otherwise, I could not have ordered a better one to be retreaded in, to hide away in.

For a while I thought the best feature about the body was that its sexual organs worked. I laughed hysterically when I felt my first stirrings in that region. Michael, who naturally had not known about the infirmity of my previous life, wondered at the laughter. When I got out of the interrogation rooms, away from him, I finally achieved what I had wished for so many years before, the enjoyment of the lascivious life. For a while it was the only thing kept me going. I had so many women I lost count. I developed a reputation as a satyr. And I loved it. It was marvelous. I could not even allow my sins, my past, my treason, to affect that. Although occasionally I thought of Ben and the surgery he had promised me, and became amused. Ben would have been amused, too, I knew. I could almost hear him cheering me on at each new sexual encounter, could almost see him nod approvingly with each penetration.

I went from city to city. In each place I generally searched out only the women, only the pleasures. I did not look very often at what was outside dark rooms. I did not want to be recognized, even though I told myself it was impossible for anybody to recognize me in a new body. But, no, that was not true. Ben would recognize me. He would recognize me if I returned in the body of a hunchbacked fisherwoman.

Of course all that could not last. I had to face myself eventually.

Stacy kept coming into my dreams. He'd look around whatever the setting was, stare at me and say, "I died for this?" and I'd laugh and he'd laugh and then he would talk a blue streak, saying what he explained as everything he had never been able to say before. I never could recall, when I woke up, what he had said.

When he had visited my dreams too often, I knew it was time to search for Alicia. It was not enough to face myself, I had to face her. As it turned out, she was not too difficult to find. Once inside radical circles and trusted (the trust came from my performing a trio of particularly ugly tasks), I asked a few discreet questions, traced Alicia to Denver. I had been afraid that the information I had supplied Michael might have enabled his agents to find her. But she had already given up her Alicia-identity, and was now completely within the underground, without a fake identity in the outside world.

17

Ben was in Denver, too, and I saw him first. As I had expected, he recognized me right away, this time with a bit more shock than before.

"Never thought you'd return. Although I confess I heard there was some controversy about your disposal. At official levels."

"Some."

"What happened?"

I told him. In his professional manner, he listened. I had difficulty telling him about the Michael part.

"And you feel guilty for, as you say, turning us in?" he said, after I had finished.

"Some."

"Some? A lot, I hope."

"You know that. At first I didn't want to see you again. You or Alicia."

"I'm glad you changed your mind. Perhaps Alicia'll be glad, too. She's a bit more of a hardliner than I. But I think . . ."

"What?"

"I don't know. All I can say is what I always say when you return after a long time. I'm glad to see you, Voss."

"Okay."

"Just don't ask for forgiveness just yet."

"I won't."

I asked what had happened to him during the last dozen years. He was reluctant to go into detail, but I worked a few things out of him. He had attempted to continue his dual role with the government and with the radical elements. Eventually a government investigation team uncovered a link between Stacy and June Albright and, through that, the link between her and Ben. She had not worked for Ben for some time, and in fact knew little about his dual role. However, she knew just enough to make them suspicious of Ben, and they began to watch him too closely. So, when there was too much heat for him to continue in the government advisory role, he abandoned it. Went completely underground.

"Good thing, too, from what you tell me. We've done a lot. There's more to do. We're making more cracks, causing more trouble. Whatever we do, it must be working. Latest reports show there're fewer bodies available than ever before. You copped a good one again, by the way. You seem to have what they call lucky resurrections. I'd insist on giving you a complete checkup but I'm a bit limited in equipment these days. It could be arranged, however."

"No matter. I checked out fine. No sabotage this time."

"Not on your body, anyway. I assume you'd like to see Alicia?"

18

Unlike Ben, she did not recognize me immediately. Ben's talent for perceiving the former individual in his retread body was rare.

I watched her from a distance. She was writing something in a well-used frayed notebook. Frequently she looked off to her left, searching for a new phrase or thought.

She had changed. There was gray in her hair, deep lines around her mouth, shadows around her eyes. Her skin seemed grainy. I assumed she must have seen a lot of outdoor life in whatever her activities now were. But the change in her face did not seem caused as much by age lines and gray hair as by an assumption of sadness. She looked unhappy. If she smiled, she would look unhappy. Her body was still slim, but there was a curve in her shoulders I did not remember. They seemed bent forward, altering subtly the design of her torso, making her small breasts look smaller, their outline not even discernible beneath the loose drab blouse she was wearing. She saw me watching her, and smiled the way people do at strangers. Ben had left me outside the door to the room, so she had no clue to who I was.

"You're new here."

"Sort of."

"I'm Alicia."

"I know."

"And you're . . . ? You don't want to tell me."

"I do. It doesn't come easy."

"Look, I'm busy, if you–"

"My name's . . . Vossilyev Geraghty. Voss, Alicia."

"Damn it! You're not, you can't be."

"I'm afraid I–"

"Shit. I've aged. I've–I look terrible. I must look terrible to you."

"No."

"Don't lie to me."

"You look different."

"The polite way of saying awful."

"Alicia–"

"What do I care how I look? I didn't know I was so vain. Come here, let me hold you. Why do you stand there?"

"I can't touch you, not until I've told you some things."

"Okay. You sit there. I'll sit here. My heart is racing. I don't know what to say to you. Why didn't you tell me you were coming here?" Why the hell didn't you tell me you were alive again? Why the hell don't you stop me asking questions?"

I told her. Everything I had told Ben, but in more detail. She did not like it.

We sat across from each other for a long time after I had finished. The lighting of the room made her face look sallow. She reached a hand into her blouse, scratched at her collarbone. Then, without a foreshadowing of it, she smiled.

"You look good, Voss."

"New body, I guess."

"We look close to the same age. Convenient, I suppose."

"Why do you say that?"

"Things seem to work out for us. Perhaps we're blessed. All that worrying about the future, and what happened is you came out retreaded at about my age. Like I say, convenient."

"I don't understand."

"You're dense. Look, I don't care for what you've done, any more than you do, I suspect. Things got really hot for me there, for a while, and I couldn't figure why. But it's over, and we're sitting here across from each other. That's pretty good, I'd say. I think about you a lot."

"I didn't know whether to search for you or not."

"No, I'd have trouble with that problem, too. Funny."

"What's funny?"

"Around the eyes, you still look the same. Similar mouth, too."

"I thought they were different. Meaner."

"Maybe you didn't know how mean you looked before. Anyway, I can get used to looking at you, changes and all. But there are, well, situations."

"Tell me."

"For one thing, and I've imagined myself telling you about this hundreds of times, I've been with Ben for most of the time since you've, well, since you died. We had no reason to expect that your death was not final. Although I think we both hoped. It's the stuff of comedy, I suppose."

"Do you love Ben?"

"About in the same way you do, and that's quite a bit. But it's no real problem. In spite of the fact that we had no reason to expect it, Ben's been awaiting your return as eagerly as I. We won't mind."

"If you'd rather stay with him—"

"I'd rather, as you put it, *stay* with both of you, but we can discuss that later. Especially after you've found out if you want to stay with me."

"I do."

"How can you tell, after so much time?"

"I can tell."

"I'm not pretty any more."

"That's debatable."

"Ah, but at least you admit the possibility."

"I'm not pretty any more either."

"You're still coy, but that's all right. I've gotten used to it."

"How much longer are we going to continue to be this awkward about everything?"

"A little longer. It's comfortable for me. I have to still get over the nightmare of coming back to that apartment and seeing Triplett kill you. There was so much blood, I thought—well, it doesn't make any difference what I thought."

"Last thing I saw, Triplett was turning to kill you."

"I don't think he had the desire to kill me. He was all wrapped up with the revenge on you. His reflexes were gone by the time he turned toward me. He moved his hand at the last second and fired past me. I just went on screaming."

"They said they found him dead."

"I killed him. But don't ask me about that. I just did it, okay?"

"All right."

"Anyway, did you know you're some kind of underground cult figure? There'll be hundreds who'll cheer at your retreading, expect you to descend immediately into another charnel house and wreak havoc left and right. You're almost as big as St. Ethel these days. Even here in Denver—where the whole cult originated, after all."

"Well, let's not tell anybody who I am. Or was. I don't think I could stand the company of St. Ethel, even on mythic terms."

"Still, we must continue to fight in her armies. There're all kinds of indications we're getting somewhere. There's a lot we can do, you can do."

"I don't know if I—"

"Of course you don't. That'll come later. You don't have much choice, really. Not if you want me. And, speaking of that, my room is two doors from here. Not very comfy, but convenient."

"I'm beginning to hate that word, convenient."

"Maybe we should stop talking."

We started with a few old-fashioned romantic rituals, a little wine, a little whispering, but they all seemed false. There was nothing, we decided, but to get to bed and get over the awkwardness of it. Except that, as it turned out, it wasn't awkward. Not at all. Every other time, with every other person, was awkward. Viewed from Olympian heights, it was just as ridiculous as any other mating of man and woman, but Fate had insulted us enough already and we were not hampered by any Olympian insights. When it was over, and we lay holding each other as if we could not risk ever letting go, Alicia whispered:

"You know, it was worth it."

And we both began to laugh.

"It was," she said, the laughter-tears running down her face. "It was. It was. It really was."

"I know. I agree. But that can't keep me from laughing."

"We shouldn't."

"Of course we should."

"Oh, of course. Of course. Let's do it again, before I stop laughing."